Sou'westers

John Dillon

January 2015
Copyright © 2015 John Dillon (book and photographs)

ISBN-13: 978-1492374992
ISBN-10: 1492374997

Order additional copies from Amazon.com.

Comments to cynddylans@hotmail.co.uk

FILM CAREER OF AUTHOR, JOHN DILLON
In "front" and "behind"

A movie actor, John Dillon had the lead in *Mind on the Run* and BBC TV *Sadwrn* in 1965, and had bit parts in *Solomon and Sheba, King of Kings, El Cid,* and *Custer of the West.* He also had roles in many TV and radio plays. In 1968, John ended his film career as Assistant Director for Lieder Films. Following are his credits:

- *Solomon and Sheba* for Sam Bronston Films, plus stunting for Terry York and Frank Howard (1958/1959)
- *King of Kings,* four "bits", uncredited (1959)
- *El Cid,* Lazarus the Leper, credited (1960)
- BBC Radio plays (forgotten titles) (1960s and 1970s)
- BBC TV play (title forgotten), credited (1964)
- *Dr. Who, Episode 3,* credited (1965)
- John Beckett series, credited (1965/1966)
- BBC Wales, *Sadwrn,* Lead (Boyo). First ever "live" play in Welsh on TV (1965)
- *Custer of the West* for Sam Bronston Films, uncredited (1965)
- *Death Happens to Other People,* credited (1966)
- Behind camera as Assistant Director, Sound, Lights, and Camera for *Jonty Moor* (1966/1967)
- Moor; K.Z.O. for CoI
- *Mind on the Run* film for Sim Scott Films; J. Moor, Director, credited (1966)

CONTENTS

PART ONE, EPISODE ONE

A QUAYSIDE IN CORNWALL DURING THE MACKEREL SEASON, IT IS JUST GETTING LIGHT. A LOT OF NOISE AND SHOUTS AS BOATS ENGINES ARE STARTED. BOATS PULLING AWAY FROM THE QUAY.

ZOOM IN ON ONE BOAT, THE 'SEA CELT', AS THE BOAT ALONGSIDE HER REVS UP AND STARTS TO PULL AWAY, ENGULFING THE 'SEA CELT' IN SMOKE.

MARTIN: Hey Janner – why'nt you get your injectors sorted? Worse than that bloody pipe you smoke!

JANNER'S GRINNING FACE APPEARS AT THE WHEELHOUSE WINDOW, WITH PIPE STUCK IN HIS MOUTH AND HE STICKS TWO FINGERS UP AT MARTIN AS HE GIVES HIS ENGINE THE GUN AND ROARS OFF.

MARTIN RETURNS JANNER'S GRIN AND SALUTE AND TURNS BACK TO HIS OWN BOAT, WHERE FRED IS BUSY BOLTING ON STRIPPERS TO THE GUNWALES.

THE BOAT ROCKS SLIGHTLY AS ANOTHER FISHERMAN STEPS ON BOARD, A LITTLE FLUSHED AND OUT OF BREATH.

IAN: Sorry Martin – sodding car wouldn't start again.

MARTIN: That's the fourth time, and you've only worked on the boat a few weeks. You'd better get rid of that banger, mate, or one of these mornings we'll be shoving off without you.

IAN: (GRUDGINGLY) Yeah, well – sorry.

MARTIN: Right then, get the ropes aboard and let's shove off. Push her bows out Fred!

IAN AND FRED COMPLY WITH THE WISHES OF THE SKIPPER AND THEN THEY COME BACK INTO THE WHEELHOUSE AS MARTIN MOVES THE BOAT OUT.

MARTIN: Stick the kettle on Fred. I hear it's a bit lumpy out there today so we may as well make use of the next half hour. (SAYS TO IAN) I want all the gurdies and strippers set up by the time we reach St. Anthony's Head.

IAN: (OFF HE GOES ON DECK) Right.

MARTIN: (REACHING FOR THE RADIO TRANSMITTER MIKE) Seven Stars, Seven Stars – Sea Celt here – anyone about?

JOHN: Sea Celt, Sea Celt – what's she like then, matey. Late again! You wanna try putting a little water in it my 'andsome.

MARTIN: Yeah – funny you should say that. What's doing then – where you to?

JOHN: Yeah – well we're an hour South East o' the light and it's getting a bit lumpy. Nothing showing on the paper so we're turning off towards Black Head. Colin just came through and told me some of the Penzance boys are pulling 'meds' (mediums) over there.

MARTIN: Right oh matey – see you there later on. Thanks. Over and out.

JOHN: Cheers and Gone.

DISSOLVE TO SHOT OF BOATS COMING BACK FROM THE DAY'S FISHING. SEA CELT AND SEVEN STARS ALONGSIDE EACH OTHER WITH A FAIR BIT OF FISH ON BOARD – THE CREWS STILL SORTING AND BOXING-UP.

SHOT OF FISH BEING WEIGHED UP AND PUT ON LORRIES AT THE QUAY.

MARTIN AND JOHN GETTING THEIR TALLY TICKET.

MARTIN: Come on then. Chain Locker! Tide's on the flood so we'll be OK for water on the North Quay for another 3 hours.

JOHN: You're on – thank God it's Friday.

SHOTS OF JOHN AND MARTIN WALKING DOWN THE STEPS TO GET INTO THEIR BOATS.

INTERIOR OF CHAIN LOCKER PUB ON FALMOUTH'S CUSTOM HOUSE QUAY – LOTS OF PEOPLE IN THE BAR, IT BEING FRIDAY NIGHT. MANY FISHERMEN STILL IN THEIR WORKING CLOTHES BUT WITHOUT THEIR WATERPROOF GEAR ON. ZOOM IN ON MARTIN AND JOHN SQUASHED INTO A CORNER AWAY FROM THE BAR.

MARTIN: Not a bad week John. How did you do?

JOHN: Five hundred stone o' meeds at £1.20 a stone which makes £600. Take out £65 for diesel and the fishfinder, £23 for gear which leaves – um – er – just about £500 – one third for the boat which leaves about £350 to split between us, making about £120 each. With my boat's share I've made roughly £280.

MARTIN: Yeah, well we're about equal then. Not a bad week. (PAUSE) Listen, if you're still in need of some antifouling I've got some in the store you can have. Fell off the back of a container ship.

JOHN: (WITH A LAUGH) Proper job. Right I'll stick her on the dinghy hard tomorrow morning, on her legs, and get the damned job done. Should see her through the rest o' the season.

MARTIN: Right oh matey – tell you what, I'll bring the antifouling down at 9 o'clock and I'll give you a hand as well.

JOHN: Thanks matey, I appreciate that. What you 'avin?

MARTIN: Another pint of Cornish, please.

CUTS OF SHOTS OF PEOPLE IN CONVERSATION AND DÉCOR OF THE PUB.

JOHN: (COMING BACK WITH THE DRINKS) Tell you what matey – you can have those six pollocks we caught this week. I stuck 'em in the deep freeze.

MARTIN: Oh, handsome, boy 'ansome. The missus loves pollock and we haven't had any for ages. Where did you get them?

JOHN: Down towards Black Head from the hotel at Coverack about half a mile offshore – you know where those big peaks show up on the fish finder!

MARTIN: Oh yes, I know – must have been Tuesday in that calm spell then. God it was lovely that day.

JOHN: Remember that day the pilot whales appeared?

MARTIN: Wasn't it a handsome day. For two pins I'd have taken off my clothes and joined the whales.

JOHN: Yeah. I know what you mean. Isn't it amazing the way they seem to stand up in the water and look at you.

MARTIN: I know. I told Fred they'd taken a fancy to him and to keep an eye on the female. (LAUGHS) Don't think he appreciated it much.

JOHN: Well – better get home to supper then. My mother's going to a WI meeting so I mustn't be late tonight – see you tomorrow morning. G'night Martin.

MARTIN: Right oh matey – see you in the morning. I'll be off myself soon.

JOHN: Cheers and gone.

EXTERIOR.
DINGHY HARD AT 10.00 HRS.
JOHN SCRUBBING DOWN AND SCRAPING HIS HULL BELOW THE WATERLINE. MARTIN ARRIVES LUGGING A BIG CAN OF ANTIFOULING.

MARTIN: What's she like then?

JOHN: Lo mate – nearly ready.

MARTIN: Right, I'll start stirring this stuff up a bit. I left it upside down all night, so that should have helped.

PASS TO SHOTS OF SAILING BOATS AND VIEWS OF THE HARBOUR ETC.

IT IS 12.30. WE COME BACK TO THE SHOT OF MARTIN AND JOHN FINISHING OFF THE ANTIFOULING.

JOHN: Right then, that's it. (THROWING HIS BRUSH AND ROLLER INTO A BUCKET) She'll be alright here till closing time then I'll come aboard and get my head down in the bunk till she's afloat. Chain Locker?

MARTIN: (IN AFFIRMATIVE REPLY) Chain Locker.

INTERIOR OF THE CHAIN LOCKER.
A GOOD SING-SONG IN PROGRESS. SMOKEY AND THE BOYS ON THEIR INSTRUMENTS – THIS GOES ON FOR ABOUT TWO MINUTES. MARTIN AND JOHN ARE IN THEIR USUAL PLACE.

MARTIN: You were talking about the Russian factory ships – well over there, now come in, are two real live Russians matey.

JOHN: Where to?

MARTIN: Over there next to the Harbour Master.

JOHN: (AFTER A LONG LOOK) Well they don't seem to have two heads or pointed ears or anything.

MARTIN: No – they seem like ordinary blokes to me too. You can't be hard on them – they're only obeying orders and in any case, the Scots and the English are selling fish to them, so what the Hell!

JOHN: Yeah – you can't blame them for buying fish for pity's sake. If I had my way it's the purse-seiners and stern trawlers I'd ban. Good God man they'll kill all our stock in another two years. Do you know that nothing can escape from a purse sein – nothing! And as for the stern trawlers – well! I think it's disgusting – they tow right through a shoal o' mackerel and scatter them to hell – and what's left for us? – and that's apart from nearly running right over one of us every few months.

MARTIN: Things are getting too crowded out here matey. Old Roger over there was putting down his long lines a few months ago off the Lizard and a bloody coaster ripped right through the lot and nearly smashed him to Hell – missed him by about 10 foot.

JOHN: Well when this season's over, I'm going to take a long look at things and I'll go one of two ways. I'll either go for a bigger boat in steel or I'll sell the old Seven Stars and take up lorry driving.

MARTIN: You can't mean that John. You wouldn't leave fishing would you?

JOHN: I have been giving it some thought Martin. Everything seems to be crowding in on us these days. And when I hear that we are forced to dump fish accidentally caught if it's so called 'protected' species like herring it makes me bloody sad mate – what about giving it to hospitals or old people. No doubt the fellas up in England in the Government can give us good reasons but I'm just a fisherman like my father and his father before him and it seems to me that what is at stake here is not just the mackerel but our whole way of life.

MARTIN: Damn it – you just reminded me – the wife wants me to get some pork for the Sunday dinner – I'd better go and get it right away. We won't be out tomorrow, there's a gale forecast, so why don't you come and help us to eat it? And I want to have a chat with you anyway.

JOHN: Well, thanks a lot, matey. Mother's off to her sister's tomorrow so I could do with a bit of fattening up!

MARTIN: Right oh then, come around about half twelve and we'll have a couple of beers first. Right – I must be off now then. See you.

JOHN: OK matey – see you tomorrow. (STARTS TO SING WITH THE OTHERS)

IAN IN HIS CARAVAN SITTING IN FRONT OF THE TV WATCHING A SOCCER MATCH WITH A CAN OF BEER IN HIS HAND. HIS GIRLFRIEND COMES IN AND SAYS

PAULINE: Why don't you go and fix the car instead of sitting in front of that box all day?

IAN: Mind your own bloody business – it's my car – I paid for it and I paid for this television as well if it comes to that so if you've got nothing else to say piss off out to that bloody kitchen and make us a sandwich.

PAULINE: From now on make your own sandwiches – I'm off. (EXITS QUICKLY, SLAMMING DOOR)

IAN: (TO HIMSELF AFTER A MOMENT'S SILENCE) Bloody hell – done it again – haven't I. Well that's that. **That's bloody well that!**

HE SHOUTS AS HE GETS UP AND SLINGS THE TABLE AT THE TELEVISION SET AND STORMS OUT OF THE DOOR.

DISSOLVE TO CALMNESS OF THE WATER ETC AND GO IN CLOSE TO SEVEN STARS. WHEELHOUSE OPENS AND JOHN COMES OUT, SCRATCHING, OBVIOUSLY HAVING JUST GOT UP AFTER HIS NAP.

GOES TO FAR GUNWHALE, SITS DOWN, CLAPS HIS HANDS ON TOP OF HIS HEAD AND STRETCHES AND YAWNS. GETS PAPERS AND TOBACCO OUT OF HIS POCKET AND STARTS TO MAKE HIMSELF A CIGARETTE. RELAXES – LOOKING OUT OVER THE WATER. IT'S ABOUT 3PM AND DUSK IS NOT FAR AWAY. PAULINE IS WALKING ALONG THE DINGHY HARD AND SEES JOHN.

PAULINE: Hello sailor!

JOHN: (LOOKING UP) Hello, my dear – how are you – haven't seen you for a long time. What you up to around here?

PAULINE: Oh, I don't know – came down to look at the water – it always helps me forget my troubles.

JOHN: Well, that doesn't sound too good. Come aboard and have a cup of tea if you don't mind getting your feet wet.

PAULINE: Well – why not – best offer I've had today.

JOHN: Hang on then while I put the ladder down along side the stern. She's still aground so it'll only come up to your knees.

SHOT OF PAULINE TAKING OFF HER SHOES AND STOCKINGS. CUT AWAY TO BLOKES REPAIRING OR PAINTING DINGHIES WHO GET AN EYEFUL OF HER SHAPELY LEGS – JOHN CATCHES A FLASH OF WHITE THIGH ALSO.

JOHN IS NOW HOLDING THE LADDER IN POSITON WHILE PAULINE WADES GINGERLY OUT TO THE BOAT – SHE SUDDENLY SLIPS AND LANDS UP SITTING IN THE WATER. THE SHOCK OF THE COLD WATER REGISTERS ON HER FACE AS GUFFAWS OF LAUGHTER REACH HER FROM THE SHORE.

CUT AWAY TO PEOPLE LAUGHING.

BACK TO PAULINE UPON REALISING THAT THE LAUGHS ARE AT HER AND SHE STARTS TO CRY.

JOHN IS DOWN THE LADDER AND AT HER SIDE IN A FLASH AND HELPING HER UP PUTS HIS ARMS AROUND HER TO COMFORT HER.

JOHN: Hey come on – it's only a drop of water.

BY NOW SHE IS SOBBING TERRIBLY.

CUT TO LAUGHERS WHO ARE NOW SHAMEFACEDLY GUILTY AND VERY SORRY TO HAVE ADDED TO HER MISERY.

JOHN NOW HELPS HER TO THE LADDER AND GIVES HER A HAND UP.

JOHN: That's it – up you go my 'andsome. I'll light the gas and soon get you warm.

HELPS HER OVER THE GUNWHALE AND TAKES HER INTO THE WHEELHOUSE. OPENS THE DOOR INTO THE ACCOMMODATION WHERE THERE ARE TWO BUNKS AND A CALOR GAS FIRE – GOES IN AND HELPS HER DOWN. GIVES HER A BLANKET AND SAYS

JOHN: Here you are love – take your wet things off after I light the fire than I'll go make you a cup of tea.

5

JOHN GOES UP TO THE WHEELHOUSE

JOHN: (CONT'D) Look I've got a better idea, I'll put the kettle on then go to the charity shop and get you some things to wear. What size are you?

PAULINE: (IN A TREMBLING VOICE) Fourteen – but you needn't bother.

JOHN: It's only 50 yards – I'll be back before the kettle's boiled. Hang on there now.

AND HE GOES.

CUT BACK TO PAULINE WHO NOW COLLAPSES ON THE BUNK SHAKING WITH TEARS.

FADE TO SHOT OF JOHN IN A CHARITY SHOP WOMAN SERVING HIM.

WOMAN: There you are, lovey, your girlfriend will be pleased with these I can tell you. That will be £1.50 please.

JOHN: (COLOURING A LITTLE AND PAYING UP) They're not for my girlfriend.

WOMAN: (WITH A GIGGLE) Ah well – they say it takes all sorts today.

JOHN, NOW FLUSTERED, MAKES A HASTY RETREAT WHILE THE LADIES IN THE SHOP HAVE A LAUGH.

SHOT OF JOHN CLIMBING OVER THE GUNWHALES AND GOING INTO THE WHEELHOUSE; PUTS THE CLOTHES ON A SEAT AND GOES ABOUT PUTTING TEA IN THE POT THEN, KNOCKING THE DOOR THROUGH, SAYS

JOHN: How are you now, Pauline? Cup of tea coming up soon.

THE DOOR OPENS AFTER A WHILE AND A VERY TEAR-STAINED FACE LOOKS OUT WITH A BRAVE SMILE AND PAULINE SAYS

PAULINE: Recovering a little thanks, John but I'm still soaking wet.

JOHN: Well look here now at these nice things I just got you – and no need to say anything – they're cleaned and ironed from the charity shop so they were only a few pence. (SHOWS THE WOOLLEN UNDERWEAR IN ONE HAND AND THE DRESS IN THE OTHER)

WHEN PAULINE SEES THE LOVELY DRESS AND THE WOOLLEN UNDERWEAR HER FACE STARTS TO CHANGE – EVENTUALLY TURNS TO A SMILE AND STARTS TO LAUGH AND GOES ON LAUGHING FOR A MINUTE.

 EVENTUALLY COLLAPSES BACK ON THE BUNK.

PAULINE: Oh John – how marvellous – oh you have bucked me up. Hand them down to me. Do you mind if I dry myself with your blanket?

JOHN: Not at all my dear – you carry on. I'll get the tea ready.

PAULINE CLOSES THE DOOR.

JOHN NOW PUTS THE BOILING WATER INTO THE TEAPOT AND OPENS A TIN WHICH HAS BISCUITS IN IT. SELECTS A COUPLE OF MUGS – TAKES A CLEAN HANDKERCHIEF FROM HIS POCKET AND CLEANS ONE MUG UP SO THAT IT LOOKS FAIRLY RESPECTABLE. LOOKS OUT OF THE WINDOW AND STARTS TO WHISTLE. THE SUN SUDDENLY COMES OUT AND, AS IT DOES, PAULINE APPEARS IN THE DOORWAY.

PAULINE: Da Daah!

LIKE A TRUMPET BLAST. THE SUNLIGHT CATCHES HER DRESS AND HER BEAMING FACE AND JOHN IS REALLY TAKEN ABACK – HE HAS NEVER SEEN ANYTHING SO LOVELY.

CUT TO JOHN'S REACTION

PAULINE: Well, go on then – say something.

JOHN: Um – your tea's ready.

PAULINE LAUGHS AND CLIMBS INTO THE WHEELHOUSE.

PAULINE: Right – it's my turn now. You sit down and I'll pour the tea. Ooh – chocolate biscuits – how lovely!

THEY BOTH SIT DOWN OPPOSITE EACH OTHER.

PAULINE: Well – you were clever to have got me this lovely dress. Do you know it's beautiful –but the underwear is something else (GIGGLING AGAIN) I must say Thank You again, John.

PAULINE: (CONT'D) I'm sorry to have caused you so much trouble and embarrassment. I was stupid to break down like that.

JOHN: That's alright love, but I must say I've never seen anyone break up like that before from getting a wetting.

PAULINE: Oh no, John – it wasn't just that it's well, it was the last straw. Things have been pretty bad lately what with one thing and another (PAUSE). I lost my job when the fish plant closed and I've been getting a lot of stick from my bloke lately – so – this afternoon I walked out on him and I reckon all that crying was the reaction. Still – it's over and done with now and I'm feeling like a new woman already – thanks to you John. (BOAT ROCKS) Oh! What was that!

JOHN: Ah –we're afloat. C'mon I'll take you for a trip around the harbour – if you fancy it.

PAULINE: (CLAPPING HER HANDS TOGETHER) Oh – I'd love it – yes please!

JOHN: Right oh then, just you sit tight while I get the legs aboard and then it's "All aboard for the Skylark".

JOHN GETS UP AND GOES ON DECK.

PAULINE: (TO HERSELF) Skylark? Hm – you may be right my handsome boy – you may be right.

CLOSE UP ONTO HER FACE – DREAMY.

THE NEXT DAY HALF AN HOUR PAST MIDDAY AT <u>MARTIN'S</u> HOUSE. <u>MARTIN</u> AND HIS WIFE <u>SUE</u> AND THEIR LITTLE GIRL OF 4 ARE IN THE LIVING ROOM. SUE IS HEAVILY PREGNANT. THE LITTLE GIRL IS PLAYING AN ABC GAME ON THE TABLE WITH HER MOTHER. <u>MARTIN</u> IS READING THE FISHERMAN'S NEWS WITH PENCIL IN HAND. THE DOORBELL GOES.

<u>MARTIN</u>: Ah, that'll be John. (GETS UP AND GOES OUT)

<u>MARTIN</u> COMES BACK WITH <u>JOHN</u> AND <u>PAULINE</u>. <u>SUE</u> AND <u>MARTIN</u> EXCHANGE LOOKS QUICKLY – <u>MARTIN</u> RATHER APOLOGETIC.

<u>JOHN</u>: Hello Sue. I'm sorry – I was going to ask if could take a rain check on the dinner as I had Pauline with me but Martin insisted that we both come in.

<u>MARTIN</u>: Yeah – silly that would have been – plenty here for another one ain't there dear!

<u>SUE</u>: Bless you – course there is my dears and welcome. Come and sit down. Mary – put that game away now my love and let's make room for the young lady.

<u>PAULINE</u>: (WITH A LAUGH) I don't know about the 'young lady' bit my name is Pauline.

<u>SUE</u>: (SHAKING HANDS) Hello my dear. It's nice to see John with a girl is what I meant and I'm sure he wouldn't pick anyone but a lady.

<u>MARTIN</u>: Hear, hear, I'll drink to that. What'll you have Sue – John – sherry – beer?

<u>PAULINE</u>: Sherry for me, please.

<u>MARTIN</u>: And John'll have beer, I know. Orange juice my dear?

<u>SUE</u>: (WITH A SMILE) Oh yes, I'd better. Can't spoil the ship for a haporth o'tar – not at this stage anyway? Only two weeks to go.

<u>MARTIN</u>: (HANDS DRINKS ALL AROUND) Here you are then. Cheers.

<u>SUE</u>: Well, where are you from my dear – are you local?

<u>PAULINE</u>: Well I'm from Penzance actually but I've been living near Penryn till yesterday.

<u>SUE</u>: Till yesterday? Why what on earth happened yesterday?

<u>PAULINE</u>: Well (COLOURING A LITTLE) what I should have said was that my boyfriend up to yesterday lived in a caravan near Penryn but now we've finished so I don't live there anymore. I only knew him for a month anyway.

<u>SUE</u>: Oh you poor dear – I know it must be very difficult being a young girl these days. There seem to be so many more problems than when I was a girl.

<u>PAULINE</u>: Well it's over and done with now anyway. I feel like a different person anyway.

<u>SUE</u>: But where are you living now, my dear?

<u>PAULINE</u>: Nowhere – I'll have to start looking in the morning.

<u>SUE</u>: Yes, my dear but where will you sleep tonight I mean.

MARTIN: Sue – why don't you have a look how that pork is getting on – I'm sure Pauline's worried enough as it is without us adding to it.

SUE GIVES MARTIN A FUNNY LOOK AND THEN LOOKS OVER AT JOHN AND PAULINE.

SUE: What I was thinking of Mr Cleversticks was that there's a spare bed in Mary's room – so don't you get all superior with me, my 'andsome!

SUE EXITS

MARTIN: Well now – that's quite a thought eh? What do you say to that then – you two?

PAULINE: (TAKEN ABACK AND OVERWHELMED AT SUCH KINDNESS. STARTS TO CRY) Well, I don't know what to say. Thank you.

MARTIN IS NONPLUSSED AND POKES HIS HEAD AROUND THE KITCHEN DOOR AND CALLS SUE BACK. JOHN COMFORTS PAULINE AND MARY SAYS

MARY: Mummy – mummy the lady's crying.

SUE: There, there my dear. Come upstairs with me – and I'll show you the bed in Mary's bedroom and if you like it you can stay here until the baby comes and maybe longer. God knows I'll need a helping hand here then.

THE TWO EXIT

MONDAY – MID MORNING. AT SEA OFF THE MANACLES, 40 OR 50 BOATS PULLING STRINGS OF GOOD FISH – MOSTLY LARGE – SOME EVEN JUMBOS. IT'S A VERY CALM SEA – THE WEEKEND'S GALE HAS FINISHED. ALL CREWS INTENT ON THEIR WORK WITH THE OCCASIONAL RIBALD SHOUT FROM ONE BOAT TO ANOTHER AS A LINE BREAKS AND LINE AND FISH ARE LOST. CLOSE IN ON SEA CELT AND SEVEN STARS. JOHN AND HIS ONE CREWMAN PULLING IN A LOT OF FISH BUT PERSPIRATION FLOWING FROM UNDER JOHN'S BOBBLE-CAP.

MARTIN: What you been up to this weekend then, matey? You're sweating like a pig there. Been up to something no doubt. (ALL THIS WITH A TWINKLE IN HIS EYE)

JOHN: (IN A HALF-JOKING HALF SERIOUS MANNER) You rotten bastard – go on tell the whole bloody world.

MARTIN: Don't have to matey – one look at you and end of story! Ha – ha!

JOHN: Ha bloody ha – rotten sod. Nice bit of pork that was, mate. (REFERRING TO THE SUNDAY DINNER AND TRYING TO CHANGE THE SUBJECT)

MARTIN: (WITH A TWINKLE IN HIS EYE) What bit are you referring to?

JOHN: Boody Hell – mate, give it a rest will you?

MARTIN: Yeah – alright matey – only taking the piss that's all. Nice girl that, John.

JOHN: Oy, I don't want the whole bloody fleet to know my business.

MARTIN: Sorry mate – oops what the hell we got here? Bloody hell. Hey Fred – bring your line in and get the gaff – I've got a bloody monster on here (CONTINUES WINDING IN) - pollock by the feel of it.

MARTIN: Hope this line holds.

FINALLY BRINGS TO THE SURFACE A HUGE POLLOCK WHICH MUST WEIGH 20LBS.

MARTIN: Hey look at that boys – hook him Fred. Lovely – thanks. (BRINGS THE FISH OVER THE GUNWHALES AND ONTO THE DECK) Wouldn't mind a few of those. Well lads we've had a good day and we're nearly up to quota – what do you say – shall we head for home?

IAN: Yeah – why not – let's piss off and get a few pints in.

MARTIN: Right oh then, wind your gear in.

THEY ALL WIND UP AND TAKE THEIR LINES OFF THE ROLLER AND WIND THEIR HOOKS AROUND THEIR GURDIES.

MARTIN: John! John oh!

JOHN LOOKS UP

MARTIN: We're going back in – see you later!

JOHN LIFTS HIS LEFT HAND AND SMILES AS HE IS WINDING IN A STRING OF LARGE ONES.

PULL BACK TO TAKE IN WHOLE FLEET AS SEA CELT MOVES AWAY.

FISH QUAY
WEIGHING UP JUST FINISHED, BOXES BEING PUT BACK ABOARD SEA CELT. IAN AND FRED TAKING OFF THEIR OILSKINS.

IAN: I'll get off here and walk up town, Martin.

MARTIN: Yeah, that's alright boy. Fred and I can take her up the river, no bother – see you tomorrow.

IAN: Right – see you.

IAN MOVES OFF THE FISH QUAY.

DISSOLVE TO IAN WALKING UP THE MAIN STREET OF THE TOWN. SUE SUDDENLY COMES OUT OF A SHOP IN FRONT OF HIM AND BENDS DOWN TO HELP YOUNG MARY AND BUMPS INTO IAN – HE SAYS SORRY AND THEN CATCHES SIGHT OF PAULINE ALSO COMING OUT OF THE SHOP.

IAN: Where the hell have you been to these last few days? Been on the bloody razzle have you?

SUE: Hey – look here – I don't know who you are and don't want to know neither, but just you keep a civil tongue in your head, young fella me lad or you'll have me to contend with.

IAN: Ah, shut up you old bag or I'll stick another one in your belly.

A VERY SHOCKED REACTION FROM SUE.

PAULINE: Don't you dare speak to her like that – you scum. (RAISES HER HAND TO SLAP HIM)

AT THIS POINT IAN JUMPS FORWARD TO GET AT PAULINE BUT KNOCKS SUE OVER IN THE PROCESS – PAULINE SCREAMS AND BENDS TO HELP HER BUT IS KNOCKED BACK INTO THE SHOP BY IAN.

THE PEOPLE IN THE SHOP START TO SHOUT – Help – Police etc.

IAN TAKES FRIGHT AND RUNS AWAY, LEAVING SUE ON THE GROUND IN GREAT PAIN, GASPING FOR BREATH, THE CHILD SCREAMING IN FEAR.

DISSOLVE TO AMBULANCE SIREN AND INTERIOR OF AMBULANCE. SUE ON ONE BUNK – ATTENDANT, PAULINE AND YOUNG MARY ON THE OTHER.

ATTENDANT: Don't worry – it'll be alright – you'll see – just try and relax.

WIDE SHOT OF MARTIN AND FRED PUTTING THE FINISHING TOUCHES TO THE TIDYING UP OF SEA CELT AND JOHN JUST BRINGING SEVEN STARS UP ALONGSIDE HER. SEVEN STARS GOES INTO REVERSE TO BRING HER ALONGSIDE WITHOUT A BUMP AND MARTIN STEPS OVER TO MEET JOHN WHO HANDS HIM A SHORT BREAST ROPE. MARTIN MAKES IT FAST TO ONE OF SEA CELT'S CLEATS.

MARTIN: You weren't long then matey.

JOHN: No – got our quota so in we came. Thought I'd come up to your place and see how Pauline was getting on.

MARTIN: I think Sue was taking her out shopping this afternoon – seems she left the few clothes she had at her previous digs – wherever that was. Who's the bloke she used to knock around with – do you know?

JOHN: No idea – 'cept that he's a fisherman. None o' my business anyway – what's bygones is bygones.

MARTIN: Yeah, quite right mate – quite right. Anyway she seems a good 'un to me.

JOHN: I hope so – I bloody hope so. Look – I've been thinking about going to look at a steel boat advertised in Penzance. The girls have gone shopping, do you feel like coming to have a look at her? Sea Celt is steel so I thought you might know what to look for.

MARTIN: Yeah – why not. Can we take young Fred with us? Poor little bugger never gets a chance to go anywhere. Gets a tough time with his father.

JOHN: Of course he can come. We'll have a pasty and a pint later on – he'll enjoy that.

MARTIN: (TURNING TO FRED UP THE OTHER END OF THE BOAT) Fred!

DISSOLVE TO THE THREE OF THEM LOOKING AT A WELL BUILT STEEL BOAT CHOCKED UP ON A QUAYSIDE.

MARTIN: Well – she'll do you matey. I like that winch. What's made up your mind so quickly then?

JOHN: About what?

MARTIN: About going for a steel boat now and forgetting the lorry driving. Couldn't be Pauline – could it?

JOHN: Well – in a way – yes. These last couple o' days everything seems to be much – well it's difficult to explain, but even – colours and sounds seem to be sharper.

MARTIN: Sounds to me like you got a dose of 'flu comin' on. (LAUGHS)

JOHN: (ALSO LAUGHS) John matey – everything is real now – like I've been in a fog all my life up to now.

MARTIN: Oh dear, oh dear. Yes I believe you've gone and done it. (SHAKING HIS HEAD) Yes, I think you've got bells ringing in your head lad. Well I hope you're right. It does happen in a flash sometimes. But there they say that marriages are made in Heaven so there's not much we mortals can do about it.

MARTIN: (TURNS ROUND LOOKING FOR FRED WHO IS PEERING AT THE PROPELLOR) Fred – come on - this kind gentleman is going to buy us a pint and a pasty.

FRED: 'Andsome – I'm bloody starving!

DISSOLVE TO INTERIOR OF A PUB AND THREE FISHERMEN SITTING AROUND A TABLE.

MARTIN: What's up with Ian then Fred? He's a bit quiet this morning.

FRED: Dunno – didn't say much 'cept that he was 'avin woman trouble and he was goin' to sort her out if he found her.

MARTIN: Silly boy – time he grew up. Likes his pint too much – that's his trouble. (TURNS TO JOHN) We've had to wait for him a few times this month 'cos of his car breaking down.

FRED: On no – 'twasn't only his car – sometimes the farmer would leave his tractor in the road and Ian would have to move it before he could get out.

MARTIN: I didn't know he lived on a farm.

FRED: Gives the farmer £10 a week – I wouldn't mind getting a caravan myself if ………

JOHN: (INTERRUPTING HIM) A caravan you say? Whereabouts?

FRED: Up the top somewhere – near Mabe I think. Dunno, exactly.

JOHN: (WITH SOME ANXIETY NOW SHOWING IN HIS EYES, ASKS IN A CONTROLLED VOICE) You don't happen to know his girlfriend's name do you?

FRED: Yeah – Pauline I think!

MARTIN: (QUIETLY) God Almighty.

JOHN PUTS HIS PASTY DOWN AND PUSHES HIS PINT AWAY.

TO JOHN

MARTIN: Easy now – could be a coincidence.

FRED: What's the matter – what have I said?

MARTIN: Nothing boy – nothing – don't you worry now. Come on – finish up and let's get back!

JOHN IS ALREADY ON HIS FEET. MARTIN GETS UP AND FRED QUICKLY SWALLOWS WHAT'S LEFT OF HIS PINT, PICKS UP JOHN'S HALF EATEN PASTY AND HIS OWN AND THEY ALL THREE MAKE AN EXIT. FRED STILL EATING.

MARTIN'S HOUSE – PAULINE IS MAKING TEA FOR MARY AND HERSELF – LAYING IT ON THE TABLE. THE DOOR OPENS AND MARTIN AND JOHN WALK IN.

MARTIN: There you are mate – I told you there was nothing to worry about – she's here safe and sound.

JOHN GOES OVER TOWARDS PAULINE.

MARY: (STANDING ON HER CHAIR QUICKLY HOLDING HER HANDS OUT TO MARTIN) Daddy – Mummy's gone to Hostipelt and that nasty man hit her!

MARTIN: What – what are you talking about? (LOOKS AT PAULINE) What's this about?

PAULINE: She was pushed over in the Main Street and we had to rush her to hospital in Truro.

MARTIN: Is she alright – I mean is there any danger?

PAULINE:They don't know yet – she's being kept quiet and under observation.

PAULINE: (QUIETLY) Martin – it's my fault that she's there. It was my ex-boyfriend who did it trying to get at me and (STARTS TO CRY) Sue stuck up for me.

AFTER A MOMENTS SILENCE.

MARTIN: My dear – what's to be is to be. I'll say it again. I'm glad you're here. Now may I ask you two questions – is your ex-boyfriend a fisherman?

AN AFFIRMATIVE NOD OF THE HEAD FROM PAULINE.

MARTIN: And is his name Ian?

PAULINE: (IN A SOB) Oh yes, yes.

MARTIN AND JOHN EXCHANGE GLANCES.

JOHN: (COMMANDINGLY AND POINTING FINGER AT MARTIN) Your duty is at the hospital. I Know where mine is.

JOHN TURNS TO LEAVE BUT MARTIN HOLDS HIM BY THE ARM.

MARTIN: Steady now – don't go off like that – that's the way to Disaster. Please, please stay here with Pauline and look after Mary while I go to the Hospital – I need you to stay, I need you to stay, John.

JOHN: (AFTER A GOOD LONG MOMENT, RELAXES HIS HARD LOOK AND NODS) Alright, alright – I will but it's not what I want to do.

MARTIN: Thanks mate, thanks – there's plenty of time for the other – don't you worry! (HE GIVES THE CHILD TO JOHN AND GIVES HER A KISS) There, you keep Uncle John happy for an hour while I go and see Mummy. (TURNS TO PAULINE AND PUTS A HAND ON HER SHOULDER) Don't you worry my girl.

MARTIN EXITS

JOHN TURNS TO PAULINE AND TAKES HER HAND. SHE PRESSES HER HEAD AGAINST HIS ARM. (SHE IS STILL SITTING)

PAULINE: Oh John – I am sorry – it's all my fault.

JOHN: (HAVING CALMED DOWN NOW) Well Mary, like your Daddy said, what's to be is to be.

MARY: A bee, a bee!

JOHN AND PAULINE LOOK AT EACH OTHER AND BEGIN TO SMILE – PAULINE THROUGH HER TEARS.

JOHN: That's right Mary, my love – a big lovely buzzy bee, flying from flower to flower. Buzz, buzz – buzzy wuzz!

MARY LAUGHS AND THEY ALL LAUGH.

MARY: Buzzy-wuzz!

FADE TO TWO HOURS LATER IN THE SAME ROOM. PAULINE IS PUTTING MARY'S NIGHTDRESS ON IN FRONT OF THE FIRE, WHEN THE FRONT DOOR SLAMS, THEN MARTIN COMES INTO THE ROOM AND STANDS THERE WITH A SMILE ON HIS FACE. HE HAS EYES ONLY FOR MARY WHO RUSHES TO HIM.

MARY: Daddy, Daddy!

MARTIN: Hello, my sweet. I've got a lovely surprise for you.

MARY: Some sweeties?

MARTIN: No sorry my love – didn't have time; but I can tell you that you've got a lovely little baby brother.

JOHN AND PAULINE JUMP UP.

PAULINE: And how's Sue – is she alright?

MARTIN: Yes, she's fine. The doctor said she wasn't injured in the fall and that it was the shock that probably brought the baby on. It was due in ten days time anyway – so all is well that ends well. Mother and son both doing well – and she asked me to tell you not to worry and would you look after things till she came back!

PAULINE: But of course I will – oh I am so relieved, (TEARS TRICKLE OUT OF HER EYES) and how big is the baby?

MARTIN: Half a stone – by God – imagine what he'd have been like in another ten days!

PAULINE: Half a stone indeed – he's not a fish you know! (HALF SCOLDINGLY, LAUGHING)

MARTIN AND JOHN HAVE A GOOD LAUGH.

JOHN: (GIVING HIS HAND TO MARTIN) Congratulations Martin – I'm glad it's turned out with such a happy ending!

MARTIN: So am I, I can tell you. Now then, up to bed with you, young maid, and then I'll come back down and we'll have a little celebration!

EXITS WITH MARY

PAULINE: Thank God, oh thank God, the baby is alright. I never dreamed that the baby might be born today. Oh isn't it wonderful.

BY NOW SHE IS IN <u>JOHN'S</u> ARMS AND HE IS STROKING HER HAIR.

JOHN: Yes, thank God it's a happy ending. You know of course, that there is still some unfinished business.

PAULINE: Oh John – no- please. No more violence.

JOHN: There won't be my dear. I'll only hit him if he asks for it and then it's over and done with.

PAULINE: How do you know? – he might hurt you badly and then I'd be the one going to Hospital to see you.

MARTIN: (COMING IN AGAIN) Oh – sorry to butt in!

PAULINE: Go on with you! – Martin, John says he's got some unfinished business – (URGENTLY) can't you talk to him?

MARTIN: You haven't known John very long have you, my dear? Well, I can tell you that when he has something to do, he does it and does it properly with the minimum of fuss – so trust him. That's all I can tell you.

GOES TO THE CUPBOARD AND GETS GLASSES AND A BOTTLE OF WHISKEY FILLS THEM UP AND RAISES HIS GLASS GIVING THE OTHERS THEIRS.

MARTIN: Mother and Son, God Bless Them!

CHORUS: Mother and Son, God Bless 'Em.

JOHN: (DRINKING HIS DOWN IN ONE) Right then. Now if you don't mind I've got something to attend to – so I'll get going.

PAULINE: Oh John – take care.

MARTIN: Don't forget my share mate.

JOHN: I shan't.

EXITS, KISSING <u>PAULINE</u> LIGHTLY.

DISSOLVE TO SHOT OF <u>JOHN</u> ENTERING A PUB AND LOOKING AROUND THE DOOR. SEES YOUNG <u>FRED</u> AND COMES RIGHT IN. GOES OVER TO <u>FRED</u>.

FRED: Hello John, what's she like then?

JOHN: Fine matey, fine.

FRED: Would you like a drink, John?

JOHN: Well, yes please, I'd love one – half o' bitter please.

FRED: Go on – you can't drink halves in here.

JOHN: No, just a half please Fred. I've got things to do.

Fred: (TURNS TO THE BARMAN WHO BRINGS THE HALF OVER) Right oh, mate, whatever you like!

JOHN: (INNOCENTLY) Any of the boys out tonight?

FRED: Seen a few in 'The Grapes' and saw Ian going into the 'King's Head' an hour ago.

JOHN: (PURPOSELY NOT REGISTERING INTEREST) Oh aye. Bit too windy to go out drinking anyway, I suppose.

FRED: (WITH A LAUGH) Go on you must be joking.

JOHN: (FINISHING HIS HALF) Well I must be going – see you tomorrow Fred.

FRED: (SURPRISE ON HIS FACE AT SUCH A HASTY DRINK AND FAREWELL) Er – yeah, OK mate, see you!

FADE TO 'KING'S HEAD'.
JOHN, THREADING HIS WAY THROUGH THE CROWD TO THE BAR, GETS A WHISKY AND FINDS HIMSELF NEXT TO AN OLD FRIEND WHO IS AN ENGINEER ON A LARGE FREIGHT VESSEL.

JOHN: Hello, Andrew – back in port then!

ANDREW: (PUTTING HIS ARM AROUND HIS SHOULDERS) John, my 'andsome! How are ye? What ye 'avin?

JOHN: Just got one thanks. How long you been back?

ANDREW: Three weeks my 'andsom and settin' sail tonight.

JOHN: Oh damn, what pity, we could have had a few drinks together.

ANDREW: And we will, boy, we will believe me. Listen, we're havin' a bit of a party on board tonight as the old skipper's just been paid off here and the new one is being introduced to the ship – why don't you come along?

JOHN: Don't think I can old mate – got things to do.

ANDREW: Damn what a pity, I should like to have had a few drinks with you.

JOHN: Sorry about that Andrew – what time are you setting sail anyway?

ANDREW: 0300 hrs. But we must be on board by 11 o'clock.

JOHN: Well, good luck to you anyway in case I don't see you again tonight. I got to look for someone now but might come and say goodbye later on.

ANDREW: Right oh my bird – hope to see you later.

JOHN: Right.

SIDLES HIS WAY AROUND AND THROUGH THE CROWD UNTIL HE SEES IAN STANDING AT THE BAR. SQUEEZES IN TO STAND NEXT TO HIM.

IAN: 'Lo mate.

JOHN: Hello – oh yes you work on the Sea Celt don't you?

IAN: That's right – pays me enough money to buy my beer every night and that's about all. Boats and fish – who the hell wants any of 'em. I'd rather have a good piss up anytime.

JOHN: Yeah – I suppose so if that's what you fancy. Personally I love the sea.

IAN: Well I sodding well hate it – give me a bottle of whisky and a rave-up anytime.

THE GLIMMERINGS OF A PLAN START TO SHOW ON JOHN'S FACE.

JOHN: What are you having – whisky?

IAN: (WITH A BIG LAUGH) Heaven sent that's what you are. Yes – just pour it in matey – pour it in.

JOHN: (TAKING A FIVER FROM HIS POCKET AND GIVING IT TO IAN) Hang on a minute, I think I can get us into a party here – get one for me as well will you.

IAN: (AS JOHN MOVES OFF, LAUGHS AND, HALF TO HIMSELF, SAYS) Fucking idiot. (AND LAUGHS AGAIN)

IAN ORDERS THE DRINKS FROM THE BARMAN AND PUTS THE CHANGE IN HIS POCKET AND LAUGHS AGAIN – DRINKING HALF JOHN'S DRINK AND THEN SOME OF HIS OWN.

JOHN: (BY NOW BACK WITH ANDREW) Here I am again mate – is that offer still open and can I bring another bloke?

ANDREW: Why yes, my 'andsome, yes of course, bring him over.

JOHN MOVES OFF TO GET IAN, ARRIVES THERE AND SAYS

JOHN: Got an invitation to a party on board ship; if you want to come along as well.

IAN: (LAUGHING AGAIN IN A VERY COCKY WAY) Yes, don't mind if I do. Didn't think you were a party goer.

JOHN: (PICKS UP HIS GLASS) Oh I get some strange notions in my head sometimes. Bon Voyage.

IAN: (LAUGHING) Yeah, whatever you say, just bring on the whisky and the women.

JOHN: (WITH GLASS TO LIPS) Yeah. (AND HIS FACE HARDENS BUT HE QUICKLY RECOVERS).

DOCKSIDE AT NIGHT; A LARGE SHIP IS ALONGSIDE, THE GANG PLANK IS DOWN AND PEOPLE ARE STAGGERING UP – ANDREW, JOHN AND IAN INCLUDED. IAN SINGING AT THE TOP OF HIS VOICE. PARTY IN FULL SWING IN A LARGE SALOON ON BOARD SHIP. MANY OFFICERS PRESENT IN UNIFORM, SOME WITH JACKETS OFF. QUITE A FEW GUESTS IN VARYING FORMS OF DRESS – SOME DOCKSIDE-TYPE WOMEN, AND THE ODD BLATANT WHORE. THERE IS MUSIC AND SOME PEOPLE DANCING. IAN IS DANCING WITH A VERY WILD LOOKING BIRD, AWAY FROM HER, ARMS IN THE AIR ETC.

JOHN IS LEANING AGAINST A WALL, WATCHING THE 'GOINGS-ON'. ANDREW COMES UP TO HIM.

ANDREW: How are you enjoying yourself, John – alright ain't it?

JOHN: Marvellous party Andrew – it's enough to make me want to sign on with you myself for a couple of trips.

ANDREW: Love to have you aboard any time John. You're a good man with an engine and, what's more I know you're reliable. But, tell me something, who the hell is that bloody idiot you've got with you? I've not seen you with the likes o' that before!

JOHN: Well to tell you the truth, I've got a bit of a problem there – can I talk to you frankly? I need your help, pal, I really do.

ANDREW LISTENS AS JOHN STARTS TO TALK.

FADE TO – TWO HOURS LATER.
BY THIS TIME IAN IS VERY DRUNK AND SLUMPED IN AN ARMCHAIR. THE GIRL HE WAS DANCING WITH SUDDENLY STARTS TO DO A STRIP-TEASE WHICH GOES ON FOR ABOUT TWO MINUTES. IAN SUDDENLY GETS EXCITED, STRUGGLES UP FROM HIS CHAIR AND ATTEMPTS TO PULL HIS TROUSERS OFF, TRIPS, THUMPS ON TO THE DECK AND IS OUT COLD. EVERYONE LAUGHS.

ANDREW: Alright, alright, leave him to me, it's time he was leaving anyway. (LOOKS UP) John, come on, you brought him, you can take him away!

JOHN STEPS FORWARD AND BENDS DOWN TO LIFT IAN WITH ANDREW.

ANDREW: Come on then, up he comes.

ANDREW AND JOHN DRAG IAN OVER TO AND THROUGH THE DOOR, CLOSES IT BEHIND THEM.

ANDREW: OK – Now down the port side on this deck and then down another two decks – come on.

CUT BACK TO GIRL DANCING AND THEN FADE TO ANDREW AND JOHN OPENING A CABIN DOOR WHERE THERE IS A BUNK.

ANDREW: On that one (PUFFS AND GASPS). There – that'll do. Look at him – out cold. Right I'll leave the rest to you. I'll wait at the bottom of the companionway. Oh, by the way (PULLS TWO BOTTLES OF WHISKY FROM HIS POCKET) A nightcap for him.

ANDREW (GRINS AND EXITS).

JOHN UNDRESSES IAN DOWN TO HIS UNDERPANTS AND THROWS THE LOT OUT OF THE PORTHOLE. THEN PROPS IAN UP AND SLAPS HIS FACE UNTIL HE OPENS HIS EYES.

JOHN: Here we are then – a nightcap for the little feller. (HE UNSCREWS THE TOP AND PUTS THE NECK TO IAN'S LIPS AND TIPS IT UP) One for your Uncle John – that's it, now a little rest then one for Sue, and then one for the teeny weeny baby, one for Martin, your old skipper, and the last one for Pauline – you rotten little bastard.

(FINALLY LETS IAN'S HEAD DROP ON THE PILLOW AND SCREWS THE TOP BACK ON THE BOTTLE, THEN LEAVES BOTH BOTTLES UNDER IAN'S ARMS. OPENS THE CABIN DOOR, LOOKS BACK AND SAYS) Have a nice party. And the best of British luck to you mate, you're going to need it where you're going!

EXITS AND FADE TO <u>ANDREW</u> AND <u>JOHN</u> UP IN THE SALOON AGAIN TALKING.

<u>CAPTAIN</u>: Ladies and Gentlemen – Ladies and Gentlemen- please! As most of you are aware yesterday was my last day as Master of this vessel and Captain Hughes has kindly thrown this party in my honour for which I would like to sincerely thank him. (CLAPPING AND CHEERS) Many thanks, Captain! May I also take this opportunity to say a thank you to the people of Falmouth who have been so kind to myself and my ex-crew whenever we came to this port. I know Captain Hughes has to weigh anchor at 3 o'clock and, as it is now 2.15, I think it's time we left and allowed this old lady to get on her way so – (CLAPPING AND CHEERS AS ALL START TO LEAVE) if you'd all like to follow me down the gangplank, I'll wish Captain Hughes and his crew the best of luck, a safe return and God speed.

TURNS TO THE CAPTAIN, SHAKES HIS HAND.

<u>ANDREW</u> AND <u>JOHN</u> EXIT.
AT THE TOP OF GANGPLANK.

<u>ANDREW</u>: You sure that will do you now? We can dump a stowaway anywhere you know!

<u>JOHN</u>: No, thanks a lot, Andrew. Buenos Aires will do fine – he'll find a lot of his own sort there. You're a bloody good mate – thanks a lot.

<u>ANDREW</u>: Well, we've been good mates in the past and I owe you a few favours.

<u>JOHN</u>: Thanks, Andrew. Thanks. I'll wait on the dockside till you go. God Bless.

<u>ANDREW</u>: Yeah. Tug's alongside now. In 45 minutes we'll be under our own steam. Cheers matey. (WAVES)

<u>JOHN</u> BY NOW ON DOCK – WAVES UP TO <u>ANDREW</u> WHO DISAPPEARS. <u>JOHN</u> WALKS ALONG TO WATCH THE GANGPLANK BEING LIFTED, ETC AND DISSOLVE TO

PENRYN QUAY – EARLY MORNING.
<u>MARTIN AND FRED</u> ARE ON BOARD SEA CELT. <u>JOHN</u> ARRIVES LOOKING SHATTERED.

<u>MARTIN</u>: Morning, John – you alright matey? You look shagged!

<u>JOHN</u>: Oh boy – I feel it – didn't get to bed till 4 o'clock.

<u>MARTIN</u>: Well there's a gale forecast so we'll only get a couple of hours at sea. I don't know if it's worth going honestly.

<u>JOHN</u>: Well if there's a gale coming up I shan't go, not like this. The fish'll keep till tomorrow.

<u>MARTIN</u>: Right then, come on back to my place and we'll get Pauline to make us breakfast later on.

<u>JOHN</u>: You're on, mate. (TURNS TO HIS CREWMAN) Go on home, I'll see you alright for turning up this morning.

<u>MARTIN</u>: Fred, if you feel like hanging on a bit, you can clean out the fish hold and give her a general scrub down.

<u>FRED</u>: Right oh Martin – that's fine by me. Morning John – you must have drunk a lot of half pints to get in that state!

<u>JOHN</u>: Lo, Fred – well it turned out to be quite an evening – and a morning. (LAUGHS)

MARTIN: (QUIETLY SO THAT FRED DOESN'T HEAR) What's happened then? Ian hasn't showed up this morning!

JOHN: Tell you when we get to your place.

LIVING ROOM OF MARTIN'S HOUSE.
MARTIN AND JOHN SITTING DOWN WITH MUGS OF COFFEE, LAUGHING UNTIL TEARS RUN DOWN THEIR FACES. MARTIN, BETWEEN HIS LAUGHS, TRYING TO SING "SOUTH OF THE BORDER', WHICH MADES JOHN LAUGH AGAIN.

PAULINE SUDDENLY APPEARS, BUTTONING UP HER CARDIGAN IN THE DOORWAY.

PAULINE:Hey, you two, you've woken the child up. They can hear you out at sea.

MARTIN: (STILL WITH TEARS IN HIS EYES, SAYS HALF CHOKING) Well, it seems that some people out to sea won't be waking up for another 24 hours.

JOHN FALLS OF THE CHAIR, LAUGHING AND MARTIN DOUBLES UP AGAIN.

PAULINE:Well, I can see I'm not going to get any sense out of you two so I may as well start cooking breakfast.

LOTS OF 'OH DEARS, AAHS, I DUNNOS ETC FROM THE TWO MEN AS THEIR LAUGHTER GRADUALLY DIES DOWN.

MARY COMES DOWN AND HER FATHER SAYS

MARTIN: Hello, my dear – give us a kiss. Mmm! What are you up to today!

MARY: Poorleen is going to take me to playschool and then when I come home she's going to take me to see my Mummy and my baby in the Hostipelt.

MARTIN: Oh – Poorleen is going to is she? Good girl Poorleen. (HE WINKS AT JOHN)

PAULINE: Come on then Mary – here's some cornflakes and some orange juice for you – what do you happy fellas want for breakfast – bacon, egg, sausage, fried bread and tomatoes suit you?

MARTIN: Suits me fine, my dear.

JOHN: Sounds fantastic to me!

FADE TO LATER ON DURING THE BREAKFAST WHICH IS NEARLY ENDING.

MARTIN: Well John – you still as keen on a new boat?

JOHN: Yes indeed. I should get about £6,000 for Seven Stars which will give me about half of what I need for that boat we saw yesterday.

MARTIN: You wouldn't think of going bigger – say a sixty footer?

JOHN: Come on Martin – where would I get the money from to put down on a boat of that size?

MARTIN: Well – I've been thinking for quite a while now about things. If I'm poking my nose in then tell me to shut up and we'll say no more about it.

JOHN: I don't know what you're talking about yet. Go on.

MARTIN: Well – I've got enough money in the bank to buy 25% of a decent 60 footer and so have you if you sell Seven Stars. If we become partners it means we'll only have half the purchase price to find and the White Fish Authority will back us with a loan and a grant.

JOHN: (WITH A LOOK OF ASTONISHMENT ON HIS FACE) Hell mate, you've just about flattened me with that.

MARTIN: 'Well, what do you think? I can get Fred to fish the Sea Celt if you had no objection; he'd jump at the chance and I'd also have two strings to my bow. What do you think?

JOHN: (STILL STAGGERED BY THIS SUGGESTION) Martin, let me think about if for a while will you?

MARTIN: Yes, of course. You'll want to do your own mathematics on it. As far as I'm concerned it means that I'll be able to fish mackerel, bottom trawl, long line, gill net, even pair trawl I suppose. Think it over.

PAULINE:(COMING IN) I couldn't help overhearing. It's a marvellous opportunity, John, for you – isn't it?

JOHN: Yes it is dear and now that that silly business of yesterday is out of the way I'll be able to think more clearly.

PAULINE: What do you mean 'out of the way'?

JOHN: Well, let's just say that that little feller won't be bothering you anymore. He's – er – gone on a cruise. (CHUCKLE) And he won't be back again.

MARTIN: (LAUGHING) No, he won't be back, have no fear.

JOHN: And before you ask – I didn't use any violence or threats at all. In fact you might even say he drank the baby's health! Ha, ha.

JOHN AND MARTIN LAUGH AGAIN.

PAULINE: Well – I shan't ask questions at all. I'm only grateful that it's over. Now then, I'll leave you two now and take Mary to her playschool. See you later.

MARTIN: Right, thanks Pauline.

JOHN: Well, Martin, if it's alright with you, I think I'll have snooze in this chair for an hour.

MARTIN: Right oh, mate, I'll go down and see how Fred is getting on with the painting and I'll put a few feelers out on how he'd like to skipper a boat - See you. (EXITS)

AN HOUR LATER.

PAULINE COMES IN HAVING TAKEN MARY TO PLAYSCHOOL AND DONE SOME SHOPPING. SHE SEES JOHN SLEEPING AND GOES TO TIPTOE PAST HIM BUT HE WAKES UP.

JOHN: (OH-HOHING, YAWNING AND STRETCHING) Oh you look good – good enough to eat – c'mere. (HE GRABS HER AND PULLS HER ON TO HIS LAP)

PAULINE: John – Martin might come back – stop it.

JOHN: No he won't, he'll be on the boat for another hour or more so - - - -

THERE FOLLOWS A TWO MINUTE SCENE WHICH I CAN LEAVE TO THE IMAGINATION BUT WHICH MAY EASILY BE WRITTEN IN IF REQUIRED.

AN HOUR LATER ON THE QUAY, JOHN AND PAULINE ARRIVE TO SEE MARTIN AND FRED PAINTING AND SCRAPING ETC. THEY WALK TO THE EDGE OF THE QUAY.

JOHN: What oh, boys.

FRED: (WITH A GRIN) Recovered then!

MARTIN: Ah, just the bloke. Hang on and I'll be up in a minute.

THEY MOVE BACK FROM THE EDGE OF THE QUAY. MARTIN APPEARS AND BEFORE HE HAS A CHANCE TO SAY ANYTHING JOHN SAYS

JOHN: I've had a think and Pauline and I have had a chat and we think your suggestion is a damned good one – here's my hand on it.

MARTIN: (TAKING HIS HAND) Good man, I knew you'd make that decision. I've already told Fred of the possibility. Hang on while I shout down to tell him. (GOES TO EDGE OF QUAY) Fred – ahoy, Fred. What we were talking about earlier on – well you're on. You take her over in six weeks' time.

A REBEL-TYPE YELL COMES UP FROM BELOW AND IMMEDIATELY AFTER IT A PAINT CAN AND BRUSH COME FLYING UP IN THE AIR AND FALL BACK FROM WHENCE IT CAME WITH A BIG CLATTER AND SHOUTS.

FRED: Bloody hell – oh - yukk, ouch! etc.

MARTIN TURNING BACK TO JOHN AND PAULINE, SHAKING WITH MIRTH SAYING

MARTIN: Silly sod – it went to his head – all over it!

THEY ALL LAUGH.

AS THEY TURN TO WALK UP THE QUAY THERE'S A SHOUT OF "Look Out" AND WE SEE A ROPE GO TAUGHT AS A WOMAN IS ABOUT TO STEP OVER IT. SHE FALLS ARSE OVER TIT. HER HUSBAND (WHOSE BOAT IS ON THE END OF THE ROPE AND WHO IS STANDING ABOUT 10 YARDS AWAY) RUNS FORWARD TO PICK UP HIS WIFE (ONE WOULD THINK) BUT NO. GRABS THE ROPE AT THE OTHER END OF THE BOAT, WHICH HAS PARTED. HE PULLS AND DIGS HIS HEELS IN, STOPPING THE BOAT FROM SWINGING OUT INTO THE RIVER AND POSSIBLY BEING DAMAGED; PULLS HER IN AND TIES HER UP AGAIN. TO THE AMUSEMENT OF EVERYONE ELSE ON THE QUAY SHE STARTS SHOUTING

You rotten bastard! – wouldn't pick your wife up but you'd save your boat from scratching the paint. Fishermen!! By God! You should all take your bloody boats to bed with you.

THE QUAY COLLAPSES WITH LAUGHTER AND JOHN TURNS TO PAULINE AND SAYS

JOHN: We're not all the same, my love, well, not all the time anyway.

FADE, PULL BACK TO POSSIBLY SHOT OF SEAGULL SQUAWKING ETC.

(1 Hour)

PART ONE, EPISODE TWO

HARMONIES

Harmonies is a restaurant where the only music played is classical music.

CHARACTERS

Martin
John - Fishermen partners (from A Sailor's Farewell)
Sue (from A Sailor's Farewell)
Pauline
Grandpa – in his last 80's
Hugh (his son) – the owner of the restaurant
Rachel (Hugh's wife)
Mark (Hugh's son)
Emma (Hugh's daughter)
Jack (their hired help)
Tony (Antonio), Hugh's restaurant manager – a Spaniard
Henry (Fish quay manager)
Fred (Sea Celt crew, from a Sailor's Farewell)
Fred's Father

END OF MARCH – A WARMISH DAY.

GRANDPA, IN HIS 80'S, SITTING ON A GARDEN SEAT, BACK TO THE KITCHEN LISTENING TO 'IT'S A LONG WAY TO TIPPERARY' ON 'DESERT ISLAND DISCS'. HUGH, HIS SON OF 50, IS SITTING NEARBY AND EMMA, HUGH'S DAUGHTER OF 6, IS PLAYING ON THE LAWN.

GRANDPA: Terrible days, my boy, terrible!

HUGH: Terrible? ! Why we've never had it so good!

GRANDPA: No, no, not now. Then!

HUGH: (WITH PUZZLED LOOK ON HIS FACE) Then? ! - When?

GRANDPA: (BECOMING IRRITATED AND A LITTLE PURPLE AROUND THE GILLS) In the war, dammit!, and don't say what war – you know what war I'm talking about!

HUGH: (NOW TRYING TO PLACATE HIS FATHER) Hey, hey, Pa – calm down now. There's no need to get all het up; my mind was on other things.

GRANDPA: (STILL IRRITABLE AND RATHER CAUSTIC) That new house o' yours' no doubt.

HUGH: (TRYING TO GET THE CONVERSATION ONTO AN EVEN KEEL) Well, yes, as a matter of fact. It's only natural that my mind should be on it. There's a lot that needs doing.

GRANDPA: (STILL BRISTLING) You should never have bought it. What do you want with a house in town anyway?

HUGH: (NOW STARTING TO GET IRRITABLE HIMSELF) I've already told you – I need an unearned income of £100 a week to keep ahead of the cost of living. It's an investment as a hedge against inflation.

GRANDPA: (NOW ASKING A GENUINE QUESTION) What about the two cottages I gave you? What have you done with those?

HUGH: Don't you remember, Pa, I sold those three years ago because they needed so much doing to them!

GRANDPA: (REALISING THAT HIS MEMORY HAS BEEN AT FAULT) Oh – er – yes, that's right. So you did.

HUGH: I quite agree with you though, the 14-18 war was a terrible thing. What a waste of life. Those responsible should have been shot themselves.

GRANDPA: (GETTING IRRITATED AGAIN, ANGERED BY MEMORY AND BITTER AGAINST THE 'LEADERS') By God yes, Generals! Leaders they called themselves – Huh! And what happened? Did they get hauled over the coals for their mistakes? No sir – they did not! They became heroes – bloody heroes.

HUGH: Never mind, Pa; we must learn not to do it again.

GRANDPA: (INSISTENTLY) But we have my boy we did it again in 1939. Will we never learn. I had a sergeant under me who got blown up on the Somme. I had to write to his widow – poor woman; and do you know what – the poor woman's only son was shot down in 1942 and died in the same place. (SADLY) I could tell you a score of similar cases.

HUGH: (GENTLY) I know Father, you've told me before.

GRANDPA: I thank God you weren't old enough my boy, it upset your dear mother enough when you did you National Service – (A QUAVERING IN HIS VOICE NOW. PAUSE WITH MOIST EYES) I miss her so much some days – Oh she would have loved little Emma so much.

FROM THE KITCHEN WINDOW – SINGING OUT

RACHEL: Tea's ready. Are you coming in or what?

GETTING UP AND HELPING HIS FATHER TO RISE

HUGH: We'll come in, dear. Come on Pa. Come on Emma. Tea.

****

IN THE DRAWING ROOM. TEA IS IN PROGRESS. EMMA CARRIES A WOBBLY PLATE OF CREAM TO HER GRANDFATHER AND THEN THE PLATE OF SCONES AFTER TRYING TO GIVE HIM ONE WITH HER FINGERS.

RACHEL: Help Grandpa to more cream, Emma. Good Girl. An now offer him a scone from the plate. No Emma! Carry the plate over. That's right dear. Thank you.

EMMA: (VERY NICELY AND PROPERLY) Would you like some more Grandpa?

GRANDPA: (WITH A TWINKLE IN HIS EYE) No thank you, my dear, I have some I shan't have more.

RACHEL: (IN A WHISPER) Emma, you must not ask people to have more. That's bad manners.

EMMA: (LOUDLY ALMOST ACCUSINGLY) But my teacher at school says it Mummy!

RACHEL: (BEGINS SCOLDINGLY AND THEN GIVES UP AS IF ACCEPTING THE DECLINE IN MANNERS) Well, she shouldn't – oh I don't know – everything seems to get worse with this education system.

HUGH: (THOUGHTFULLY) Isn't it strange; all this welfare state stuff seems to have brought standards down to make all men equal.

GRANDPA: (REFLECTIVELY AND PONTIFICATING RATHER) Yes, I know what you mean, but don't forget the other side of the coin. I can remember coming over to Britain when I was a boy – and I can tell you that the conditions of the ordinary working man were disgusting!

HUGH: (RATHER HOTLY) I don't know how you can say that and not remember how things were in Argentina!

GRANDPA: (SMUGLY) But they weren't half as bad as they were here!

HUGH: (VERY FRANKLY AND POLITELY LETTING HIS FATHER KNOW THAT HE HAD ALL HIS FACTS RIGHT) How would you know?! You came straight off the camp – spent the night in a 1st class hotel in B.A. and then got on the ship as a 1st class passenger – got off and then made a grand tour of all the clubs, hotels and pubs in London! You're bound to have seen more poverty here by virtue of the fact that you spent most of your time here in a city! In Argentina you hardly moved off your own estancia!

GRANDPA: (REALISING, PERHAPS, THE VALIDITY OF HUGH'S ARGUMENT) What do you ………? Well – Well – I suppose you could be right. Do you know – I never thought of it like that before ---------- Well – at least we treated **our** men **well.**

HUGH: Of course you did, Pa. But that's more than can honestly be said for the greater part of the country – unless you lived in Patagonia where the Welsh co-operatives flourished. (ROUNDING OFF THE DISCOURSE AND ATTEMPTING TO PUT A HUMOUROUS END TO IT. LAUGHS) And that wouldn't have been much use to you either if you couldn't speak Welsh!

GRANDPA: (NOSTALGICALLY) I remember – I remember! Ah – but they were grand days on the estancia. Work hard – play hard, and **everybody** enjoyed themselves probably because they **gave all** of **themselves**. Ah well – it was a long time ago.

HUGH: (SOOTHINGLY) Yes, Pa – it was, but the spirit is still within us – it's only the circumstances that change and remember your motto 'the only constancy in life is flux!'

GRANDPA: (AFFIRMATIVELY) Amen.

HUGH: Very well, then. Come on, let's go and watch the evening news on television.

RACHEL: (A LITTLE RESIGNEDLY) Emma, will you please help me take the dishes away, now that the men have put the world to rights once again

RACHEL AND EMMA BUSY THEMSELVES TAKING OUT THE TEA THINGS FOR SOME MOMENTS. THE PHONE RINGS, AND RACHEL GOES TO ANSWER IT IN THE HALL. RACHEL PICKS UP THE RECEIVER. HER SON HAS REVERSED CHARGES.

RACHEL: Hello – hello – yes it is – what? – yes of course – Hello. Mark! Hello darling. How are you? A LONG PAUSE……………. but of course, you silly thing. Yes, but Mark, Mark! Wait – go straight to the restaurant – yes – you can have a meal there and Daddy'll bring you back here when he's finished. Yes, alright then. – Mark – is everything alright – yes – yes – alright then! Bye darling!

FACE BECOMES A LITTLE TROUBLED. PUTS THE PHONE DOWN AND PAUSES THOUGHTFULLY AT THE PHONE TABLE BEFORE GOING INTO THE SITTING-ROOM.

RACHEL: Hugh, dear! That was Mark phoning from Tilbury. He's on his way down and will come straight to the restaurant tonight.

HUGH: (REGISTERING SURPRISE) Mark, coming home? - ! But I thought this trip was an 'in and out' job and straight on to South America!

RACHEL: (LOOKING CONCERNED AGAIN) Yes, I know. I think something's wrong, Hugh. He didn't sound himself.

GRANDPA: Hope he's alright. Never know – he might be bringing a belly-dancer back with him! (CHUCKLES)

RACHEL: (CROSSLY AND DISAPPEARING BACK TO THE KITCHEN) Grandpa.

HUGH: (ADMONISHINGLY) Steady on Pa, you know how she feels about Mark! (THEN TURNS BACK TO TV AS INTERSTING ITEM APPEARS ON THE NEWS) Hello – what's this?

BACK IN THE KITCHEN

EMMA: Is Mark coming to stay for a long time Mummy?

RACHEL: (WONDERING) I don't know darling. I think he might be.

EMMA: (DRYING A PLATE AND ASKING SWEETLY) Do you think he'll bring me a nice present?

STILL WONDERING AND THEN PULLING HERSELF TOGETHER. BRINGS IN BOB, THE BOXER DOG.

RACHEL: I don't know – ah – yes of course, dear, I'm sure he will, there, give these left overs to Bob.

RACHEL: (GOING FROM THE KITCHEN TO THE SITTING ROOM ASKS) What time are you leaving Hugh?

HUGH: Another few minutes. No need to be too early otherwise I might hurt Tony's pride; (REFERRRING TO TONY, HIS MANAGER, A SPANIARD) managers tend to be a bit jealous of their territory you know. Tony's certainly been a bit prickly of late.

RACHEL: Very well, I'll go out and start the milking then as Jack's got the day off. Back soon Grandpa.

EXITS

GRANDPA: Alright my dear. I'll just sit and watch this for a while.

****

BEGINNING OF APRIL. PENRYN QUAY. IT IS SATURDAY.
JOHN IS JUST FINISHING HOSING DOWN THE BOAT. WIPES HIMSELF WITH A TOWEL – TAKES HIS OILSKINS AND WELLIES OFF, PUTS SHOES ON. PUTS FRESHWATER IN A BOWL WITH A BAR OF LIFEBUOY SOAP, HAS A QUICK WASH OF HANDS, FACE, NECK, ARMPITS. DRIES OFF. PUTS ON A DECENT GUERNSEY, A BRETON CAP. SLINGS HIS REFFER JACKET ON TO THE QUAY AND CLIMBS THE LADDER. GETS TO THE TOP JUST AS MARTIN, PAULINE AND YOUNG MARY ARRIVE IN MARTIN'S OLD ESTATE CAR.

JOHN WALKS OVER TO THE CAR

MARTIN: Ready mate?

JOHN: (A LITTLE DOUBTFULLY) Yeah, as long as you're sure he'll be there this time.

MARTIN: Well, it don't matter if he isn't, our time's our own and we can always look at the other boats.

COMING ROUND TO THE PASSENGER SIDE AND OPENING THE DOOR, GETS IN TURNS ROUND TO PAULINE AND MARY. MARTIN PUTS THE CAR IN GEAR AND BEGINS TO MOVE OFF THE QUAY.

JOHN: Well, if he's not there today he can keep his boat. Plenty on the market. Hello love – hello Mary – don't you look pretty.

DISSOLVE TO SHOT OF MARTIN AND CO LATER THE SAME DAY SITTING IN A CAFÉ IN MEVAGISSEY HAVING TEA ETC. JOHN IS A LITTLE DISAPPOINTED BUT THANKFUL HE'S HAD A GOOD LOOK AT THE BOAT.

JOHN: I'm not sorry he didn't turn up - gave us a chance to have a better look at the boat. Lucky it was low water otherwise we'd never have had a look at her bottom. I don't think she's had anodes on her for two years. Criminal to treat a boat like that. Anyway she's out o' the question so what's the next one on the list?

MARTIN: Well the only one near here is up at Fowey and I hear he's asking too much anyway. I dunno, looks like a proper dead end to me. Never mind, the money you got for Seven Stars is increasing everyday for you in the bank. As long as you're happy working on Sea Celt with me there's no problem. In one way it's a good thing; Fred could never have taken her over so soon; this way he's doing it gradually and building up his confidence more and more every day. Mind you **my** old man would have said "Throw him in at the deep end" but that wouldn't have worked with Fred.

JOHN: Yeah, well we're in to good fishing on the long lines now alright so it's not urgent. But I'm just itching to get my fingers on a decent sized boat. I hear that a couple of fellers in Plymouth have converted their boats to beamers and are making a bomb on the scallops.

MARTIN: Yeah, but converting to beaming means extra money again. Anyway, let's wait and see.

PAULINE: You fishermen! Can't you every talk about anything else?!

MARTIN: Reckon we don't my dear. Ain't nothing more important to us than family and fishing.

MARTIN: Well, we may as well get back, I suppose.

JOHN: (PICKING UP THE BILL) Yeah alright. I'll get this matey!

THE DUGDALE HOUSE – THE NEXT DAY (SUNDAY).
TEA IS OVER AND <u>MARK</u> IS HELPING HIS MOTHER TO WASH AND DISINFECT THE MILKING UTENSILS AND MUCK OUT THE BENCHES THE GOATS ARE MILKED ON.

<u>MARK</u>: It's all very well for you to say that Mother, but you've never been through it. There's not one of the chaps that I could call friend – all I seem to get are remarks about Public Schoolboys being pampered little prigs from privileged backgrounds. I wouldn't mind so much if they were masters of their craft but they weren't, mind you, not one of them was from Cornwall and not one of them was a country type.

<u>RACHEL</u>: (RATHER CRITICALLY) You really are bitter – aren't you?

<u>MARK</u>: (CONTEMPLATING) Not really Mother; I suppose it's the boredom of being here for the last couple of weeks.

<u>RACHEL</u>: (IN MOCK ANGER) Well, thank you very much!

<u>MARK</u>: Sorry, Mother. I didn't mean it like that. I meant that I'm fed up with **me** – I must get started on something big soon.

<u>RACHEL</u>: (CRITICALLY) The sea is big, Mark and you soon got fed up with that.

<u>MARK</u>: There's no need to be sarcastic, Mother. I've told you all about that – deep sea sailing is not for me.

<u>RACHEL</u>: (SARCASTICALLY) In that case you'd better start taking trips up the river in a pleasure boat or catching fish or something but please try to do **something** while you're home. (RELENTING HER TONE AND BECOMING THE MOTHER AGAIN) Your father thinks you're just enjoying a little holiday, but I believe you're searching for yourself, - and moping around here won't occupy your mind and body in doing **something**. I'll help – **whatever** it is you want to do!

<u>MARK</u>: Would you, Mother? Help – that is.

<u>RACHEL</u>: Of course, darling.

<u>MARK</u>: Well, I know all about mental stability and that – I'm not quite an adolescent any more.

<u>RACHEL</u>: (QUICKLY) Of course you're not, dear!

AN UNCERTAIN PAUSE

<u>MARK</u>: Well, I have been thinking quite a lot recently and – well – well – what if I told you I wanted to be a fisherman.

<u>RACHEL</u>: (TRYING TO APPEAR UNSHAKEN) Mark! – that's terribly hard work and I'm always reading of fishermen being drowned or involved in terrible accidents.

<u>MARK</u>: (ADMONISHINGLY) Mother – not a minute ago you told me you would help!

<u>RACHEL</u>: (AT A LOSS) Yes dear but –

<u>MARK</u>: Mother – **come on**!

<u>RACHEL</u>: (TILL SHAKEN) Oh Mark! Let me think about it – it's such a – well, a shock I suppose. You weren't brought up to be a fisherman for one thing.

MARK: (WITH RESTRAINED ANGER – MOCKINGLY) Ah yes – here we go – expensive education and now I'm thinking of throwing it away and all that. Well, Mother – there are people working in fishing boats all over the country who have honours degrees in Classics, Physics and all the rest of it. (REASONABLY) Just because a man's a fisherman it doesn't mean he's stupid, or unthinking; - come on Mother – the world is changing! More and more people – thinking people – are going back to learning basic skills and finding out what they themselves are made of through their new way of life.

AFTER A LONG PAUSE IT DAWNS THAT MARK IS REALLY A DEEP-THINKING YOUNG MAN. GOING TO HIM AND PUTTING HER ARMS AROUND HIM AND THEN HOLDING HIM AT ARMS' LENGTH FOR A MOMENT, HER EYES GETTING MOIST, TURNS AND EXITS SAYING - -

RACHEL: Well – Mark – I didn't realise that you had thought so much and so deeply about things. You really have – haven't you …… You remind me more and more of my Father. If he were still alive he would have said exactly that – people finding themselves.

MARKS LOOKS AFTER HER SADLY, FONDLY.

A FEW DAYS LATER. THE FISH QUAY MID-MORNING 10.30.
SEA CELT IS UNLOADING BOXES OF FISH. CRABS – RED MULLET – A FEW DOVER SOLE – QUITE A BIT OF LEMON SOLE – THE ODD COD AND WHITING AND ONE LARGE TURBOT.
MARTIN AND JOHN MARKING TICKETS. ANTONIO IS WANDERING AROUND LOOKING AT FISH.
MARTIN AND TONY GO TO WEIGH THE TURBOT ON THE SCALES TWO YARDS AWAY.

MARTIN: After some fish are you mate?

TONY: Yes, but I am waiting for my friend who sells me his fish always. But I like this big fish – how much money will this be?

MARTIN: Well - let's go and weight 'im up – soon see. ,,,,,,,,,,,,,,,,,, Well – now – there you are. How about £15 for cash?

TONY: Very good, thank you.

MARTIN: That's alright mate – there you are – I'll even throw in a cardboard box.

TONY: Thank you.

PRODUCES MONEY AND PAYS. WITH A GRIN PUTS THE FISH IN A CARDBOARD FISH BOX.
TONY TAKES THE BOX AND MOVES ON UP THE QUAY.

FRED COMES ON THE QUAY.

MARTIN: Well – I never sold fish to a tourist before.

FRED: He ain't a tourist Martin – got a restaurant somewhere. I seen 'im on the quay before.

THE BOYS TIDY UP, A FEW MINUTES GO BY. WE SEE TONY WALK BACK PAST CAMERA AND GO INTO THE OFFICE.

TURNS TO MARTIN

JOHN: I'll just go and see if they've got my gloves in the office.

MARTIN: Yeah. Get 'half a dozen pair, John and stick 'em down on the boat's account.

JOHN GOES TO THE OFFICE. LOOKS AT THE VARIOUS ITEMS FOR SALE AT THE OFFICE – GLOVES, WELLIES, OILSKINS, DIESEL PRICES AND OVERHEARS CONVERSATION.

MANAGER: And in any case you should be buying your fish through me – not straight off the boat – it'll be the same price anyway – so why don't you?

TONY: (JUST A LITTLE FLUSTERED) I'll think about it – I am sorry to have given you problems.

THE MANAGER IS ABOUT 55-60 AND LIKES THINGS NEAT AND TIDY. IS A LITTLE OFFICIOUS WITH STRANGERS - IS FROM THE LONDON AREA.

MANAGER: There's no problem, Sir, it's just that we keep everything ship-shape here and you'd get a record of your account at the end of every month. I would have thought it would be to your advantage.

TONY: (EVASIVE) Not exactly – but I will think about this matter.

MANAGER: Of course, if you had some spare capital I would recommend that you bought your own boat and sold the surplus to us – there are quite a few for sale here.

TONY: (NOW ANXIOUS TO END THIS CONVERSATION – IS SIDLING TOWARDS THE DOORS. CUT TO JOHN'S FACE – LISTENING, TAKEN ABACK). Thank you – no, but we already have a sixty foot boat which has been lying idle for two years.

MANAGER: Good Lord, why on earth don't you get her working?

TONY: I don't know – there seems to be certain problems with the engine. Anyway – I must go now – I shall have to come back to try to see my friend tomorrow. Goodbye. (LOOKING AT HIS WATCH. EXITS)

JOHN ENTERS THE OFFICE.

JOHN: Six pairs o' gloves, please Harry.

MANAGER: Hello, John; have a good day?

HARRY HAS STARTED PICKING UP HEAVY DUTY RED GLOVES.

JOHN: Yeah – not bad at all in fact. No blue ones. That's it. Thanks. Who was that bloke then?

MANAGER: (MUMBLING AS HE GETS THE ACCOUNT BOOK MARKED 'SEA CELT' FROM THE SHELF). He says he owns a restaurant in town – I think it's called 'Harmonies' - right down the end of town somewhere – never been there myself – told it's a bit pricey. Right – six pairs fishing gloves. Thanks John.

JOHN: Thanks Harry. Don't get up – I'll get them myself.
LOOKING TO MAKE SURE JOHN ONLY TAKES 6 PAIRS. EXIT JOHN - MOVES OUT TO TALK TO MARTIN.

JOHN: Hey Martin – that bloke you just sold the turbot to – he's got a sixty foot fishing boat – it's been laid up for two years!

MARTIN: (GREAT INTEREST) Has he by God! Why's it laid up?

JOHN: He was just telling Harry about it – said it had engine problems.

MARTIN: Well – what do you think?

JOHN: Worth looking at isn't she!

MARTIN: (HALF ASHAMED GRIN SPREADING OVER HIS FACE)
Alright then, but it can't be today. Wedding anniversary today. Going to buy Sue a little present and splash out on a good meal tonight.

JOHN: (TAKING THE MICKY. PAUSE) Oh! – special day then! Best suit and all that! Hey – I've got a good idea! Why don't you combine business with pleasure?! That bloke who owns the sixty footer owns a restaurant as well.

MARTIN: (BECOMING INTERESTED) Does he? Whereabouts?

JOHN: Far end o' town – place called 'Harmonies'. Pricey though.

MARTIN: (SHAKING HIS HEAD AND WITH A GRIN) I don't know how you mastermind all these plans matey, but they always make good sense. Tell you what – why don't you and Pauline come as well – on me.

JOHN: (SHAKING HIS HEAD) Oh no matey – couldn't do that, especially on your anniversary.

MARTIN: Don't be silly – if Sue and I go we'll just sit there saying nothing to each other all night – come on – let's make it a bit of a lively do. Come **on**.

JOHN: (SHAKING HIS FINGER AT MARTIN) Alright then – on one condition - **I** pay for the drinks!

MARTIN: You're on mate! You're on!

SAME DAY

BACK AT THE DUGDALE'S. RACHEL AND MARK ARE WORKING ALONGSIDE JACK, THE HIRED HAND, TENDING TO YOUNG PLANTS IN THE GREENHOUSE.

RACHEL: How are your lettuce coming along there Jack?

JACK: They're doing alright, Mrs Dugdale – and I shall have some radish ready for Mr Dugdale by next week along with the Spring onions.

RACHEL: Marvellous. Well done Jack.

JACK: Tain't me, Mrs Dugdale – 'tis them goats o' yours. Wait till you see what that there dung 'ave done to my onions. (RACHEL AND MARK EXCHANGE A SMILE) Bet you I gets a prize at the show!

IN ASTONISHMENT – HURRIEDLY PICKS UP HER BITS AND PIECES.

RACHEL: Look how the time's going! Goodness! Come on, Mark dear; come and help me get the lunch or Grandpa'll be champing at the bit!

EXIT

DISSOLVE TO LUNCH TABLE. GRANDPA, RACHEL, MARK EATING. BREAD AND CHEESE, PATE, PICKLES, CHUTNEY. A HALF-FULL BOTTLE OF WHITE WINE ON THE TABLE, AND A BOWL OF FRUIT.

GRANDPA: (REALLY ENJOYING HIS REPAST) Don't know why you don't do this everyday for lunch, my dear. Excellent! Good brown bread, cheese and an apple – all washed down with a glass of wine. What more could Man ask of the Gods!

A NOISE FROM THE KITCHEN. JACK'S VOICE APOLOGETICALLY AS RACHEL GETS UP AND GOES TO THE KITCHEN.

JACK: Mrs Dugdale – Oh Mrs Dugdale! Sorry to disturb you but just come to let you know that I'll go home for my crowse today and pick up that spade from the blacksmith's – if that's alright with you.

RACHEL: Why certainly Jack, of course.

JACK: Right oh then – I'll get along.

EXITS AND BEFORE RACHEL HAS TIME TO SIT DOWN THE TELEPHONE RINGS, SO SHE GOES TO THE HALL. PICKS UP PHONE – CALLS OUT TO MARK. MARK REPLIES.

RACHEL: Hello – hello darling …………… yes ……………… hang on, I'll just ask him …………Mark! Oh Mark – Daddy wants to know if you can give him a hand tonight' he's short-handed ……

MARK: (THROUGH A MOUTHFUL) Yes, of course.

RACHEL: (AGREEING) Yes dear – he can – yes alright. Bye. (PUTS PHONE DOWN)

GOES BACK TO THE LUNCH TABLE. ALL THIS TIME GRANDPA IS HUMMING TO HIMSELF AND ENJOYING HIS LUNCH.

RACHEL: Well, that'll keep you amused for the evening anyway, darling. I must say I've enjoyed it every time Daddy's needed me to go in.

MARK: Never know – might find myself a girlfriend.

RACHEL: (COMRADELY CHIDING) You sailors are all the same!

HARMONIES RESTAURANT THE SAME EVENING. MARTIN, SUE, JOHN AND PAULINE HALF-WAY THROUGH THEIR SOUP. MARK ARRIVES AND SHOWS BOTTLE OF WINE TO MARK THEN GOES AROUND THE TABLE TO JOHN AND SHOWS IT TO HIM.

MARTIN: Show it to that kind gentleman there – he's buying the drinks.

MARK: Sorry ………… there you are, Sir.

JOHN: Looks alright to me my 'andsome.

MARK UNCORKS THE BOTTLE, SMELLS THE CORK AND LOOKS INTO THE BOTTLE NECK. SEES THAT ALL IS WELL – TURNS UP JOHN'S GLASS AND POURS IN ENOUGH TO TASTE.

MARK: Would you like to taste it, Sir?

JOHN: (TASTING THE WINE) Seems alright to me.

MARK GOES ROUND, FILLING EVERYONE'S GLASS

MARTIN: Is the owner free to have a word, do you know?

MARK: I'm afraid he's rather busy right now. May I help? I'm his son.

MARTIN: You don't look Spanish.

MARK: (PUZZLED THEN TWIGS THE MIX-UP) Spanish? Oh – it's the Manager you want to see – Tony.

MARTIN: Well it's whoever it is who owns a sixty foot fishing boat.

MARK: That's my father – it's our boat. How did you get the impression it was Tony's?

MARTIN: Well this Tony feller bought £15 worth of fish from us this morning and my mate there got the impression it was his boat.

MARK: (WITH A SMILE) Yes, well I'm sure he'd like to think it was his. I'll tell my father. Do you fish?

MARTIN: (LAUGHINGLY – AS IT IS PATENTLY OBVIOUS) How did you guess?!!!! Yes – we both do. That's my partner there.

MARK: (SMILES AT JOHN) Please don't think I'm being rude but what exactly is it you wanted to know about the boat.

MARTIN: I was told that she's been alongside the quay for a couple of years and I was wondering if she was for sale. Mind you I haven't seen her so I may be chasing moonbeams but if she **is** for sale we'd like the chance of looking at her.

MARK: Well – I'll certainly tell him at once. Excuse me.

PUTS BOTTLE IN THE BASKET AND GOES TO THE BACK OF THE RESTAURANT. OPENS THE KITCHEN DOOR, STOPS, HALF LOOKS BACK, IN THOUGHT; HIS EYES START TO LIGHT UP AND HE SMILES AND GOES THROUGH THE DOOR.

MARTIN: Nice polite lad, wasn't he!

SUE: Good-looking too, I'd say.

PAULINE: So would I.

GIGGLES FROM THE LADIES.

MARTIN
JOHN: Hey - steady on there etc.

THE OFFICE – A SMALL ROOM BESIDE THE KITCHEN AND BEHIND THE BAR. MARK KNOCKS AND ENTERS.

MARK: Daddy – there are two chaps in the restaurant who want to talk to you. It's about the boat.

HUGH: (SURPRISED, HE LAUGHS) About the boat! Dear me, I'd almost forgotten we had a boat! Right – I'll be out in a minute. Just checking these invoices.

MARK DOESN'T LEAVE BUT KEEPS LOOKING AT HIS FATHER AS IF ABOUT TO SAY SOMETHING BUT CHANGES HIS MIND AND EXITS TO THE NOISE OF THE KITCHEN WHERE TONY IS BUSY WORKING AND ISSUING ORDERS AND LOOKING AT DISHES ABOUT TO GO OUT.

A FEW MINUTES LATER HUGH EMERGES FROM THE OFFICE. MARK SEES HIM AND GOES OVER.

MARK: There they are Dad – the table for four in the corner.

HUGH: Thanks. What do they want?

MARK: Just that they'd heard the boat was laid up and wondered if it was for sale.

HUGH: (IN SURPRISE. SUDDENLY REALISING A POSSIBLE SOLUTION TO HIS NEED FOR CASH TO CONVERT HIS NEW HOUSE) For Sale? -!!!!! For Sale! Of course! Mark – this may solve my bedsits problem if – well let's not cross our bridges. The boat! Who'd have thought it – under my very nose all the time. (MUTTERING – LEAVES MARK AND GOES OVER TO THE TABLE) Ladies and Gentlemen – is the meal to your expectations?

MARTIN, JOHN, ETC: Lovely, marvellous, Mmm etc.

HUGH: My name's Hugh Dugdale – I believe you gentlemen wanted to talk to me but perhaps I should come back later when you've finished.

MARTIN: (STANDING UP AND SHAKING HUGH'S HAND. HUGH MUTTERING 'HOW DO YOU DO' TO ALL OFFERING HOSPITALITY WITH A WAVE OF HIS HAND). Oh no, Mr Dugdale. Pleased to meet you, this is my wife. John Trelawney, my partner and his fiancée – Pauline, and my name is Martin Polglaze. Why don't you sit down and have a glass of wine with us Mr Dugdale – if you're not busy that is ……..

HUGH: (WARMING TO THIS MAN). Why thank you Mr Polglaze – it's not often I'm invited, I can tell you! Thank you very much.

HUGH GETS A GLASS FROM THE NEXT TABLE AND SITS DOWN. MARTIN FILLS THE GLASS.

HUGH: Your very good health. Ladies – gentlemen.

MARTIN AND OTHERS: Cheers etc

HUGH: My son tells me you are interested in the old boat.

MARTIN: Well – we heard she was laid up – by the way you say 'old' – how old?

HUGH: I believe she was built in Holland in the 1950's.

MARTIN: Well yes, that's a fair age for a working boat but if the steel is – she **is** steel is she?

HUGH: Yes – oh yes.

MARTIN: Well as long as she has all the proper protection against electrosis and rust she shouldn't have come to too much harm. What's the engine like.

HUGH: Well, to tell you the truth I simply don't know. I had someone do the engine up – you know – new rings etc then she ran the bearings. I had the same chap do her up again and the same things happened **again** so I tied her up to the quay and apart from sending someone down there every few months to see that she's not sinking that's all I can tell you.

JOHN: That's a hell of a thing to happen twice. Sounds strange to me.

HUGH: Well, there you are. As far as I'm concerned the engine's written off although the chap who goes and looks at it every so often says he puts oil in the bores and turns the engine over –I think he uses a crow bar – of all things.

JOHN: Proper job, sounds as though he knows his stuff.

HUGH: (HAS A HIGH OPINION OF JACK) Yes, salt of the earth – an ex tin miner – used to fish as well in the old days (ALMOST APOLOGETICALLY) works for my wife mainly, keeping the land in order. We have a vegetable garden and some goats.

MARTIN: Well, Mr Dugdale, it sounds as if you might not be sad to part with her.

HUGH: Do you know, the idea had not occurred to me until a few minutes ago but the more I think about it the more I'm inclined to agree with you.

MARTIN: Well – can we go and have a look at her, and by the way I'm sorry to talk business to you here but it's our wedding anniversary and I thought I'd kill two birds with one stone.

HUGH: (WITH A LAUGH – PAUSE) Well done – a pragmatist – I like it! In that case would you please accept a small token of congratulations from me!

MARTIN: Oh no – Mr Dugdale please!

HUGH: Come, come my dear Sir. This is the first time in many months that I've been invited to sit at a customer's table. Please allow me to show my thanks.

(MARK ARRIVES) Mark, would you go into the office and bring one of the bottles from the crate at the bottom of the cupboard – Rothschild!

MARK HURRIES OFF.

MARTIN: Well thank you very much, Mr Dugdale. I don't know much about wine but I know the name of a good one when I hear it.

HUGH: I tell you what I'll do Mr Polglaze. I'll arrange for the man who's been keeping an eye on the boat to come and show you over her - his name's Jack by the way, Jack Menhenniot.,

PAULINE: Why my father's brother is called Jack Menhenniot. Lives over to Carnon Downs way.

HUGH: Well! I believe it may be the same man. Congratulations to you then, my dear – you come from a decent and honest family!

PAULINE: (FLUSHING WITH PLEASURE) Well thank you Mr Dugdale.

HUGH: (HANDSHAKING AND CUSTOMERS GREETING) Ah! There you are Mark. Mrs Polglaze Miss Menhenniot – may I introduce my son Mark. Mr Polglaze, Mr Trelawney. Mark was at sea until quite recently but gave it up.

JOHN: (LOOKING AT MARK.) One of us then ain't he!

MARK: (BEAMING SMILE) You bet I am!

MARTIN: Will you join us in a drink Mark? My name's Martin by the way; that's John, my wife Sue and John's lady, Pauline.

MARK: (EXPERIENCING DIFFICULTY) Thank you Martin. I'd love to if I can open this damned bottle.

HUGH: Mark!

THEY ALL LAUGH. POP! BOTTLE OPENS – MARK POURS SOME FOR HIS FATHER WHO TASTES AND NODS. MARK FILLS ALL OTHERS AND GRABS A GLASS FROM THE NEXT TABLE. HUGH MAKES THE TOAST.

HUGH: Well God Bless you both and keep you safe to enjoy many more anniversaries.

MARK: God Bless.

OTHERS: Cheers, etc. Thank you's etc.

HUGH: Well now Mark, Mr Polglaze. Thank you Mr ………… Martin! Martin and John are going to have a look at the boat. I'll arrange for Jack to take them down – oh it seems that Jack is Miss Menhenniot's uncle – he'll show them over the boat. Incidentally, you have complete "carte blanche" to carry out whatever tests you require to make.

MARTIN: Oh thank you Mr Dugdale.

HUGH: Hugh!

MARTIN: Thank you Hugh.

HUGH: Do you have a boat now, Martin?

MARTIN: Oh yes and if we find the boat we're looking for I shan't sell her either – my crewman will take her over – he's getting pretty confident now. So we'll let him take her over, look for new crew for the new boat and off to go!

MARK: Would you take on a novice I mean someone who was new to fishing but knew his seamanship.

MARTIN: Yes – why not? Why do you ask?

MARK: Well – I'm applying for the job!

THEY ALL LAUGH AT HIS CANDOUR AND FORTHRIGHTNESS. HUGH TAKEN ABACK, SEEING HIS SON ANEW. NODDING HIS HEAD.

MARTIN: When you've got something to say, you come right out with it don't you!

MARK: Right!

MARTIN: Are you keen?

MARK: It's the only thing I've thought about since coming home!

HUGH: Mark – I've never heard you say anything about it before!

MARK: No – sorry Dad. I'm afraid it's one of those things – well I didn't know if you'd approve.

HUGH: Approve? – ! My dear boy, I'm absolutely delighted! Absolutely! Well what a marvellous evening and all from a chance enquiry.

MARTIN: Not really – if it hadn't been for your Manager buying £15 worth of fish from us this morning we might never have come here!

HUGH: (CHORTLING. SLIGHTLY LOSING HIS GOOD HUMOUR).
Well, well, "great oaks from little …………" What did you say – how much?

MATTER OF FACT. STAY ON MARTIN'S FACE AS HE LOOKS FROM HUGH TO MARK AND BACK AGAIN; FINAL CUT TO HUGH'S FACE, EMBARRASSED AS HE REALISES TONY'S FIDDLING.

MARTIN: Fifteen pounds.

FADE

THAT NIGHT. FRED'S HOME. HIS FATHER IS GIVING HIS MOTHER A BAD TIME, SHOUTING AT HER FROM THE LIVING ROOM WHILE SHE IS WASHING CLOTHES BY HAND IN THE KITCHEN. SHE IS A FADED BEAUTY, BUT NOW DOWNTRODDEN. FRED IS FINALLY OVERCOME BY IT AND TEARS START TO POUR DOWN HIS FACE. HE IS WHITE; GETS UP AND GRABS HIS FATHER BY THE THROAT CRYING AT HIM THROUGH CLENCHED TEETH, BANGS HIS HEAD AGAINST THE WALL THREE TIMES AND THEN STARTS TO HIT HIM AROUND THE ROOM. SMASHES HIM ALL OVER THE PLACE – FURNITURE GOING TO PIECES – NOW ALMOST SCREAMING. FRED'S MOTHER COMES SCREAMING OUT OF THE KITCHEN CRYING PULLING FRED AWAY. IT FINALLY STOPS AS THE FATHER COLLAPSES TO THE FLOOR UNCONSCIOUS. THEY BOTH STAND THERE, MOTHER IN FRED'S ARMS. FRED BREAKS DOWN, SOBBING TERRIBLY.

FRED: No – no – you can't do it any more – I'm going to fuckin' kill you – you bastard – you bastard – you bastard …………You're not going to touch her again. You're not going to touch her again. You're not going to touch anyone again ……. I'm goin' to make fuckin' sure o' that you fuckin' bastard – I'm goin' to fuckin' kill you! …………!!

FRED'S MOTHER: Fred – no Fred – no don't – you'll kill him – don't - for **God's** sake Fred!

FRED: I couldn't help it Mother. I had to – I had to – I couldn't let him lay a 'hand on you again – I 'ope I've killed 'im!

MOTHER: (ARMS AROUND HIM NOW TIGHTLY). Oh Fred – o' my darlin' boy- my boy – my boy. (THROUGH HER TEARS) 'e wasn't always nasty my darlin' boy.

FRED'S FATHER GROANS, FRED IS SPURRED ON AGAIN BY THIS – JUMPS – GRABS HIS FATHER BY THE LAPELS – DRAGS HIM UP AGAINST THE WALL – SLAPS HIS FACE SHOUTING.

FRED: Open your eyes you bastard, open your eyes! (FATHER'S EYES OPEN SLOWLY AND FRED SAYS SHOUTING) If you ever so much as raise your **voice** in this house again at my mother I'll fuckin' kill you – do you understand! …….?

FATHER: (THROUGH BRUISED MOUTH) Argh – yes ………

FRED: (SHOUTING AGAIN – BANGS HIS FATHER'S HEAD TWICE AGAINST THE WALL AND LETS HIM SLIDE DOWN. TURNS HIS BACK ON HIM.). Right – don't you – **fuckin'** – forget!

GOES OVER TO THE FIREPLACE. PUTS HIS HANDS ON THE SHELF AND LETS HIS HEAD REST ON THE WALL SLUMPING FORWARD AND THEN STRAIGHTENS UP.

FRED: I'll go down to the boat, mother. I'll stay there for a while – don't worry – You'll be alright now. (HOLDING HER ARMS, THEN LOOKING AT FATHER).

MOTHER: Oh Fred – take care – I'll take care of him – don't you worry neither – he'll **need** me now!

FRED: (KISSING HER FOREHEAD SLOWLY – THEN EXITS). I'll go now Mother – you know where to find me.

CUT BACK TO MOTHER'S FACE.

FADE TO
FRED ON THE QUAY STEPPING ON TO THE BOAT. GOES TO THE DOOR TAKES KEYS FROM HIS POCKET TO OPEN THE DOOR – SUDDENLY LEANS HIS HEAD AND HANDS ON THE DOOR, CLENCHES TEETH, NARROWS NOSTRILS AND BREATHES DEEP BREATHS FAIRLY SILENTLY.

BACK TO FRED'S HOUSE. HIS MOTHER HAS A POT OF TEA ON THE TABLE AND SOME CAKE, SHE HAS A DAMP CLOTH IN HER HANDS AND IS JUST WIPING AWAY THE REMAINDER OF THE BLOOD FROM HER HUSBAND'S MOUTH; STROKES HIS HEAD AND KISSES HIM ON TOP OF THE HEAD, GIVES HIS HEAD A QUICK HUG AND SAYS

MOTHER: Oh my dearest love.

FRED'S FATHER DOES NOT LOOK UP; EYES LOWERED HE FUMBLES FOR A PIECE OF CAKE, PUTS A PIECE IN HIS MOUTH – SLOWLY AS HE EATS, HIS MOUTH STARTS TO PUCKER – HE FINALLY STARTS TO CRY WITH A HIGH-PITCHED MOANING SOUND AND PULLS HIS JACKET UP OVER HIS HEAD AND ENVELOPS HIMSELF. SOUNDS CONTINUE.

CUT TO MOTHER'S FACE – TEARS POURING DOWN SILENTLY, LOOKING AT HER HUSBAND.

FADE TO
AT SEA – NEXT MORNING – THE WARPS OF THE BOTTOM TRAWL TRAILING OUT ASTERN OF THE BOAT. JOHN IS ON DECK DOING SOMETHING, MARTIN AND FRED ARE IN THE WHEELHOUSE. FRED AT THE WHEEL CONSTANTLY CHECKING COURSE ON THE DECCA – SOME DECCA TECHNICAL TALK ABOUT GREEN LANES, PURPLE LANES ETC.

MARTIN: You alright Fred?

FRED: Yeah – alright.

MARTIN: Bit quiet today, mate.

FRED: (AFTER A PAUSE) Yeah – well – had a bust up with my old man last night.

MARTIN: Oh sorry mate – I didn't mean to stick my nose in.

FRED: No – that's alright Martin – it had to happen someday I suppose ………..(PAUSE) I slept on board last night Martin – hope you don't mind?

MARTIN: Not at all, old mate. Thought the wheelhouse was nice and warm this morning! (PAUSE) – look Fred – if you need any help or anything ……….

FRED: (LOOKING AHEAD TIGHTENING HIS JAW ANOTHER PAUSE)
No, no thanks Martin. I just got to live with it now, that's all.

MARTIN: Well – you're quite welcome to live aboard as long as you like, Fred, but I reckon you'd better come and have a meal with us now and then.

FRED: (FROWNING) Oh no need for that, Martin.

MARTIN: No – you come and eat three times a week with us matey and that's an order. Starting tonight!

FRED: (TIGHT-JAWED) Thanks Martin.

THAT NIGHT AT MARTIN'S HOUSE QUITE A BIT OF LAUGHTER.

MARTIN: Yes – and when Fred tried to get up off his backside he slipped and kicked a monkfish straight across the deck and the next thing we knew was that John was doing an Indian rain-dance round the deck shouting at the top of his voice – and I shan't tell you what he was shouting either!

THE LADIES LAUGH WITH MARTIN AND FRED.

JOHN: (HUMOUROUSLY – TURNING TO THE LADIES) I don't know why I go to sea with you two, really I don't! You'd think a man's mates would jump to help when a bloody great monster fish has wrapped its teeth around his wellie-boot!

MORE LAUGHTER

MARTIN: (HALF SMILING BUT BECOMING SERIOUS) Yeah – a joke's a joke but I tell you what, John – oh – if you hadn't been wearing miners wellies it would have been a different story.

JOHN: Just what I was thinking mate.

SUE: (INNOCENTLY) Was it dangerous then? (THE MEN LAUGH).

MARTIN: I'll bring you home a monk head one day and you can see for yourself, my dear! …….When shall we go and see this boat of Mr …….Hugh's, John?

JOHN: I thought he was going to arrange it with Jack Menhenniot …..!

MARTIN: Oh yes – that's right ……… Marvellous night wasn't it!

CHORUS FROM THOSE CONCERNED Yes

PAULINE: John – when you go to see this boat can I come please. I haven't seen my Uncle Jack since I was a little girl.

JOHN: Why not? - be nice for you to see one o' your family – wouldn't it!

PAULINE: Yes …….. **'course** it would!

SOME DAYS LATER (MORNING). 'HARMONIES' RESTAURANT.
HUGH AND TONY ARE IN THE MIDDLE OF A CONVERSATION ABOUT THE ORDERING OF MEAT, WINE, FISH ETC IN A VERY DELIVERATE VOICE, SLOWLY. TONY'S FACE IS A PICTURE. HE JUST DOES NOT KNOW WHERE TO PUT HIMSELF.

HUGH: And while we're on the subject Tony, I want a copy of all the wine and fish purchased this last financial year. The accountants had cause to get in touch with the fish quay over some discrepancy or other, and there seems to be no record there of our having purchased **anything** – so would you see to that by the end of the week please – oh and they would also like the names of the dealers from whom you have been buying wine ………

TONY DOES NOT ANSWER.

HUGH: Well … Very well then.May I suggest that you occupy yourself doing that the whole of today. I shall go down to buy fish from my own source so please don't concern yourself with any restaurant purchasing. (COLDLY) Thank you – that will be all

TONY RETREATS FROM THE OFFICE CLOSES THE DOOR, AND WE SEE FEAR IN HIS EYES. WE SEE HIM GO UP THE STAIRS FROM THE KITCHEN TO WHERE HE HAS A FLAT – HUGH HEARS THE NOISES AND KNOWS WHAT IS HAPPENING AND SMILES. TWO MINUTES LATER TONY COMES DOWN VERY QUIETLY WITH A SMALL OVERNIGHT BAG AND SLIPS OUT OF THE BACK DOOR. HUGH, STILL COCKING AN EAR NODS, PICKS UP THE PHONE AND DIALS.

HUGH: Hello, Harmonies Restaurant here …… yes, that's right. Look here ……. I need to have all the locks changed here today. Can you cope with that – would you? Oh how very kind. Thank you so much – oh – it'll be cash by the way. Yes – quite. Don't want all that VAT and stuff do we. Quite – fine – thank you again. Goodbye.
(PICKS UP THE PHONE AND DIALS AGAIN) Hello – Mark – yes – look here – would you come and spend the day here for me please? Yes. I'm having all the locks changed and I'd rather like you to be here while the workmen are here. By the way, if needed, could you cope with managing the restaurant? – Ha – yes well I don't think we'll be seeing him again. I'll tell you about it when you get home – but do you think you could cope if he doesn't reappear? Good, excellent – see you in half an hour. Oh and Mark, do you think you could get your mother to arrange with Jack to show Martin and John over the boat – yes and arrange for it to happen on Saturday ….. what? Yes Saturday ……. No, no Mark! Fine fisherman you'll make! Don't you know there's more to fishing than catching the fish! Oh and by the way – do be sure that Jack knows his niece will be there ……. Thanks ……Bye.

SCENE OF QUAY TUCKED AWAY UP A CREEK (COULD BE GWEEK). MARK AND JACK ARE THERE. MARTIN, JOHN AND PAULINE ARE JUST GETTING OUT OF THE CAR.

PAULINE GOES OVER TO HER UNCLE JACK. JACK KISSES HER, STEPS BACK AND LOOKS AT HER.

JACK: Pauline – my dear girl. My – but you 'ave changed – what a beauty you turned out.

PAULINE: (LAUGHS) You look pretty good yourself Uncle Jack.

JACK SMILES AND PUTS HIS ARM AROUND HER SHOULDERS,

JACK: Well, we shall 'ave a chance of a little chat in a minute when we've finished here. (GOES OVER TO THE MEN - WITH A SMILE) and who's the lucky man who's courtin' Pauline then?

GOING FORWARD, SHAKES HANDS. JACK LOOKS HIM OVER AND SMILES.

JOHN: My name's John – John Trelawney and this is my partner Martin.

SHAKES WITH MARTIN. JACK RECIPROCATES.

MARTIN: Pleased to meet you.

JACK: Well, now where do you want to start?

JOHN: Well, let's have a good look at the hull first and we'll see if she's worth looking at further. Has she got anodes on?

JACK: Oh yes they were put on eighteen months ago when that feller was messin' around with the engine.

JOHN: (TURNS TO JACK) Right wellies on! – How deep is the mud here?

JACK: Six inches if that – the river runs down this bank.

JACK: (TURNS TO MARTIN) Right – got your screwdriver Martin?

MARTIN: Yes, right on!

THEY GET ON THE BOAT AND JOHN TURNS BACK TO JACK.

JOHN: What's her name – anyway?

JACK: 'Foretrekker', but it's properly spelt 'VOORTREKKER'.

THEY ALL LAUGH

JOHN: Quite a mouthful!

THEY GET THE SHIP'S LADDER, PUT IT DOWN AND GO OVER THE SIDE. JACK TURNS TO
PAULINE. MARK STAYS ON BOARD LEANING OVER THE SIDE LOOKING AT THE OTHERS.
MARTIN AND JOHN COME UP WITHIN A FEW MINUTES.

JACK: Well now young lady, come and tell me about your father and mother.

PAULINE: Alright?

jOHN AND MARTIN: Aye all OK.

JACK: What's next then – engine?

JOHN: Yes please.

THEY FOLLOW JACK. CUT TO INTERIOR OF ENGINE ROOM. JACK PRODUCES A TORCH AND
TURNS IT ON. THE INTERIOR IS SPARKLING WHITE AND ALL THE COPPER AND BRASS IS
SHINING.

JOHN: Good God Almighty …….

MARTIN: I've never seen an engine room like this before – who did it?

JACK: Well – I spend a couple of days on the boat every couple o' months and I can't stand being idle so
I give her a shine and a lick o' paint now and then.

STILL LOOKING INCREDULOUS. WE SEE ABC ON THE ENGINE – IT'S MAKE.

JOHN: Is the rest o' the boat like this?

JACK: Well – yes – suppose it is.

JOHN: (SHAKING HIS HEAD) Well – I never – I never! ……. Mr Dugdale said you barred the engine
over every now and then.

JACK: Oh yes – there's the bar.

GOES TO THE ENGINE – LOOKS AROUND IT MAKING APPRECIATIVE NOISES. PICKS UP A STEEL BAR PAINTED WHITE EXCEPT FOR THE END 6". JOHN TAKES THE BAR, HOLDS IT UP FOR MARTIN TO SEE – GRINNING. MARTIN GRINS AND SHAKES HIS HEAD. BARS HER OVER AFTER DECOMPRESSING. CALLS UP TO MARK.

JOHN: Right then – let's try her over – well – just look at that – sweet as a nut. Mark – your father said we could go ahead and do whatever we wanted to so I'd like to work on this engine for a couple of hours – is that alright?

MARK: Yes, of course.

JOHN: Right we'll come up.

ALL GO BACK ON TO THE QUAY. JOHN AND MARTIN GET THEIR OVERALLS AND TOOLS FROM THE ESTATE.

MARTIN: Sorry to keep you hanging around Pauline.

MARK: Why don't we leave you and John here Martin – and we'll go and have some tea up the road?

MARTIN: Proper job – take the car if you like.

MARK: Fine, see you later.

MARK, PAULINE AND JACK. THEY ALL THREE GET IN. THEY DRIVE OFF. MARTIN AND JOHN DON THEIR OVERALLS AND CARRY THE TOOL BOX ON TO THE BOAT. JOHN STOPS AND GOES BACK TO THE CAR AND COMES BACK WITH A POWERFULL TORCH AND A GAS LAMP.

JOHN: Tell you what Martin – if you inspect and test the hull inside down to the keel I'll get on with stripping the engine down.

GOES FORWARD TO THE FOC`SLE...

MARTIN: Right.

JOHN: Oh Martin! You know what she's made of – don't you.

MARTIN: Very old thick steel, far as I can see!

JOHN: No matey – she's made o' Lowmoor.

MARTIN: Lowmoor? But that's black iron ain't it? ....Of **course** – that's why she's riveted!........(WITH A GRIN, STICKS HIS THUMB UP AT MARTIN AND GOES TO THE ENGINE ROOM).

JOHN: Sure is matey – sure is.

ONE HOUR LATER – IN THE ENGINE ROOM – WE SEE JOHN STRUGGLING WITH AN OBSTINATE NUT – IT SLIPS AND THE SPANNER FALLS INTO THE BILGES BETWEEN THE GRATINGS. AT THAT MOMENT MARTIN COMES DOWN.

MARTIN: Trouble – matey?

JOHN SITS BACK ON HANDS, SWEAT ON HIS FACE.

JOHN: Haven't got to the bottom of it yet – everything's perfectly lubricated though – Do me a favour mate – pass up that spanner I just dropped in the bilges – I'm fair knackered! (PUFFS)

MARTIN: Yeah – sure – I want to look at this end o' the boat anyway. STARTS TO LIFT UP THE HEAVY METAL GRATINGS – SHINES HIS TORCH DOWN.

MARTIN: Quite a bit of oil down here John.

JOHN: No harm Martin – good for the metal – that stuff.

MARTIN PULLS HIS SLEEVE UP KNEELS DOWN AND PLUNGES HIS ARM INTO THE OOZE. BRINGS UP A LARGE TAP, THEN A LARGE NUT, SOME WASHERS, A DIP STICK AND FINALLY **THE** SPANNER.

MARTIN: (STRUGGLING, CHUCKLES) Yuugh!

JOHN HAS BEEN CASUALLY OBSERVING THE TROPHIES.

MARTIN: Yuugh – if I reach deep enough – I might get the lucky dip!

JOHN ALSO CHUCKLES AT MARTIN'S REMARK BUT, AS HE GOES TO PICK UP THE FOUND SPANNER NOTICES THE DIP STICK – FROWNS, OPENS HIS EYES A LITTLE MORE AS AN IDEA HITS HIM.

JOHN: Martin! Martin – do some praying while I just try something. Bring your torch over here! Point it right there – that's right.

URGENTLY! MARTIN BRINGS HIS TORCH OVER. TAKES THE EXISTING DIP-STICK OUT OF ITS SOCKET IN THE ENGINE AND CLEANS IT OFF ON HIS SLEEVE. PEERS CLOSELY AT IT. TAKES HIS RAG AND CLEANS THE DIP STICK HOLE IN THE ENGINE, FEELS THE HOLE, LOOKS AGAIN AT THE DIP-STICK, PICKS UP THE DIP-STICK FOUND IN THE BILGES, CLEANS IT OFF WITH HIS RAG – PEERS AT IT. SAYS QUIETLY BUT EXCITEDLY.

JOHN: Martin – look here. Look at this dip-stick that was in the engine – see – look – flat on one side and round on the other.

MARTIN: (WONDERING) Yes.

JOHN: No look at the hole for the dipstick in the engine – feel it!

MARTIN: Not quite understanding. Yes – it's round.

JOHN: Now look at this dipstick you now found in the bilges. Round – ain't it!

MARTIN: Well – yes.

JOHN: (EXCITEDLY NOW) Hang on now for the final test –

PUTS THE NEWLY FOUND DIPSTICK INTO THE HOLE AND IT DROPS IN LIKE BUTTER.

JOHN: (SHOUTS) There! What did I say!

MARTIN: (VERY PUZZLED NOW) You haven't said anything yet mate!

JOHN: But don't you see! It's a different dip-stick!

MARTIN: (BEGINNING TO GET ANNOYED) I can bloody see that. So what! The engine has two dipsticks – one drops in the bilges and the engineer uses a spare one!

JOHN: (PATHETICALLY, WITH MOCK TEARS IN HIS VOICE) Martin, Martin! Pull out that dip-stick and compare it with the other one – go on – I'll hold the torch! (MARTIN COMPLIES) Well?

MARTIN: Well – indeed. Two dipsticks, one dipstick longer than the ……….. (LONG PAUSE AS HE REALISES THE TRUTH) Good God! Good God John! Are you sure?! ……..

JOHN: (EAGERLY) Dip them both in the hole one after the other!

MARTIN COMPLIES – THE ROUND ONE COMES UP DRY, THE HALF-ROUND ONE COMES UP WITH OIL AT THE CORRECT LEVEL.

JOHN: Right, stand back now while I get the sump inspection cover off.

HALF A MINUTE TO DO THIS. THEN WIPES HIS RIGHT HAND **ABSOLUTELY** CLEAN TO ALMOST WHITE. PUTS HIS HAND IN – GASPING SLIGHTLY AT THE ODD ANGLE AND THE STRAIN.

JOHN: Right – now then – here we are – follow the crank – here's the bearings – slide my hand around the bearings to underneath – right! And gently back out again. There! Dry! (SHOWS THE BACK OF HIS HAND TO MARTIN) If that dipstick was showing the correct oil level the bearings and my hand should have been covered!

MARTIN: (IN AMAZEMENT AND ADMIRATION FOR JOHN) So that's what it was that knackered the bearings two times running!

JOHN: Right – some engineer Hugh had! Probably couldn't find the other one when he dropped it……. and got that one from a scrap lorry!

THEY BOTH SIT BACK GRINNING AND START TO LAUGH.

JOHN: Right then – as soon as we get a new set of bearings it can get stuck in.

MARTIN: You're sure that's all it was John? There couldn't be anything else that might have knackered the engine?

JOHN: Absolutely mate! That's it!

MARTIN: (SMILING) Well, I reckon we'd better get cleaned up then and go and talk to Hugh Dugdale!

FADE

MORNING THE SAME SATURDAY. FRED'S HOME – A WEEK AFTER 'THE INCIDENT'. FRED HAS COME IN VIA THE BACKYARD LOOKS INTO THE KITCHEN, SEES HIS MOTHER BAKING, TAPS THE WINDOW, HIS MOTHER RUSHES TO OPEN THE DOOR, SMILING AND HUGS HIM.

MOTHER: Oh you've come back, my love.

FRED: Where's Father?

MOTHER: (QUICKLY) He's reading' the paper in the front room. He's a changed man Fred …….. The first two days it was terrible to see 'im but then 'e seemed – (HER FACE MARVELLING) well – you'd hardly recognise him as the father you knew. It's like we had only just got married again. He don't think bad o' you either Fred – you wait here now!!

FRED: (FRIGHTENED) No Mother …….

BUT SHE GOES THROUGH THE OTHER DOOR. MOTHER COMES BACK IN HALF A MINUTE WITH THE FATHER. TURNS TO FRED.

MOTHER: Sit down Fred and you too Father ……….Your Father wants to talk to you Fred – just listen – **please**. (GOES TO KITCHEN TO MAKE TEA) AWKWARD PAUSE – SLOWLY – NOT LOOKING AT FRED.

FATHER: I want you to know that …….. what you did that night was …….. killed that rotten bastard who called himself your father. I don't know much about sayin' things but whatever it was that happened was a miracle. I feel like your mother and me 'have just got married again and that all that time in between then and now just got wiped out – like God had wet 'is thumb and wiped the slate clean - can't tell you more than that Son except to say that whatever 'appened I 'ad it comin – 'an I 'ope from now on – that you an' me's goin' to be mates. That's it. Son – honest.

FRED'S EYES ARE FAIRLY FULL OF TEARS BY THIS POINT AND HE GOES OVER AND HUGS HIS FATHER SLAPPING HIM GENTLY ON THE BACK.

'HARMONIES' THAT LUNCH TIME. MARTIN, JOHN AND HUGH ARE AROUND A TABLE AT THE BACK. THEY'VE JUST SAT DOWN. HUGH SUPPLIES THE DRINK.

HUGH: God Bless – mmm – it's good to see you two again – breath of fresh air that's what you are.

JOHN AND MARTIN: Cheers, Cheers.

MARTIN: Well, Hugh – we had a look at the Voortrekker and we thought we'd come and talk. We've seen enough we think, and have a good idea of what needs doing, but before we start talkin' money I'd just like to say that Jack Menhenniot has kept that boat looking like the Queen Mary – every bit of the interior is painted, polished and like a mirror. I know that what I've just said may go against us in the price but it had to be said!

HUGH: Thank you Martin – thank you for your honesty – I much appreciate that. Do you know that I haven't been down to look at her for eighteen months. It makes me feel rather small knowing that Jack has worked so hard on her.

JOHN: I don't think Jack would take it amiss, Hugh, he just loves to do it.

HUGH: Thank you John …… Well then the big question ….. I know what the boat has cost me altogether and I must **not** sell her for less than that. I've made a few notes these last few days and I know she's not the prettiest boat in the world and she's rather old – well – oh dam it I hate talking money to people – sixteen thousand pounds ……..!

HE IS OF COURSE, OLD FASHIONEDLY RELUCTANT TO MENTION THE PRICE. ALMOST SPITS THE PRICE OUT. RELAXES ALMOST EXHAUSTED. MARTIN AND JOHN LOOK AT EACH OTHER IN AMAZEMENT.

MARTIN: Are you serious? ……..

HUGH: Why – yes – of course.

MARTIN: Hugh – do you mind if John and I go and chat at another table for a minute?

HUGH: My dear boy stay here – I've got something to do behind the bar anyway.

GETS UP AND LEAVES.

MARTIN: Well?

JOHN: (IN A FORCED WHISPER) I can't **believe** it!

MARTIN: Isn't it amazing – do you know what I think he is? An old fashioned Christian!

JOHN: (LAUGHS) He certainly seems so, matey!

MARTIN: Right. We're agreed – are we? on the price?

JOHN: By God yes!

MARTIN: Right – well he's been straight with us and I reckon I'd like to replay that courtesy.

JOHN: What did you have in mind?

MARTIN: Mark. He wants to learn to fish! Why don't we offer him a job at a guaranteed minimum of £50 a week for the next year? Even if he proves to be no good we'll still have the boat for £10,000 less than she's worth.

JOHN: (FEELING EXPANSIVE) Yeah – why not – he's a good lad anyway – I like 'im.

MARTIN: (TILTS HIS CHAIR BACK) Right-o then – let's do it.

HUGH COMES BACK

MARTIN: Hugh – I'd like to order the best bottle of brandy you've got in the place!

HUGH, MARTIN AND JOHN SHAKE HANDS AND SMILE WARMLY.

FADE TO END WITH 'HARMONIES' USUAL CLASSICAL MUSIC.

PART TWO, EPISODE ONE

SCENE OPENS ON SHOT OF 35FT YACHT "WANDERER" COMING IN TO A SECLUDED CREEK – PERHAPS THE PERCUIL AT HIGH WATER. SHE STANDS A LITTLE OFF-SHORE AND DROPS HER ANCHOR ON THE PORT HAND OF THE CREEK. THE SAILOR GETS HIS INFLATABLE DINGHY OUT, PUTS HIS KEDGE ANCHOR IN IT AND ROWS ASTERN OF THE YACHT FOR 30 YARDS AND THEN DROPS THE KEDGE. PUTS BACK TO THE BOAT AND TAKES UP THE SLACK A LITTLE AND TRIMS THE BOAT UP AND THEN PUTS THE LEGS ON.

WE NOTICE THERE IS A 20FT FISHING BOAT THE OTHER SIDE OF THE CREEK - A FAIRLY TATTY, CARVEL PLANKED TOSHER WITH A MAST AND AN OLD PETROL ENGINE. THERE ARE A FEW HULKS DOTTED AROUND THE HIGH WATER MARK ON THE SHORE.

MICHAEL WILLIAMS GOES DOWN BELOW AND WE HEAR NOISES OF THE KETTLE BEING PUT ON – THEN HE EMERGES WITH BITS OF CLOTHING, HAVING SEEN TO ALL THE SAILS ETC FIRST – HANGS THE CLOTHING AROUND THE BOAT TO DRY OUT – BEDDING, SLEEPING BAG ETC. KETTLE STARTS TO WHISTLE. HE GOES BELOW AND MAKES HIS TEA, COMES BACK AND SITS IN THE COCKPIT TO DRINK IT AND RELAX AND LOOK AROUND. IT'S A LOVELY PEACEFUL SETTING – NO NOISE ONLY BIRDS. CLOSE IN TO MICHAEL'S FACE – SATISFIED SMILE (HE IS 30 YEARS OLD) SOFTLY NODS TO HIMSELF – HE WILL STAY HERE FOR A LONG TIME. WE LINGER AND DISSOLVE TO A SHOT OF THE SUN GOING DOWN.

NEXT DAY. THE BOAT IS HIGH AND DRY ON A SHALE BEACH – THE WATER IS AT LOW EBB. WE SEE MICHAEL CLEANING THE BOTTOM OF HIS BOAT WITH A LONG HANDLED BRUSH. HE STOPS, GOES UP THE LADDER AND FINDS THAT HE NEEDS WATER – GOES BACK DOWN THE LADDER CARRYING AN EMPTY 5 GALLON PLASTIC CONTAINER.

GOES UP THE BEACH – LOOKS TO LEFT AND RIGHT – WONDERING WHICH WAY TO GO – FINALLY GOES RIGHT AND DISSOLVE TO A SHOT OF HIM COMING INTO A FARMYARD, LOOKS AROUND, GOES TO EACH OF THE SHEDS IN TURN. SUDDENLY AROUND THE CORNER COMES A WOMAN OF 25-28, CARRYING TWO HEAVY BUCKETS FULL OF MILK. SHE IS SOFT-FEATURED, ALMOST AS TALL AS MICHAEL WITH HAIR AS BROWN AS HIS – SHE IS STRONGLY BUILT. SHE STOPS SHORT IN SURPRISE, NOT USED TO STRANGERS SHE BLURTS OUT.

MARGARET: What do you want? Who are you?

MICHAEL: (HE IS CONCERNED AT THE FRIGHT HE HAS GIVEN HER) I'm sorry to have startled you. I was wondering if I might be able to get some water here.

MARGARET: (STILL STARTLED) Water? What do you want water for? …….. Why are you looking for water? It's a long way from the road!

MICHAEL: (LAUGHS APOLOGETICALLY) Oh, of course, ……I **must** apologise – I should have explained – I'm moored down in the creek and, well …… I've run out of water ……sorry!

MARGARET: (WITH RELIEF AND A LITTLE NERVOUS LAUGH) Oh……I see ……of ……yes ……of course ……(VISIBLY RELAXES) I **am** sorry, but you gave me such a fright.

THEY BOTH LAUGH, SHE PUTS DOWN THE BUCKETS.

MICHAEL: (GOING FORWARD) Look, let me give you a hand with those buckets.

MARGARET: No – no that's alright I'm used to it.

PICKS UP THE BUCKETS AND WAITS FOR MARGARET TO MOVE.

MICHAEL: Come on – it's the least I can do after giving you such a fright. ……Bringing on a few calves are you?

MARGARET: (IN MILD SURPRISE LEADING THE WAY) Why yes – that's right ……you know a bit about calves do you?

MICHAEL: (NOT VOLUNTEERING TOO MUCH INFORMATION) Yes – just a little.

RECOVERING COMPOSURE. HEADS INTO CALF-SHED.

MARGARET: Well – you'd better come and tell me what you think about these ladies.

A FEW MINUTES LATER, DISSOLVES TO SEE THEM EMERGING.

MICHAEL: Well – congratulations. I must say I've not seen as good for quite a while. Will you bring them on as milking replacements or sell them?

MARGARET: Oh no – we shall keep them on.

MICHAEL: You think milking is worth it obviously!

MARGARET: Yes, of course, ……why?

MICHAEL: Well – it's just that I can see difficulties coming up with the Common Market. They're being very strict on the continent. Some farmers have even been stopped from milking by the enforcement of EEC regulations. I used to have something to do with farming – but there – I'd better not go on – I'll let you get back to your chores.

MARGARET: Well – it's been nice seeing someone around the place for a change – especially someone who knows his calves.

MICHAEL: Will it be alright then ……for the water? ……?

MARGARET: Yes, of course – and there's actually a tap above the cattle trough in the field to the left of the creek. If you don't want to come all the way up here – that is.

MICHAEL: Well – thank you very much ……and sorry to have given you the fright.

MARGARET: (LAUGHING) Yes – well …….Will you be down in the creek for long?

MICHAEL: For ever – if it were possible – it's absolutely lovely here.

MARGARET: Well – we'll meet again then.

MICHAEL: Yes – I hope so.

MARGARET: I'll try and arrange a cup of tea next time.

MICHAEL: Well – thank you – that would be marvellous! Bye now then!
(TURNS AND MOVES OFF WITH HIS EMPTY 5 GALLON CAN)

MARGARET: Bye!

MICHAEL STOPS AND TURNS APOLOGETICALLY.

MICHAEL: Oh ……my name is Michael, by the way, Michael Williams.

MARGARET: (SMILING) And I'm Margaret Jenkins.

WITH A WAVE THEY BOTH MOVE OFF.

DISSOLVE TO PENRYN QUAY – SEA CELT ALONGSIDE. FRED SITTING ON THE EDGE OF THE QUAY EATING A PASTY. MICHAEL COMES UP IN HIS INFLATABLE ASTERN OF SEA CELT AND SPEAKS TO FRED.

MICHAEL: Afternoon.

FRED: (NODS HIS HEAD) Alright then?

MICHAEL: Is it OK to tie up alongside this boat for an hour or so?

FRED: Help yourself my bird, she aint going anywhere today.

STARTS TO TIE UP AND SEES ROPE AROUND THE PROP.

MICHAEL: Thanks and incidentally, don't think me nosey but from down here I can see she's got some rope and nylon line wrapped around the prop shaft.

FRED: (AGHAST) What? 'ang on and I'll be down.

MICHAEL: Here – jump into my dinghy and you'll see better.

PUTS HIS PASTY ON THE QUAY AND CLIMBS ON TO THE BOAT, JUMPS INTO DINGHY AND PEERS AT PROP, SEES A MARE'S NEST OF ROPE AND MACKEREL GEAR.

FRED: By God! …… 'ang on while I get a knife.

MICHAEL: Wait a minute I've got one here (UNSHEATHED A SHARP KNIFE AND STICKS HIS ARM IN THE WATER. TAKES SWEATER AND SHIRT OFF AND LEANS OVER SIDE) - now then – phew – no – here will you hang on to my belt while I lean over.

MICHAEL: Phew …… not quite there – won't be long though ………. (TAKES A DEEP BREATH AND SUBMERGES WHOLE OF HIS UPPER HALF FOR HALF A MINUTE AND COMES UP. TAKES A BREATH, GOES BACK OVER AND EVENTUALLY SURFACES TRIUMPHANT) There! Phew …….. that's better – lucky I saw that!

FRED: Lucky for me you mean. You needn't have done that my 'andsome – that was my job.

MICHAEL: (STILL PUFFING SLIGHTLY AND SQUEEZING THE WATER OUT OF HIS HAIR) Yes, but my reach is longer than your's I'm sure, and I'm used to holding my breath under water, most fishermen aren't – I know.

FRED: Well, thanks mate …… Fancy a cup of tea?

MICHAEL: Yes – I'd love one – do you make it on board?

FRED: No – not alongside the quay – too lazy – besides there's a good café on the quay – oh I forgot my pasty – ah here it is – got to watch the seagulls here – take a pasty out o' your 'and the bastards! (GRINS)

ALL THE TIME WALKING OVER TO THE CAFÉ.

MICHAEL: I expect they're worse at sea.

FRED: Hey! You never take a pasty to sea my 'andsome 'tis very bad luck …… Oh yes! There's a lot 'o things that's bad luck at sea. You never whistle, never wear anythin' green, don't allow a vicar on board and never, ever, mention the name o' those furry things with long ears and a little white fluffy tail.

MICHAEL: (GOING TO SAY "RABBIT") You don't mean ……… ?

FRED: (PLEADINGLY) Don't say it for God's sake.

MICHAEL: Hey – you're really serious?

THEY GET TO THE CAFÉ.

FRED: Oh yes my 'andsome – come on – after you.

INSIDE THE CAFÉ A FEW FISHERMEN – FRED GETS THE TEAS. MICHAEL LOOKS AT THE PRICE LISTS AND LOCAL "ADS", BOATS FOR SALE ETC.

MICHAEL: Thanks – seem to be a few boats for sale ……

FRED: Looking for a boat then?

MICHAEL: Well I'd like to get an unsinkable dinghy to take the place of my inflatable.

FRED: What you want – GRP, wood or what?

MICHAEL: I don't mind what it is as long as it'll take the ground and will last me the next ten years without trouble.

FRED: I know just the thing for you – there's a bloke down the road who has just started building unsinkable aluminium boats – and I tell you what – they-re cheaper than GRP.

MICHAEL: That sounds interesting – any idea how much?

FRED: About £350 for a 10 footer.

MICHAEL: In that case I'm definitely interested.

FRED: What you doing anyway – that you need a dinghy?

MICHAEL: Nothing really, though I wouldn't mind a job on a fishing boat. I'm living up a creek over near St Mawes.

FRED: Ever fished before?

MICHAEL: Yes – I used to fish on the West Coast of Scotland – not full time, mind you, but I know the work and I can handle the gear and a boat.

FRED: Well, in that case, I might be able to offer you something in a week's time. My skipper and 'is partner are taking over another boat – so I'll be skipper and I'll be looking for crew. I'm only thinking of taking one man on anyway, now that we're into the summer.

MICHAEL: Well – thanks a lot – that sounds perfect – when will you know definitely?

FRED: (WITH A GRIN) Right now mate – I'm the new skipper and I gets the crew I want – alright.

MICHAEL: Right.

FRED: You'll be on one week's trial OK?

MICHAEL: Fine by me – but I don't think you'll have any complaints.

SUBJECT OVER FRED OFFERS -

FRED: Well – if you fancy looking at those aluminium boats I'll show you where they are – meet the man himself.

MICHAEL: Great.

THEY GET UP AND LEAVE.

DISSOLVE TO WORKSHOP, 6 OR 7 "ALLY" BOATS OF VARYING SIZE AND TYPE LYING AROUND. THE MAESTRO HIMSELF IS BUSY WELDING. THEY WAIT UNTIL HE STOPS AND PUSHES HIS HELMET BACK. FRED AND MICHAEL WALK OVER TO HIM.

FRED: 'Lo mate – still 'ard at it then?

STAN: (WITH A QUIZZICAL AND HUMOUROUS LOOK) Can't stop man, once I finish one I just bash on to the next – it's like a drug man – I love it. (ALL WITH A TWINKLE IN THE EYE) Well come on don't piss me around man – have you come to chew the fat or see a genius at work?

FRED: (RECIPROCATING) We actually came to drink some o' that bilge piss you call tea!

STAN: (MOCKINGLY TAKES A PUNCH TO FRED'S CHEST) Well – why didn't you say so in the first place! Come on into my executive suite! ....

ALL TROOP INTO A SMALL OFFICE WITH STUFF EVERYWHERE. STAN FILLS KETTLE AND SWITCHES IT ON.

FRED: Got a man here who might be interested in one o' your floatin' mess-tins!

STAN: (LOOKING AT MICHAEL – STILL HUMOUROUS) Well – what's his name then – rank and serial number – what's he want – what for and why! ....!

MICHAEL: Michael Williams .... I'm interested to see what you've got that I can use as a general purpose dinghy and as a tender to my boat.

STAN: Right. Will it need to take hard ground? Not that it matters anyway so forget that question. (HUMOUROUSLY AND RESIGNED) I don't know what I'm talking about half the time – I work all day and I'm out of touch with reality. Okay – you want an all-purpose unsinkable. Do you want it to rest on your deck?

MICHAEL: On top of the coach roof if I have to go anywhere.

STAN: Right what's the length and width of your coach roof?

MICHAEL: Nine foot by four.

STAN: OK – I can make you a nine foot dinghy with a beam of four foot for £300 to clip on to your coach-roof. Do you want it to plane or do you want to sail it?

MICHAEL: Planing would be quite useful though I've only got a 6 horsepower outboard.

STAN: Adequate – perfectly adequate. My dinghies plane with a four horse.

MICHAEL: That sounds find to me but what were you going to say about the coach roof?

STAN: (TURNS TO TURN OFF THE KETTLE, POURS INTO THE CUPS WITH TEABAGS. POURS IN MILK AND SUGAR AND HANDS THEM ROUND. Just that I can make you some handy clips that you can bolt through your coach roof so that you'll never lose your dinghy in a blow.

MICHAEL: OK – Can you show me some to give me an idea.

STAN: Yeah – we'll go and see to that when we've finished the serious business of drinking tea – ugh! (TAKES A SIP) For £300 you are treated to this rare experience and titillation of the taste buds. (IRONICALLY) I'll throw the boat in for nothing ......! (BITTERLY) Tea bags – ugh! ......!

WE MOVE TO HARMONIES RESTAURANT. MICHAEL IS SITTING DOWN AT THE BAR ENJOYING A GLASS OF DRY SHERRY WHILST WAITING FOR HIS LUNCH. GRANDPA IS AT A TABLE NEAR THE BAR. THEY ARE THE ONLY TWO IN THE RESTAURANT.

GRANDPA: Young man! come and share my table – a little conversation will help the day along!

MICHAEL: (LOOKING AROUND IN SURPRISE, TAKES HIS DRINK OVER, SITS. Why yes, I'd love to. Thank you! How kind of you.

GRANDPA: Not at all, I think it a cardinal sin for people to dine alone!

MICHAEL: (SITTING – PAUSE) What a rare place this is. It's not often that one can enjoy good music **and** good food...... (WITH A SMILE) Perhaps I shouldn't cross my bridges as I haven't yet sampled the cuisine.

GRANDPA: Oh I can vouch for the cuisine – have no fear. My son owns this place and I brought him up correctly. You'll enjoy it – you'll see!

HUGH: (COMING IN) Are you comfortable, Sir? Has my father been looking after you?

MICHAEL: Oh yes indeed – he's just been extolling the virtues of your cuisine!

HUGH: (WITH A HAND ON HIS FATHER'S SHOULDER) Thank you father. Would you care to join my father and me in a glass of sherry?

MICHAEL: (APPRECIATELY) Why, thank you, it's a particularly good dry sherry.

HUGH: Ah yes – I'm afraid it's knowing where to buy these days.

MICHAEL: I hope you'll excuse my attire but I just came ashore across the road there.

GRANDPA: My dear boy – the days of correct attire have long gone – and I must say I'm rather glad – still it gave one something to do, I suppose.

HUGH: What kind of vessel do you have?

MICHAEL: Well – I've actually just bought a little aluminium tender – unsinkable ……

HUGH: (INTERRUPTING) From Stan the Man?

MICHAEL: Why yes! I must say he is a wizard – goes twice as well as my old inflatable and ten times as safe. And not only that – it's about half the price.

HUGH: I know, I know! I've just sold a trawler to some fishermen and they've been looking around for an inflatable – but they're all fairly pricey. Thing is they're so compact when deflated and they can stow them in a locker.

MICHAEL: Well – my old one's for sale if they'd care to look at it.

HUGH: (GOES TO GET THE SHERRIES) Fine – well I'll let them know.

AFTER A PAUSE.

GRANDPA: Do you live locally?

MICHAEL: No, just arrived. I've moored up a creek the other side.

GRANDPA Ah, it's lovely over there – some good farming land too.

MICHAEL: Yes, I was thinking that myself.

GRANDPA: Are you a farming man then?

MICHAEL: Basically yes, but I've had a rather longish holiday and I've found myself wondering about land down here these last few days. It seems to be so much milder!

GRANDPA: Yes it is, but we do get all the wind in creation sometimes it seems!

HUGH RETURNS WITH DRINKS. DISTRIBUTES DRINKS. ALL LIFT THEIR GLASSES.

HUGH: There we are Sir, father; your good health Sir!
MICHAEL: And yours Sir.
GRANDPA: God Bless.

PAUSE.

MICHAEL: (THINKING ABOUT FARMS) Do you have a telephone I could use please? It's a London call.

HUGH: But of course. Come into the office – ask for ADC that's easiest. (TAKES HIM TO THE OFFICE AND LEAVES)

MICHAEL: (LIFTS PHONE AND SPEAKS TO OPERATOR) ADC please – yes ……

HUGH: Nice chap – not seen him in before.

GRANDPA: Yes – good stock, I've no doubt!

IN THE OFFICE.

MICHAEL: So if I find anything I can buy it using the name of the London registered company...... Yes ...... No ...... but I think there's some good farming land down here and quite honestly, I like it here ...... No ...... of course not – I'll let you know by phone immediately ...... yes! ...... name, location and price ...... Yes of course. Fine – as long as everything is clear for me to go ahead if I wish. Good – thank you Simon. Yes – Goodbye. ......

PUTS PHONE DOWN, RETURNS TO TABLE. THANKS HUGH.

MICHAEL: Thank you very much

HUGH: Not at all, Sir.

MICHAEL: Would you add it on to the bill please?

HUGH: Yes, of course, (PHONE RINGS AND HUGH GOES TO ANSWER IT) ...... ah that'll be the operator now.

PENRYN QUAY. SOME DAYS LATER.
MARTIN, JOHN AND FRED TIDYING UP THE BOAT.

MARTIN: So why did you tell him you'd take him on?

FRED: Well I only said he could have a week's trial Martin.

MARTIN: Yeah, well you haven't seen 'im since, have you!

FRED: No – but I think he's the kind of chap you can trust.

MARTIN: Never mind. ...... look why don't you come over to the Voortrekker this afternoon? Give us a hand just to polish the brasses an' that before the girls come on board tomorrow for their look-around.

FRED: Yeah alright – I 'aven't 'ad a good look at her anyway.

MARTIN: Well – we'd better get cracking then as Hugh's sending a bloke over with an inflatable this afternoon. Don't want to miss that – not at the price he's askin.

THE SAME DAY.
BACK AT THE FARM MICHAEL HAS JUST ASKED MARGARET IF SHE'D LIKE A TRIP ACROSS THE RIVER, SHE GOES BACK INTO THE HOUSE – INTRODUCES HIM TO HER FATHER WHO IS ARTHRITIC.

MARGARET: Come in Michael ...... Father – this is the gentleman whose boat is in the creek, Michael Williams. This is my father Michael.

MICHAEL: How do you do, Sir.

MR JENKINS: Pleased to meet you young man. Are you alright down there?

MICHAEL: Oh yes thank you – it's beautiful there.

MR JENKIN: Well, you want to watch yourself if it starts to blow from the South. Can get a bit nasty. How's my old boat there – is she still afloat?

MICHAEL: Is that the twenty footer?

MR JENKINS: Yes – the little Tosher – lovely little boat if she were cared for, but my arthritis makes it impossible now.

MICHAEL: Well – I'll look her over for you tomorrow. Make sure she's alright.

MR JENKINS: Oh I think she's probably long past her days – bit like me I suppose.

MICHAEL: I don't believe that for one minute, not of either of you – but I'll have a look at her anyway – I hope you don't mind me asking your daughter out for the afternoon, but as it's such a beautiful day I thought we might go across and up the Helford – I've got to deliver an inflatable there – and it should be a lovely trip.

MR JENKINS: Not at all my boy – not at all. High time she had a day out – it's not good for her to be working around the place all day **and** looking after me. Besides I've got to go and tell the auctioneers exactly where the boundaries lie.

MARGARET: What about, Father?

MR JENKINS: Oh, it's next door dear. They're putting it up for auction next month. …… (TO MICHAEL WHO PRICKS UP HIS EARS) You'd think that 30 acres would pay these days, but there, it seems that some so called farmers seem to have high-fallutin' ideas. New cars, new tractors, new outbuildings. Huh! No wonder they've gone bankrupt!

MICHAEL: Well – there you are Mr. Jenkins – some people will never realise what farming is all about.

MR JENKINS: Quite right – we used to say that farmers were born – not made.

MICHAEL: And I think that's the truth of it, Mr Jenkins – well, I'm afraid we must go if we're to be there in time ……… It was nice meeting you, Sir.

MR JENKINS: And you, my boy.

MICHAEL AND MARGARET TURN, LEAVE AND WALK DOWN THE YARD. FATHER LOOKS AFTER THEM THOUGHTFULLY. MARGARET TURNS AND WAVES – HE RAISES HIS HAND AND SMILES.

THE QUAY WHERE "VORTREKKER" IS MOORED. THE BOAT NOW LOOKING SPIC AND SPAN. IT IS HIGH WATER – THE ENGINE IS RUNNING SWEETLY. JOHN IS IN THE WHEELHOUSE, MARTIN ON DECK COCKING AN EAR TO THE ENGINE. JOHN GIVES HER A FEW SHORT BURSTS ON THE THROTTLE. MARTIN SMILES – SHAKES HIS HEAD TO ONE SIDE, GRINS AND WINKS AT JOHN.

FRED IS OVERAWED BY THE WHOLE SET-UP. UP THE RIVER COMES MICHAEL AND MARGARET TOWING THE INFLATABLE AT ABOUT 10 KNOTS. MARTIN LOOKS UP.

MARTIN: Ah here he comes I hope.

ALL LOOK.

FRED: It's Michael Williams, Martin – the bloke I asked to be crew on the "Sea Celt".

MARTIN: It's not is it? - !

FRED: 'Tis – honest.

MARTIN: Well – we shall be able to kill two birds with one stone then.

MICHAEL PUTS ALONGSIDE AND THROWS A ROPE UP AND, AS HE DOES SO ......

MICHAEL: Well – I never expected to see you here Fred!

FRED: Nor you, Michael. How's the dinghy then?

MICHAEL: First class. Thanks for that Fred – that's one I owe you!

MARTIN: (NODDING TO MICHAEL) that inflatable **is** the one Hugh Dugdale told me about is she.

MICHAEL: Yes – here she is. You must be Martin Polglaze – I'm Michael Williams.

MARTIN: I know – Fred's told me about you – come aboard – here you are, if you hand the lady up I'll help her over.

MARGARET: (SMILES UP AT HIM WHILE BEING HANDED UP) Ooops – oh – an – thank you ...... oh what a smart boat. (LOOKS AROUND AND MICHAEL FOLLOWS).

MICHAEL: Yes isn't she – what a lovely boat; this is the one you've just bought from Mr Dugdale.

MARTIN: That's right. We took her over last week and we start fishing her in a few days time, if all goes well ...... Fred tells me he asked you to crew "Sea Celt".

ALL THIS TIME JOHN HAS BEEN CHATTING TO MARGARET AND SHOWING HER OVER THE TOPSIDES AND FRED JOINS THEM.

MICHAEL: Yes – that's right. I've been meaning to come over and get more details from him these last few days but I've had a few things that needed doing. However – I'm here now so we can talk.

MARTIN: Well – Fred takes over the "Sea Celt" full time, day after tomorrow. Will you be ready by then?

MICHAEL: Yes indeed I shall.

MARTIN: Look – I may as well be honest with you – I don't know what your experience is or how much you know about boats.

MICHAEL: Well I appreciate that you must be concerned – "Sea Celt" is a valuable work-horse but I can assure you that there is nothing to worry about where I'm concerned. Incidentally, now that you've brought this one will you be hanging on to "Sea Celt" or what?

MARTIN: Well – I'll hang on to her for the moment but what's your interest anyway.

MICHAEL: Nothing really, it's just that the idea of having a fishing boat again appeals to me. Anyway – we can chat about it at some later date – now let's have the inflatable up so that you can inspect it. (TURNS TO LOOK AT THE INFLATABLE).

MARTIN AND MICHAEL REACH OVER AND PULL ON THE PAINTER AND BOAT AND GET IT ON BOARD AND INSPECTS IT.

MARTIN: Hup ....! Well – she seems fine – How old is she?

MICHAEL: Not more than eighteen months old. She's never leaked but I have an emergency kit that goes with her.

MARTIN: Hugh told me you were asking £100 for it – is that right?

MICHAEL: That's right.

MARTIN: (REACHES INTO HIS BACK POCKET AND GIVES HIM MONEY WITH A CHUCKLE COUNTING IT OUT IN £5'S.) Well – in that case – here you are – I had to squeeze it out o' the wife this morning.

MICHAEL: Thank you.

MICHAEL TAKES THE MONEY AND GIVES HIM BACK £5. MARTIN PUTS HIS HANDS UP. NOT TAKINGTHE MONEY YET.

MARTIN: What's that for?

MICHAEL: That's your "luck money"!

MARTIN: Luck money? What's that?

MICHAEL: It's an old Celtic custom – you give some money back for luck – both for the purchaser and the vendor!

TAKES THE £5 FINALLY. SPITS ON THE FIVER AND PUTS IT IN HIS POCKET.

MARTIN: Didn't know **you** were a Celt! – anyway – from one Celt to another – thanks, thanks a lot!

MICHAEL: Well – what time do you want me to turn up Fred?

FRED: Half-past five on the quay, day after tomorrow.

MICHAEL: I'll be there. Oh – incidentally – can we tow my dinghy astern do you think?

FRED: Yeah – I should think so though she might get a bit of a bashing about!

MICHAEL: That's fine then – I'll be there! - are you ready to go Margaret?

MARGARET: (TURNS TO JOHN AND MARTIN) Yes – thank you for letting me see your boat – she's so pretty!

THEY BOTH GO OVER THE SIDE AND SHOVE OFF. MICHAEL STARTING THE ENGINE AND MOTORS OFF WAVING.

MARTIN: (THOUGHTFULLY WATCHING THEM GO). H'm – that's a bloke who knows what he's about I reckon!

FRED: (MORE A STATEMENT THAN A QUESTION) Think he's alright then Martin.

MARTIN: (CLAPPING FRED ON THE SHOULDER) Reckon so, matey, reckon so!

DISSOLVE TO MICHAEL AND MARGARET SITTING DOWN IN A CAFÉ.

MARGARET: Well that **was** a treat and thank you so much for the lovely head-scarf it's beautiful.

MICHAEL: (TAKES HER HAND) It was all my pleasure, believe me – you know where this is heading us don't you! We seem to be getting fonder of each other in leaps and bounds – we're both mature but we can't stop seeing each other every day – do you feel it too?

MARGARET: Yes Michael.

MICHAEL: Well I'm too old fashioned and mature, as you are yourself, to rush anything. As long as we are happy in each other's company the next few months will tell us both what steps we should take – do you agree?

MARGARET: Yes, Michael I've always treasured the thought of a ………….

MICHAEL: Don't be afraid to say it, my dear – a secure marriage?

MEANING HIS SEEMINGLY LACK OF A MEANS TO MAKE A FORTUNE. THEY BOTH GET OVER THEIR NERVOUSNESS BY LAUGHING.

MARGARET: Yes – and don't worry about – well – you'll be starting fishing now – soon, so everything will be alright …………… and Daddy's fond of you too!

MICHAEL: Yes …… Come on, I'd better get you back in case he starts wondering where you are.

DISSOLVE TO AUCTIONEER'S.

THE NEXT DAY – AN AUCTIONEER'S OFFICE. MICHAEL IS TALKING TO THE CHIEF PARTNER.

MR EVANS: Well, it's slightly more than that Mr Williams – it's actually 32 acres or 13 hectares – and the owner has **not** been declared bankrupt, luckily; that's just hearsay. The truth is that he overstretched himself in stocking the place and renewing all the machinery and didn't leave himself enough money to operate. I've seen it before – a new hand at the game hoping he'll be able to muddle through once everything's up-to-date. (WITH A SIGH) Well – there you are. Oh – and, incidentally, there's also some land that was bought by the mother-in-law which borders this land – it's about 7 acres – or 2.8 hectares in Heathen terms – a nice little dwelling – 2 beds – outbuildings. The land goes down to the water's edge – has an old quay on it badly in need of repair of about 15 yards in length and (WITH A SMILE) I don't **know** what it would be in metres! As you might imagine the mother-in-law doesn't want to stay if the rest of the family is going back up country so she has put her place on the market also. I believe they will pool their resources and buy something small and manageable up-country.

MICHAEL: Well that sounds splendid – I must say …… I'm definitely interested Mr Evans but can you give me any idea of what the whole should fetch?

MR EVANS: I should hate to be held to a price Mr Williams but if you estimate £1,000 per acre and a further £30,000 for the larger dwelling and £25,000 for the smaller that should give you a rough guide.

MICHAEL: I see – so that makes a total of – um - £94,000 – quite a sum …… what stock does he have on the place?

MR EVANS: There's a small milking herd and about 20 year old pure Aberdeen heifers that he bought for breeding purposes. Apart from the stock there are excellent outbuildings and barns all very expensively renovated and quite a few pieces of new machinery – a tractor – harvester – baler and so on.

MICHAEL: Mr Evans, before we go any further, I'd like to say that whatever business we do will have to be done in my company's name. I don't want **my** name brought into it yet. There are no **really** important reasons but I would just like to remain anonymous for the time being.

MR EVANS: Very well, Mr Williams – that's not an unusual request I can assure you.

MICHAEL: Good. Well – in that case would the present owner accept an offer prior to the auction – for the whole lot – lock, stock and barrel?

MR EVANS: I shall certainly enquire for you Mr Williams.

GETTING UP
SHAKES HANDS AND PARTS.

MICHAEL: Fine. Thank you – until Saturday then.

DISSOLVE TO MICHAEL IN A PHONE BOX TALKING TO SIMON.

MICHAEL: Yes – it's got to be worth that. Look I should like to be able to hand a cheque over on Saturday morning – he might jump at it! Yes quite – and money's hard to come by these days. Oh and Simon – I don't think I want to hang on to the Australian property any more so would you arrange to let that go? It'll more than cover this purchase. Yes - well I'll leave you to juggle that – a simple transfer I would have thought. Fine – I'll phone you first thing Saturday morning to confirm …… excellent – thank you Simon, oh and Simon ……   (WARMLY) come down for a weekend when it's all over and done with …… great. Bye.

AT SEA THE NEXT DAY. WE ARE ON BOARD "SEA CELT" FRED AND MICHAEL HAVE JUST HAULED UP THE COD-END. FRED UNDOES THE ROPE THAT FASTENS IT – PULLS AND A NICE MIXED BAG CASCADES ON THE DECK.

FRED: That's not bad for our first haul together Michael – right – give it a shake. Let's tie her up again and let's have another go. (MAKES THAT SPECIAL KNOT)

THEY BOTH GO ABOUT THE BUSINESS OF GETTING THE TRAWL OUT AGAIN, THEN THE DOORS AND MICHAEL GOES TO OPERATE THE WINCH WHILE FRED GOES TO THE WHEELHOUSE AND MOVES THE BOAT AHEAD UNTIL THE WARPS ARE TIGHT.

MICHAEL: (SHOUTING) Right ho Fred, I've let the same amount of warp out.

FROM THE WHEELHOUSE. MICHAEL MOVES IN.

FRED: That's it mate – come on inside! - Happy to be fishing again?

MICHAEL: I should say so – marvellous out here, Fred. She's a damned good boat isn't she!

FRED: She **is** boy – best in the fleet – I reckon, and John keeps that engine sweet as a nut. She'll do! Reckon you will too matey!

MICHAEL: Well – thank you Fred.

A SILENCE
THEN

FRED: Where you from then, Michael? You speak a bit posh like so you could be from anywhere! - No offence meant mate!

MICHAEL: That's alright Fred. Well – I was born in Scotland, my family's well-off you could say so I was sent to one of those strange schools which are anything but Public. But originally my great-grandfather came from Cornwall, although **his** grandfather came from Wales, so I have **some** Cornish blood in my veins, you see!

FRED Well you ain't an Emmett anyway!

MICHAEL: What's an Emmett?

FRED: (LAUGHS) A tourist-type bloke from up-country …… There was a lorry driver on the quay the other day, chap from Helston. Do you know Helston?

MICHAEL: No.

FRED: Well – Helston gets proper jammed wi' traffic in the summer – anyway, e' was sayin' as 'ow the new word for Emmets was "aemorrhoids" – 'cos they comes down here all red an' close packed and gives us a pain in the arse! …… (BOTH LAUGH). An then an English bloke asks 'im what e' calls piles then if 'aemorrhoids is Englishmen and – know what e' said? (GUFFAWS).

MICHAEL: No. what?

FRED: Asteroids!

BOTH FALLING ABOUT LAUGHING.

DISSOLVE TO MICHAEL APPROACHING HIS BOAT IN HIS DINGHY. TIES UP ALONGSIDE – GOES ABOARD, BRINGS A PAN OF WATER ON DECK, STRIPS DOWN, WASHES, DRIES OFF. THROWS WATER AWAY, GOES BELOW AND EMERGES LATER IN A CLEAN SHIRT, TIE, FLANNELS AND JACKET. GETS INTO THE DINGHY AND ROWS OVER TO THE SHORE. PULLS UP ON THE HARD. EXCHANGES WELLIES FOR SHOES AND WALKS UP TO THE FARM – IT IS 6.30 PM. HE KNOCKS THE FARMHOUSE DOOR. IT IS OPENED UP BY MARGARET AND HER FACE LIGHTS UP.

MARGARET: Michael! Oh **do** come in …… Daddy here's Michael come to see us!

MR JENKINS: Oh good – it'll give me an excuse to open that bottle of whisky by way of saying "thank you" for cleaning up my old "Tosher".

MICHAEL: Not at all Mr Jenkins – I enjoyed it – she's beautifully built and actually, once I'd cleaned up and dried the magneto, the old engine went well.

MR JENKINS: (INCREDULOUSLY) You got her going? ……! But she hasn't been started for three years!

MICHAEL: (LOOKING AT MR JENKINS QUICKLY) Just goes to show what the old ones are made of! …… I actually came to ask if you'd like to come out to dinner tomorrow evening Margaret, if it's possible!

MARGARET: (ALSO LOOKING AT HER FATHER) Oh – I'd love to – that would be alright wouldn't it Daddy if I got Ben to come up to do the milking?

BEN IS AN OLD FARM-WORKER WHO HELPS OCCASIONALLY.

MR JENKINS: You go on, my dear, don't you bother about me. I shall be fine and Ben will come in after and have a cup of tea. Yes, of course it'll be alright Michael. I don't mind telling you she's been a different girl these last few weeks!

MARGARET: Daddy!

MR JENKINS: Now, now, my dear – it's done my heart good to see the change that's come over you. I'm sorry Michael – I didn't mean to embarrass you, but when a man gets old and incapable and has an only child – a daughter – he takes kindly to someone who obviously makes her happy. (MARGARET GETS A LITTLE MOIST EYED). Come now – open that bottle my boy, and let's have a drink together.

MICHAEL SMILES MOST SYMPATHETICALLY AND GETS THE BOTTLE – MARGARET SETS 2 GLASSES.

MICHAEL: There we are then …………aren't you having one Margaret?

MARGARET: No thank you.

MR JENKINS: Well, God Bless you, my boy!

TAKES A SIP EACH.

MICHAEL: And you Sir!

MR JENKINS: Why don't you have supper with us tonight! It would be quite a treat to have company at the table.

MARGARET: Yes – why don't you Michael! We've got some ham that I boiled the other day and some of last year's chutney!

MICHAEL: I accept, I accept – it's too much! ……..!

ALL LAUGH.

LATER THAT EVENING THE SUPPER THINGS ARE BEING CLEARED AWAY BY MARGARET – THE MEN ARE STILL AT THE TABLE.

MR JENKINS: Margaret tells me you are going to start work on a fishing boat.

MICHAEL: I've started today actually.

MR JENKINS: (IN AMAZEMENT) Well! Not tired or anything?

MICHAEL: I expect it will hit me tomorrow morning when I get out of my bunk.

MR JENKINS: Are you alright down there, by the way? I don't imagine it can be very easy for you if you hope to fish for a living so if there's anything you need or anything we can do – please don't hesitate to ask.

MICHAEL IS REALLY HIT BY THIS KINDNESS. THEY REALLY BELIEVE HE ISN'T WELL-OFF.

MICHAEL: I …… thank you very much Mr Jenkins, I'll remember that …….. .

DISSOLVE TO LATER THE SAME EVENING, MARGARET AND MICHAEL ARE WALKING DOWN THE LANE TO THE CREEK.

MARGARET: I'm so glad I walked you down – I love this little creek and it's funny smells and the cry of the curlews.

STOPPING AND TURNING TO FACE HER.

MICHAEL: So am I …… Margaret …… we've seen each other every day for the past few weeks and I think you know already that I love you, but there's something I ought to tell you (SEEING THE LOOK IN HER EYES) – no – no, there's no one else – I'm not that kind, but after what your father said to me this evening I feel a little ashamed – I had to tell you **that** now, …… (PAUSES) but I can't tell you what it's about until tomorrow ………   You may feel differently towards me after I tell you but, believe me – I love you.

MARGARET: (SOFTLY) And I love you Michael. I trust you – I don't think you would harm anyone willingly.

THEY KISS TENDERLY.

MICHAEL: Until tomorrow then – I'll meet you here at half-past six.

THEY KISS LIGHTLY AGAIN.

MARGARET: Tomorrow ………   Goodnight Michael.

MICHAEL: Goodnight Margaret.

MARGARET EXITS.

CLOSE UP OF MICHAEL'S FACE – TROUBLED AS HE LOOKS OUT OVER THE RIVER – CRIES OF THE CURLEWS. FADE.

AUCTIONEER'S OFFICE THE NEXT DAY 12 O'CLOCK.

MR EVANS: Will you have a cup of coffee Mr Williams? (PICKS UP PHONE, AND PRESSES BUTTON) Two coffees please, Kathy.

TURNS BACK TO MICHAEL.

MR EVANS: Well – I thought you might have changed your mind and weren't coming in.

MICHAEL: No – I had a few things to clear up by phone first.

MR EVANS: Well then – I've been in touch with Mr Morris the present owner and he says he would welcome the chance of selling you the 32 acres, stock and machinery but that he has already accepted an offer for the cottage and seven acres at the water's edge, an offer, as he put it, impossible to refuse. (MICHAEL'S FACE SHOWS THE DISAPPOINTMENT) So I'm afraid that our discussion is now confined to the 32 acres; - a pity but there, that's how these things go so very often.

MICHAEL: Damn! I should have come in sooner. Damn it!

MR EVANS: My **dear** Sir – don't go chastising yourself. You never know – this new purchaser may put it on the market again in a few years' time and then you will be able to jump in. Now then – the 32 acres and dwelling etc are you still interested?

MICHAEL: (STILL RECOVERING) Well – yes, I suppose I am – (BUCKING UP) Yes – of **course** I am!

MR EVANS: Very well then. Mr Morris' instructions to me are as follows – the 32 acres and dwelling, the machinery and all the stock are on the market for £90,000.

MICHAEL: (THOUGHTFULLY, PRODUCES PAPER AND CHEQUE BOOK) Well now ....Mr Evans, I have here my credentials and cheque book and I should like to write a cheque for £85,000 and then go to the outer office and drink my coffee while you phone Mr Morris and discuss it. - It is the one and **only** cheque that I shall write Mr Evans. If Mr Morris does not accept then I shall go elsewhere for land .... there we are – I shall be next door!

WRITES CHEQUE AND HANDS IT TO <u>MR EVANS</u> WHO IS RATHER TAKEN ABACK BY THIS BEHAVIOUR. <u>MICHAEL</u> GETS UP AND LEAVES. <u>MR EVANS</u> IS LEFT STARING AT HIM UNTIL HE REACHES FOR THE PHONE.

DISSOLVE TO A FEW MINUTES LATER <u>MICHAEL</u> ENJOYING HIS CUP OF COFFEE.
THE DOOR OPENS AND <u>MR EVANS</u> SAYS

<u>MR EVANS</u>: Do please come in Mr Williams ....

GOES IN

Well I'm happy to tell you that Mr Morris has accepted your offer. Congratulations! You now possess one of the nicest little farms in the area.

<u>MICHAEL</u>: Thank you Mr Evans – oh and, by the way, I shall want to dispose of the milking herd soon and I may ask you to buy me some sheep and more Aberdeens.

<u>MR EVANS</u>: Very well, Sir, whatever you wish.

<u>MICHAEL</u>: Good – oh and would you get in touch with my Solicitors please? It's all there in those papers – and you can arrange things between you. I'm in no hurry to move in – give Mr Morris a month or so – I'll go over and chat to him tomorrow evening .... Right – I must be off now – oh, by the way, who's the chap who bought the seven acres?

<u>MR EVANS</u>: His name is Bishop, Teddy Bishop.

<u>MICHAEL</u>: Well – I shall probably meet him sooner or later, I suppose. Now then – I must get off. Thank you again Mr Evans. Goodbye now.

SHAKES HANDS. EXITS. DISSOLVE TO STREET.
WE SEE <u>MICHAEL</u> COME OUT OF DOOR, STOP, TAKE A DEEP BREATH, SMILE AND GO MARCHING OFF.

PENRYN QUAY THAT AFTERNOON – <u>FRED, JOHN AND MARTIN</u> ARE SITTING ON THE GUNWALES OF "SEA CELT".

<u>MARTIN</u>: Well – that wasn't a bad week Fred – not with novice hand an' all.

<u>FRED</u>: He's no novice Martin, I can tell you that. Knows what 'es doin' all right.

<u>MARTIN</u>: Well – that's a load off my mind – anyway. What's 'e like otherwise, Fred? What do you reckon makes 'im tick?

<u>FRED</u>: I dunno …… 'ard to say. 'e's a damn nice bloke an' all that but I gets the impression that 'e don't care – no that's not right – almost like 'e don't have to work – like.

MARTIN: Yeah – I know what you're gettin' at Fred an you know what it's called in proper English? "An underlying supreme confidence". Comes from knowing what you want and having what it needs to get it. I reckon 'is family educated him properly. I don't mean sendin' 'im to a posh school – I mean they probably showed him that he mattered and that he was important to them – tell you what – he reminds me a bit of Hugh Dugdale.

JOHN: Yes – he does in a way – now you come to say it!

MARTIN: But I'll tell you the basic reason why he's turned out as he has. It's because his family probably had the spare time – that's where they score mate – that's where they score. Mind you on the other hand I know plenty around here with spare time and they don't spend it with their families – no sir – they're on the piss all the time. Anyway – what the hell am I doing talking about somebody else's business – I got plenty o' my own to worry about. The main thing is you're happy with 'im Fred! ....?

FRED: Oh **yes** – Martin!

MARTIN: That's alright then 'cos if you wasn't now's the time to speak especially as he's just walked on to the quay.

FRED IS STARTLED AND GRINS – THEY ALL DO. MICHAEL APPROACHES A CHORUS OF "HALLOS".

MICHAEL: Afternoon all.

FRED: What's she like then Michael?

MICHAEL: Fine, fine couldn't be better!

MARTIN: Well – seems like you did alright your first week then.

MICHAEL: You'd better ask Fred his opinion on that.

MARTIN: I did – 'e said you did okay – so that's alright by me mate! – well – what are you up to tonight then? We're all going out for a bit of a celebration – how do you fancy comin' along?

MICHAEL: Oh dear – I'm sorry but I've already made plans for this evening. I can't alter them I'm afraid, as it involves someone else – damn – that **is** a pity as I would have enjoyed that!

MARTIN: Not to worry – not to worry – there'll be other times, I've no doubt – it should be quite a night though, but there we are – next time, mate. ....(GETS UP) well, better get back and face the missus I suppose. She's goin' on something chronic these last few days says as 'ow I should 'ave bought a bigger house not a bigger boat (THEY ALL LAUGH) - no it's no laughin' matter I can tell you – she means it – was at me like a "Force Ten" last night. Oh yeah, Michael, you won't be goin' out tomorrow there's a big blow comin' up from the South East, so 'ave a lie-in.

MICHAEL: OK suits me. If you're walking up the road – I'll walk with you.

MARTIN: (GETS ON TO THE QUAY) OK Mate! – right oh, Fred keep the fish comin' in (GRINS AND TAPS HIS HEAD) oh I forgot – I'm seein' you tonight – ain't I – see you later then boys – cheerio!

CHROUS OF "CHEERS". MARTIN AND MICHAEL WALK OFF THE QUAY.

DISSOLVE TO SHOT OF THEM WALKING ALONG THE MAIN STREET.

MARTIN: Fancy a pint before your dinner mate?

MICHAEL: good idea – why not?

INSIDE OF PUB SEEN IN PREVIOUS EPISODES. GO UP TO BAR.

MARTIN: Bitter?

MICHAEL: Yes please.

MARTIN: (TO THE BARMAN) Two pints o' bitter please.

MICHAEL: (LOOKING AROUND) My word – somebody likes collecting brass!

MARTIN: (PAYS FOR PINTS. LOOKING AROUND AT THE VARIOUS GIRLS. Yes -...........................
the ornaments aren't bad either!

MICHAEL: (GRINS AND RAISES HIS GLASS) God Bless.

MARTIN: (APPRECIATIVE SIGH) Cheers – ah – just what I need to go and face the missus! – you
married or anythin' Michael.

MICHAEL: (SKIRTING AROUND THE QUESTION) No – not yet, you mentioned earlier, on the quay,
that a move to a larger house might be imminent ……..

MARTIN: (WANDERLINGLY) No! – not yet – what I said was that the **missus** wanted a larger house!
She's right too – as it happens. (WITH A LAUGH) Why – you got one for sale then?

MICHAEL: No – but I just thought you might be thinking of putting the boat on the market.

MARTIN: No – don't you worry mate I wouldn't whip the boat from under your feet like that – I know
work's hard to find these days!

MICHAEL: (LOOKS A BIT UPSET) I appreciate your kindness, Martin, but no what I meant was that I
happen to have some spare cash today and if she were for sale ………….

MARTIN: Spare cash - ! What the hell are you talking about! "Sea Celts" worth eight thousand pounds
of anyone's money!

MICHAEL: I'm sorry – but perhaps I should have said that I have some money; - however in case I've
hurt your feelings let me simply ask you if she's for sale.

MARTIN: (HIS ANGER SUBSIDED) Yes, of course, she is, every boat on the quay's for sale – you
should know that!

MICHAEL: Well, in that case, how much do you want for her?

MARTIN: I don't know what to make o' you, you know! You haven't fished on the boat for a week yet and
'ere you are askin' me if she's for sale as if it was peanuts!

MICHAEL: I don't want to waste you time Martin, I've got plenty of other things to buy with my money –
and you're right – money doesn't mean a lot to me – but a way of life does and the longer the inshore
fisherman survives the better it'll be for everyone. I'm not just a Celt, Martin, I'm British and I'm British
first – and if I have to spend all my money preserving our way of life in farming and fishing then, by God,
I'll do it! Now then, how much do you want for "Sea Celt"?

MARTIN: (AMAZED BY THIS PATRIOTIC OUTBURST) Eight thousand quid.

MICHAEL: With all the gear?

MARTIN: Yeah – of course – with all the gear.

MICHAEL GETS HIS CHEQUE BOOK OUT OF HIS POCKET AND A PEN AND WRITES A CHEQUE.

MICHAEL: There's your cheque – do you want to shake on it? .... For your peace of mind – we'll wait till the cheque is cleared before we finalise. (MARTIN IS SPEECHLESS – HE LOOKS AT MICHAEL, THEN THE CHEQUE ON THE BAR – THEN SUDDENLY BURST OUT LAUGHING. MICHAEL SMILES ALONG WITH HIM). I'm sorry – please accept my apologies, I didn't mean to sound like a pompous patriot though I **do** feel quite deeply about it. Look here – I simply want to invest some money in a fishing boat. Your boat fits the bill and Fred is a chap I trust as a skipper – if he'll work for anyone other than you – that is.

MARTIN: (STILL CHUCKLING) Here's my hand mate – if you're keeping Fred on that's good news – he's a good boy! – well, well – wait till I tell the missus!

MARTIN: (STILL SHAKING HIS HEAD AND LAUGHING) Well – I never. I reckon we shall have to have a pint tonight now!

MICHAEL: I tell you what – I'm taking a young lady to Harmonies tonight – would you like to meet us there before dinner for a drink?

MARTIN: (NOT UNDERSTANDING) When? - before dinner? But it's dinner time now ......oh yes I see, yes, of course, that'll be good. Yes – we'll have one with Hugh as well ...... Just wait till the Missus sees this! (LAUGHS AGAIN)

MICHAEL: Well – if you're happy then we have a deal. I'll be going, I've got to go and have a look for a car this afternoon – it's time I bought one! (THEY SHAKE HANDS)

MARTIN: I'll see you this evening.

MARTIN: (SHAKING) Bye then Michael – we'll be there!

MICHAEL EXITS.

SAME EVENING.
HARMONIES RESTAURANT. PEOPLE EATING AT TABLES – 6/7 PEOPLE AT THE BAR.
CLASSICAL MUSIC SOFTLY IN BACKGROUND
MARGARET AND MICHAEL ARE SITTING AT GRANDPA'S TABLE WITH MARK. HUGH IS FLITTING TO AND FRO AND SERVING BEHIND THE BAR. MARK OCCASIONALLY IS CALLED TO HELP. THEY ARE SHORT STAFFED.

MICHAEL: But I think that the big difference is that Cornwall has such a lot of people from other parts of the country and traditionally so – it's certainly had it's fair share of immigrants this last 150 years – perhaps that's what makes it such a refreshing place to live in – I certainly know that I love it here and shall put my roots down here like my great grandfather did.

MARGARET: I didn't know you had family in Cornwall Michael!

MICHAEL: (WITH A SMILE AND RAISING HIS GLASS TO HER) Oh yes – but they left in my grandfathers day – and now I've come home!

GRANDPA: What do you plan doing with the rest of your life then, young man?

MICHAEL: (SKIRTING AROUND IT) Well – there are certain things that I'm just getting under way but there – it's all in the lap of the Gods.

MARK: How's the fishing going?

MICHAEL: Fine – it's good to be doing something again – how's the "Voortrekker"?

MARK: She's a marvellous old girl – I'm beginning to regret father sold her – but I'd never have got the chance to fish if things had been different anyway ......We'll be starting five-day trips this next week. Makes much more sense – in and out every day would soon put the fuel bills up. The French have always done long trips and look how successful **they** are; - mind you it's our coast they've come to for the best fishing anyway! I'm told there is even a book that's published in France which tells them what fish are where and at what stage of the tide – all with charts and details of wind and temperature! Why – **we** haven't got that. Now **that** is what I call fishing professionally!

MICHAEL: I find that incredible! ...... Has anyone ever got hold of one of these books?

MARK: I've not **seen** one.

MICHAEL: Well – why don't we try to get hold of it and translate it! – what do you say Mark?

HUGH COMES UP TO THE TABLE.

MARK: You're on – I'll get cracking on getting a copy.

HUGH: (LAUGHS) Hello – fishing again! That's all we hear these days – fish, fish, fish!

MARK: That's nothing – I even had a dream last night that we had a hold full of fish and couldn't get back to the fish quay because we were too low in the water to get up the channel – I woke up in a sweat!

HUGH: Well – that's what being professional does to you. I remember a very famous professional wine-taster who had to give up going to church – he used to have this recurring nightmare of taking the communion wine, swishing it around in his mouth, spitting it out and saying to the Priest "Definitely full-bodied!"

THEY ALL BURST OUT LAUGHING.

THE RESTAURANT DOOR OPENS AND IN COMES MARTIN, FRED AND JOHN. THEY GO OVER TO THE BAR – THEY'VE ALREADY HAD A FAIR AMOUNT TO DRINK. THEY GET DRINKS FROM HUGH WHO GOES TO SERVE THEM. THEY COME OVER TO THE TABLE, HUGH BRINGING A BOTTLE OF WINE.

HUGH: For Mr Williams and party with the compliments of Mr Polglaze.

FRED: (SHAKES WITH MICHAEL, INCREDULOUS AND PLEASED CRIES ALL ROUND) And I'd better shake hands with the new owner of "Sea Celt".

MARTIN: Still happy Michael?

MICHAEL: Absolutely.

MARGARET: (INCREDULOUSLY) You've bought a boat? ......!

MICHAEL: Yes – I've just bought her from Martin.

MARGARET: (LAUGHING) And I thought you were struggling to make a living.

MICHAEL: Not exactly!

MARGARET: So that's what you were going to tell me today!

MICHAEL: No, in fact, it wasn't – I'll tell you all about that over dinner – well – come on let's get on with the serious part. (TURNS BACK TO THE OTHERS, POURS DRINKS OUT).

HUGH: Mark – would you come and give me a hand please and find out if Mr Williams' meal is ready yet – (MARK GOES TO KITCHEN – TO THE OTHERS) - it's absolute hell here these days – I can't get a decent reliable girl at all …… I've looked everywhere. Plenty of girls who'll take the job for a few months but not one of them want a permanent job. I don't know what's got into the young people these days.

MARK COMES BACK, CARRYING MICHAEL AND MARGARET'S FIRST COURSE AND PUTS IT ON A TABLE THE OTHER SIDE OF THE ROOM, NODS AT MICHAEL. CHORUS OF "YEAH" "SEE YOU LATER" ETC AND MICHAEL AND MARGARET GET UP AND GO TO THEIR TABLE.

MICHAEL: Will you excuse us please – it's time for us to eat now.

JOHN: Hugh – my Pauline's looking for a job – a permanent one – would you like me to tell her you've got a vacancy?

HUGH: My dear John – if your Pauline is looking for a job, tell her to look no further, she's on starting tomorrow.

JOHN: Right – I'll tell her – that'll buck her up no end. Thank you Hugh.

HUGH: Thank **you** – John!

OVER TO MICHAEL'S TABLE – POURING WINE, LIFTS GLASS.

MICHAEL: To you my dear.

MARGARET: It should be to you on your recent purchase.

PAUSE.

MICHAEL: ………… Margaret - I don't know how you're going to take what I'm going to tell you now but I want you to be the first to know ……… .

PULL BACK – THEIR VOICES FADING – MUSIC COMES UP AND WE SEE MARGARET'S REACTION – SHE TAKES MICHAEL'S HAND IN BOTH OF HERS, HER FACE SHINING. MICHAEL GRASPS HER HAND – BRINGS IT TO HIS LIPS AND KISSES IT. MUSIC UP AND PULL BACK TO SHOT OF WHOLE RESTAURANT – ALL GROUPS HAPPY AND VIBRANT.

END CAPTIONS

PART TWO, EPISODE TWO

PENRYN QUAY ONE FINE AFTERNOON. A FEW BOATS ARE ALONGSIDE, SEA CELT ONE OF THEM. ON BOARD ARE MICHAEL, FRED, ALF, DANNY. DANNY IS ABOUT TO REPLACE MICHAEL ON THE BOAT AS HE IS FULLY OCCUPIED WITH THE FARM.

FRED: ……. and what do I do if anything's needed on the boat? It's not as if you lived just up the street or anything.

MICHAEL: I've thought about that and it seems to me that it might be easier all round if I were to start an account with the fishing chandlers up the road. Sign for whatever you need and they'll bill me each month. How does that sound?

FRED: Fine Michael. Makes it easy.

MICHAEL: Right then (LOOKING AT DANNY) Are you alright to start tomorrow, Danny?

DANNY: Yeah - start right away if you like.

MICHAEL: Well, what do you say Fred? Is there anything else that needs doing?

FRED: Well we could get the spare trawl out on the quay and have a look at it; I'm pretty sure it needs mending up. Best do it while Father's still here as well.

MICHAEL: Fine – well I'll get off now then I've still got a lot to do at the farm. I'll see you later in the week Fred 'bye for now. (JUMPS ON TO THE QUAY, GETS INTO HIS CAR AND DRIVES AWAY)

FRED: Well Father will you give us a hand with this trawl?

ALF: Sure thing my boy.

FRED: …… Danny! Lift this hatch-cover up with me and jump down in there and hand me up the first bit of net that you see. Father, if you go onto the quay I'll hand the net on to you. Pull it across the quay as far as you can and then we can get it sorted out.

DISSOLVE TO HALF AN HOUR LATER – THE TRAWL IS ON THE QUAY. THE THREE MEN ARE ON THE BOAT DRINKING TEA).

FRED: Not so much to do as I thought!

DANNY: Oh I wish every day was as nice as this!

FRED: Yeah lovely ain't it!

DANNY: With any luck we'll have another Summer like '76.

ALF: Oh don't say that! I never suffered so much in my life as I did that Summer! Fair near killed me it did. No matter what I tried I couldn't keep cool. Sweat? ! I must have lost a stone and a half just walking back and fore from the pub! (BOTH LADS LAUGH) Seriously though, sometimes I thought I'd never draw the next breath. I reckon that bloody mine did more to me than bust my hip.

DANNY: What mine was that Alf?

ALF: Wheal Clifford.

DANNY: Was it hard in the mines then Alf?

ALF: Hard? It was bloody diabolical, boy!

FRED: Hey! Before this turns into a lecture on the old days in the mines, lets get that trawl back on board else we'll be here all day.

ALF and DANNY LAUGH AND THEY ALL GET UP.

CUT TO WORKSHOP OF STAN THE MAN. MARTIN POLGLAZE AND JOHN TRELAWNEY ARE ORDERING AN ALUMINIUM BOAT.

STAN: Well come on! It's make your mind up time! Twelve foot or fourteen foot?

MARTIN: Well John, what do you think? Fourteen would be handy, wouldn't it!

JOHN: Yes, why not? Go ahead Stan, make it fourteen.

STAN: OK, when do you need it?

MARTIN: Couple of weeks be alright?

STAN: Yeah sure thing buddy. (LOOKS UP AS TWO MEN WALK INTO THE WORKSHOP). Oh – Oh look out fellers the ferrocement kings have arrived!

JOHN: 'Lo Stuart. 'lo Alan. Don't tell me you're switching to aluminium!

ALAN: No not at all! We've come to issue an invitation to the Maestro here.

STAN: Hey -! Invitation already! Any blondes involved?

ALAN: Nothing like that I'm afraid, old mate. We've just completed our ferro boat and want you to come and see what she's like, if you and your wife fancy a picnic on Saturday!

STAN: Hey right up my street man. Great! When did you finish her?

STUART: Yesterday. We just motored her down to the main quay this morning.

STAN: What engine did you put in her?

ALAN: Ford.

STAN: Fine. Plenty of spare parts for that breed.

STUART: Hey! I hope we shan't need any for a year or two!

STAN: (LAUGHING) Well, you know what I mean. Come on let's have cup of tea.

MARTIN: Well we've got to go now if you don't mind Stan.

STAN: No, that's alright! The boat will be ready for you in two weeks but leave it as long as you can so I can show it to some potential customers.

MARTIN: Alright mate we'll do that. Cheerio Stan and thanks!

STAN: Thank you! 'bye now. (MARTIN AND JOHN EXIT) Well come on, lets get the kettle on.

MOVE INTO STAN'S OFFICE.

STAN: Well tell me about this boat!

STUART: She's basically a Colin Archer with slight modifications. 38' long, 12' beam, 5' draft. She's lovely Stan! Wait 'til you see her!

ALAN: We want to take her out for a spin on Saturday to see how she responds and within the next few weeks we'll take her over to France for a proper maiden voyage.

TEDDY BISHOP WALKS INTO THE WORKSHOP AND LOOKS AT BOATS.

STAN: Hang on a minute, lads, while I see what this chap wants. (GOES TO THE DOOR AND STICKS HIS HEAD OUT). Hello! Anything I can do for you?

TEDDY: I was told that I might see some decent little dingies here, but I don't seem to be able to.

STAN: In that case, buddy, you must have shit in your eyes! (SLAMS DOOR SHUT AND COMES BACK IN). Well that takes care of that customer. Silly bastard! (FALLS INTO A CHAIR). You were saying? ....? (BOTH LADS FALL ABOUT WITH LAUGHTER).

DISSOLVE TO LAUGHTER IN HARMONIES RESTAURANT. MARK AND HUGH ARE ENJOYING A JOKE WITH SOME CUSTOMERS. DOOR OPENS AND HELEN BISHOP WALKS IN (TEDDY BISHOP'S WIFE).

HELEN WALKS IN LOOKING AROUND UNCERTAINLY. MARK GOES TO HER.

MARK: May I help you?

HELEN: (SHYLY) Oh no thank you, my husband was going to meet me here but I see he hasn't arrived.

MARK: Were you intending to have a meal here?

HELEN: Yes, I think so.

MARK: Well in that case why don't you come and sit at the bar until he arrives.

HELEN: Well I don't think I .....

MARK: It's alright we aren't pirates! (TAKES HER ARM AND USHERS HER TO A BAR STOOL) Now, what may I get you, Sherry, Gin and Tonic?

HELEN: Oh no I couldn't .... - perhaps a lemonade please.

MARK: Certainly! (GETS DRINK AND RETURNS).

HELEN GETS OUT HER PURSE.

MARK: (Contd) No, that's alright, it's on the house.

HELEN: (NOW BLUSHING) Oh ! ......But ......Thank you (QUIETLY).

MARK: It's a pleasure! .... Are you on holiday?

HELEN: No, my husband .... I mean we have just bought a place across the river.

MARK: Well done!; you've come to the next best place to heaven.

HUGH: (STEPPING IN) Welcome to Harmonies, Madame! Did I hear you say you have just moved here?

HELEN: Yes.

HUGH: Would it be terribly ill-mannered of me if I were to ask whereabouts?

HELEN: Not at all! It's just the other side of the river, at the waters edge, a place called Creekside.

HUGH: I know that place! A lovely spot with a little quay. I've always loved that little house. There's some land as well as far as I remember.

HELEN: Yes, seven acres.

HUGH: Well that's what I call a decent start in the area I'd say. I wish you all the best of good wishes with it, Madam! Now, may I offer you a glass of something?

HELEN: (MORE AT EASE NOW) No thank you. Goodness! This gentleman has already been too kind! Thank you.

HUGH: Good! This is my son Mark, actually, and my name is Hugh Dugdale. If there's any way in which we may help, you have only to ask. We are, after all, nearly neighbours. Our place is only a few miles from Creekside.

HELEN: (REALLY THAWED OUT NOW) Oh how marvellous! It's been such a worry, you know, having no idea who or what the neighbours are like. It's such a relief meeting you both (SMILING).

HUGH: Well, look here my dear, you must come and meet my wife, she'll give you any help or information you may need, ... introductions, and all that. I'm sure you'll find her useful to you in settling in!

HELEN: Oh thank you so much! Yes I'd very much like to take you up on that. My name is Helen Bishop, by the way.

HUGH: Well now, I feel that Harmonies is living up to her reputation today. I can feel it's going to be one of those days filled with light and happiness.

ENTER TEDDY BISHOP FACE LIKE THUNDER. GOES TO HELEN.

TEDDY: (SARCASTICALLY) Oh I see you've already made some little friends!

HELEN: Yes, these gentlemen have been very kind and ....

TEDDY: (INTERRUPTING) Hm! I just had a conversation with a local 'gentleman! Little swine! I hope all his aluminium boats collapse! Come on! (PULLS HER OFF THE STOOL). Let's go and sit at a table where we can get some privacy! (PULLS HER AWAY FROM THE BAR).

HELEN: I …… (THROWS AN EMBARRASSED AND APOLOGETIC LOOK AT <u>HUGH AND MARK</u> AS SHE'S PULLED AWAY).

HUGH: (SOFTLY) Oh dear, oh dear! I think there's a problem marriage there. And such a sweet little thing too.

MARK: What was that you said about 'light and happiness'…..?

HUGH: Quite!

PAULINE: MOVES INTO CONVERSATION.

PAULINE: What was all that about?

HUGH: Oh I don't know, seems as though he'd been to see Stan the Man, and you know what Stan can be like sometimes…… but, in any case, there's no excuse for behaving like that in public.

PAULINE: Huh! You should have seen him in the supermarket the other day, after one of the assistants, ……. ! If the supervisor hadn't been on the spot quick I think it would have been nasty and embarrassing. And in 'public' too, mind you! He's a bit loopy if you ask me! STARTS TO GATHER UP GLASSES, SHAKES HER HEAD AND GIGGLES) 'In public' …….! (MORE GIGGLING AS SHE PUTS THE GLASSES IN THE SINK AND STARTS TO WASH THEM UP).

DISSOLVE TO WASHING UP IN PROGRESS AT JENKINS' FARM.

JENKINS: …… and I don't know for the life of me why people cut hedges in the Spring these days. Spoils everything, takes away the cover for the birds and small animals …… and it looks so unsightly and unprofessional!

BEN: Yes, beats me too Mr. Jenkins, you can't better a proper cut and laid fence, done Winter-time. Only needs a trimming off every winter after that and it's good for twenty years. ……. Those mechanical hedge-trimmers are frightening things!

JENKINS: Terrible! Oh and by the way, Ben, would you have a look at the roofing timbers in the buildings? I haven't had them treated for seven or eight years, and I heard one of the corrugated sheets rattle the other day in that gust of wind.

BEN: Certainly, I'll do that now if you like.

JENKINS: Thank you Ben.

BEN: Right then I'll get on with that. (GETS UP) Thank you for the tea Margaret.

MARGARET: You're welcome Ben; and thank you for your help. I don't know how we'd manage sometimes without you.

BEN: It's a pleasure. (EXITS)

JENKINS: Do you know Margaret, it's 62 years since I first met Ben Tripp and I've never heard him utter a harsh word, he doesn't seem to change. Never alters his pace, just plods on and gets the job done, come hail or shine.

MARGARET: Yes he's marvellous, isn't he.

JENKINS: And how about your Mr Marvellous? Is he coming to see us today?

MARGARET: Daddy!

JENKINS: I was only teasing my dear. He's a good man and I'm very fond of him but I still don't understand why he didn't let us know that he was going to buy the farm or why he led us to believe that he was virtually penniless.

MARGARET MOVES TO THE TABLE AND SITS.

MARGARET: Now listen to me Daddy! ....! Michael told me he didn't want to be known as a man with plenty of money. He believes that a man should be taken on his merit not by the size of his bank balance; and that too many people with money sit back and enjoy it without having to make any effort and thereby lose the best part of life; winning by one's own efforts. He's a good man Daddy, and I should hate it if you started to have strange thoughts about him and .... well .... I think that Michael will soon ask me to marry him.

JENKINS: (SURPRISED) My dear! Isn't it a bit soon! ....?

MARGARET: It's alright Daddy, don't worry. We've both got our heads screwed on. Michael and I are both hard workers and we'll make a good marriage.

JENKINS: Well now, you do realise that there'll be two farms to work if you get married? ...... ?

MARGARET: Yes Daddy, and, in fact, I don't see why they couldn't be run as one. It's the obvious and simple answer; after all there's only a hedge and some wire which divides them at present. Also I know that Michael is going to breed Aberdeens and sheep, so both farms could drop out of milking before amalgamating and receive the Common Market's Golden Handshake, which is not something to sneeze at!

JENKINS: (A LITTLE DAZED) My word Margaret, you've certainly thought things out very thoroughly.

MARGARET: (REACHING ACROSS THE TABLE TO CLASP HER FATHER'S HANDS) Yes I have. .... Daddy, I hope with all my heart that you will come and live with us. There are 5 bedrooms, so you needn't worry yourself on that score, and I know that Michael will need your help in the planning of the amalgamation and in your local knowledge of what was planted where in the old days. He doesn't like the modern methods of farming, you see; he'd rather plant crops without any spraying of Pesticides and all those new-fangled chemicals. Anyway, I know that Michael would need your help.

JENKINS: Thank you my dear, but when do you think Michael will ask you to marry him?

MARGARET: Within the next few days, ... but he doesn't know yet! ....

JENKINS IS TAKEN ABACK BY THIS REMARK BUT REALISES IT'S HALF IN JEST AND HAS A GOOD LAUGH.

MARGARET: Daddy I want you to be near me always; you know that. Now, if I don't hurry up I'll not have tea ready by the time Michael arrives. (THERE'S A KNOCK ON THE DOOR) Come in!

BEN: I've had a quick look at the timbers Mr. Jenkins and some of them are rotten clear through.

JENKINS: Oh dear! Is there any way in which they could be patched up in case of a storm?

BEN: Well you've got some 3 x 2 in the old barn that's never been used. I could strap that alongside the existing timbers. ....That would help it along for a few months as long as we don't get one of the hurricanes! (GRINS)

JENKINS: Good. Thank you Ben. I'd forgotten about those 3 x 2's. Yes, by all means, go ahead whenever you can.

BEN: Right oh then, I'll get started now and I'll need some of those special nails for corrugated roofing by tomorrow afternoon.

JENKINS: Fine Ben, fine. I'll see to that.

BEN EXITS. WE HEAR A CAR DRAW UP AND BEN'S VOICE SAYING 'IN THE HOUSE'.

MICHAEL: (ENTERS) Hello everybody (KISSES MARGARET ON THE CHEEK). What a lovely day. How are you Mr Jenkins?

JENKINS: Well, thank you; and what have you been up to then?

MICHAEL: Oh I had to go down and see Fred's new crewman this morning and then I had a bit of shopping to take care of in town. It's such a lovely day I'd like to take the boat out for a sail!

MARGARET: Oh yes it's a perfect day for sailing!

MICHAEL: Well come on then ……… what are you waiting for?

MARGARET: We could go after tea I suppose.

MICHAEL: Will you come with us Mr Jenkins?

JENKINS: My dear boy, I couldn't even get down the lane to the creek, with my arthritis.

MICHAEL: Well what if I were to borrow Mr Morris' Land Rover to take us all down to the creek? I could easily lift you on board from there!

JENKINS: (LAUGHS) No no, thank you all the same. I appreciate the thought but you two go ahead. It would be too much for me.

MICHAEL: Well look, if it's a nice day on Saturday why don't I take the boat down the river to Creeekside's quay, while Margaret drives you round there by road? All you'd have to do would be to get out of the car and walk ten steps to the boat, and, if I time it just right by the tide you merely have to step straight on board.

JENKINS: Alright, alright. It's a lovely idea, thank you Michael. I shall look forward to that.

MICHAEL: Right! That's decided then. It'll also give me the opportunity of meeting the new people.

MARGARET NOW GETS A FOLDED TABLE CLOTH OUT OF THE DRAWER AND FLAPS IT IN THE AIR TO COVER THE TABLE.

DISSOLVE TO SAIL FLAPPING ON BOAT GOING ABOUT ON THE OTHER TACK.

MICHAEL: Margaret! How do you fancy a drink in a waterfront bar?

MARGARET: Sounds like a good idea to me.

MICHAEL: Perhaps we could get something to eat as well.

MARGARET: Better still.

MICHAEL: Right then sailor! Port your helm and make for Customs House Quay!

MARGARET: Aye-aye, Sir. (PUTS THE HELM OVER AND THE BOAT SHOOTS OFF TO STARBOARD)

CUT TO THE CHAIN LOCKER PUB'S INTERIOR. MICHAEL AND MARGARET HAVE JUST WALKED IN.

MARTIN POLGLAZE: Hello there Michael, come and join us!

MICHAEL: Hello Martin. Thank you we'd love to. Margaret, you remember Martin …………

MARGARET: Yes, of course. How's your pretty boat?

MARTIN: Turning a pretty penny, thank God. …… You haven't met my wife Mary, and these drunken pirates here are Stuart, Alan, Ron the Lifeboat coxswain, and this is Bert (IN CUSTOM UNIFORM)..(MARGARET AND MICHAEL SAY HELLO TO EVERYONE).

MARTIN: (Contd) Well what would you like to drink Margaret?

MARGARET: A glass of white wine, please if that's possible.

MARTIN: In this place anything's possible! Michael?

MICHAEL: A pint of bitter please.

MARTIN: Right! (TURNS TO BRIAN THE BARMAN) Hey, come on, stop drinking the profits and give some service here!

BRIAN: Yes Sir, immediately Sir!

MARTIN: Glass of white wine, please and a pint of bitter. Oh, and have one yourself and fill the others up as well.

BRIAN: God Bless you Sir! fine gentleman and scholar that you are!

ALAN: Been out for a sail, Michael?

MICHAEL: Yes. Couldn't resist it. Such a lovely evening! Are you a sailing man yourself?

ALAN: Yes, Stuart and I have just finished building our's.

MICHAEL: Oh that sounds as if you know a good deal about boats. What's the one you've just finished?

ALAN: She's a 38ft Colin Archer type in ferrocement.

MICHAEL: Ferrocement? Does that mean she's actually made of cement?

ALAN: Yes, indeed. It's a cement plaster laid into a weldmesh frame with steel rods for reinforcement.

RON: Yes, we know all about ferro boats in my line of business!

BERT: Yeah, don't you believe what he's telling you now. It's all made out of hollow breeze blocks and they fill it with polystyrene foam to stop it sinking!

ALAN: Gerroff you bloody Heathen. A properly constructed ferro boat is as strong as eggs.

BERT: Strong as eggs? Now I know you're nuts! What the hell are you talking about? Strong as eggs! ………… Huh! ………… .

ALAN: Well, you know ……… has the same strength as an egg when compressed point to point.

BERT: Well, you bloody lunatic! Anybody can squash an egg!

ALAN: Oh is that so! Point to point?

BERT: You're not trying to tell me that I can't do it are you?

ALAN: Well let's just see, shall we? Brian! Give us a box of eggs mate (TURNS TO BRIAN WITH WINK).

BRIAN: Sure thing mate (GOES AND GETS EGGS) there you are!

EVERYBODY IS INTERESTED BY NOW

Bert: Hey, come on Alan, if you say you can prove it how do I know that you'll be putting enough pressure on?

ALAN: In that case, if you don't trust me you'd better do it your bloody self, hadn't you!

BERT: Damned right I will. Right! What are we having on it?

ALAN: Oh, cocky with it! Alright then, I'll back it up with a pound note. Here you are, then. I guarantee that you will not break this egg if you hold it in your palms, fingers outstretched and squeeze with all your might!

BERT: Bollocks! …… Give it here! (GRABS THE EGG, ASSUMES THE POSITION AND STARTS TO SQUEEZE. GRUNTS AND GROANS, GOES RED IN THE FACE, FINALLY STOPS). Hey, come on, this is a dummy egg. Come on I saw you winking at Brian!

ALAN: Would you credit it! Give me the egg. Come on, hand it over. (TAKES THE EGG, TURNS TO THE BAR, GRABS AN EMPTY WHISKEY GLASS, CRACKS THE EGG ON THE RIM AND EMPTIES IT INTO THE GLASS, LIFTS THE GLASS UP AND LETS THE EGG SLIDE INTO HIS MOUTH). There you are Bert, you shouldn't give up so easily!

BERT: Give up? I didn't say I was giving up! Give me another egg. (HE'S GIVEN ANOTHER EGG, AND HE IMMEDIATELY STARTS TO PRESS IT).

ALAN: (TO BRIAN) Hey, that bloke over this is smoking Pot!

BERT: (STILL SQUEEZING, HALF TURNS TO SEE WHERE ALAN IS LOOKING AND THE EGG SMASHES TO SMITHEREENS IN HIS HANDS. IT GOES ALL OVER HIS UNIFORM) Aargh……… Oh ……… Bloody Hell ……. Oh Shit! now look what you've …… (EVERYBODY BURSTS OUT LAUGHING, BRIAN HANDS HIM A CLOTH, ALAN RECOVERS HIS COMPOSURE AND STICKS HIS HAND OUT).

ALAN: Come on, cough up, where's my Quid!

BERT: Hang on you rotten sod (GETS A POUND OUT OF HIS POCKET AND GIVES IT TO ALAN) there's your bloody quid!

ALAN: Hey! Come on what about the betting tax? See that lads? Her Majesty's Custom & Excise, Revenue Men, by God! Trying to evade the betting tax! (ALL LAUGH AGAIN).

ALAN: (TURNING TO BRIAN, GIVES HIM THE POUND NOTE). Two large Scotches please, Brian. (BRIAN COMPLIES. ALAN HANDS ONE GLASS TO BERT, RAISES HIS GLASS WITH A GRIN 'CHEERS'; BERT RAISES HIS GLASS TAKES A SWIG, LIFTS HIS HEAD LOOKING AT THE CEILING, STARTS TO LAUGH, SPRAYS WHISKEY OVER ALL AND FINALLY BURSTS OUT LAUGHING. ALAN AND BERT END UP, HANDS ON EACH OTHERS SHOULDERS, SOBBING WITH LAUGHTER. THE WHOLE PUB JOINS THEM).

MICHAEL: (WIPING HIS EYES) Oh dear, I don't think I've seen anything so funny in years. Would you like a drink, dear, or would you rather go and eat?

MARGARET: I think 'd prefer to eat.

MICHAEL: Fine. …… Martin, Margaret and I are going to have some food now. May I buy you a drink before we leave?

MARTIN: No, that's alright, you go ahead. We'll see you again.

MICHAEL: Rightho then, we'll be off. 'Bye now, cheerio, nice to have met you all.

CHORUS OF GOODBYES.

CUT TO SHOT ON BOARD 'WANDERER'. IT IS DUSK.

THE COUPLE ARE IN THE COCKPIT, DRINKING BRANDY FROM TOUGH LITTLE GLASSES. THE SKY IS AFIRE WITH THE SETTING SUN.

MARGARET: What a wonderful day it's been, Michael; thank you for taking me to that Italian restaurant; the food was quite delicious.

MICHAEL: Margaret, …… I have a surprise for you (DUG IN HIS POCKET AND BROUGHT OUT A TINY BOX, OPENED IT, AND BROUGHT OUT A RING WITH A GOOD-SIZED DIAMOND. HE TOOK MARGARET'S HAND AND SLIPPED THE RING ONTO THE THIRD FINGER. THERE WAS AN INTAKE OF BREATH FROM MARGARET AND MICHAEL SAID SOFTLY) Will you marry me, my dear Margaret? (THEN HE KISSED HER GENTLY).

MARGARET: Oh Michael, you know I will.

MICHAEL: Darling ……… (THEY KISS AND CLING TO EACH OTHER) Shall we make it soon, my dear?

MARGARET: I think we'd better, don't you? (SMILES)

MICHAEL: (SMILING TOO) It would be wise. …….. the end of the month?

MARGARET: (CLOSES HER EYES GENTLY IN AFFIRMATION, OPENS THEM AGAIN) The end of the month. (SOFTLY)

FADE TO DUGDALE'S GARDEN.

JACK MENHENNIOT: (SITTING DOWN TO EAT A PIECE OF BREAD AND CHEESE ON A WOODEN BOX. MARK APPEARS WITH A JUG OF TEA AND MUGS). Hello Mark, my boy. Not gone to sea yet then?

MARK: No we're catching the evening tide.

JACK: How's John Trelawney doing then?

MARK: Fine. He's a wizard with engines.

JACK: Good. I like that boy; seems like just the right match for Pauline.

MARK: Yes, they're a perfectly matched couple I'd say.

JACK: She's the spitting image of my mother you know. …… I've never had a family, 'though I nearly did get married once but then something happened and I went to Australia for seven years; but whatever little I've got in the world when I die well, I'd like to think it would go to my own kin. ………. Anyway, what I got don't amount to much; only that old cottage of mine and some mining shares I was silly enough to accept instead of wages. Huh …… ! The company went bust a few weeks later and there was me and one other man left with useless shares. He, poor chap, got caught in a rock fall; didn't give him compensation or anything just more worthless shares. They were terrible unfeeling people Mark, those mine owners. Ha! It was all a long time ago now anyway. Hope I've got a few more years before I have to start thinking of wills and that kind of thing.

MARK: I jolly well hope so Jack; I might buy a boat one day, and who can I trust to do her up if you're not around!

JACK: I'd enjoy doing that for you Mark!

(GRANDPA AND RACHEL DUGDALE APPEAR, HOLDING A MUG AND FOOD)

RACHEL: I've brought another guest to your picnic, Jack. Do you mind? He's brought his own mug of tea and bread and cheese.

GRANDPA: Thank you my dear, (RACHEL EXITS) Hope I'm not intruding. Thought I'd come and get some sunshine.

JACK: No, no. Come you on Mr Dugdale.

MARK: (GETTING UP) Here Grandpa come and sit here.

GRANDPA: Thank you my boy. What a lovely day Jack! How are you? It must be 2 weeks since I saw you last. Goodness. How time passes!

JACK: It's all on account of the weather Mr Dugdale. The sun's only come out these last few days. We could do with some of that Argentinian weather of yours.

GRANDPA: Not mine Jack, not mine. Argentina ceased to have any meaning for me when that man Peron took over. And now we're talking of taking the Endurance away from the Antarctic! Damned fools! Don't they know the Argies will be rubbing their hands with glee with the thought of all those easy pickings left for them? …… . The Falklands, South Georgia, our slice of Antarctica, the oil, the minerals, the richest fishing grounds in the world? …… ! Why haven't we got any Shackletons in this country any more? …… ! What we need I'm afraid is an enormous slump or a war; then, perhaps, some of our people will get up off their backsides and start putting this county on the map again! …… (PAUSES) (LOOKS APOLOGETIC)

79

I'm terribly sorry, I've been sounding off again. Hmph! Well come on Mark, fill the mugs up again, there's a good chap.

MARK: (GETTING UP AND FILLING THE MUGS) Much of what you say is true Grandpa, but I think that our modern society is too sophisticated to think in terms of pioneering and, also I think too many people are too busy trying to make a living to have the luxury of thinking of putting Britain back on the map again. Don't get me wrong, I believe that the majority of people have immense courage in knuckling down to the everyday tasks. Just think of those people who have to do the same thing every day of their lives on some production line or other. God, just living in one of those towns would be too much for me. And yes, I know that these things have always been so, but I don't think we had so much complacency in the old days, neither did we have complacency's newest ally, ... television.

ENTER EMMA

EMMA: I've brought you your pipe and your tobacco, Grandpa.

GRANDPA: Thank you my sweet. (TAKES THEM AND PUTS EMMA ON HIS KNEE) Are you feeling better now?

EMMA: Yes thank you.

GRANDPA: Tummy not hurting any more?

EMMA: Only a little bit.

GRANDPA: Nasty little things these tummy bugs, aren't they!

EMMA: Yes, they're disgusting. (ALL LAUGH) (JUMPS OFF LAP) I'm going to look at my tomato plant. (EXITS)

GRANDPA: Well Jack, I think you've got a young apprentice there.

JACK: Oh she loves her gardening does Emma. Goes around every evening watering her plants. Did you see the Scots Pine she planted?

MARK: Yes. It looked as if someone had put it in with a bulldozer.

THEY ALL LAUGH.

JACK: Well, she worked all morning digging the hole for it. Determined little lass that.

MARK: Especially when she's trying to get me out of bed in the morning. (LAUGHS AND GETS UP) Well I've got a few things to do so I'd better get cracking. ...... Jack, can I give you a lift home? It'll be via the quay, if you don't mind the round trip.

JACK: No I'd enjoy that Mark, thank you.

MARK: Right, I'll go and get the car out. (EXITS)

DISSOLVE TO QUAY. MARK'S CAR COMING TO A HALT.

MARK GETS OUT OF CAR WITH JACK, WALKS OVER TO WHERE 'VOORTREKKER' IS TIED UP, SEES NO-ONE ON BOARD, SO WALKS ALONG TO 'SEA CELT' WHERE FRED, ALF AND DANNY ARE DOING SOMETHING)

MARK: Hello Fred.

FRED: 'Lo Mark, off tonight then?

MARK: Yes with a bit of luck. Haven't seen John, have you?

FRED: Yes, he was on the quay an hour ago, said he'd be back soon.

MARK: Oh fine, in that case I'll hang on here for him. (TURNS TO JACK WHO IS TEN YARDS BEHIND HIM). Jack! Do you mind hanging on for a while, till John comes back?

JACK: No not at all, my boy. I always enjoyed being around boats, anyway. (ALF, WHO HAS BEING DOING SOMETHING ON THE BOAT SUDDENLY STOPS, LOOKS MORE KEENLY AT JACK).

ALF: Jack! Jack Menhenniot! Is that you

JACK: That's my name, yes. Why? Do you know me, then? Can't say that I .... no! It can't be! Alf! Alf my old mate! Just you come on up that ladder and shake my hand! (ALF CLIMBS THE LADDER, WHILE JACK IS MUTTERING). Well, well, I never ....

ALF: (FINALLY GETTING THERE). (THE TWO CLASP EACH OTHER ROUND THE SHOULDERS AND SHAKE HANDS). Well I didn't ever think I'd see you again, Jack.

JACK: Last time I saw you I didn't think I'd see you again either, especially as there was three tons of rock covering you!

ALF: I'll never forget it Jack, nor what you did. (PUMPS JACK'S HAND UP AND DOWN AGAIN WITH VIGOUR. TURNS HIS HEAD AND SHOUTS) Fred! Come up here and meet the man who saved my life down the mine!

JACK: Now Alf, there's no need for that. You would have done the same for me. Do you know, it's very strange but I was only talking about those shares this morning. How you and me were the only idiots to accept them instead of wages.

ALF: Well we weren't to know they'd go bust the next week were we! Still, it doesn't matter now. By God, Jack, it's good to see you! Got a family now, I suppose!

JACK: No Alf, I never did get married. You took the only decent girl around and I was never one to be satisfied with second best.

ALF: (CONSTERNATION NOW APPEARING IN HIS FACE). Jack, my old mate!

FRED AT LAST COMES ON THE QUAY AND GOES OVER TO THE TWO MEN.

ALF: Fred this is ...... this is Jack Menhenniot. (JACK AND FRED SHAKE HANDS)

JACK: I'm glad to meet you. I see you've got Martin Polglaze's old boat.

FRED: Yes, but how come I've never met you before if you know Martin?

JACK: Oh Martin and John came round to the Voortrekker one day in the Sea Celt when Mr Dugdale had her round the other coast.

AS <u>JACK</u> HAS BEEN TALKING TO FRED IT HAS SLOWLY DAWNED UPON HIM THAT THE BOY BEARS A STRONG SIMILARITY TO HIMSELF. SUDDENLY HE LOOKS AT ALF, LOOKS BACK AGAIN AT FRED AND THEN BACK AT ALF AGAIN, HIS EYES CLOSE, HE GOES WHITE AND STARTS TO SWAY.

<u>FRED</u>;: Hey! Hold him! (<u>ALFAND FRED</u> BRACE HIM UP). Mr Menhenniot, Mr Menhenniot! Are you alright? Mr ………

<u>ALF</u>: Jack! Jack boy!

<u>MARK</u> IS THERE BY NOW BUT <u>JACK</u> NOW RECOVERS.

<u>JACK</u>: Alright, I'm alright. Just leave me alone to walk around the quay for a while. I'm alright, alright ……… (HE PUSHES THEIR ARMS AWAY AND SLOWLY WALKS ABOUT 30 YARDS AWAY AND SITS ON A LOBSTER POT).

<u>MARK</u>: I think I'd better go to him.

<u>ALF</u>: No it's alright, I know what's the matter. Leave it to me I'll go and see to him.

<u>ALF</u> WALKS SLOWLY TO <u>JACK</u> AND STANDS AT HIS SIDE AND PUTS HAND ON HIS SHOULDER.

<u>ALF</u>: We couldn't find you Jack. I tried but by the time Sarah knew she was having the baby you'd upped and gone to Australia …… and, Jack, you had no need to go …… that night before my accident …… the night you saw me and Sarah out walking …… there was nothing in it Jack, upon my life …… there never was. Twas only when I came out of hospital that I found out about Sarah from her mother …… and, well, you'd saved my life, Jack, and …… it was part feeling sorry for Sarah, and part saying 'thank you' to you – that's why I asked her to marry me. (TEARS ARE TRICKLING DOWN <u>JACK</u>'S FACE, <u>ALF</u> HAS BEEN LOOKING AHEAD DOWN RIVER ALL THE TIME HE HAS BEEN SPEAKING). I never thought I'd see you again. I had no idea you'd come back. …… He's a good boy, Jack, and he worships his mother. Strange, you know, …… you'd think that being brought up as my son, he'd have taken on some of my character, but no, he's you Jack, never seen any reason to tell him. ………… I don't bear no grudge, Jack, we were good mates too long for that and I hope we still can be. (<u>JACK</u> PUTS A HAND UP AND CLASPS <u>ALF</u>'S WITHOUT LOOKING UP) ……… And Jack, …… let's leave it as it is for now, cos I know that I haven't go long to go now. ……… Reckon you've come back just in time, old mate.

<u>JACK</u> NOW LOOKS UP AT <u>ALF</u> WHO IS STILL STARING AHEAD DOWN THE RIVER, GETS UP AND PUTS BOTH ARMS AROUND HIM.

FADE TO CREEKSIDE QUAY.
SATURDAY. YACHT WANDERER HAS JUST COME ALONGSIDE.

<u>MICHAEL</u> HAS JUST STEPPED ASHORE WITH A STERN ROPE; MAKES FAST GETS THE HEAD ROPE AND STARTS TO MAKE THAT FAST WHEN <u>TEDDY BISHOP</u> COMES OUT OF THE HOUSE AND GOES OVER TO <u>MICHAEL</u>.

<u>TEDDY</u>: And what do you think you're doing?

<u>MICHAEL</u>: (LOOKING UP, SURPRISED AT THE TONE, BUT WISHING TO MAKE THE EFFORT TO GET OFF ON THE RIGHT FOOT WITH HIS NEW NEIGHBOUR, HOLDS HIS HAND OUT). You must be the new owner of Creekside.

<u>TEDDY</u>: I should have thought that was patently obvious!

<u>MICHAEL</u>: I was merely tying up in order to ………

TEDDY: Then you can jolly well untie it again!

MICHAEL: Hang on a minute, I was about to say ……

TEDDY: I don't wish to hear what you've got to say. You are on my property without my permission. You are trespassing! Now just untie that rope and get off my quay!

MICHAEL: But you don't seem to understand!

TEDDY: I only understand that you are on my quay! - !Get your ropes off or I'll cut them off! (TAKES HIS SHEATH KNIFE OUT)

AT THIS POINT MARGARET AND MR JENKINS DRIVE ON TO THE QUAY AND MAKE A CIRCLE, PULLING UP TWO YARDS FROM MICHAEL AND TEDDY).

MARGARET:(SMILING UP AT MICHAEL THROUGH HER OPEN WINDOW). Timed it just right didn't we!

TEDDY: I'm afraid you did. Now kindly put your car in gear and go back the way you came!

MARGARET: There must be some mistake. Don't you know who we are?

TEDDY: I don't care who you are. Now just Get Off My Land. ……! And you! ……You untie those ropes. At once!

MICHAEL: (LOOKING CONSOLINGLY AT MARGARET). It's alright, dear, I'll meet you back at the house.

MARGARET GLARES AT TEDDY AND DRIVES OFF. MICHAEL UNTIES THE HEAD ROPE AND THROWS IT ON BOARD, UNTIES THE STERN ROPE, RUNS IT THROUGH THE RING AND TAKES THE END ON BOARD WITH HIM AND MADES FAST TO A CLEAT, SO THAT HE CAN UNDO THE ROPE ON BOARD AND PULL IT THROUGH THE RING. HE BENDS DOWN IN THE COCKPIT TO START THE ENGINE, STARTS IT WITHIN 20 SECONDS, AND STRAIGHTENS UP TO UNTIE HIS ROPE ONLY TO FIND THAT IT HAS BEEN CUT AND THAT HE IS FLOATING DOWNSTREAM. HE QUICKLY PUTS HER IN GEAR AND INCREASES THE REVS.

MICHAEL: You bloody idiot ! - !

TEDDY: Some of you people will never learn that an Englishman's home is his castle!

MICHAEL: If you're an example of being English then Thank God I'm British!

MICHAEL MOTORS UPSTREAM.

HELEN: (COMING OUT OF THE HOUSE) I thought you'd left the house to go out in the boat, I didn't realise you were talking to someone. **Are** you going to go out in the boat?

TEDDY: No. (STILL WATCHING MICHAEL, HIS GAZE IS TAKEN BY THE BOAT PASSING MICHAEL'S, BUT COMING DOWNSTREAM. HE SEES THAT STAN THE MAN IS AT THE HELM. HIS FACE BECOMES WILD) Oh yes I am!

JUMPS INTO HIS OWN LARGE AND FAST 'GIN PALACE', CASTS OFF STERN ROPE, GOES AND STARTS ENGINE, TRIES TO UNTIE BOW ROPE, FAILS, CUTS IT AND GOES TO THE WHEEL. HE GIVES THE ENGINE ALL SHE'S GOT, THE BOAT REARS UP AND SLEWS AROUND, CRUNCHING HER AFTER END AGAINST THE QUAY AND THEN RACES OFF AFTER STAN AND OTHERS IN THE FERRO BOAT. HE CATCHES UP WITH THEM IN 30 SECONDS AND CUTS ACROSS HER BOWS, COMES BACK TO THE ATTACK AGAIN AND CUTS ACROSS AGAIN, THIS TIME CORNERING AND GOES AROUND THE BOAT TWICE BEFORE ROARING OFF LAUGHING.

THERE ARE SHRIEKS AND SHOUTS FROM FERRONUFF AS SHE'S THROWN ALL OVER THE PLACE BY THE WASH. THE ENGINE STOPS.

STAN: Alan the anchor! Quickly!

ALAN: Stuart, where's the anchor?

STAN: In the forepeak.

ALAN: Come on then; hand it up to me! (THEY EXECUTE THIS QUICKLY).

SOPHY: (STUART'S GIRL, PANICKING) Oh, what's happened?

STAN: The engine's stopped. (HE LIFTS THE COVER OFF THE ENGINE AS THE LADS COME AFT AGAIN) (FEELS THE ENGINE). Well she's not hot anyway. Right, let's have a look at the bleeder.

JANE: (STAN'S WIFE. SURPRISED BY THE WORD). Stanley!

STAN: (WITH HURT EXPRESSION) What now!

JANE: That word! And you haven't bothered to ask us if we're alright even!

STAN: Alright, I'm sorry …… are you alright ladies?

AFFIRMATIVE ALL ROUND. THE LADS ARE CHUCKLING OVER JANE'S MISUNDERSTANDING OF 'BLEEDER'.

STAN: (Contd) I don't know who that idiot was but I shan't forget his boat, leastways.   !

ALAN: As soon as we get downriver I'm going to get in touch with the Harbour Master. This is a job for him and his Constable, I reckon.

STAN: It sure is, the man's a lunatic! Can I get stuck into this engine now Jane? Or do you want me to swim ashore and get you some fish and chips?

JANE: Go on with you. You embarrass me sometimes, you do!

STAN: Alan, pass me that adjustable spanner, mate. (HANDS IT). Right lets try this one first – (SLACKENS BLEEDER AND FUEL WITH MANY BUBBLES SPLUTTERS OUT). There you are. Air lock in the diesel. Where's the header tank?

ALAN: We didn't install one.

STAN: Well, …… look no further then. That's the problem. …… Why not Alan? ……?

ALAN: Dunno …… lazy I suppose.

STAN: You'll have to do it Alan, otherwise every time you go over a bump with a part filled fuel tank you're going to have this problem.

ALAN: Quite right Stan, yeah let's get it in tomorrow, Stuart.

STUART: Suits me. Anything to make her a safer vessel, mate. It's a long way to France!

STAN: Do you two want a hand in putting in the tank tomorrow?

ALAN: No thanks Stan, we can manage. Well then, shall we go on?

STAN: Yes of course. What do you say ladies?

LADIES CHORUS 'YES, OF COURSE'.

DISSOLVE TO LATER AT JENKIN'S FARM.

MICHAEL: (HAS JUST GOT THROUGH TO MR MORRIS ON THE 'PHONE) …… yes I seemed to remember something like that in the deeds. Well, would you mind if I came and had a look at your map this afternoon, mine hasn't yet been returned by me solicitor. ……… Thank you very much. I'll be up shortly. (PUTS 'PHONE DOWN AND TURNS TO MARGARET AND MR JENKINS). Well that's confirmed it. There's no Right of Way through from Rosebrawse to Creekside.

MR JENKINS: (FROWNING IN THOUGHT) You're quite right. Yes, I'd forgotten all that trouble; yes – it's all coming back to me now. ……… Creekside was an isolated property originally, built by a sea-captain in the 1800's; nobody liked him so he finished his days in loneliness. After his death the property became a ruin until the 1930's when John Tripp, who owned Rosebrawse at the time, made it habitable and put his newly-married son in there. There was a wall right around the property in those days but John Tripp knocked a gap through the wall and put a gate up a few yards further down, with a little Cornish hedge each side, just to tidy it up. He then could bring all his building materials in with a horse and cart. Anyway, having gone to all that trouble, the son's wife decided she hated living in the country and the couple moved to some town up-country. John Tripp put a lock on the gate and rebuilt the stone wall, and it stayed like that until Morris came here a few years ago. He did the same thing all over again but I'm pretty sure he locks that gate for one or two weeks every year to make sure that no Right of Way is established.

MICHAEL: That's what he just told me on the 'phone - there's no Right of Way. Our charming little neighbour down the river is going to get quite a shock. **Quite** at shock!

MARGARET: Why? What are you going to do Michael?

MICHAEL: You'll soon see! I quite honestly don't think that our Mr Bishop is going to fit into the pattern of life we enjoy in Cornwall, and the sooner he leaves the better. I'm merely helping to foster that idea in his mind, you might say.

JENKINS: You may not have to bother about that. Nobody's ever stayed there for long. It's an unlucky place, that. When I was a child we used to play there; we all thought it was haunted. Even later, when I married Margaret's mother, it was …… what's the word, it made me feel uncomfortable, walking near there. It used to give your mother the horrors. I was told the story when I was a young man. …… . The sea-captain who built it brought a captured Brigantine back from the Napoleonic wars with 20 or 30 French prisoners in chains. It seems that he anchored the ship just off where the quay is now, and had the prisoners build the whole of that quay. Then he brought the ship alongside the quay and tied her up there, forcing the prisoners to build the house, using some of the topside timbers for joists, beams and so forth. The prisoners worked in shifts, half of them during the day, the other half at night. Anyway, when the house was completed, the captain locked the night shift in the cellar and shot every one of them. His man-servant didn't take to that, overpowered his master, tied him up and escaped in the ship, freeing the other prisoners. It's said that they eventually got back to France, and that the man-servant was given an estate of land in gratitude. Well, …… that's the story, for what it's worth. …… But I can tell you that we searched all through the cellars of that house when we were children and never found a trace of anything, though it was always a frightening place.

MICHAEL: What a fascinating story! Well, with any luck, the ghosts will do the job for me. ……… Look, I must be off now, please excuse me. See you later! (MOVES TOWARDS THE DOOR THEN TURNS BACK) Oh, you won't forget that we're all going to Harmonies tonight, will you? Must celebrate the announcement of our Nuptials!

JENKINS: That's something I'd never forget, my dear boy! (TAKES HOLD OF MARGARET'S HAND).

MICHAEL: Of course, I'll be back later to pick you up. (EXITS)

DISSOLVE TO HARMONIES THAT EVENING.

THERE'S QUITE A CROWD AT THE BAR, MOST OF OUR CHARACTERS IN FACT, MICHAEL AND MARGARET ARE FACING THE BAR, TALKING TO HUGH. TEDDY BISHOP AND HELEN COME IN AROUND THE BACK OF THE CROWD. HUGH WAVES THEM CLOSER, AND AS THEY APPROACH, SAYS

HUGH: I'd like to introduce you to someone, ……… Mr Williams – your next-door neighbour. (MICHAEL TURNS AROUND TO SEE WHO IT IS. TEDDY SEES MICHAEL AND THE AWFUL TRUTH DAWNS UPON HIM. HIS FACE IS A PICTURE. HE GRABS HELEN'S ARM AND USHERS HER OUT. CUT BACK TO MICHAEL'S FACE.

FADE.

PART THREE, EPISODE ONE

THE DUGDALE RESIDENCE.
IT IS BREAKFAST TIME. ALL EXCEPT MARK ARE PRESENT. LITTLE EMMA IS FEEDING HER DOLLY.

HUGH: So, at long last, there'll be some money coming in from it. There's only the top flat and what I call "the caretaker" still to let now.

MARK: (COMING INTO THE ROOM) Morning everyone. Sorry I'm late. (SITS) What was that about a caretaker, Dad?

HUGH: Oh I was just telling your mother that there are only another two flats to let in Dering Road and the house will be full and paying its way nicely.

MARK: But you're not going to put a caretaker in, are you?

HUGH: (WITH A LAUGH) No, No! I call the little bedsit the caretaker.

MARK: How big is it?

HUGH: It's just a bedsit.

MARK: (WITH HALF AN EYE ON HIS CERIALS) I know someone who'd be interested in that!

HUGH: Oh good! Who is it?

MARK: Me.

HUGH AND RACHEL LOOK AT EACH OTHER IN ASTONISHMENT.

HUGH: You? What on earth do you want with a bedsit?

MARK: I thought it might be more convenient for the fishing and, besides, it's time I stood on my own two feet.

RACHEL: But Mark, it's not as if you were taking advantage of the fact that you live here! You more than pull your weight and pay your way!

MARK: No, it's not that Mother. It's just that ……oh, I don't know, - I don't seem to be on the same wavelength as other chaps of my age. It's time I made more use of my days ashore. You know what I mean, Dad; having a few drinks with the other fishing lads and all that stuff.

HUGH: Yes, of course. I understand my boy. It must be rather dull, spending most of your time here or at Harmonies.

MARK: No Dad, Harmonies is great!

RACHEL: Oh! So you think that we are dull and boring then.

HUGH: Rachel!

MARK: There you go again, Mother. You're putting words in my mouth. Please don't take it like that. What I meant was that life here is limited, for ME!, that is. There are so many different things, different ideas going on down there that I'd like to take full advantage of them, and the only way I can really do that is to get a place of my own.

GRANDPA: Quite right, my boy. When I was a young ………

RACHEL: (INTERRUPTING) Please don't start agreeing with him it's too much! Whenever I start to give my opinion on my son's welfare you two take his side and seem to think that what I have to say is of no importance!

HUGH: That's unfair, Rachel. My father just said what I was going to say. Mark is quite right! If he thought otherwise I wouldn't think he had any spirit in him. (TURNS TO MARK) Right, my boy, the caretaker flat is yours for £10 a week!

RACHEL: Oh! (GETS UP AND STORMS OUT. EMMA IS STILL PLACIDLY FEEDING HER DOLLY, WHICH WE HEAR FROM TIME TO TIME)

MARK: (DISTRESSED, STARTS TO GET UP AND GO AFTER HER) Mother!

HUGH: (HOLDS MARK'S ARM): Stay where you are my boy. I'll handle your mother later. Just let her simmer down for a few hours, then she'll be alright.

MARK: Alright, if you say so.

GRANDPA: Terribly sorry! Didn't mean to ………

HUGH: Don't worry yourself Father, it's nothing to do with what you said. Rachel hasn't been too well these last few days.

GRANDPA Oh! ……… Oh, I see! Well I'll go and see what the papers are frightening us with today. (LEAVES THE TABLE)

HUGH: (SMILING AT HIS FATHER'S REMARK) Mark - you will keep an eye on things at Dering Road, won't you?

MARK: Of course I will Father. In fact, I'd better take some tools with me, in case of a burst pipe or whatever.

HUGH: Well, if you intend moving in on that kind of basis I'll only charge you £7!

MARK: (STICKING HIS HAND OUT AND SHAKING HUGH'S) Done!

HUGH: (LAUGHING) I probably have been! (MARK JOINS THE LAUGHTER).

   FADE TO ROSEBRAWSE SITTING ROOM.

MICHAEL: So I nailed a sheet of plywood from gatepost to gatepost and jammed four tons of rubble hard up against it with Morris' front end loader and then plonked a ton of cow muck on top of that. (SIMON LAUGHS)

SIMON: So than what happened?

MICHAEL: Oh ... ... a couple of days later I got a letter from his solicitor which I passed on to ours straight away. So the two solicitors are playing a lengthy game of legal tennis. From what I hear he won't be there much longer, then I'll arrange for someone to buy it from them immediately just in case he refuses to sell to me.

SIMON: Well that seems to take care of all my queries about the land and property. What about your father's collection of paintings?

MICHAEL: I'll keep all the ones done by my great, great, great, great grandfather, who shall herinafter be called John M Williams. All these greats are too much. (SMILES)

SIMON: Yes. (CHUCKELS)

MICHAEL: And, as for the others, I'm not sure, I think we'd better seek advice. Perhaps this restorer lady will be able to suggest something.

SIMON: Good idea! What time is she coming?

MICHAEL: Any minute now I should think.

SIMON: Right, well let's see what she has to say. I must say she's done a marvellous job on these. (LOOKING AROUND)

MICHAEL: Yes, she has, by George. I didn't recognise that one of the horse when it came back. It was absolutely black when she took it away, and now I discover that there was a goat in the picture all the time. (DOOR BELL) Ah, that must be her now. (GETS UP AND EXITS, SIMON GOES AND LOOKS AT THE 'HORSE' PAINTING. HUGH AND A WELL BUILT SENSIBLY ATTIRED LADY RETURN). Elizabeth, may I introduce my Best Man, Simon Scott. Simon, this is Elizabeth Labron.

SIMON: How do you do? I've been admiring your handiwork,

ELIZABETH: How do you do. Thank you. They're lovely paintings actually and it's always a pleasure to work on something worthwhile. (TURNS TO MICHAEL) I must say you've performed a lightning transformation here!

MICHAEL: Well, I cheated actually! Mr Morris was kind enough to give me a free hand his last two weeks here, so I got a firm of decorators in straight away. - By the time I actually moved in, everything was done.

ELIZABETH: Well, your big day is nearly upon you! No nerves yet?

MICHAEL: (SMILING) No thank God! But I may feel otherwise on Saturday! (THEY ALL CHUCKLE). - Elizabeth, Simon and I have just been discussing my father's collection of paintings by various artists and we were wondering if you could advise us.

ELIZABETH: Yes, of course, if it's within my capability!

MICHAEL: Well, the collection consists of about forty paintings by various artists and about a hundred by John M Williams.

ELIZABETH: Oh yes, one of the three I've just cleaned.

MICHAEL: Quite. He was an ancestor of mine and I should like to keep them for sentimental reasons.

ELIZABETH: You needn't be ashamed of him Michael. He was a fine artist. I didn't realise he was an ancestor of yours! Actually I rang a friend of mine in the National Gallery about him. DIGS IN HANDBAG AND PRODUCES A PIECE OF PAPER). It'll give you something to read later. Right now I'd better get your paintings in.

SIMON: Let me give you a hand. (THEY EXIT)

MICHAEL PUTS THE PAPER ON THE DESK AND READ IT. - - John Michael Williams. B. 1790. Wales. Painted in oils, mainly interesting horses of the period; some seascapes; noted for his creekside paintings which were very fashionable in the late 1800s. Painted mainly in Cornwall, where he died in 1861.

SIMON AND ELIZABETH ENTER. SIMON PUTS A LARGE PAINTING AGAINST A WALL, ELIZABETH STANDS TWO SMALL ONES ON A TABLE WITH THEIR BACKS TO THE WALL. MICHAEL LOOKS AT THE LARGE ONE.

MICHAEL: Lovely, absolutely lovely. (LAUGHS) Simon! I can't believe it! (GOES TO THE TWO SMALL ONES) Simon! Come and look at these. Do you remember what they used to look like? Goodness me!

ELIZABETH: I particularly like the Williams one for the quality of light, but the other has beautiful attention to the minutest detail. ………. Do you see how these stones are beautifully lit in the later one but lack definition.

MICHAEL: What do you mean by the later one?

ELIZABETH: The later painting of the house.

MICHAEL: No! I had no idea! ………… But no, hang on! ………. It can't be! By what you say, this one (POINTING TO THE 'RUIN' ONE) is earlier.

ELIZABETH: Yes by about 50 years. I'd say.

MICHAEL: But how could the house be complete here (POINTING TO THE WILLIAM'S ONE) and be a ruin 50 years earlier.

ELIZABETH: But it's not a ruin! No! If you were to look at it through a lens you'd be able to see that there are two wheelbarrows there, piles of sand and look here, the window frames are complete. If the house were a ruin the wooden frames would have rotted long before the walls had got down to this level. And that's another thing, the walls are level all the way along to this point here, where they drop, but then continue on, again at the same level. And look here at the point of the drop; look on the ground, there, a pile of sand and that splash of white just has to be lime. And what do you see sticking out of the sand? A shovel! Couldn't be plainer, could it! And anyway, why aren't there any rotting tree stumps around! And, if that doesn't convince you, look at this distinctive stone in the quay wall, at the foot, there. Oh yes, it's positively the same house in the process of being built! I'd stake my reputation on it!

MICHAEL: Elizabeth, but that's absolutely remarkable!

ELIZABETH: Incidentally, it may be a valuable painting. I'm not saying the Williams isn't. As you may have gathered from that printout, Michael Williams was very fashionable in the late 1800's, but this man is still very much sought after today. I'm pretty convinced that the artist was a French Naval Officer called Emil de Trapenard. You see the initials down in this corner there, E. de T. He did many paintings of sea battles during the Napoleonic Wars. You'll need the opinion of an expert in this school of painting to verify it, of course.

MICHAEL: How very interesting! ………… What do you make of the writing on the back of it?

ELIZABETH: Actually, it's painted on; which points to it's having been written by the artist himself. Hm! ………… Souvenir de l'Enfer, A memory or souvenir of Hell! Strange! And the other one has something on the back also.

MICHAEL: Yes, Crugsaeth (PRONOUNCES IT CROOGZEETH). I've never known what it meant; I thought it might be the name of the house.

ELIZABETH: I agree! And, as de Trapenard was French, I'd like to hazard a guess that this house is in France, and I wouldn't mind betting, from the name on the back, that it might be found in Brittany!

MICHAEL: Bravo! Yes I believe John Williams did go to France. Yes, of course, he must have painted it while he was over there, and brought the de Trapenard back with him.

ELIZABETH: I know I'm being rather romantic, but it would be nice to think that the two artists had met over there.

MICHAEL: Lord, yes, I hadn't thought of that. Perhaps de Trapenard gave him the painting.

ELIZABETH Well, everything is possible, I suppose. However, I must be off; and, if you need advice on your paintings in London get in touch with Naomi Lewis at the National Gallery and tell her you're a friend of mine. I'll be happy to look at the Williams paintings for you when you get them down here. Now – I must fly! 'Bye Simon, see you on Saturday.

SIMON: Yes, - rather! See you at the reception.

MICHAEL: I'll show you out. (EXIT. SIMON CONTINUES TO LOOK AT THE PAINTINGS. MICHAEL RETURNS. Phew! I need a drink! Simon?

SIMON: Gin and tonic please.

MICHAEL: Good. Same here. ……… What a woman! God! A tornado on legs.

SIMON: Is she like that all the time?

MICHAEL: When she's talking about paintings – yes, but, when she switches off she's a different person, terribly charming and very, very funny.

SIMON: Certainly knows her eggs, I should let her look at the Williams paintings. ………. Tell you what Michael, your very distant Welsh cousin, John Williams, is coming to see me in a few weeks time and I happen to know that he's coming down to Cornwall for a while. Would it be a good idea if I were to have the paintings sent down on the train under his watchful eye?

MICHAEL: Why – yes! An excellent idea. Why not invite him to stay here? I'd like to meet him.

SIMON: Well, I'm not so sure about that; he's a bit primitive.

MICHAEL: Nonsense, he's probably a good chap. You know, Simon, you're becoming too bloody sophisticated. ………… I think I'd better fix you up with one of the local farmers' daughters.

SIMON I say, Michael, I might have my own ideas about that!

MICHAEL I thought you might! Won't do though, you're too bloody far gone for restoration! (SIMON SLINGS A CUSHION AT MICHAEL'S HEAD. MICHAEL LAUGHS, GETS HIS OWN CUSHION AND WE SEE THEM BEGIN A PILLOW-FIGHT BEFORE WE FADE).

FADE TO MARTIN POLGLAZE'S HOUSE.

MARTIN, JOHN AND MARK MARCH IN AT 10AM WHILE MARY IS TENDING TO THE NEW BABY).

MARTIN: Hello, my love. An how's my little feller then?

MARY: Don't you dare put your fishy fingers all over him! God, you do smell, you lot!

MARTIN: Well then my love, what have you got for breakfast?

MARY: You'll have to wait! I'm still tending to this little man here without you big ones getting in the way! (TAKES BABY OUT)

MARTIN: Well sorry boys. Looks like we've arrived at the wrong moment. (ENTER PAULINE)

JOHN: Hello Love!

PAULINE: Hello dear. Well no need to ask what you lot are doing here at 10 o'clock in the morning. I suppose you want breakfast!

MARTIN: (SCRATCHING HIS HEAD AND LOOKING EMBARASSED) Well - um - .

PAULINE: Sausages and eggs it will have to be, you lot; is that alright? (CHORUS OF ALRIGHTS, YES, ETC) How's my Uncle Jack getting on up there, Mark?

MARK: Oh he's fine now.

PAULINE (COMING OUT OF THE KITCHEN) Why, has he been ill?

MARK: I thought you knew!

PAULINE (LOOKING ANXIOUS) No! What?

MARK: Well, he had a funny turn on the quay the other week.

PAULINE: Did he fall down, or what?

MARK: No, Fred and Alf, Fred's father held him up. Then he went and sat down on the quay and Alf went over and talked to him. I took him home afterwards. Whatever it was, it hit him hard at the time. My mother and I were going to go over the next day to check whether he was alright or not, but he turned up for work the next day. Mother is very worried about him; he seems better but he's changed quite a bit.

PAULINE: Oh dear, I'd better tell my father, in case it's serious. I'll get him to go over with me tonight.

MARK: Yes, it might be as well, Pauline, ... you never know. I'm sorry, I thought Jack would have been in touch with you.

PAULINE: No, ... never heard a word.

MARK: I'd offer to take you over there myself, but I've got people coming to see the flat this morning.

MARTIN: Oh – what flat is that Mark?

MARK: It's my father's house in Dering Road, where I've got a bedsit. I'm moving in on Saturday, if there's time before Michael Williams' wedding. (PAULINE COMES BACK OUT OF THE KITCHEN).

PAULINE: How big is this flat, Mark?

MARK: Oh, you know the sort of thing, bedroom, living room, kitchenette, WC, shower.

PAULINE: Sounds nice, would do John and me nicely.

MARK: I didn't know you two were looking for a flat!

PAULINE: John! What's the matter with you? Here's us looking for a home and you've just let one go right under your nose! How much a week is it Mark?

JOHN: Hey, hang on!

PAULINE: No, I won't hang on! I don't care what your mother might say!

JOHN: There's a couple already going to see it this morning!

MARK: If you two want it, it's yours! Don't worry about that!

PAULINE (GOING TO HIM, PUTTING HER ARMS AROUND HIM) Oh you lovely, lovely boy! (GIVES HIM A BIG KISS ON THE CHEEK AND HUGS HIM. MARK IS EMBARASSED).

PAULINE (GOING BACK TO THE KITCHEN, TURNS ………) You'll get an extra egg for that! (ALL LAUGH)

FADE TO

AT SEA – ON BOARD SEA CELT, TRAWLING. NICE DAY. FRED IS SITTING ON THE GUNWALES (KEEPING HALF AN EYE ON DANNY WHO IS AT THE WHEEL) AND TALKING TO ALF AT THE SAME TIME. ALF IS MAKING NEAT ENDS OF THE ROPES AND WHIPPING THEM.

FRED: Well, father, I'm glad you decided to come out with us, these ropes have needed doing for ages.

ALF: I'm enjoying myself! (SMILES)

FRED: I can see that!

ALF (AFTER A PAUSE) I've been thinking, Fred. How many trawls have you got in the store?

FRED: Only those three old ones. They're too far gone for me to spare any time on them.

ALF: I've got plenty of time.

FRED: How do you mean?

ALF: I could make them up for you.

FRED: What, repair them, you mean?

ALF: Yes – why not? Would give me something to do, and you'd have three useful trawls at the end of it! (PAUSE) How much does a trawl cost these days?

93

FRED: (WITH AN INTAKE OF BREATH) Expensive, Father, bloody expensive!

ALF: Well – there you are then. Makes sense – don't it!

FRED: It's a hell of a lot of work, Father!

ALF: Maybe, but I'd like to do it. Besides, I'd like to feel that I was doing something for you.

FRED: Go on with you, Father. You've no need to be saying that.

ALF: You wouldn't mind then.

FRED: Course I wouldn't. It's just that it's a lot of work, that's all.

ALF: Right then, I'll start in on it tomorrow.

THE BOAT CHANGES DIRECTION VERY SLIGHTLY.

FRED: Hey Danny! (SHARPLY) Bring her back on course!

DANNY: Shit! (TURNS THE WHEEL) Sorry Fred, the compass ………….

FRED: Never mind the bloody compass! For Christ's sake, how many times do I have to tell you? Go by the Decca. That's what it's bloody there for. You'll be sorry alright if we hit a wreck! Now keep your wits about you. (LOOKS AT HIS WATCH). Time we hauled her up anyway. (TURNS TO HIS FATHER) Right, Father, let's get her up.

DISSOLVE TO LATER THE SAME DAY IN THE CHAIN LOCKER. FRED, ALF AND DANNY ARE HAVING A PINT.

FRED: You look tired, Father.

ALF: It's all that sea air.

DANNY: Yes, gets you at first, doesn't it!

FRED: At first! ……… Listen to him – anybody'd think he'd been fishing for ten years. (SMILES) Never mind Danny – I'm only joking. Come on – drink up – you've only had three pints. By God – we'll make a fisherman of you yet! (PUSHES DANNY PLAYFULLY AND HE STAGGERS INTO RON THE RNLI COXSWAIN).

RON: Hey – look out! Don't know what's wrong with you fishermen! Go out in a force two and you're all over the place. (BEAMS A SMILE, PUTS OUT AN ARM AND PULLS DANNY TO HIM IN A FATHERLY WAY). You're alright – don't you worry, and that's more than I can say for your young brother. (DISENGAGE)

DANNY: Who, Tom? ………… What's he been up to now?

RON: Nothing **yet**, but you tell him from me to take care in that little boat of his. He was out in it the other day when he shouldn't have been. Even some of the bigger boats had come in on account of the weather. He's got to learn to respect the sea otherwise I'll be dragging him in over the side one night when I should be in bed.

DANNY: We keep telling him but he says he never goes farther than Black Rock.

RON: Black Rock? Huh – that's a laugh! I saw him coming back from up the coast the other day and that must have been more than seven miles the other **side** of Black Rock! (PAUSE) How old is he?

DANNY: Sixteen.

RON: Well, tell him to get a lifejacket at least. It wouldn't be so bad if he had an inflatable but going that far in a twelve foot clinker dinghy with a little outboard is too much for a sixteen year old.

DANNY: I'll tell him Ron, but it won't be any use. Father can't do a thing with him. None of us can.

RON: Well, let's hope it never comes to anything then … Don't mind me going on at you Danny – it's just that I think prevention is better than cure!

BERT: (CUSTOMS OFFICER) Talk about prevention. Here comes one who should have been prevented before he was born. (TURNS TO BRIAN) Give him a pint Brian before he starts going around with the cap. Alan ("EGG SEQUENCE" MAN) has come in.

ALAN: (NOT LOOKING AT BERT TAKES THE PINT AND TAKES A SWIG) Ah! Lovely. (TURNS AROUND ACCIDENTALLY ON PURPOSE AND PRETENDS TO SEE BERT FOR THE FIRST TIME). Oh! Hello Bert! Didn't see you there, thought it was a penguin come in for some smoked mackerel!

BERT: (SLOWLY LOOKING DOWN AT HIS UNIFORM, SMILES) You rotten sod, I'll bloody get one on you one day!

THEY BOTH SMILE.

ALAN: How are you my old mate? (RAISES HIS GLASS) Cheers, by the way.

BERT: Cheers Alan. RAISES HIS GLASS) Not too bad, I must say. How's things with you? Boat going well?

ALAN: Handsome. Surprised me with her speed under sail I can tell you. Goes like a train. Why don't you come out with us one day Bert?

BERT: Would love to. I've got a few days leave coming next month that would be a good time for me.

ALAN: Alright mate ……… I'll check with Stuart and arrange it.

BERT: Great. (PAUSE) Listen – did you find out who the idiot was who tried to swamp you?

ALAN: Yes, some bloke who's just moved down here; bought a place up the river.

BERT: Well, let me know the name of his boat and I'll keep an eye open for him. What did the Harbour Master say?

ALAN: Said that part of the river was outside his jurisdiction, but he's taken all the particulars and written him a letter.

BERT: Ron! Ron! (RON TURNS) Don't you think it's time for the government to bring out laws and examinations of competency for people owning boats?

RON: Wish it was possible, Bert. Wish it was possible. But I bet you there's be a public outcry if it was suggested. I'd like to see a lot of things made compulsory, like wearing lifejackets or safety harness, or having life saving equipment and radios on board, but if the RNLI were to even hint at it we'd be called all the names under the sun. We'd have people complaining that there are enough infringements on their liberty already without making laws to ensure their own safety.

BERT: Yes, I suppose you're right. Funny old country isn't it.

RON: Yes it is, in lots of ways; but, you know – it's still the best.

ALAN: Amen to that.

BERT: You're bloody right it is!

FADE TO CREEKSIDE QUAY.

TEDDY BISHOP (IN A TANTRUM, SEATED AT A GARDEN TABLE WITH PAPERS IN FRONT OF HIM. HELEN IS SEATED OPPOSITE. THEY EACH HAVE A GLASS OF SOMETHING). What kind of bloody country is this anyway, where the laws allow a man's access to the main highway to be taken away from him! And that common little twit of a Harbour Master! (TAKES A SWIG) Huh! For two pins I'd ......

HELEN: Please don't start something you'll regret later Teddy. I couldn't bear it again.

TEDDY: Oh! I suppose you're going to bring Jersey up again!

HELEN: I wasn't, but that all started with you behaving exactly as you have been this last week or so.

TEDDY: That's right! Rub it in! It's all my fault, I suppose! Well – I didn't ask to go and live in bloody Jersey, you know!

HELEN: I know, I know, but as the Trust had already been set up for me there it seemed the most convenient place to go.

TEDDY: Convenient! And what am I? Also convenient, I suppose! And I suppose it was also convenient to come here and not be able to have vehicular access! What am I supposed to do? Drive around the fucking **quay** for kicks?

HELEN: Dear God (QUIETLY, IN DESPERATION) I wish I had never bought the place!

TEDDY: That's right, that's right! **I** can't provide for you! I've **had** all that from your mother, the patronizing cow, and I'm not going to take it from **you** much longer! I shall be off! Oh yes – don't think I haven't got anywhere to go – oh no! There are quite a few little ladies who would welcome my attentions, I can assure you!

HELEN: (INVOLUNTARILY AND IN DISGUST) Uuch! (STANDS UP AND SAYS QUIETLY AND ICILY) I'm coming to the end of my tether, Teddy; and I'm getting rather bored with hearing you say you're leaving, every five minutes. (PAUSE) Stay .... or go .... Whichever it is is immaterial but whichever it turns out to be – for Christ's sake (SHOUTING) **DO IT**! (TURNS AND MARCHES INTO THE HOUSE, SLAMMING THE DOOR.

TEDDY (ASTONISHMENT ALL OVER HIS FACE. THE WORM HAS TURNED; SWALLOWS, STRAIGHTENS UP, STANDS, GOES TO HIS BOAT AND STARTS THE ENGINE, UNTIES THE ROPES AND MOVES OFF FAIRLY QUICKLY)

CUT TO <u>HELEN</u> OPENING DOOR AND LOOKING AFTER <u>TEDDY</u>. AFTER SOME MOMENTS SHE
BENDS AND PUTS ON WELLINGTONS FROM INSIDE THE DOOR, PUTS ON A TWEED JACKET
AND HEADSCARF, COLLECTS A WALKING STICK, COMES OUT, CLOSES THE DOOR AND GOES
TOWARDS THE BLOCKED_OFF GATEWAY TO ROSEBRAWSE – THE WILLIAMS' PLACE., AND
CLIMBS OVER THE WALL.

DISSOLVE TO <u>HELEN BISHOP</u> RINGING WILLIAMS' DOORBELL.

<u>MICHAEL</u> (OPENING DOOR) Hello – sorry to keep you waiting. I was at the other end of the house
(REALISES WHO IT IS). Oh – aren't you …….?

<u>HELEN</u>: Yes – Creekside. May I talk to you?

<u>MICHAEL</u>: Um………yes ……….. of course! Please come in.

CUT TO SITTING ROOM WHERE THERE ARE ALL KINDS OF PRESENTS. <u>SIMON</u> IS DOING
SOMETHING)

<u>MICHAEL</u>: Simon, do you mind if this …….. oh I'm terribly sorry – may I introduce Mr Simon Scott.
Simon this is Mrs Bishop.

<u>HELEN</u>: No – my name is White – Helen White.

<u>MICHAEL</u>: Oh – I'm terribly sorry.

<u>HELEN</u>: That's alright (PAUSE). Mr Williams- there are some things I should like to discuss with you.

<u>SIMON</u>: (SENSING THAT <u>HELEN</u> WOULD PREFER TO TALK TO <u>MICHAEL</u> IN PRIVATE). Michael,
there are a few things I have to do upstairs – would you excuse me please, Mrs White?

<u>HELEN</u>: Yes, of course. (<u>SIMON</u> EXITS) It's **Miss** White actually (TO <u>MICHAEL</u>).

<u>MICHAEL</u>: I'm sorry about the mess. I'm getting married tomorrow (SMILES).

<u>HELEN</u>: Oh, I'm terribly sorry. I had no idea! ……………… perhaps we'd better forget ………….

<u>MICHAEL</u>: No – no – I won't hear of it! Won't you sit down?

<u>HELEN</u>: Thank you. (SITS)

<u>MICHAEL</u>: May I offer you something to drink?

<u>HELEN</u>: No thank ………… why, yes please. I could **do** with a strong drink!

<u>MICHAEL</u>: Whiskey, vodka, gin, brandy?

<u>HELEN</u>: Brandy please. (<u>MICHAEL</u> GETS DRINKS)

<u>MICHAEL</u>: Here we are (SITS). Now then!

<u>HELEN</u>: Well – first of all I should like to ask that what passes between us here **remains** between **us** and
goes no further. I've made enough of a fool of myself and I would not like it spread further than these
four walls.

<u>MICHAEL</u>: But, my dear lady, of course ……… you have my word on it!

HELEN: Thank you. (PAUSE) ………. It's difficult to know where to begin – but may I first of all ask you if you are still interested in buying Creekside?

FADE TO JENKINS' FARMHOUSE.

IT IS MARGARET'S LAST NIGHT AT HOME WITH HER FATHER BEFORE GETTING MARRIED. SOME OF MARGARET'S LADY FRIENDS ARE THERE AND THERE'S A LOT OF CHATTER AND LAUGHTER. JENKINS HAS LEFT THE ROOM. MARGARET MISSES HIM AND LEAVES THE ROOM TO FIND HIM.

       CUT TO JENKINS' BEDROOM.

JENKINS IS SITTING AT THE DRESSING TABLE, HOLDING A PHOTOGRAPH OF HIS WIFE. THERE IS A KNOCK AT THE DOOR.

JENKINS: Come in! (HE'S LOOKING AT HIS WIFE'S PHOTOGRAPH)

MARGARET: (ENTERING) Daddy! I wondered where you had got to.

JENKINS: Oh – there was just something I had to say to someone in private.

MARGARET: (GOING TO HER FATHER) Daddy! (KNEELS DOWN AND PUTS HER ARMS ABOUT HIM AND LOOKS AT THE FAMILIAR PHOTOGRAPH). She **was** lovely, wasn't she!

JENKINS: (NOT REPLYING TO HER STATEMENT) There are times when I know she has never left.

MARGARET (HOLDING HIM TIGHTER) **I know, Daddy – I know. (PAUSE) Well – I'm sure she's happy today.**

JENKINS (LOOKING AHEAD, HIS EYES SHOWING THE SADNESS OF HIS THOUGHTS) It would be nice to see her face when we walk down the aisle.

MARGARET: Oh, Daddy. (KISSES HIS FOREHEAD, GETS UP AND STARTS TO GO TO THE DOOR; STOPS) Daddy – you're sure you don't mind the reception being up at Rosebrawse?

JENKINS: No – not at all.

MARGARET: You're sure now? We haven't hurt your feelings?

JENKINS: Goodness me no, child! I've got too much common sense for that! No – Rosebrawse is far more suitable in all ways. Go on with you (SMILING HE GETS UP).

MARGARET: Thank you Daddy (SMILING, EXITS).

SAME EVENING

FADE TO OUTSIDE ALF'S HOUSE

JACK MENHENNIOT: HAS JUST KNOCKED FRONT DOOR. ALF ANSWERS.

ALF (OPENING DOOR, THEY LOOK AT EACH OTHER IN SILENCE FOR A MINUTE): I reckon you'd better come in Jack.

CUT TO LIVING ROOM. THE TWO MEN HAVE COME IN WITHOUT SPEAKING.

SARAH (FROM THE KITCHEN) Who is it? Who is it Alf? (RECEIVING NO ANSWER SHE COMES OUT, WIPING HER HANDS, INTO THE LIVING ROOM).

ALF It's an old friend, Sarah; …………. an old friend come back to see us.

SARAH (IMMEDIATELY SITS DOWN AT THE TABLE, RECOGNISING JACK; HOLDING BOTH HER HANDS TO HER STOMACH – CLOSES HER EYES). Why did you have to come? Why couldn't you have left us alone?

JACK I had to, Sarah ………. There are things I have to say ……. things I have to do.

SARAH You've done enough already and I'd rather not hear what you've got to say.

ALF (SITTING DOWN) Sarah – Jack has come here with a good heart – I'm sure.

JACK It's alright, Alf – she's got every right in the world to say what she has. (TAKES OUT A LONG WHITE ENVELOPE FROM HIS INSIDE POCKET, PUTS IT ON THE TABLE. That's a copy of my Will. It's the only Will I'll ever make ………… I've left the cottage and contents to Fred along with those Wheal Clifford shares. I've also left him £2,000 and I've left £1,000 to Pauline, my brother's daughter. None of it amounts to much, but it's the only way I know of trying to undo the wrong ………… I leave it up to you whether you tell him the facts or not. He's your son, Alf ………. You brought him up, loved him, looked after him. I was only God's instrument in his making.   …………… I'm going now (PUTS HIS HANDS ON ALF'S SHOULDERS) Don't move, Alf – I'll see myself out (EXITS).

CUT BACK TO SARAH'S FACE LOOKING AFTER JACK; CLOSES HER EYES, DROPS HER HEAD, CLASPS HER FOREARMS ACROSS HER STOMACH AND SOFTLY STARTS TO CRY AND SAY

SARAH Jack …….. Jack.

CUT TO ALF WHO IS STRETCHING A HAND ACROSS THE TABLE TO HER, HIS ARM HALF COVERS THE WILL). CLOSE UP ON WILL AND

FADE TO ROSEBRAWSE.

THE WEDDING RECEPTION IS IN PROGRESS. A STAND UP AFFAIR. BRIDE AND GROOM ARE STILL IN THEIR CEREMONIAL CLOTHES.

HUGH (TO ELIZABETH LABRON) Aren't they a charming couple!

ELIZABETH Perfect – aren't they! She's such a sweet girl.

SIMON SCOTT (INTERRUPTING) Ah – there you are.

ELIZABETH Oh, hello Simon – have you two met? (AFFIRMATIVE NODS) – I thought your speech was very good – I like your sense of humour.

SIMON It gets better the longer you know me.

HUGH (STARTING TO MOVE AWAY) I somehow feel I'm rather "de trop" here – (SMILES) - if you'll excuse me I must have a word with my wife (EXITS).

ELIZABETH Well, Simon, what do you think of this part of the country?

SIMON Absolutely lovely! It's such a tremendous change from London! It's like going under water in a crowded swimming pool and when you come up you're on a sandy beach with palm trees all round..

ELIZABETH (LAUGHING) Ah! You've seen our palm trees then!

SIMON Palm trees? But I was joking.

ELIZABETH I know, but we do have palm trees.

SIMON I can't believe my ears. Palm trees – in England? ….!

ELIZABETH (WAGGING HER FINGER) Tsk! Tsk! Cornwall! England begins the other side of the Tamar.

SIMON (LAUGHING) You're very proud of living in Cornwall – aren't you?

ELIZABETH Anybody with any sense would be. Mind you, I must say that the rat race seems to be catching up with us down here. Sad really; (PAUSE) still, there's nowhere else quite like Cornwall.

SIMON I've got a bottle tucked away in one of the other rooms; actually, there's a very interesting painting there.

ELIZABETH (LAUGHING) Very well then – lead on! (THEY EXIT)

MICHAEL (WITH MARGARET, AND TALKING TO MARK, MARTIN AND FRED, SEES SIMON AND ELIZABETH LEAVE THE ROOM, TURNS TO MARGARET WITH A CHUCKLE) There – what did I say! We'll be drinking their champagne next year!)

MARGARET (LAUGHING) You men! I though it was we women who were supposed to be the matchmakers!

MARTIN Don't you believe it, my dear. Just wait till you see what I've got picked out for Fred!

FRED Hey! Less of that – I'm married to Sea Celt don't forget (LAUGHING).

MICHAEL (CLAPPING HIM ON THE SHOULDER) Well done, Fred ……… How's your father by the way?

FRED On top form. He's repairing those three trawls in the store now. Can't stop him working!

MICHAEL Is he, by Jove! Well – I'll see that he gets a fair wage for that, Fred!

FRED No – that's alright – he doesn't want anything.

MICHAEL No, no, Fred. The labourer is worthy of his hire – and must be recompensed!

FRED Oh (EMBARRASSED) Well – thank you, Michael!

MICHAEL How about you, Martin – off tonight?

MARTIN Yes- we shall catch the evening tide as long as the weather prospects hold good.

MARTIN Where are you off to this time?

MARTIN Well, Mark was going to find out about landing our fish in France. They get good prices over there (PAUSE). Where are **you** off to then, Michael?

MICHAEL Ah – now that's a closely guarded secret, but I **can** tell you that it involves islands, sand and palm trees.

MARTIN Ah – sounds exotic.

MICHAEL **We** think it is – don't we dear?

MARGARET It's Heaven, absolute Heaven. Well, darling, I think it's time we got ready.

MICHAEL Yes, of course – come on then! (QUIETLY TO MARTIN AND FRED). We're going to change now, otherwise we're going to be late. ……….. See you in a few minutes (EXITS).

MARK COMES OVER TO MARTIN.

MARTIN I think we'll be able to get away before long. Do you want a lift Fred?

FRED No – it's alright, thanks. Mark`s taking me back.

MARTIN I'll take you back if you like – save Mark the trip into town.

FRED Yes – fine by me.

MARK Oh – yes, that would be great Martin; I've still got a few things to collect from home.

DISSOLVE TO HALF AN HOUR LATER – MICHAEL AND MARGARET ARE JUST DRIVING OFF. MANY OF THE GUESTS ARE OUTSIDE WAVING.

MARK Right, I'd better get going before this crowd starts moving.

MARTIN See you later then.

MARK Right. (GOES TO HIS CAR AND DRIVES OFF).

DISSOLVE TO A FEW MINUTES LATER. MARK PASSES HELEN BISHOP ON THE ROAD, REALISES WHO IT IS, STOPS AND OFFERS HER A LIFT; SHE GETS IN.

HELEN This is very kind of you.

MARK Not at all (HE'S SLIGHTLY PISSED). It's not often that I have the pleasure of having a beautiful woman sitting in my car!

HELEN (LAUGHING) You're very kind!

MARK Not at all – I'm in deadly earnest (SMILES). Where do you want to go?

HELEN To town – I want to look for a quiet hotel for a week or so.

MARK Friends coming down on holiday?

HELEN No, it's for me, actually.

MARK Oh dear (REALISING SOMETHING HAS GONE WRONG WITH HER MARRIAGE). Is there anything I can do to help?

HELEN I'm afraid not, unless you know of a decent room where | could be left in peace and quiet for the next week.

MARK I'm afraid I don't really. I'm off fishing tonight for the next .... (THINKS). Hang on! How would a bedsit do you?

HELEN Fine. Why? Do you know of one?

MARK Yes – you can have mine for a week. I'm off to France in a few hours time!

HELEN Oh no! I couldn't!

MARK It's alright – you have nothing to worry about. In fact – I'm only moving in today .... Tell you what – have it for the week and you can pay me back by tidying it up for me!

HELEN But we don't know each other!

MARK Nonsense – you're a customer of Harmonies. That's like being one of the family – Well – go on! What do you say?

HELEN (BURST OUT LAUGHING) Yes – alright! Thank you very much! (THEY BOTH LAUGH AND FADE TO END).

Thirty minutes

PART THREE, EPISODE TWO

THE DERING ROAD HOUSE WHERE JOHN AND PAULINE LIVE, AND WHERE HELEN HAS BEEN STAYING FOR A WEEK (IN MARK'S BEDSIT). PAULINE IS JUST GOING INTO HER FLAT AND HELEN IS COMING OUT OF THE BEDSIT. BOTH FLATS HAVE THE NAMES OF THE OCCUPIER NEAR THE BELL PUSH.

THE TWO WOMEN MEET.

PAULINE Oh hello – how are you getting on?

HELEN Very well, thank you.

PAULINE Gosh – I've just noticed – you **do** look younger.

HELEN (FLUSHING AND LAUGHING) Why, thank you. I've had a marvellous rest this past week and I've done practically nothing but laze around reading, and not worrying about anything.

PAULINE I must remember that tip. Huh! (LAUGHS) Fat chance I'll ever get – you off shopping?

HELEN Yes – thought I'd go down town for a change. The corner shop is rather limited.

PAULINE They've got most things though.

HELEN Yes, but I'd rather like to get Mark an extra special present for letting me stay here.

PAULINE I know of a present that Mark needs.

HELEN Oh? What's that?

PAULINE You staying here **another** week.

HELEN But Mark is coming back today!

PAULINE That's right, my dear. (HELEN REALISES WHAT PAULINE IS SAYING AND GOES RED. BOTH GIRLS GIGGLE)   Anyway – I must go in and tidy the place up before John comes; I moved all our stuff in by myself. John would have a fit if he saw it as it is! See you, my dear. (TURNS AND PUTS THE KEY IN THE LOCK, THEN TURNS BACK TO HELEN WHO IS MOVING AWAY) Don't forget Mark's present now!

THEY BOTH GIGGLE AGAIN AND GO THEIR DIFFERENT WAYS.

DISSOLVE TO SHOPPING CENTRE IN TOWN. WE SEE HELEN STOP OUTSIDE A JEWELLER'S AND LOOK IN THE WINDOW. SHE ENTERS THE SHOP AND A FEW MOMENTS LATER THE ASSISTANT'S HAND REACHES INTO THE WINDOW AND TAKES OUT A GOODLOOKING WATCH VALUED AT £70. HELEN EMERGES MOMENTS LATER CLOSING HER HANDBAG.

CUT TO SHOT OF TEDDY WALKING ALONG THE STREET. HE SEES HELEN, DODGES INTO A DOORWAY, LETS HER WALK ON, THEN STARTS TO FOLLOW HER.

DISSOLVE TO JENKINS' FARM. ELIZABETH LABRON IS VISITING.

JENKINS Are you sure you won't have another cup, Miss Labron?

ELIZABETH Thank you, but no – I hope you didn't mind me calling.

JENKINS Delighted to see you. Margaret wrote to tell me you might call.

ELIZABETH Did she say what kind of weather they were having in the Scillies?

JENKINS Not on the card, no; but she rang me the night before last and said it was very good apart from one windy day.

ELIZABETH Oh well, that's splendid …….. so you're getting on well then.

JENKINS Champion! Ben's wife comes and cooks me a hot meal midday and does any shopping; the rest of the time I manage very well by myself.

ELIZABETH Mr Jenkins – would you mind my asking if your arthritis is rheumatoid or osteo.

JENKINS It's rheumatoid, my dear.

ELIZABETH Good! Well – I have two friends who are both fairly well on in age and they had the most crippling rheumatoid arthritis for years; the man in his hip and the woman in her shoulder.

JENKINS Go on (INTERESTED).

ELIZABETH Well – they were introduced to a man who was a registered GP and who had gone off to study Acupuncture.

JENKINS What's that?

ELIZABETH It's one of the old Chinese methods of medicine.

JENKINS Like faith healing, I suppose.

ELIZABETH Absolutely not! No! The Chinese even cure their animals with it and you can't use faith healing on animals can you?

JENKINS No, I suppose not ……… But what do they use then?

ELIZABETH Needles.

JENKINS Needles?

ELIZABETH Extremely fine needles; some so fine that you can hardly see them.

JENKINS Well, what happened with your friends?

ELIZABETH Cured. Absolutely cured!

JENKINS (LAUGHS) Well, they couldn't have had what I've got, then.

ELIZABETH Oh yes they did, and worse. You don't have to be carried anywhere do you?

JENKINS Goodness no, thank God!

ELIZABETH Well, Clifford was carried or pushed in a wheelchair for three years before he had the treatment.

JENKINS (REALLY TAKING NOTICE NOW) How long did it take to cure him?

ELIZABETH He was walking normally within six months and within the year he was digging the garden.

JENKINS What? (PAUSE) You're not imagining any of this Miss Labron?

ELIZABETH Certainly not! I've **seen** what it's done for them.

JENKINS (AFTER A PAUSE) Would it be possible for me to see this doctor?

ELIZABETH (SMILING) Yes, of course.

JENKINS Is it very expensive?

ELIZABETH (SMILING) No.

JENKINS Where does he live.

ELIZABETH London.

JENKINS (LOOKING DISMAYED) Oh, I see.

ELIZABETH Look, Mr Jenkins, may I suggest something?

JENKINS By all means.

ELIZABETH Well, I go to that part of London every month or six weeks. It would give me great pleasure to take you up and bring you back.

JENKINS Oh, dear me, I couldn't impose that much upon you.

ELIZABETH Mr. Jenkins! It would be marvellous to have someone to talk to on the drive, I can assure you. (PAUSE, SMILING AT HIM) My friends would be only too glad to put you up for the night.

JENKINS Goodness me! This conversation is like a dream. (LAUGHS) Are you really sure about all this?

ELIZABETH Absolutely, and if you get cold feet you can always back out anyway; but when you see how my friends get about I think you'll be convinced.

JENKINS Are your friends – the ones I may be able to stay with – the ones who had this treatment, then?

ELIZABETH Yes, they are. (PAUSE) I tell you what, Mr Jenkins, why don't we keep this as our little secret. It would be a lovely, if belated, wedding present for Margaret.

JENKINS My dear girl (LEANING FORWARD AND CLASPING HER HAND). How can I say my thanks?

ELIZABETH You don't need to, Mr Jenkins. I'm a restorer by nature! (THEY BOTH LAUGH HEARTILY)

FADE TO NET AND GEAR STORE OF SEA CELT. ALF IS BUSY MENDING UP NETS, HUMMING AWAY TO HIMSELF. FRED APPEARS.

FRED Hello, Father.

ALF Hello – what's up then?

FRED Bloody water pump packed up – so we had to come back in.

ALF That's a pity. Were you far out?

FRED No, luckily! We'd only just gone beyond Black Rock; - so it wasn't too bad. Missed a day's fishing though – bloody Hell!

ALF Never mind, my boy; have a rest. Stay and talk to me here for a while.

FRED Alright, Father, I'll give you a hand.

ALF No need for that – I'm on the last panel. Oh yes – tell you what you can do – have a look at the seizing on that head rope; I think some of it has perished.

FRED Right ho, Boss. (TOUCHES HIS FOREHEAD AND SMILES)

ALF (SMILING TOO) I should have tried to get a little fishing boat years ago, Fred.

FRED Why's that, Father?

ALF Well ……….. we could have been working together all that time by now.

FRED Oh ………. Yes ……… would have been alright that.

ALF Fred (PAUSE) ………. Fred - what would you say if I was to tell you that someone had left you some property in his Will?

FRED I'd say – is it worth anything? (LAUGHS)

ALF No – seriously – what would you say?

FRED Nothing much **to** say, is there

ALF Fred – I should have had a talk with you years ago. (LONG PAUSE). There's something you ought to know but your mother and me have never had the guts or, well known how to tell you. (PAUSE) ………. sit down, Fred. (FRED SITS). Well – your mother and I – oh Hell! You see, Fred …………. there's a lot I should have done for you and didn't; and I didn't treat you too well for a couple of years not too long back, and well, I've got **you** to thank for bringing me to my senses and we're better mates now than we've ever been ………. but I'm not your real father, Fred.

FRED (QUIETLY) I know that.

ALF And the thing is that it's been hard to even think of telling you that all these years even though …….(STOPS – THINKS) What did you say?

FRED I said I know that. I know you're not my real father. Gran told me that when I was fourteen, just before she died.

ALF (ABSOLUTELY AGHAST, SPEECHLESS, STARTS TO DRAW DEEP BREATHS)   I ………….. Fred ………….. (FRED GOES OVER TO HIM).

FRED Father, are you alright? What is it?

ALF (HOLDING OUT A HAND AND NODDING HIS HEAD – HIS FACE SHOWS THAT HE IS UNABLE TO REGULATE HIS BREATHING).   Fred, Fred ……….. you gave me quite a turn, my boy.   Oh! ……….. you've known all these years?

FRED (NODS) Yes, Father.

ALF And did your Gran tell you who your real father is?

FRED She did say, but I've forgotten now. Don't think I wanted to remember really. I still don't want to remember. If he left my mother in the lurch, then he's not the kind of man I **want** for a father. **You** are the man who took care of my mother when she most needed help, and you are the only father I will ever recognise **or** want, for that matter; and, if this is what all that talk about someone leaving me property is about, you can tell him to stick it up his bloody arse (SHOUTING). I don't want his bloody property, and I don't want to know his fucking name either! (HE HAS STOOD UP BY NOW AND HE KICKS A LOBSTER POT VISIOUSLY AND MARCHES TOWARDS THE DOOR AND COMES BACK). I hate him, I hate him and if he PAUSES) ………… no – I don't want to know (GOES TO ALF AND GRABS HIS COAT) Don't ever tell me I'm not your son again, never! (STARTS TO CRY BUT STOPS QUICKLY. GOES AND STANDS IN THE DOORWAY)

ALF (GETTING UP, GOES TO HIM; PUTS AN ARM ON HIS SHOULDERS). Come on, son, let's go home and get Mother to make us a cup of tea. (THEY LOOK AT EACH OTHER)   AND

DISSOLV.E TO STREET SCENE.

ALF AND FRED ARE WALKING ALONG. WE SEE A CAR STOP AHEAD OF THEM AND MARTIN GETS OUT.

MARTIN Thank you, Mark, see you tonight! (STRAIGHTENS UP – BANGS THE CAR TOP TWICE AND CAR EXITS. MARTIN TURNS AROUND AND ALMOST BUMPS INTO FRED) - Oops – oh – hello Fred, 'lo Alf.

FRED Have a good trip, Martin?

MARTIN Yes – very interesting – I got a lot of ideas in France.

FRED Oh yes, of course, France! What was it like?

MARTIN Well – they're very clever people – even little children were speaking the language. (THEY ALL LAUGH) ……… Do you know where Wellington Close is Fred?

FRED Yes – take the next left and it's the first left after that. What's up then?

MARTIN There's a house I want to have a look at. She's giving me a bit of stick about moving these days. Came down and met the boat and told me to get cracking! (GRINS). Ah well, see you then boys (EXITS).

ALF) Cheerio
)
FRED) Cheers

DISSOLVE TO MARK'S CAR DRIVING UP TO THE DERING ROAD HOUSE. HELEN IS ALSO APPROACHING FROM THE OTHER DIRECTION.

MARK Hello there. How did you get on?

HELEN Thank you so much – it's been a marvellous rest for me. It's nice to see you back. Oh – and I got you a little present to say thank you! (DIGS IN HANDBAG AND BRINGS OUT TINY PARCEL)

MARK Oh dear! You shouldn't have. It's the last thing I wanted you to do. (PAUSES, LOOKING AT HER, THEN OPENS PARCEL AND IS SURPRISED AT SUCH AN EXPENSIVE PRESENT). My God! ………… But! ………... (THROWS HIS ARMS AROUND HER AND KISSES HER CHEEK).

HELEN Here – let me put it on for you (FIDDLES) - there you are.

MARK Marvellous! I say – what a beautiful watch! ………. Well! …I think this calls for a cup of coffee, don't you? (THEY START TO WALK TO THE FLAT)

HELEN I hope you like the way I've arranged everything. I'll move my things this afternoon.

MARK No! Shan't hear of it.

HELEN But …………..

MARK No 'buts', something can always be arranged.

HELEN (PRODUCES HER KEY AND OPENS DOOR AND THEY GO IN).

CUT TO TEDDY'S FACE. HE HAS BEEN WATCHING FROM AROUND THE CORNER.

DISSOLVE TO THE QUAY

SEA CELT AND VOORTREKKER ARE TIED UP ONE AHEAD OF THE OTHER. JOHN IS REPAIRING SOMETHING ON THE WINCH. DANNY WANDERS ON TO THE QUAY.

DANNY Hello John – still here then?

JOHN Hello Danny-boy, yes – had to fix something. Just finishing up though. Be glad to get to bed. Fair knackered I am (PAUSE). What you up to then?

DANNY Said I'd meet my brother Tom on the quay; he wants me to go and have a look at an inflatable with him.

JOHN Thinking of buying one is he?

DANNY Yes.

JOHN Well – we've still got ours down below. Don't need it anymore since we got the ally one. He can have a look at it if he likes.

DANNY How much are you asking for it, John?

JOHN Oh – I don't know – about £60 or £70 I suppose ………..   Do you want to have a look at it?

DANNY Yeah – sure thing.

JOHN Hop down here then and give me a hand to get it up on deck. (JOHN OPENS UP A HATCH AND HE AND DANNY JUMP IN AND WITHIN A FEW SECONDS THROW THE DEFLATED DINGHY ON DECK. THEY BOTH CLAMBER ON DECK AGAIN AND UNRAVEL THE DINGHY. DANNY GRABS THE FOOT PUMP FROM THE BUNDLE AND STARTS TO INFLATE IT. TOM APPEARS AT THE QUAY'S EDGE).

TOM Oy – what you got there?

DANNY Half a pound of bacon, of course; what does it look like – you silly sod! (GRINS)

TOM Alright, alright – don't get all puffed up!

DANNY You come down here and puff this bugger up if you're so smart.

TOM (JUMPING ON DECK AND LOOKS AT JOHN) Just because he's working on a fishing boat now he thinks he's a bloody admiral!

DANNY (LIFTING HIS HAND UP MOCKINGLY TO CUFF TOM) Come 'ere!

TOM See? See that?

DANNY Come on Tom – don't piss around now – get your foot on this and pump.

JOHN Pump it up real hard now so that it goes ping if you flick it.

TOM Yeah – alright. LOOKS AT DANNY AND WHISPERS) For sale?

DANNY Yes.

TOM (STILL WHISPERING) How much?

DANNY £70 – maybe less.

TOM (OUT LOUD) £70! (JOHN LAUGHS TO HIMSELF) The other one is £100.

DANNY Got the money on you?

TOM I got £50.

DANNY Oh, Tom! What's the use of looking at boats if you've only got half the money on you?!

TOM Well, I thought …………. maybe …………..if you was to ……………

DANNY Oh, Tom (DESPAIRINGLY) when will you learn? (BRINGS MONEY OUT OF HIS POCKET TO SEE HOW MUCH HE HAS, LOOKS UP AT TOM AND SHAKES HIS HEAD). When will I learn, I mean! (TOM SMILES).

JOHN (WIPING HIS HANDS) Well – I'll leave you to it. Try her out and if you want her give me the money later on; - I'll be down the Chain Locker tonight. Or see Martin or Mark!

DANNY Alright John, I'll see you down there.

JOHN (JUMPING ON TO THE QUAY) Right – see you then!. Cheers and gone!

DANNY Cheers John.

TOM Thanks John.

JOHN That's alright boy (EXITS).

DANNY Come on Tom – hurry up.

TOM Hey – it's not a two minute job you know!

DANNY Got the outboard?

TOM Yes – it's on the quay.

DANNY Go and get it then, and I'll finish this.

TOM OK (GOES UP ON THE QUAY AND REAPPEARS WITH A 10HP OUTBOARD THAT <u>DANNY</u> HAS NOT SEEN BEFORE). Here Danny, give us a hand! (LOWERS ENGINE DOWN TO <u>DANNY</u>).

DANNY Hey! Where did you get this engine?

TOM A bloke sold it to me.

DANNY What bloke?

TOM Oh, you don't know him.

DANNY What did you do with the old engine?

TOM He took it in part exchange.

DANNY Did he guarantee this one?

TOM No – but it seems to be alright.

DANNY What did he allow you for the old one?

TOM I forget.

DANNY You forget? …………! So how much money did you hand over to him.

TOM £50.

DANNY Hey Tom, where the Hell are you getting all this money from?

TOM From the fishing, of course!

DANNY What fishing? You never get more than a few stone of mackerel or some grey mullet.

TOM I get more than bloody mackerel or mullet Danny (GRINS).

DANNY What else do you get then?

TOM You'd be surprised.

DANNY What the Hell, Tom! Come on – tell me. What fish do you catch that you can afford to cough up £100 in one week.

TOM I'm not telling **you** ………. **You'd** be after them as well.

DANNY You're not doing anything wrong are you Tom?

TOM What are you saying?

DANNY You're not doing anything against the law? …………..

TOM No, I'm not! If that's what you think, I'm not going to tell you any more.

DANNY Tom!

TOM I'm not doing anything wrong! Now forget it will you!

DANNY Alright then – I'll forget it for now, but you just take care.

TOM Alright! For Christ's sake!

DANNY (LOOKS LONG AT HIM) OK then! …………….. Now let's get this inflatable over the side.

DISSOLVE TO INTERIOR OF CHAIN LOCKER PUB. THERE ARE NO CUSTOMERS. BRIAN IS SITTING BEHIND THE BAR READING A NEWSPAPER. RON THE RNLI COXSWAIN COMES IN.

BRIAN (LOOKING UP AND STANDING) Morning Ron.

RON Morning Brian. Lovely day.

BRIAN Beautiful. Wish I didn't have to stand behind this bar for the next few hours.

RON Never mind, boy! It's a good place to be on a rough night.

BRIAN Usual Ron

RON Yes please Brian ……….. Tasted a bit off last night though.

BRIAN Yes, I thought that too. Mind you, you can't get a perfect barrel every time. We've had a pretty good run really – that's the first barrel that's caused any trouble for more than six months (HANDS UP RON'S PINT). Have that on the house Ron.

RON Go on now – I wasn't complaining to get a free pint.

BRIAN I know that. No, that one's on me Ron; personally.

RON Thanks a lot Brian. (LIFTS GLASS) Well – here's to you then!

BRIAN God Bless!

RON Anything in the papers today?

BRIAN Not much ………. They're still going on about taking that ship away from the Antarctic. RON
                          Huh! What we should be doing is sending an extra one down there, not taking the existing one away. (DRINKS) Ah – good pint that, Brian …………..Hello – who's that coming in to the quay? (BRIAN LOOKS THROUGH THE WINDOW)

BRIAN That must be Alan and Stuart's boat – the ferrocement one.

RON Never – is it?

BRIAN: I think it is – yes, there's Stuart on deck, look!

RON: Well, well, I'd never have known that was a ferrocement boat. She's got lovely lines. Looks like a Colin Archer to me. How did they get that finish on her Brian?

BRIAN: Epoxy, I think.

RON: Shines just like GRP doesn't it!

BRIAN: Yes – they've done a good job on her alright. Sound boat that Ron.

RON: I'd like to have a closer look at her sometime.

BRIAN: They'll be in in a minute, they'll be only too glad to show her to you, I'm sure.

RON: There must have been as much of a fuss when steel was first used to build a boat as there is now about ferrocement, I'm sure. Huh (LAUGHS) I wonder what material they'll bring out next?

BRIAN: Something from the space age, I suppose.

RON: You might be right, Brian (TAKES ANOTHER SWIG).

DISSOLVE TO LATER IN THE PUB. STUART AND ALAN ARE COMING IN.

ALAN: Good day gentlemen!

BRIAN: Hello Alan.

RON: I was admiring your boat there earlier on.

STUART: Buy him a drink Alan! (LAUGHS)

ALAN: Hey – gerroff! It's your turn to buy the drinks; I don't know what's wrong with these young lads today. (ALAN IS SLIGHTLY OLDER THAN STUART)

STUART: Two pints please Brian.

BRIAN: Coming up!

ALAN: Go on then Ron. Tell me what you like about our boat; - it's sweet music to me ears!

RON: (LAUGHING) I like her lines, Alan and I'd like to have a closer look at her sometime if possible.

ALAN: Well – of course you can! We'll go and have a look at her after this pint, if you like.

RON: (LOOKS AT HIS WATCH) Yes – that'll be fine.

TEDDY BISHOP WALKS IN AND GOES TO THE OTHER END OF THE BAR. BRIAN GOES OVER TO HIM.

TEDDY: A large Plymouth gin and water, please.

BRIAN: I'm sorry, Sir, we're out of Plymouth. We've only got Gordon's or Booth's.

TEDDY: Out of Plymouth! You should get some more then – it's only an hour and a half away (LAUGHS LOUD AT HIS OWN JOKE). In that case I'll have Booth's.

BRIAN: Very well, Sir. (GOES TO GET IT)

ALAN: Hey Stuart. Did you recognise that laugh?

STUART: I dunno; seemed to ring a bell.

ALAN: Well, I think it's that bloody maniac who tried to swamp us!

STUART: Hey – you may be right there!

RON: Do you mean the chap you reported to the Harbour Master?

ALAN: Yes, I think that's him. (PUTS DOWN HIS GLASS AND WALKS OVER TO TEDDY)

ALAN: Excuse me, but are you the chap who owns that fast cruiser and lives up the river at the water's edge?

TEDDY: Yes, why? (SNOOTILY)

ALAN: Well, in that case you're the chap who tried to swamp my boat, going round us in circles and cutting across our bows!

TEDDY: (LAUGHS) Oh that!

ALAN: (SMACKS TEDDY'S GLASS OUT OF HIS HAND, GRABS HIS LAPELS AND RUNS HIM ACROSS THE ROOM SLAMMING HIM UP AGAINST THE WALL) There were women in that boat, you little creep! And you could have caused a bad accident. Don't you know boats are not playthings! And the way you handle a boat it's definitely a lethal weapon! If I ever hear of you doing that again I'll come after you and tear you into little pieces. Now piss off back up-country where you belong! (LETS GO OF HIM AND STEPS BACK. TEDDY IS LOOKING WILD BY NOW)

TEDDY: If you ever touch her again I'll kill you……………. Don't know why you're shouting about women anyway, they're all tarts! (ALAN HITS HIM ONCE, RIGHT ON THE BUTTON. TEDDY BOUNCES OFF THE WALL AND COLLAPSES ON THE FLOOR, UNCONSCIOUS)

ALAN: Get up you scum! Get up (KICKS HIM, TRYING TO GET A RESPONSE).

RON: Alan! That's enough! (ALAN STEPS BACK)

ALAN: Little ponce had to go and lie down on me, didn't he (LAUGHS). Don't worry Brian, I'll drag the little bastard outside in a minute!

RON: Don't touch him again, Alan. Brian and I will handle that. If I were you, I'd get back on your boat. Brian and I didn't see anything, did we Brian?

BRIAN: What? See what?

RON: (WITH A SMILE) Alright! No, go on! Both of you! I'll come and have a look at your boat in 20 minutes).

ALAN: (EXHALING HEAVILY ONCE) Yes – suppose you're right old mate. Thanks. Come on Stuart! (THEY EXIT)

RON: Christ! I've never seen Alan like that before!

BRIAN: No, he only gets like that if someone insults women, or this country or takes the piss out of the under privileged. He calls it righteous indignation.

RON: Well, it was certainly his righteous hand he hit him with – not his lefteous! (THEY BOTH LAUGH, BREAKING THE TENSION). Come on, Brian! Give us a hand with this lump of misery! (THEY GO TOWARDS TEDDY).

DISSOLVE TO MARTIN POLGLAZE'S HOUSE. SUE IS PLAYING WITH THE BABY.

MARTIN ENTERS.

MARTIN: Hello my love; and how's my son and heir?

SUE: We've just been having a great game of burps and crosses. (SMILES)

MARTIN: (LAUGHING) Well now! That's why we had a gale warning on the radio then. (SLUMPS DOWN IN A CHAIR) Phew! I'm done in.

SUE: Well?

MARTIN: Well what?

SUE: The house! Did you go to see it?

MARTIN: What house?

SUE: You don't mean to tell me ....

MARTIN: Alright! Alright! Yes, of course I went to see the house.

SUE: So what did you think of it?

MARTIN: Alright.

SUE: Martin!

MARTIN: (LAUGHING) Yes, my love, it's a nice house. It's got four bedrooms, a box room and an attic which could be converted into one large room if we put dormer windows in; four large rooms downstairs and a kitchen, a large kitchen, built on to the back. Small garden in front, large garden in the back with a nice lawn, double garage and workshop.

SUE: It sounds lovely.

MARTIN: It is! No through traffic there either so it's pretty safe for the children.

SUE: Yes – that's why I asked you to go and look at it.......... What do you think, Martin? Will we be able to buy it?

MARTIN: Well, we might have to let some of the rooms as bedsits for a few years.

SUE: That doesn't matter, with a house that size we could afford to divide the house in two, which would still give us four rooms and an attic and a large kitchen. Why, that's more than we've got here! (THINKS). So .... four rooms at £15 a week each is £60 Martin.

MARTIN: My God woman – you're a walking calculator. Don't go at me too hard now – I need sleep.

SUE: Oh, I'm sorry my love – I'll make you your breakfast straightaway! (GETS UP, PUTS THE BABY IN MARTIN'S LAP AND GOES INTO THE KITCHEN). So what do you think? Shall we think about buying it?

MARTIN: I've already done it.

SUE: (SHOOTING OUT OF THE KITCHEN) What?

MARTIN: Well, I've made the old lady an offer and she seemed to take kindly to it.

SUE: (RUSHING OUT OF THE KITCHEN THROW HER ARMS AROUND MARTIN AND HUGS HIM UNTIL THE BABY COMPLAINS). Oh! I shall give you more than breakfast this morning my lovely husband!

MARTIN: Hang on now! Two's enough for the moment! (LAUGHING AND TRYING TO FIGHT HER OFF. THE BABY STARTS TO CRY LOUDLY UNTIL SUE PICKS HIM UP LAUGHING. THE DOOR BELL RINGS, AND THE DOOR OPENS. WE HEAR PAULINE'S VOICE SAYING)

PAULINE: It's only me.

SUE: Oh come in Pauline.

PAULINE: (ENTERING) Well – you are a happy family!

SUE: Yes, my love – Martin's just been to see the house I was telling you about and we might be able to buy it.

PAULINE: Oh, that's lovely! Well – that's good news, I must say!

SUE: Cup of tea, Pauline?

PAULINE: Love one please; I've been waiting for John; I heard Mark go in – so I wondered if John was here with you Martin.

MARTIN: No, my dear, there was a bit of work that needed doing and he said he'd get it over and done with now instead of tomorrow.

PAULINE: Have a good week?

MARTIN: Yes. Good fishing and we had a good time in port. The French fishermen were very kind to us, wouldn't let us put a hand in our pockets.

PAULINE: And what about the mademoiselles, then?

MARTIN: Don't see many of those in fishermen's bars, I'm afraid – never mind (SIGH) next time maybe.

SUE: I'll give you next time, my lad! (LAUGHING)

Pauline: Hey Sue – what do you think! That girl, Helen, you know that one who's a bit posh – well I happened to be looking through the window when Mark came back and she met him and gave him a watch.

SUE: No! Ooh – what did Mark say?

PAULINE: I couldn't hear what he said but he gave her a kiss and then they went into his bedsit!

SUE: Oooh, Pauline, do you think anything will come of it?

PAULINE: Well, there's not much in a bedsit except a bed – is there? (BOTH WOMEN GIGGLE)

MARTIN: I don't know! To hear you two going on about Mark and that poor girl you'd think there was some great love affair in the wind!

SUE: Well, Martin – she had left her man and Mark has been kind to her and, well – anything can happen – can't it Pauline?

PAULINE: Oh yes, Martin, you never know (EAGERLY).

MARTIN: (BURSTS OUT LAUGHING) Well – I suppose you're right; you never know.

SUE: Martin – I was just thinking – if we get this house, Pauline and John could have a flat there!

MARTIN: Hang on now, Sue; that means converting a room into a kitchen and putting in a shower and wc and all that. It would be too expensive, my dear. Best keep to the bedsit idea. It would be nice to have John and Pauline there, yes, but it wouldn't be possible – not with that house anyway (THE DOORBEL GOES).

MARTIN: (GETS UP) Seems like visitors' day. (WE HEAR HIM OPEN DOOR) Hello mate, your better half's here; you're just in time for a cup of tea. (THEY BOTH TROOP IN).

JOHN: (GOES TO PAULINE). This is where you are then! Doing the rounds, drinking tea and gossiping! (KISSES HER)

PAULINE: Don't go on about women gossiping now, you men are much worse than us.

MARTIN: Hey, hey! The man's had a hard night – look at the bags under his eyes!

PAULINE: Well, as long as it's from working I'll forgive him, but I'd better not find any mademoiselles on board (WAGGING HER FINGER AND SMILING AT JOHN) and hey! What do you think! Mark and that woman are in his bedsit together! Isn't that nice! (JOHN AND MARTIN LOOK AT EACH OTHER AND BURST OUT LAUGHING; THE BABY STARTS TO CRY AGAIN).

DISSOLVE TO SHOT OF ANTONIO THE EX-HARMONIES MANAGER GETTING OUT OF THE PASSENGER SEAT OF A CAR, CARRYING HIS SMALL OVERNIGHT BAG. HE LOOKS UNCLEAN AND IN NEED OF FOOD. WE SEE HIM WALK PAST THE QUAY AND LOOK IDLY AT THE BOATS. MARK'S CAR DRIVES ON TO THE QUAY AND MARK GETS OUT. ANTONIO DODGES BEHIND A TELEGRAPH POLE AND OBSERVES. MARK SEES DANNY AND TOM TYING THE INFLATABLE UP TO VOORTREKKER AND GOES OVER TO THEM.

DANNY: (SEEING MARK) Hello Mark.

MARK: Hello Danny, what's up then?

DANNY: We've just been trying out your inflatable. John gave it to us to try – said he was asking £60 or £70 for it. Tom's decided to have it, so we reckon on £65 – is that alright?

MARK: I suppose so, but talk to John about it.

DANNY: Well – I'd like Tom to pay for it really. If he goes wandering round town with all that money in his pocket he might spend it. I'd much rather hand the money to you right now.

MARK: Alright then, if that's what you'd prefer to do.

DANNY: Good! Tom, let's have your money (HOLDS HIS HAND OUT <u>TOM</u> GIVES HIM THE MONEY. HE FISHES INTO HIS OWN POCKET AND BRINGS OUT £15 TO ADD TO TOM'S £50, GOES UP ON THE QUAY AND COUNTS OUT THE MONEY INTO <u>MARK'S</u> HAND)

CUT TO <u>ANTONIO</u> WATCHING AND LISTENING TO THE MONEY BEING COUNTED OUT)

DANNY: 61, 62, 63, 64, sixty-five! There we are – all paid for.

MARK: Alright Danny, thank you. Well – I must get back now so I'll be off.

DANNY: Where are you heading for?

MARK: Dering Road – my father's bought the big house there and turned it into flats.

DANNY: Going to pick up the rents then! (LAUGHING)

MARK: No – not at all (SMILES). I've got a bedsit there.

DANNY: Can you give me a lift to the T-junction then, Mark?

MARK: Yes, of course. Hop in!

DANNY: (TURNING TO <u>TOM</u>) I'm off to see Fred, Tom. Remember what I said now! Watch your step. (WAGGING HIS FINGER).

TOM: Yes – alright, and thanks, Dan! (<u>DANNY</u> PUTS HIS THUMB UP. <u>MARK</u> AND <u>DANNY</u> GET INTO THE CAR AND DRIVE OFF THE QUAY)

CUT TO <u>ANTONIO</u>, WATCHING THEM GO. HE WALKS ON TO THE QUAY AND OVER TO VOORTREKKER.

ANTONIO: Good morning!

TOM: (LOOKING UP) Oh aye!

ANTONIO: I have an important message for Mark Dugdale from his father. He said he would be here at this time.

TOM: Oh – you've just missed him; he's gone a few minutes ago.

ANTONIO: Oh, what a pity! It is a very urgent message!

TOM: Well, I heard him tell Danny where he lived – if it's really urgent.

ANTONIO: Oh yes, it is terribly important that he is told soon!

TOM: Right then! Well he lives in the big house in Dering Road – got a flat there or something.

ANTONIO: Thank you very much! You have been most helpful. Excuse me I must go quickly!

TOM: That's alright.

ANTONIO: Goodbye now.

TOM: Cheers!

DISSOLVE TO FERRONUFF – THE FERROCEMENT BOAT. STUART AND ALAN ARE TALKING TO A POLICE SERGEANT – A GOOD OLD-FASHIONED ONE WHO'D RATHER ADMINISTER THE LAW ON THE SPOT AND FORGET IT THAN TAKE THE PERSON TO COURT.

ALAN: Come on, Dave – what the Hell would you do if an idiot like that put your woman's life at risk?!

DAVE: Probably exactly what you did, but I wouldn't do it in a public place.

ALAN: But nobody saw what happened. I only went to help him when he slipped (WITH A CHEEKY SMILE).

DAVE: Hey! Hey! Come on now! (BECOMING STERN) No need to take the piss! I know what happened as well as you do. Just because I would have done the same and nobody saw you (REPEATS IRONICALLY) nobody saw you, doesn't alter the fact that what you did was wrong. Question of time and place. (SMILES AND SLAPS ALAN ON THE KNEE) Hot-headed bastard! I think the best way out of this is if I tell him that proceedings will be initiated to prosecute him for that business with the boat if he continues with pressing the charge of assault. He hasn't really got a leg to stand on if there are no witnesses anyway. (WE HEAR THE NOISE OF SOMEONE JUMPING ON BOARD AND HEAR STAN'S VOICE)

STAN: Anybody home?

ALAN: (SHOUTING) Down here! (STAN APPEARS)

STAN: Hello Dave! Found that silly sod with the Gin Palace then?

DAVE: (SMILING) Well – we found what was left of him after Alan had finished with him!

STAN: (SURPRISED – GOES AND THUMPS ALAN IN THE CHEST) You rotten bastard! Why didn't you wait for me? Fine buddy you are! (THEY ALL LAUGH)

DAVE: Well, I like your boat, lads. What are you going to use her for; - charter or what?

ALAN: Smuggling marijuana, of course!

DAVE: Christ! Don't say that. It's not a joke right now. Some bastard's doing it and doing a lot of it! There's a Hell of a flap on. It's coming in here somewhere! ……… Drug Squad are going mad! – If you see anything lads let us know will you?

ALAN: Of course we will. You know that.

DAVE: Thanks (PAUSE). I think we can forget that little business this morning, but next time do it after dark when nobody's watching! (GETS UP AND BUMPS HIS HEAD). Ouch! (GRINS) You didn't build this boat with members of the Force in mind, I see! (RUBBING HIS HEAD) Well – cheerio then boys. (CHORUS OF CHEERIOS).

ALAN: And thanks, Dave.

DAVE: That's alright, boy. (EXITS)

DISSOLVE TO 'HARMONIES' RESTAURANT. HUGH IS BUSY CHECKING BOTTLES. THE PHONE RINGS. HUGH ANSWERS IT)

HUGH: 'Harmonies' .... Mark! How did it go? .... Good .... You've got a bottle of what for me? .... Calvados! Bless you, my boy! .... What? Good Lord, has she been there all week? .... No, Pauline hasn't said a thing................. but, of course .... and Mark! .... Do you think you could give me a hand tonight? Pauline's having the night off .... Yes, well, bring her up with you ....fine, I'll be up myself soon .... Hang on! better still .... I'll pick you both up and we can come straight back here at 8 o'clock .... yes .... invite her to have a meal here .... yes, quite, she is .... I look forward to that .... right .... See you in half an hour. (PUTS THE PHONE DOWN; REMEMBERS AND PICKS IT UP AGAIN, DIALS). Hello dear. Mark's just phoned to say he'd like to come home for a few days............. No – he's fine. It seems that he's been giving refuge to that sweet girl who moved into Creekside.......... husband's a nasty bit of work, I believe .... What? .... I don't know! and it's not the kind of question I would ask him .... Rachel! Don't be silly! .... I'm bringing her up soon with Mark so please, please don't start worrying about that kind of thing. Well .... See you soon. Bye. (PUTS PHONE DOWN, SHAKES HIS HEAD AND EXHALES)

DISSOLVE TO DERING ROAD. "THE HOUSE" IS IN THE DISTANCE. ANTONIO IS IN A SECLUDED HIDING PLACE WHERE NO ONE CAN SEE HIM. HE IS WATING FOR MARK TO COME OUT AND DRIVE AWAY. IT IS DUSK. IT WILL BE NIGHT IN A FEW MINUTES. THE STREET LIGHTS ARE ALREADY ON. ANTONIO IS SMOKING FURTIVELY, CUPPING THE GLOWING END INSIDE HIS HAND. HE HAS VERY LONG FINGERNAILS. HUGH DUGDALE'S RECOGNISABLE CAR PULLS UP OUTSIDE "THE HOUSE". HUGH GETS OUT AND WALKS TO THE BEDSIT DOOR AND RINGS THE BELL; THE DOOR OPENS AND MARK APPEARS, TALKS FOR A SECOND OR TWO, GOES BACK IN, EMERGES AGAIN WITH HELEN AND ALL THREE WALK TO THE CAR, GET IN AND THE CAR MOVES TOWARDS ANTONIO. AS THE CAR GETS LEVEL WITH ANTONIO, MARK'S FACE IS SEEN QUITE CLEARLY. ANTONIO QUICKLY LEAVES HIS HIDING PLACE, WALKS TO MARK'S BEDSIT DOOR, LOOKS AROUND, REACHES INTO HIS POCKET, TAKES OUT SOME KIND OF TOOL, FIDDLES WITH THE LOCK AND QUICKLY OPENS THE DOOR, GOES IN AND CLOSES THE DOOR.

DISSOLVE TO INTERIOR OF A PUB. TEDDY IS THERE DRINKING HEAVILY, BUT THE SPIRITS ARE NOT HAVING ANY EFFECT ON HIM. HIS LIP AND JAW SEEM PUFFED UP AND BRUISED. HIS NORMALLY SATURNINE APPEARANCE IS NOW ONE OF POSITIVE EVIL. HE LOOKS AT HIS WATCH. GULPS DOWN HIS DRINK AND WALKS OUT. THE BARMAN CALLS AFTER HIM.

CUT TO BARMAN.

BARMAN: Goodnight, Sir! (RECEIVES NO REPLY, LOOKS AT ONE OF HIS CUSTOMERS AND GRINS TOSSING HIS HEAD IN TEDDY'S DIRECTION). Bloody headcase, that one.

DISSOLVE TO TEDDY WALKING UP DERING ROAD. HIS EYES ARE ICE COLD SLITS. HE IS CARRYINGA THREE FOOT LENGTH PIECE OF THICK WOOD, QUITE OPENLY. HE GETS TO MARK'S BEDSIT, GOES TO THE WINDOW AND LISTENS.

DISSOLVE TO INTERIOR OF JOHN AND PAULINE'S FLAT'S LIVING ROOM. THE REMAINS OF A MEAL AND A BOTTLE OF WINE ARE ON THE TABLE. PAULINE AND JOHN ARE SITTING IN ARMCHAIRS WATCHING THE TELEVISION.

PAULINE: Don't you think it's time we got into bed? (THERE'S NO ANSWER. PAULINE LEANS FORWARD TO LOOK AT JOHN'S FACE. HE IS ASLEEP). Well – we'll soon see about that. (LEAVES THE ROOM)

DISSOLVE TO A MINUTE LATER, PAULINE COMES BACK IN A FLIMSY DRESSING GOWN AND AN EVEN FLIMSIER SORT OF NYLON NIGHTIE OPEN AT THE FRONT, BUT TIED WITH A BOW AT THE TOP. THE BED IS CLEARLY VISIBLE THROUGH THE OPEN DOOR. SHE GOES TO A PILE OF RECORDS, SELECTS THE ONE SHE WANTS, PUTS IT ON THE RECORD PLAYER, TURNS THE TELEVISION OFF. STARTS THE RECORD PLAYER AND TURNS THE VOLUME UP. "THE STRIPPER" BOOMS OUT INTO THE ROOM BY WHICH TIME PAULINE IS GYRATING UNDER THE TOP LIGHT IN THE BEDROOM. SHE TAKES OFF HER DRESSING GOWN AS JOHN OPENS HIS EYES AND SEES WHERE SHE IS.

CUT TO JOHN'S FACE.

CUT BACK TO PAULINE. SHE UNDOES THE BOW OF HER NIGHTIE, SHRUGS IT OFF, BUT RETAINING HOLD OF IT IN ONE HAND. HER BEAUTIFUL, LARGE BREASTS ARE FREE AND WOBBLING FROM SIDE TO SIDE. SHE HAS MARVELLOUS LARGE HIPS AND BOTTOM WHICH WE SEE CLEARLY AS SHE TURNS AROUND. SHE HAS A G-STRING ON. WHEN SHE TURNS AROUND TO FACE JOHN AGAIN, SHE HOLDS HER NIGHTIE IN BOTH HANDS, TWO FOOT APART, AND BRINGS IT UP UNDER HER BREATS ELEVATING THEM AND LETTING THEM HANG OVER THE NIGHTIE WHICH IS NOW AS THIN AS A COIL OF ROPE. SHE BRINGS BOTH ENDS OF THE NIGHTIE UP AROUND HER HIP AND STANDS THERE, GYRATING HER BOTTOM HALF AND WOBBLING HER BOOBS BACK AND FORE.

CUT BACK TO JOHN – HIS FACE IS ONE OF WONDER. HE SPRINGS UP FROM HIS CHAIR, TEARS HIS SHIRT OFF AND RUNS TOWARDS PAULINE.

DISSOLVE TO EXTERIOR OF HOUSE. "THE STRIPPER" MUSIC IS CLEARLY HEARD. TEDDY IS STILL LISTENING AT THE WINDOW. SUDDENLY HE STIFFENS AND WALKS QUIETLY TO THE CORNER OF THE WALL. WE HEAR THE BEDSIT DOOR OPEN AND CLOSE AND A FIGURE BEGINS TO COME INTO VIEW. TEDDY BRINGS THE LENGTH OF WOOD VICIOUSLY DOWN ON ANTONIO'S HEAD. ANTONIO FALLS TO THE GROUND. TEDDY HITS THE PRONE FIGURE FOUR OR FIVE TIMES ON VARIOUS PARTS OF THE BODY. HE STOPS, LETS THE LENGTH OF WOOD FALL FROM HIS HANDS AND STANDS THERE, HEAD BOWED, BREATHING HEAVILY.

DISSOLVE TO HEAVY BREATHING IN PAULINE'S BEDROOM. WE SEE SOME OF THE LOVEMAKING AND THEN

FADE TO END.

PART FOUR, EPISODE ONE

HARMONIES. THE RESTAURANT HAS OPENED. IT IS THE SAME NIGHT AS ANTONIO'S "ACCIDENT" AT THE HANDS OF TEDDY BISHOP. THERE ARE FEW CUSTOMERS. HELEN BISHOP AND MARK ARE EATING AT A TABLE TUCKED AWAY IN A CORNER. HUGH IS HAVING A GLASS OF WINE WITH THEM, OCCASIONALLY GETTING UP TO SEE TO DRINKS AT THE BAR. IT'S A QUIET NIGHT. THE DOOR OPENS AND DAVE, THE POLICE SERGEANT, WALKS IN WITH ANOTHER TWO CONSTABLES. HUGH GETS UP.

HUGH Good evening, Sergeant.

DAVE Good evening, Mr Dugdale.

HUGH Is this an official visit? (SMILING)

DAVE I'm afraid it is, sir. (HUGH'S SMILE VANISHES). Do you own a property in Dering Road converted into flats?

HUGH (LOOKING ANXIOUS NOW) Yes, I do, why? What's happened?

DAVE I'm afraid there's been an accident, sir.

HUGH Accident? What? Is anyone hurt?

DAVE I'm afraid so, sir. A man has been attacked by an unknown assailant.

HUGH How bad is the man? Who is he? Is it one of my tenants?

DAVE No, he's not anyone known in the house, though Mr Trelawney said the man's face was familiar. Mr Trelawney was first on the scene. He was in bed and heard him moaning.

HUGH What did the man say?

DAVE He's in no state to say anything. He's in hospital on the critical list.

HUGH My God! .... My son has the ground floor bedsit there. Would you like to speak to him, Sergeant?

DAVE Indeed I would.

HUGH He's over here (HUGH LEADS THE WAY) .... Excuse me, my dear. Mark, it seems that somebody has been attacked outside your bedsit and the Sergeant wants to ask you some questions.

MARK Good Lord! What happened?

HUGH This is my son Mark, Sergeant.

DAVE Good evening, Mr Dugdale.

MARK Good evening, Sergeant. How can I help you?

DAVE Just routine questions, Sir. Have you been at the house in Dering Road today?

MARK Yes. My father picked me up there this afternoon and took me home. He brought me straight back here at 8 o'clock.

DAVE So you weren't there after 8 o'clock?

MARK No. What time did you pick me up, Father?

HUGH It must have been about 4 o'clock.

DAVE Very well, Sir. It's nothing that need bother you then.

MARK But who's been hurt?

DAVE We don't know who he is and he may not be able to tell us for some time, if ever.

MARK He didn't fall or anything?

DAVE (WITH A SMILE) I'm afraid not; the back of his head has been smashed in and he's got several broken bones. The weapon was lying beside the body – sorry – beside the injured man. Sorry, Miss, I didn't mean to upset you (HELEN HAD UTTERED A LITTLE CRY). I'D BETTER GO NOW. We have to try and establish this man's identity.

MARK I'll certainly do that.

DAVE Would be very helpful if you would, Sir. Thank you all. I'm sorry to have disturbed you.

HUGH Not at all – I'm so sorry this poor man has been hurt.

DAVE Well, goodnight all.

HUGH)Goodnight, Sergeant.
)
MARK)Goodnight.

(THE POLICEMEN EXIT. HELEN STILL SITS THERE WHITE AND SILENT)

HELEN I don't think I want to go back there tonight, Mark. Do you mind if I book into a hotel?

HUGH No, no, my dear; you'll come home with us.

HELEN Oh, but ....

HUGH Say no more! We have two spare bedrooms and Rachel would love to have you there. She took to you instantly the first time she met you. She'll be very glad of your company, I promise you.

HELEN You're very kind – thank you.

HUGH That's settled then. You need a brandy, my dear, so do I, come to that (GOES TO GET BRANDY).

MARK I wonder what on earth could have happened?

HELEN It's too dreadful to think about.

MARK I think I'd better go up there and see what's happened.

HUGH (COMING BACK) Here we are my dear, ……….. Mark.

MARK Not for me thanks. I think I'll go and find out what's happened.

HUGH Yes, quite right. See what you can find out. You never know, it might be something to which we could supply and answer.

MARK Right. May I borrow your car please, Dad?

HUGH But of course. Here (DIGS IN HIS POCEKT). Here are the keys – you know which ones.

MARK Yes. I'll try to be as quick as possible.

HUGH Oh I don't think you need hurry. Doubt if we'll get any more people needing a meal now.

MARK `Bye Helen ………… Oh – is there anything of yours you'd like me to bring back?

HELEN Oh, of course; I'd forgotten in the shock of it all. Yes please, some night clothes and my sponge bag.

HUGH Haven't you anything else to get?

HELEN No – I left Creekside in a hurry. I brought the night clothes when Mark kindly lent me his bedsit. ………… I don't see any reason to buy any clothes when I have all I could ever need at Creekside.

HUGH Quite right, my dear. Extravagance is not a vice to encourage.

MARK Well, if that's all that needs bringing I'll be off.

HUGH See you soon, Mark.

HELEN Mark! …….. Take care!

MARK Yes, of course. Thanks. (HUGH LOOKS AT HELEN AFTER HER LAST REMARK. MARK EXITS.

HUGH There's no need to worry about anything, me dear. This is probably one of those petty feuds over money or women that certain orders of society get themselves into.

HELEN (LOOKING EVEN MORE SHAKEN, QUICKLY TAKES A SIP OF BRANDY, PUTS THE GLASS DOWN, NOT LOOKING).

CLOSE UP ON HER EYES AND

DISSOLVE TO A QUIET QUAY, THE SAME NIGHT. HARRY THE FISH QUAY MANAGER IS SITTING IN A SMALL VAN. WE SEE TOM, DANNY'S BROTHER, COME INTO VIEW, OUT OF THE DARKNESS, IN HIS INFLATABLE. HARRY GETS OUT OF THE VAN AS TOM COMES IN TO THE QUAY. HARRY WALKS TO THE EDGE WHILE TOM TIES UP TO THE LADDER. TOM HANDS UP A SACK, AND ANOTHER AND ANOTHER AND WHISPERS.

TOM Empty these into your box and throw the sacks back down. I've got more here. (HARRY DOES THIS AND GHROWS THE EMPTY SACKS BACK DOWN. TOM GOES ABOUT FILLING THE SACKS AGAIN AND WE SEE THAT HE IS FILLING THEM WITH BASS. HE FINISHES AND HANDS THE SACKS UP AGAIN, CLAMBERING UP HIMSELF AFTERWARDS)

HARRY What the Hell you been doing Tom? Scooping them up in a bucket?

TOM Yeah – a good night alright!

HARRY It's going to take time to weigh them all, Tom, and I don't want to hang about too long. I tell you what – I'll go by your tally. We can always adjust it either way later.

TOM Alright then! Well there are 57 there and they're all over two pounds in weight.

TOM Make it £70.

HARRY Alright £70 and we call it quits.

TOM OK.

HARRY (GETTING OUT A BUNDLE OF NOTES COUNTS THEM OUT INTO TOM'S HAND) ....
£65, £70. There you are mate.

TOM Thanks! That's paid for my inflatable.

HARRY I'm glad to see you've got one at last.

TOM: Have you got any gear in the van?

HARRY: What kind?

TOM: Hooks, monofilament, all that stuff. I've nearly run out of everything.

HARRY: Hang on then. (REACHES INTO THE VAN AND BRINGS OUT A BOX WITH ALL THOSE THINGS). Here – give me a fiver.

TOM: (PEELING OFF A FIVER AND HANDING IT OVER) Thanks. (PAUSE)   When do you want some more?

HARRY: Best leave it two or three days. Give me a ring when you're on the quay ready to go and we'll fix a time to meet here.

TOM: OK then. Well, I'll be off now. Thanks (CLAMBERS DOWN THE LADDER).

HARRY: take care now, Tom. Don't go taking silly risks just because you've got an inflatable now.

TOM: (LOOKING UP FROM HIS DINGHY WHICH HE HAS UNTIED) Piece of piss, now! (GRINS) (STARTS THE OUTBOARD FIRST TIME AND ZOOMS OFF)

DISSOLVE TO JOHN AND PAULINE'S FLAT

MARK: And you say his face looked familier?

JOHN: Well – I wouldn't say that, but there was something about it that rang a bell. There was too much blood about anyway.

PAULINE: John (COVERING HER FACE, SHE IS FULLY CLOTHED BY NOW).

JOHN: Sorry love! Come on – you'd better get to bed. Try to stop thinking about it.

PAULINE: Oh, it was horrible!

MARK: Well, I've got to go now anyway. I'm just going to pick up some things for Helen; oh and Danny gave me £65 for the inflatable; I'll just go and get it. I left it next door (GETS UP AND GOES).

DISSOLVE TO A FEW MINUTES LATER. MARK COMES BACK.

MARK: It's not there – nor the watch.

JOHN: What do you mean?

MARK: The money is not where I put it! It's gone! And Helen gave me a watch today and that's gone too!

JOHN: Mark, I think you'd better ring the police – it may have something to do with what happened tonight!

MARK: Yes, you're right! May I use the phone?

JOHN: Of course, (WAVES HIS HAND AT THE PHONE) help yourself! (MARK PICKS UP THE PHONE).

DISSOLVE TO PHONE TYPE RECEIVER BEING USED BY CUSTOMS OFFICER ON BOARD THE CUSTOMS LAUNCH.

OFFICER: He's heading for that little quay behind the wood yard...... Yes .... No, we can't get up there; his inflatable's a dam sight more shallow drafted than we are .... Fine! Thank you Sergeant; let us know what you find. Over and out.

DISSOLVE TO HARMONIES HALF AN HOUR LATER. THERE ARE NO CUSTOMERS.

HUGH: Well that makes it even more imperative that you come home with us.

HELEN: Oh – it's all too ghastly!

MARK: Yes – it's quite a shock to me too! Do you know it's not so much that something's been stolen as that someone has been inside one's own place and probably looked through all the drawers and, well – I suppose it's just – I don't know – it makes me feel dirty!

HELEN: Exactly! It's a terrible feeling isn't it!

HUGH: (GETTING UP) Well, we may as well get on home. Ah yes (REACHING UNDER THE BAR) a kind person brought me this bottle of lovely Calvados back from France! I think a nightcap of this at home will do us all the power of good!

DISSOLVE TO NEXT DAY. THE LOCAL POLICE STATION.

MARK WALKS IN, SEES DANNY THERE.

MARK: Hello Danny. How are things?

DANNY: Bloody bad!

SERGEANT DAVE: Morning Mr Dugdale!

MARK: Good morning, Sergeant. I called in to give you any information that might be needed with regard to my watch and the money.

SERGEANT: Well, we've got someone in the cells now.

MARK: What – he's not admitting to it. No Sir! We found £65 on him but no watch; and he won't tell us where he got the £65.

MARK: How do you know it's the right chap then?

SERGEANT: We don't! We picked him up last night after being alerted by the Customs, they've had their eyes on him for some time; - it seems he's always coming into the harbour late at night. We're hanging on to him until the Customs & Excise have finished with him. That's his brother there!

MARK: (LOOKING ASTONISHED) What? You don't mean Danny's brother is your man? (SERGEANT NODS) But he's only a boy! He's a nice lad! God – I sold him a boat only yesterday!

SERGEANT: Oh yes Sir? Was it an inflatable?

MARK: Yes, it was!

SERGEANT: If you wouldn't mind me asking Sir, how much money did he pay you?

MARK: £65 (AS HE SAYS IT HIS FACE REGISTERS THAT <u>TOM</u> COULD BE THE THIEF).

SERGEANT: Did you tell him where you lived?

MARK: No I did not! (REMEMBERS THAT HE TOLD <u>DANNY</u> AND THAT <u>TOM</u> WOULD HAVE HEARD).

SERGEANT: Are you sure you didn't tell him, Sir?

MARK: (LOOKING AT <u>DANNY</u>) No – I didn't tell him.

SERGEANT: Very well, Sir ………… Well – there's nothing else you can do here, Sir. Don't forget to call at the Hospital if you have the time!

MARK: I'm on my way there now.

SERGEANT: Good. Appreciate that, Sir.

MARK: Goodby, Sergeant (TURNS AND STARTS TO LEAVE. <u>DANNY</u> GOES WITH HIM).

CUT TO POLICE STATION EXTERIOR.

DANNY: Thanks, Mark!

MARK: Well, I don't see how Tom could possibly have done it, so there was no need to tell the Sergeant any more than the truth.

DANNY: Thank you, Mark. Tom wouldn't have done that – especially to a fisherman!

MARK: Well, let's hope the Customs go easy on him. They can be pretty tough sometimes. ……………
I'd better be off Danny – can I give you a lift?

DANNY: No thanks, I'm waiting till my Dad arrives, then I can go.

MARK: OK then. See you ……………

DANNY: Cheers Mark and thanks again! (MARK WAVES HIS HAND SIGNIFYING "DON'T MENTION IT", GETS INTO HIS CAR AND DRIVES OFF)

DISSOLVE TO TEDDY IN LOCAL YACHT BROKER'S OFFICE. TEDDY AND THE BROKER RESEMBLE EACH OTHER.IN FEATURES AND CHARACTER.

BROKER: Well, quite honestly, Mr Bishop, it's not the kind of thing we normally do. If we were to part exchange boats and receive the difference in money that would be alright, but to part exchange and pay out the difference would be contrary to all business practices, unless, of course, it happened to be very little. Now …………… if you were interested in a more expensive yacht it might be different, 'though I must point out to you that the kind of boat you have is not in demand down here. We're sailors in this area! (WITH A SMILE) You may find a ready market a few hundred miles up the coast, I would have thought …………… Yours is the ideal craft for nipping across to France from Folkestone or Rye, after all.

TEDDY: Mm! I see (GENTLY FEELING HIS BRUISED MOUTH WITH A FINGER). Well – what else do you have to offer then? Something coming nearer to the value of mine, I mean!

BROKER   Well – again, you see, if you want a yacht, the value of yours brings you up to something with a lot of sail area. How big is your normal size of crew?

TEDDY: (GETTING A LITTLE FLUSTERED NOW) I don't have a crew.

BROKER: Do you mean to say you want something you can sail single handed?

TEDDY: Well – yes, I do.

BROKER   I see! (THINKS) Look – I tell you what we've got which may suit you down to the ground, and that's a converted French trawler. She has mast and sails and could be sailed single handed, but she also has a thumping great Baudoin engine in her which would get you out of any trouble. She's been beautifully converted at great expense. The accommodation is absolutely palatial. Standing headroom all the way through. The Master's cabin is the most beautiful I've ever seen. Now – I want to be honest with you. This vessel, in terms of what it has cost to be converted is worth twice as much in value as yours, but it is a vessel which is not sought after down here. When we start to advertise her in the National magazines this coming Summer I'm sure we'll sell her and at much more than we're asking now. However – if you're really desperate to acquire that kind of vessel I would be only too pleased to make a sacrifice and make a straight swop with you. After all, you live locally; ……… you did say you lived locally?

TEDDY: Yes – up the river at Creekside!

BROKER: Well (EXPANSIVELY) in that case – no more to be said – when you see her you'll realise that we are making a sacrifice and I've no doubt that you will come back to us again and again. After all – it's the basis of good business! The satisfied client returns.

TEDDY: Well – I rather think I'd like to have a look at this vessel.

BROKER: (LOOKING AT HIS WATCH) Very well. I've got an appointment in an hours time, but I'll put him off as you're an important client.

TEDDY: (LOOKING VERY SMUG NOW) Fine – yes – I think I've got time to look at her now.

BROKER: Right – I'll just get my secretary to bring you in some coffee and biscuits while I arrange some things in the other office (GETS UP). Oh! I'm terribly sorry – would you like a glass of brandy with your coffee?

TEDDY: Yes – thank you!

BROKER: HELPS TEDDY TO A BRANDY. Well – if you'll excuse me for a few minutes – There are lots of boating magazines there, please help yourself. (EXITS)

DISSOLVE A MOMENT LATER TO THE BROKER ENTERING ANOTHER OFFICE.

BROKER: (SPEAKS TO HIS MALE COLLEAGUE) Hey! I've got a punter in the other office who's got a lovely gin palace and I've sold him the idea of a straight swop on that heap of French junk.

COLLEAGUE: What! The converted trawler?

BROKER: Yes (CAN'T SPEAK FOR GIGGLING). Listen – get Jim to drive down there toute-suit with a couple of diving air bottles and fill up the air bottle on board and start her up and run her for twenty minutes then stop her. I'll be down there with the punter in about 45 minutes and I'll get him to look at the accommodation while I go and start her up. That way he won't know the engine's warm and that there's anything wrong with the air system – OK? Got that?

COLLEAGUE: Yes! Bloody great! Well done – hang on Nigel!

BROKER: What?

COLLEAGUE: Is she clean?

BROKER: Yes – I'm positive.

COLLEAGUE: OK then – I'll get Jim straight away (GETS UP AND THEY BOTH GO OUT OF THE OFFICE).

DISSOLVE TO MARK WALKING ALONG A HOSPITAL CORRIDOR. COMES UP TO A UNIFORMED POLICEMAN AND A PLAIN CLOTHES MAN.

MARK: Excuse me, but is this where the man is who was assaulted last night (POINTING TO THE ROOM).

PC: That's right.

MARK: I told the Sergeant at the police station that I'd come over and see if I recognised him. You see, it happened outside my flat.

PC: Don't know about that. Wait here a minute (GOES INTO THE ROOM, SPEAKS TO ONE OF THE PLAIN CLOTHES MEN INSIDE AND COMES OUT WITH ONE OF THEM)

DETECTIVE: Would you be Mr Dugdale?

MARK: That's right.

DETECTIVE: You know what's happened, I take it (GOING INTO THE ROOM).

MARK: (FOLLOWING) Yes, he was attacked outside my bedsit.

DETECTIVE: And that's all you know?

MARK: Yes.

DETECTIVE: Right, well, I'd like to get a few more details please. Take a seat (BRINGS A CHAIR FROM NEAR THE SCREEN WHICH SURROUNDS THE BED AND PUTS THE CHAIR NEXT TO ANOTHER CHAIR AT A TABLE UPON WHICH ARE VARIOUS ARTICLES WITH LABELS ON THEM, AMONGST WHICH IS MARK'S WATCH AND ANOTHER ONE).

MARK: My watch!

DETECTIVE: Which one?

MARK: (POINTING The diver's one ………… That and £65 have been missing from my room since yesterday afternoon.

DETECTIVE: Well, well (TURNS TO THE GROUP OF MEN) Boss! (A MAN COMES OVER). This is Mr Dugdale who owns the flat where it happened last night.

BOSS: Mr Dugdale.

DETECTIVE: This is Detective Inspector Taylor.

MARK: How do you do!

DETECTIVE: Mr Dugdale says this watch is his.

BOSS : Oh! Is that so Mr Dugdale?

MARK: Yes.

BOSS: Is there anything else here that you recognise?

MARK: No.

BOSS : Well – look carefully now. (MARK STARTS TO GO THROUGH THE RHINGS. KNIFE, SMALL CHANGE, BUNCH OF KEYS AND A BOTTLE OPENING/CUM CORKSCREW WITH THE NAME 'HARMONIES' STAMPED ON IT).

MARK: Christ!

BOSS: What's the matter?

MARK: That (POINTING) - it's one of ours – we hand them out to our good customers.

BOSS: Interesting. Anything else you can tell us?

MARK: No – not really.

BOSS: How did you come to lose your watch Mr Dugdale?

MARK: It was stolen from my bedsit yesterday.

BOSS: Was anything else stolen?

MARK: Yes - £65.

BOSS: Was there anything distinctive about the £65.

MARK: How do you mean

BOSS: Well, were they fivers or tenners or what?

MARK: (THINKING WITH EYES CLOSED) Yes – there were ten fivers and fifteen £1 notes.

BOSS: Good! Anything else about them?

MARK: Well, they were a bit fishy, smelt of fish, I mean; oh yes, and I made them into a roll with a yellow rubber band around them.

BOSS: (PICKS UP A PLASTIC BAG AND EMPTIES IT ONTON THE TABLE AND OUT FALLS A ROLL OF MONEY WITH A YELLOW RUBBER BAND AROUND IT) Like this?

MARK: Good Lord!

BOSS: Have you taken a statement, Robbie?

DETECTIVE: Not yet, Boss, but they've got a report down at HQ. He was nowhere near at the time of the attack.

BOSS: Well – we can get one later if needs be. Now then Mr Dugdale – in view of the fact that that corkscrew has your restaurant's name on it, you'd better come and see if you can identify the body. It may be one of your customers.

MARK: (STANDING UP AND TAKING A STEP BACKWARDS, CLATTERS THE CHAIR. HIS EYES ARE WIDE OPEN). You mean ………….?

BOSS: I'm afraid so – it's murder now!

CUTS TO MARK'S FACE – PAUSE – AND BACK TO THE INSPECTOR'S

Boss: It's alright, there's nothing to be afraid of (TAKES HIS ARM AND WALKS HIM OVER TO THE SCREEN) Sergeant! Help this gentleman to identify the body please. (ANOTHER PLAIN CLOTHES MAN COMES OVER TO MARK AND TAKES HIM BEHIND THE SCREEN AND OVER TO THE BED)

CUT TO MARK'S FACE AS THEY PULL THE SHEET DOWN.

MARK: Oh my God! (TURNS AWAY QUICKLY AND GOES QUICKLY TO A CHAIR IN THE CORNER WHERE HE SITS DOWN AND BURIES HIS FACE IN HIS HANDS, ELBOWS ON KNEES. THE INSPECTOR GIVES HIM A MOMENT OR TWO TO RECOVER AND GOES OVER TO HIM)

Boss: Well, Mr Dugdale – did you know hik?

MARK: (LOOKING EMOTIONALLY DRAINS, SOFTLY) Yes, his name is Antonio Fuentes, he used to be the manager at Harmonies.

BOSS: Thank you, Mr Dugdale. You've been most helpful. I'm afraid that we'll have to ask you a lot more questions about him now. - Do you feel up to it?

MARK: (NODS HIS HEAD).

BOSS: Good man! (CLAPS HIM ON THE SHOULDER) Robbie! Accompany Mr Dugdale down to Harmonies and get as full a picture as you can (TURNS TO MARK) Will that be alright with you, Mr Dugdale?

MARK: (STILL SHAKEN) Yes, of course.

BOSS: Thank you very much. (MARK AND ROBBIE EXIT; BOSS GOES OVER TO THE TABLE AND LOOKS AT THE CORKSCREW) I expect Robbie will get a few in while he's at it (GRINS). Nice food there!

SERGEANT: Yes – quite a price too!

BOSS: Not as much of a price as this poor bastard paid, and what the Hell have we got to go on – one plastic button! One button! I ask you!

DISSOLVE TO LATER IN THE POLICE STATION. THE DETECTIVE INSPECTOR COMES IN AND GOES TO THE DESK WHERE DAVE THE SERGEANT IS ON DUTY.

INSPECTOR: Morning Dave!

DAVE: (LOOKS AROUND) Hello Mac – how are things coming along?

INSPECTOR: Got a positive identification anyway!

DAVE: That's something; I heard the poor sod snuffed it.

INSPECTOR: Yes – pity. There we are! No news come through on that button, do you happen to know?

DAVE: Not anything to go on but the lads were in for a cup of tea earlier and said that the button had been resewn on to the material since leaving the manufacturers, and whoever had resewn it had used very good quality, strong thread. The important things was the few threads of the material that were attached to the sewing thread. That's narrowed the field considerably if we find a suspect, that is.

INSPECTOR: Yes; "if" it is, I'm afraid – there's still a lot puzzling me about all these strong associations with Harmonies restaurant.

DAVE: Oh, by the way, was it the Dugdale son who identified the body.

INSPECTOR: Yes. The deceased turned out to be the restaurant's ex-manager.

DAVE: I see what you mean.

INSPECTOR: That's not the end of it! We found young Dugdale's missing watch and money!

DAVE: Eh? ………….. Where?

INSPECTOR: In the pockets of the deceased!

DAVE: By God, Mac. Gets fishier and fishier! ………….. Oh well! I'll have to let that boy go then.

INSPECTOR: What boy?

DAVE: A lad we brought in last night on information received from Customs & excise. They're still with him now. ………….. He happened to have £65 in his pocket, and wouldn't tell us where he got it. Gutsy little bugger too.

INSPECTOR: (LAUGHS) Ah well – a night in the cells won't have done him any harm. Prevented many a life of crime that has.

DAVE: Thank God.

INSPECTOR: Well – let's hope it stays that way. I'm going to have some food Dave. If the boys come in, tell them I'm in the canteen.

DAVE: Righto Mac! (EXIT INSPECTOR)

DISSOLVE TO CHAIN LOCKER. THE USUAL CROWD ARE THERE.

BERT: He didn't.

RON: He bloody did! He only gave him one. Smack! And off he went, sailing through the air like a flying trapeze until the wall stopped him going any further.

HOOTS OF LAUGHTER.

BERT: I didn't know he could get like that!

RON: (CHUCKLING) Opened my eyes I can tell you!

ALAN: (COMING IN TO THE CONVERSATION) Alright! Alright! Come on now – it was only a bit of fun.

BERT: Hey, what about that murder then! (SILENCE)

ALAN: What murder?

BERT: Some poor bugger got done in last night up Dering Road.

ALAN: Poor sod! Did they get who did it?

BERT: No – not a trace!

ALAN: That's bloody bad that! I don't mind a bit of fun but when somebody kills someone, then it's a bit bloody bad! What the Hell's wrong with people that they have to go and do something like that! Makes me sick! Poor bastard!

BERT: Yeah …………. Danny's brother got run in last night too.

RON: Danny off the Sea Celt?

BERT: Yes. Our launch has been watching this boat putting into harbour these last few weeks. Well – I say boat, but it's an inflatable really. Anyway it's always been at night so we thought it might be one of these fellers bringing drugs in. Well – the long and short of it is that the police picked him up. He was clean, of course, but he had some money on him he couldn't account for so they kept him in all night. Poor little sod, he's not much more than a kid.

RON: Glad to know he's got an inflatable at last anyway! I should hate to wake up one night thinking about him.

BERT: (LAUGHS) Ron, do you remember the time ....

AS THIS CONVERATION GETS UNDER WAY, BRIAN LEANS OVER TO ALAN.

BRIAN: (QUIETLY) Alan!

ALAN: Yeah!

BRIAN: Have you ever seen Ron when he gets one of his turns?

ALAN: No – what do you mean?

BRIAN: Well – you know! He gets, like a premonition!

ALAN: Hey yes! Someone was trying to tell me about it the other night.

BRIAN: That was me you silly sod!

ALAN: Oh shit (GIGGLES) must have been pissed again!

BRIAN: You bloody were too! Anyway – listen .... About half an hour before something is going to happen at sea Ron will go all quiet and go down to the lifeboat and wait for the boys to come running!

ALAN: Go on! Every time!

BRIAN: No, no – I'm not saying that! No! But sometimes it does happen. I've seen it happen here four times now in the last – well, how long have I been behind this bar?

ALAN: Not so fucking long as you should be behind iron ones (LAUGHS).

BRIAN: Hey, come on now – I'm trying to tell you something!

ALAN: Alright then, alright (MUMBLING).

BRIAN: Well – Ron will just go quiet and his eyes go sort of staring for a second and then he's off out of the door and the first thing he does is hold on to those railings and look out over the sea taking deep breaths.

ALAN: Now – come on Brian – stop taking the piss!

BRIAN: I'm not, Alan! I swear it! Ask half the boys here today. Let me finish now will you! Bloody Hell!

ALAN: Sorry! Sorry!

BRIAN: Well, when Ron goes all quiet, all the chaps who know what's going on put down their glasses, wait till Ron's had his deep breathing exercise and gone round the corner then they leg it out of that bloody door (LAUGHING NOW) as fast as they can bloody go, jump into their cars and drive like maniacs up to the point, trying to get to the best lookout place first and get a packet of crisps and an ice cream from the ice cream van – if it's in the afternoon that is, of course. (ALAN HAS BEEN GIGGLING ALL THOUGH THE LAST PART OF THE STORY).

ALAN: You're really not taking the piss now? (LAUGHING)

BRIAN: (HOLDING HIS HANDS UP) If God were to strike me down dead right now! Of course I'm not taking the piss! You wait! You'll see it one day. Anyway – there it is! .... Strange! Sort of like water divining and all those sores!

ALAN: What sores?

BRIAN: Pint of bitter thanks Alan! - thought you'd never ask! (GRABS A GLASS AND DRAWS A PINT AND ONE FOR ALAN WHILE ALAN IS DOUBLED UP WITH LAUGHTER, LIFTS HIS GLASS) Cheers, mate!

ALAN: (PUTS A £5 NOTE ON THE COUNTER) Well – the pint's worth it for the story! (GIGGLING).

BRIAN: (SERIOUSLY AND HOLDING ALAN'S ARM) No! What I told you about Ron is true. Honest!

DISSOLVE TO THE FRENCH TRAWLER. TEDDY AND THE BROKER ARE ON DECK.

BROKER: Well – what do you think of that for accommodation, Mr Bishop? (CONFIDENTLY)

TEDDY: It's certainly spacious – twice as much as I've got now.

BROKER: Yes – one could use it as a houseboat if necessary.

TEDDY: Yes! Yes – indeed!

BROKER: I apologise for the lack of polish, but we've been rather busy with repair work recently. You noticed, of course, the craftsmanship of the accommodation. What marvellous joinery! Can't tell you want it would cost at today's prices! Now – let me show you the wheelhouse (LEADS THE WAY).

CUT TO INTERIOR OF WHEELHOUSE. TEDDY AND THE BROKER ENTER.

BROKER: There we are – all mod cons, two radios – one with all the channels you'll need; the other's a bit old fashioned, but the previous owner left it in for use as an ordinary receiver. He loved moving along under sail listening to radio three (SWITCHES ON AND FIDDLES). There's still a lot of juice in the batteries anyway. (FIDDLES UNTIL HE GETS THE LOCAL STATION). And here we have an intercom set up with the various parts of the ship – sorry, I meant boat, but she is rather like a ship, don't you think? (THE BROKER'S VOICE DRONES ON).

CUT TO TEDDY'S FACE.

WE HEAR THE RADIO ANNOUNCER'S VOICE "A REPORT HAS JUST COME IN OF A VICIOUS ATTACK ON A MAN BY AN ANKNOWN ASSAILANT. THE MAN IS IN HOSPITAL IN A CRITICAL CONDITION. THE ATTACK OCCURRED LATE LAST NIGHT IN DERING ROAD "X TOWN". WOULD ANYONE WHO WITNESSED THE ATTACK PLEASE GET IN TOUCH WITH THE LOCAL POLICE STATION" TEDDY SMIRKS. THE BROKER TURNS AROUND AND SEES THE HALF SMILE ON TEDDY'S FACE.

BROKER: I see you're enjoying yourself. It's a lovely wheelhouse, isn't it!

TEDDY: (SUDDENLY BLOSSOMING INTO COCKINESS). Yes, yes! Lovely.

BROKER: Just listen to that engine – you can hardly hear it. (COCKS AN EAR). Beautiful ....
Well, Mr Bishop – do you think she'll suit you? She's quite a lovely little ship, you know. Occasionally I bump into the previous owner and he speaks quite nostalgically about her........... Between you and me I happen to know that quite a few weird parties took place on board. He used to anchor her off the beach in the Summer time and just sit back and wait for the ladies to swim out. I'm afraid she's rather well known to a number of ladies who come down here regularly for their Summer holidays! (TEDDY'S FACE LIGHT UP) If you take her on you may feel you'd like to change her image! (HE KNOWS DAMNED WELL THAT TEDDY IS INTERESTED IN THE LADIES FROM HIS REACTION). For myself, I'm rather partial to the dear little things; in fact some to them are coming down next week .... I say .... Would you mind awfully if I brought them on board? They do so love this little ship!

TEDDY: By all means! I'm not unknown for my own particular brand of hospitality!

BROKER: Thank you, Mr Bishop; thank you very much.............. Well – I'd be honoured if you would be my guest for dinner, we could discuss the formalities and do whatever signing of documents over coffee and brandy.

TEDDY: An excellent idea!

BROKER: Very well then! I suggest we go back to the office and pick up the relevant papers. I'll introduce you properly to my secretary and she can go over them with you first; and perhaps we might take her on to dinner afterwards. A very interesting lady –very interesting. Has a charming flat positively filled with all sorts of articles and photographs. My dear chap I can't begin to tell you what fun we have with her. (TEDDY, BY NOW IS EAGER TO GET ON WITH THE DEAL AND BE INTRODUCED TO THIS VERY INTERESTING CIRCLE OF FRIENDS). If you'll allow me .... (LEADS THE WAY OVER THE SIDE AND ON TO THE QUAY.

DISSOLVE TO BROKER'S OFFICE.

BROKER AND TEDDY HAVE JUST COME IN. TEDDY IS LOOKING AT PHOTOGRAPHS OF BOATS ON THE WALL. BROKER, STANDING UP TOO, BEGINS TO OPEN DRAWERS LOOKING FOR PAPERS. THE DOOR OPENS AND THE SECRETARY COMES IN. SHE'S GOT A GOOD BONE STRUCTURE, WHEARS GLASSES AND IS QUITE SLIM.

JENNY: I heard you come in!

BROKER: Ah Jenny! I'm sorry my dear I didn't have time for proper introductions before! May I introduce Mr Bishop?

TEDDY: Teddy!

BROKER: This is Jenny. (JENNY GOES OVER TO TEDDY AND SHAKES HIS HAND) Mr Bishop (TEDDY INTERRUPTS).

TEDDY: Teddy please!

BROKER: (SMILING) Teddy then! My name is Nigel , by the way! Teddy's buying that lovely French motor sailer.

JENNY: How lovely! I'm terribly fond of that boat!

BROKER (Nigel): Yes – I was telling Teddy earlier that we'd had some lovely parties on board.

JENNY: Oh absolute Heaven!

BROKER Nigel: Well, I think we might have a spot of something to liven up our afternoon. Teddy – brandy?

TEDDY: Oh – thank you. (JENNY HELPS HIM TO SHRUG OFF HIS COAT AND SMOOTHES IT DOWN OVER HER ARM, DASHING OFF BITS OF DUST).

JENNY: Oh dea, you've got a button missing! I've got some buttons and the rest in my office – I'll just go and sew one on for you! (TEDDY BEGINS TO REMONSTRATE BUT JENNY GIVES HIM A LOVELY SMILE AND WALKS OUT OF THE OFFICE WITH THE REEFER JACKET OVER HER ARM. TEDDY LOOKS AT NIGEL, SMILES, OPENS HIS ARMS AS IF TO SAY 'THERE WAS NOTHING I COULD DO')

Nigel: (LAUGHING) Don't worry, Teddy! Jenny'll fix more than your button for you, wherever it happens to be! (LAUGHING. TEDDY LAUGHS TOO, TURNS TO LOOK OUT OF THE WINDOW).

CUT TO TEDDY'S FACE AS HE REALISES THE SIGNIFICANCE OF THE MISSING BUTTON.

DISSOLVE TO LATER THAT EVENING. AN OFFICE IN THE POLICE STATION. THE DETECTIVE INSPECTOR IS THERE WITH SOME OTHERS. THERE IS A PLASTIC BAG ON THE TABLE WITH "THE BUTTON" INSIDE.

Inspector: So what's the final report on it. Anything we can pin our hops on?

ROBBIE: (READING FROM THE LABORATORY REPORT). Well – a few things really. Shall I give you a rough summary Boss?

INSPECTOR: Yes – and I wish you would stop calling me Boss!

ROBBIE: Very well, Sir! ………. Well – number one – the button itself is a standard one purchased by a top quality manufacturer in Jersey for sewing on to very expensive reefer jackets. They sell thousands every year.

INSPECTOR: Just as I bloody thought!

ROBBIE: Hang on Boss – it gets better! – Sorry – Sir! Number two – this particular button has a slight fault in the attachment of the fitting at the back – you know – the eye that the thread goes through!

INSPECTOR: Go on.

ROBBIE: Well, the eye was put in wrongly by the machine in the factory so that the shoulders of the eye cause a ridge in the back of the button. Yes?

INSPECTOR: Ah ha! At last!

ROBBIE: Well – apart from that, there is the bit of material still attached to the button and the thread with which the button was resewn on – it's black embroidery silk.

INSPECTOR: Well – get on to the Jersey lot and ask them if they could possibly give us a lead on retailers of high class reefer jackets. If they show willing, hop over there and see what you can dig up. There's got to be a lead there somewhere!

ROBBIE: I agree sir!

INSPECTOR: You would! (SMILING) I bet you've got a little jaunt and a few birds already on tap!

ROBBIE: (LOOKING INNOCENT BUT GUILTY) Well – I have been in touch with the Jersey Police and they've offered me a lot of help and quite an intensive itinerary!

INSPECTOR: Go on! (SMILING AND WAVING HIS HAND) Get out of here! (ROBBIE GETS UP, OPENS THE DOOR) And bring back some results!

ROBBIE: Yes Boss! (CLOSES DOOR QUICKLY)

DISSOLVE TO JENNIE'S FLAT THAT NIGHT.

JENNY AND HER FLATMATE DIANE, A BUXOM GIRL, HAVE JUST CLEARED AWAY THE DINNER THINGS AND TEDDY HAS JUST SIGNED THE CONTRACT FOR THE BOAT).

NIGEL: Well – that's that then! Well done Teddy – you've got a nice little ship there!

TEDDY: Thank you! And thank you Jenny and Diane for the best meal I've had in years.

JENNY: There's more to come yet!

TEDDY: I couldn't eat another thing!

JENNY: Wait and see!

NIGEL: Would you make me one of your special cigarettes Jenny darling? (JENNY MOVES TO A CUPBOARD AND TAKES OUT A BOX) You don't mind do you, Teddy?

TEDDY: Sorry! – mind what?

NIGEL: If we smoke some pot! Gets us into the party spirit – you know!

TEDDY: (EAGERLY) No! Not at all! It's a long time since I smoked any actually!

NIGEL: Ah! What did I tell you, Jenny! He's one of us – you see! Thank you, my dear! (JENNY HAS BROUGHT HIM A JOINT AND NOW HOLDS A LIGHTER TO IT AS NIGEL PUTS IT IN HIS MOUTH. NIGEL TAKES A LONG PUFF AND HANDS IT TO TEDDY, WHO, IN TURN, TAKES A DRAG. JENNY AND DIANE COME AND SQUAT DOWN IN FRONT OF THEM. JENNY TAKES THE JOINT FROM TEDDY). You know, Teddy, I think we might be able to work out some kind of financial agreement between us if you fancy making some money.

TEDDY: Yes, indeed!

NIGEL: Well, if you're interested, it involves taking your boat out to sea every two weeks or so. Absolutely hush hush, of course, and rather exciting – especially when these lovely ladies come along.

TEDDY: Sounds first class to me!

NIGEL: Fine. In that case we'll say no more now until the time comes. (LOOKS AT HIS WATCH) I'd like to catch what's left of the news if nobody has any objections. (GETS UP AND SWITCHES ON THE TELEVISION). Why don't you girls go and put your party clothes on and welcome Teddy aboard?

THE GIRLS GET UP AND LEAVE AND WE HEAR SQUEALS AND GIGGLES COMING FROM THE OTHER ROOM AS THE NEWS GOES ON. THE LOCAL NEWS HAS JUST STARTED – BLAH – BLAH – BLAH .... "THE MAN TAKEN TO HOSPITAL LAST NIGHT IN A CRITICAL CONDITION HAS SINCE DIED. HE HAS BEEN IDENTIFIED AS ANTONIO FUENTES, THE EX-MANAGER OF A LOCAL RESTAURANT". TEDDY LETS OUT AN INVOLUNTARY CRY AND JUMPS UP, WHITE AS A SHEET. NIGEL STARES AT TEDDY IN AMAZEMENT THEN REALISES THAT WHAT THE ANNOUNCER HAS SAID, AND IS STILL SAYING – "IF YOU HAVE ANY INFORMATION" ETC" – HAS A VERY S TRONG AND FRIGHTENING ASSOCIATION FOR TEDDY, AND MISTAKING THE REASON FOR TEDDY'S BRUISES, QUITE RIGHTLY ASSUMES THAT TEDDY IS THE MURDERER. HE GETS UP, PUTS THE JOINT BETWEEN TEDDY'S LIPS, PUTS AN ARM AROUND HIS SHOULDERS.

NIGEL: (SOFTLY) I think you and I are going to be of immense help to each other, my dear Teddy, immense help. (TEDDY LOOKS AT HIM. REALISES THAT NIGEL HAS GUESSED THE TRUTH FROM HIS REACTION TO THE NEWS ANNOUNCEMENT).

THE BEDROOM DOOR OPENS, SHOWING A HUGE BED UPON WHICH DIANE IS LYING WITH THE FLIMSIEST OF NIGHTES. JENNY IS STANDING AT THE SIDE OF THE BED WEARING A BIZARRE LEATHER OUTFIT AND A MASK.

NIGEL   Shall we join the ladies?

FADE TO END.

PART FOUR, EPISODE TWO

SCENE OPENS IN THE WHEELHOUSE OF SEA CELT. FRED AND DANNY ARE SETTING OFF FOR A DAY'S TRAWLING, GOING DOWN THE RIVER.

FRED I bloody hate late starts – especially when it's my fault (SOURLY).

DANNY (GRINNING) That's what old age does to you.

FRED (GIVING HIM A DIRTY LOOK) Think I've got a dose of 'flu coming on.

DANNY (OPENING THE DOOR) Well, I don't want to catch the bloody thing.

FRED Shut the door!

DANNY I don't want to catch your 'flu!

FRED (PUSHING DANNY ON DECK) Stay on deck, then, but keep that bloody door shut!

DANNY (LOOKING VERY SURPRISED) All right! All right! No need to lose your flaming temper!

FRED (SHOUTING NOW BUT TURNING HIS ATTENTION BACK TO THE CHANNEL) Piss off! (THE RADIO MESSAGES BACK AND FORE FROM BOAT TO BOAT ARE GETTING ON HIS NERVES SO HE SWITCHES THAT OFF). And you can bloody well piss off as well! (UP AHEAD WE SEE AN INFLATABLE. AS SEA CELT GETS NEARER THE OCCUPANT STANDS UP AND WAVES HIS ARMS AT THEM) Oh Jesus Christ! What now! - ?!

DANNY (COMING BACK TO THE WHEELHOUSE TAPS THE WINDOW) It's Tom, Fred!

FRED I can bloody see it's bloody Tom! (STARTS TO THROTTLE BACK AND GRADUALLY COMES GENTLY UP TO THE INFLATABLE. TOM GRABS HOLD OF SEA CELT'S RAIL AS DANNY GOES OVER TO HIM).

TOM (GRINNING) 'Lo Dan!

DANNY What's up then – motor conked?

TOM No! Want a lift that's all.

FRED (COMING OUT OF THE WHEELHOUSE) What's up? You in trouble?

TOM Can you give me a lift past Black Rock, Fred?

FRED Give you a .... (HIS GROWING ANGER HAS DROPPED TO ZERO, HE SUDDENLY SMILES WANLY AND LEANS BACK AGAINST THE WHEELHOUSE. HE IS BATHED IN PERSPIRATION).

DANNY GRABBING FRED'S ARM AND PEERING INTENTLY AT HIM) You alright, Fred? (FRED NODS WITH A HALF SMILE WHICH SUDDENLY CHANGES. HE OPENS HIS EYES WIDE AND JUMPS TO THE GUNWALES AND VOMITS INTO TOM'S INFLATABLE).

Tom Aah – shit! What the ....

DANNY Shut up Tom! Come up here and give me a hand with him! (DANNY HANGS ON TO FRED SO THAT HE WON'T FALL OVERBOARD AND TOM JUMPS ABOARD AND TIES HIS INFLATABLE TO THE GUARDRAIL). Here – help me sit him down on the hatch cover with his back to the wheelhouse. (THEY STRUGGLE) That's right Tom. Now hang on to him! We're going back in! (DANNY GOES INTO WHEELHOUSE, GIVES HER THE GUN AND SPINS THE WHEEL ROUND AND GOES BACK UP THE RIVER).

DISSOLVE TO THE QUAY SOMETIME LATER; AN AMBULANCE IS JUST PULLING AWAY AS MARK, MARTIN AND JOHN DRIVE ON TO THE QUAY IN MARK'S CAR. IT PULLS UP AND THEY GET OUT.

MARTIN What was that for?

DANNY Fred. He got took ill on the way out so I brought her back and rang the ambulance; I felt a bit of a fool, but I didn't know what else to do; besides it would have taken me half an hour to go up and bring his father down.

MARTIN You did quite right boy. (CLAPS HIM ON THE SHOULDER). Well done Danny! ……………… Did he faint or anything?

DANNY Well, sort of, and vomiting.

JOHN Yes, there's some kind of nasty bug going around. My auntie got taken to hospital with it the other day. One old lady died from it in the same ward.

DANNY Oh bloody Hell! (THINKING OF FRED)

MARTIN (WITH A CHUCKLE) Hey! Come on now, Fred's a strong lad, not an old woman …………… so – what are you going to do now then Danny?

DANNY I don't know.

MARTIN Well – I'll tell you what. Why don't you go up the store-shed and see if Fred's father is there and if he isn't, go to his house and tell him. It won't be any use going to the hospital; tell him to ring them in an hour's time, not before. Give them a chance to do their job first. John and I will see that Sea Celt's OK ………. Alright?

DANNY Yes – thanks Martin.

MARTIN That's alright my boy – that's what mates are for.

DANNY Cheers then. Coming Tom?

TOM Yeah; - 'course. (EXITS)

MARTIN Come on then, let's see to Sea Celt!

MARK Do you need me Martin?

MARTIN No, that's alright, you go on home. Take care though, in case you fall over any bodies (LAUGHS).

MARK Don't remind me about last week for God's sake. I'd rather forget that that week ever happened.

JOHN Have the police stopped sniffing around us yet, d'you know?

MARK Not yet. They want the receipt for the watch now – that's all ……… That lad Tom is very strange, you know. He didn't want to admit that he'd paid me £65 for the inflatable and there was another £65 he had in his pocket. He just would not tell the police where he got it!

MARTIN Tom? ……… Tom wouldn't tell you where the wind was coming from! Not that he's a bad lad mind – no – he's very generous in fact, but never ask him questions! He just clams up like a scallop!

MARK Yes – but you'd think he'd have used his head where the police were concerned!

JOHN (WITH A KNOWING LOOK TO MARK) Maybe he did!

MARK (WITH A LAUGH) No – I don't think Tom's the kind to get up to skulduggery!

JOHN You never know, Mark.

MARK No ………… It's possible, I suppose, but not Tom – no ………… Well see you later then.

MARTIN See you later.

JOHN Cheers Mark.

MARK Bye now (GETS INTO HIS CAR AND DRIVES OFF)

MARTIN AND JOHN WALK OVER TO SEA CELT TO START PUTTING THINGS IN ORDER.

DISSOLVE TO MINUTES LATER ON SEA CELT.

JOHN (CHECKING ENGINE OVER) This pulley's a bit slack here, may as well tighten it up. (WALKS TO WHEELHOUSE, REACHES IN AND BRINGS OUT TOOLBOX).

MARTIN I think I'd better ring Michael. Fred won't be back for a couple of weeks, perhaps.

JOHN Good idea. Do you think Danny could take her out by himself?

MARTIN Oh yes, but who would he get as crew?

JOHN His brother, I suppose.
]
MARTIN. Hm. Not much of a choice – is it?

JOHN No ………………… Trouble is Tom's such an independent little cuss!

MARTIN That's right.

JOHN What about Janner?

MARTIN What about him?

JOHN His boat's been sold.

MARTIN The owner needed the money, I suppose!

JOHN What do you think?! Fishing's gone to Hell. It's time all those foreigners buggered off – otherwise we'll have no bloody fish stocks left.

MARTIN Yeah! Sad, boy – sad! .... Where does Janner live now? Same place?

JOHN (POINTS WITH HIS CHIN) Just up the hill there.

MARTIN Yeah – that's it. Look, John, I'll just go and ask him if he'd take over Sea Celt if I can get in touch with Michael. Alright?

JOHN Yes .... I'll be a few minutes here anyway.

DISSOLVE TO MARTIN ON TELEPHONE IN PUBLIC CALL BOX. JANNER'S OUTSIDE.

MARTIN I got the number from Mr Jenkins................ In a way – yes! .... Fred has just been taken to hospital .... no, nothing like that! It's probably this virus that's going around .... Yes, she's alright; John and I are just seeing to her now ....not at all, Michael. Now listen .... Do you know Janner? .... Yes (GRINS) that's right – the feller with the pipe! Well he hasn't got a boat these last two weeks and I think he's the chap to take over Sea Celt for you .... Yes, I've already talked to him. I hope you didn't mind me doing all this, but it's a shame for her to be lying alongside the quay for the next few weeks .... go on, you'd do the same for me wouldn't you. Listen now, Janner can start tomorrow. If you like I'll go and tell Danny he's got a new skipper for a while .... Alright.................... Good! Cheers! (BZZZZZZZ AS PHONE GOES DEAD. TURNS TO JANNER WHO'S WAITING OUTSIDE). You're on mate! (CLAPS HIM ON THE SHOULER)

JANNER Oh thanks, mate. You're a bloody good mucker Martin.

JOHN (COMING UP TO THE TWO) Alright Martin?

MARTIN Yes – all fixed. Janner takes her over tomorrow.

JANNER Thanks again, Martin!

MARTIN Not al all Janner. Shame to see her sitting alongside the quay.

JOHN Yeah – a boat not at sea's the same as a woman sleeping alone. A crime against Nature!

THEY ALL LAUGH.

MARTIN I suppose you could be right mate!

DISSOLVE TO POLICE STATION.

MARK IS TALKING TO ROBBIE THE DETECTIVE IN AN OFFICE.

ROBBIE Come, come Mr Dugdale – it's a very small request and there is a case of murder under investigation! Please don't forget that!

MARK Yes – I'm terribly sorry, but I personally would not like to involve the person who gave me the watch. Look, I'll be seeing her – damn! – alright, yes, it's a lady! (SIGHS). I'll be seeing her in half an hour and I'll ask her to bring it in herself. I know she won't refuse but I can't – I couldn't possibly implicate her without her consent.

ROBBIE Very well, Sir; I can understand your feelings in the matter, but do make sure she comes in this afternoon!

MARK Yes – I'll tell her.

ROBBIE Fine – well, that's all for now then. Thank you for coming in. (LEANS BACK IN HIS CHAIR)

MARK (GETTING UP) Bye now then.

ROBBIE Goodbye Mr Dugdale. (WATCHES HIM GO OUT AND GOES BACK TO HIS NOTES)

DISSOLVE TO MALAMUC – TEDDY'S "NEW" FRENCH TRAWLER.

HIS BRUISES ARE GONE BUT HE HAS A GAUNT, HAUNTED LOOK ABOUT HIM AND THERE ARE DARK SHADOWS UNDER HIS EYES. ALL THESE ARE NOT ONLY DUE TO HIS LAST WEEK'S ORGY OF DRUGS AND WOMEN, ALTHOUGH IT HAS GONE ON EVERY NIGHT AND DAY, SOMETIMES. THE MURDER IS HANGING OVER HIS HEAD. HE'S PUTTING TINS OF FOOD IN THE BILGES – TAKING THE PAPER OFF AND WRITING THE NAME OF THE CONTENTS ON THE METAL. HE'S PREPARING FOR A LONG VOYAGE AND MUTTERING TO HIMSELF.

TEDDY Huh! I'm a jump ahead of you, laddie! All I need now is you on board with your passport in your pocket! (GRINS TO HIMSELF. THERE'S A NOISE AGAINST THE HULL AND HE QUICKLY PUTS THE LAST TIN IN AND BOOTS THE BOARDS BACK. WE HEAR FOOTSTEPS WALKING ON DECK. HE KEEPS ABSOLUTELY STILL. WE HEAR THE FOOTSTEPS GO DOWN INTO THE ENGINE ROOM AND SOUNDS OF SOMETHING MOVING AROUND. TEDDY CREEPS TO THE DOOR IN THE BULKHEAD AFTER A FEW MOMENTS AND GENTLY OPENS THE PEEPHOLE AND WATCHES FOR QUITE A LONG TIME. HE THEN TAKES OFF ALL HIS CLOTHES, STILL VERY QUIETLY, OPENS THE DOOR TO THE ENGINE ROOM AND CLOSES IT, STILL WITHOUT NOISE AND TAKES A FEW STEPS).

CUT TO DIANE LYING ON THE ENGINE ROOM FLOOR, SMEARING HERSELF IN OIL, ALL OVER. SHE IS WRITHING AROUND AND THE OIL IS ALL OVER HER NAKED, BUXOM BODY. SHE IS MAKING MOANING SOUNDS. SHE SUDDENLY SEES TEDDY STANDING OVER HER AND OPENS HER MOUTH AND PUTS HER ARMS OUT, HER HANDS MAKING CLUTCHING MOTIONS, LIKE TALONS OPENING AND CLOSING.

DISSOLVE TO A QUAY ALONGSIDE A BOAT YARD.

ALAN AND STUART ARE CHECKING RIGGING, FASTENINGS ETC ON FERRONUFF.

STUART All good on the rigging Alan!

ALAN Good. Well, that's it then apart from the engine. We'll get Stan to do a final check on that for us before we go. (SIGHS) Oh, just think of all that lovely wine just waiting for us!

STUART And all those lovely birds who'll bring it to us!

ALAN: Lucky things – they don't know that Heaven is soon to fall on them!

STUART Fall is bloody right! By the time we get there we'll be fairly knackered.

ALAN Or de-knackered if our women have their way – (LOOKS UP) – Oh! Oh! – Talk of the Devil! (STUART LOOKS UP AND HIS GIRLFRIEND SOPHIE(?) APPEARS ON THE QUAY)

SOPHIE (NOT SAYING 'HELLO' AND LOOKING FAIRLY MISERABLE, LOOKS AT STUART). You're still going? ………………

STUART Of course! .... What's the matter with you Sophie? For Christ's sake we've been planning this trip for months now! (TEARS START TO TRICKLE FROM HER EYES AND SHE TURNS AND WALKS A FEW PACES AWAY AND PUTS HER HAND OVER HER EYES).

STUART (SOFTLY) Oh shit! What now! (HE GOES UP ONTO THE QUAY. GOES TO SOPHIE, PUTS HIS ARM AROUND HER SHOULDERS AND THEY MOVE AROUND THE QUAY VERY SLOWLY. SHE SEEMS TO BUCK UP A BIT, STUART TAKES HER IN HIS ARMS, KISSES HER AND WATCHES HER WALK OUT OF THE YARD. HE THEN COMES BACK TO THE BOAT LOOKING A BIT WORRIED AND STEPS ON BOARD).

ALAN What's up mate?

STUART You'll never bloody guess!

ALAN(LOOKING AT HIM FOR A WHILE SUDDENLY BURSTS OUT LAUGHING AND POINTS A FINGER AT HIM, CONTINUES LAUGHING)

Stuart It's not that funny!

ALAN(STILL CHUCKLING) Oh! Sorry! .... Daddy!

STUART (LOOKING AROUND FOR S0METHING TO HIT ME WITH – GRINNING NOW – PICKS UP A MOP AND BRANDISHES IT AT ALAN) You rotten piss-taking bastard! (HOOTS OF LAUGHTER FROM ALAN).

DISSOLVE TO SEA CELT ALONGSIDE THE QUAY.

JANNER IS TALKING TO JOHN AND MARTIN).

JOHN No – you've got no need to worry about the engine; I put it in myself and she had a good overhaul not so long ago. I don't know about the anti-fouling though ....

MARTINNor do I – still it won't come to any harm. We gave her a good coating last October – didn't we John?

JOHN Yes .... What do you want to do with her then Janner.

JANNER (CONFUSED BY THE QUESTION) Fish, of course! What do you mean?

JOHN (WITH A SMILE) I know that you daft ha'porth, but are you going to leave her as she is – trawling? Or what?

JANNER Oh, I see! (GRINS AND SCRATCHES HIS HEAD) Well – I dunno, I'm not much good at this Decca lark, I'd rather go lining.

MARTINHell! I didn't know that, Janner! I thought you had Decca on board your old boat!

JANNER Yeah we started using it, but I wasn't too clever with it, so what with that and the cost of hiring it the owner decided to send it back.

MARTINDamn! I didn't think about this – oh I am a twit!

JANNER That's alright Martin, I've got my own! Don't worry on that score!

MARTINI thought those belonged to the boat!

JANNER Did they Hell! No! The owner didn't want to spend any more money so I bought my own and took 50% of the profit.

MARTIN Hell!

JANNER Don't worry Martin! I don't want to do that with Sea Celt. No! I'm bloody grateful to have the chance to be fishing again. No – I'll lend my baskets of lines to Sea Celt. When the owner comes back we can have a chat and see if he wants me to get his own fixed up and used, or what.

MARTIN Phew! You had me worried there for a minute, Jenner. I was beginning to think I'd made a right mess of things. ………………. Well, the best thing you can do is borrow a van to get your baskets down to the quay and take the nets back up to the store-shed. Alf works there doing a bit of mending most days………. he'll take care of them ………. He won't be there now though, - not with Fred going to hospital …………. Tell you what – we're just off now anyway – I'll give you a lift up there! – OK.

JENNER Lovely job!

MARTIN Right then – let's go! (they all clamber over the gunwales).

DISSOLVE TO NIGEL AT THE YACHT BROKER'S OFFICE

NIGEL You do understand – don't you Teddy, that this has got to go absolutely to plan!

TEDDY Of course, I do! I'm as keen to do this without any slip ups as you are. (TURNS TO GO) Right – I'll just go back on board and check that my passport's not out of date.

NIGEL (LAUGHING) Passport? We're not going on a jaunt to France, you know!

TEDDY (TURNING BACK WITH AN INCREDULOUS LOOK ON HIS FACE) Good God man! You've just been going on at me about slip ups! Christ Almighty! What if the Customs men board us on our way out? This isn't exactly the best time of year for people to go on a jaunt round the bay – is it! If we've got our passports it'll make a damned sight more sense – they'll think we're off to France and we shan't incur any further investigation. I don't want to teach my grandmother to suck eggs, Nigel but I would have thought this kind of thing elementary to the success of the operation!

NIGEL (NOT WITHOUT SOME ADMIRATION) I – er – you're quite right, of course, Teddy; a bad slip on my part there! ………….. I'll come over an hour before the off and we'll go over everything for a final check.

TEDDY Good. Are we taking the girls?

NIGEL No – not on this trip. We'll have a celebration when we come back.

TEDDY I shall look forward to that. Right! Passport! (HALF TO HIMSELF TURNS AND LEAVES THE OFFICE. NIGEL OPENS A DRAWER AND TURNS THINGS OUT UNTIL HE FINALLY FINDS HIS PASSPORT AND THROWS IT ON THE DESK).

DISSOLVE TO THE DUGDALE RESIDENCE.

MARK IS TALKING TO HELEN.

HELEN No, no Mark. Don't be silly. It's perfectly alright ………….. What time are you going back down again?

MARK As soon as I've got a few things together.

HELEN I'll come back down with you then.

MARK I shan't be able to give you a lift back I'm afraid.

HELEN That's perfectly alright – I can always get a taxi.

MARK Well – if you're sure!

HELEN Perfectly sure!

MARK Fine! Have you any idea where my mother is?

HELEN I think she's around the greenhouse or somewhere.

MARK Well, if you'll excuse me, I'll just go and find her.

HELEN Of course. (MARK EXITS)

DISSOLVE TO DUGDALE'S GARDEN.

RACHEL (COMING OUT OF A SHED) Mark! I **do** wish you wouldn't shout like that.

MARK (SMILING) Sorry Mother, I didn't know where you were. I've just come to say that I won't be home tonight. We've got to move the boat around to where she used to be when Daddy owned her. We've got a leak in the stern gland and John wants to have a look at it.

RACHEL Sounds positively revolting!

MARK (LAUGHING) Mother!

RACHEL (SMILING) Well, you must admit it sounds rather surgical!

MARK (SMILING) I'd never thought of it like that before!

RACHEL Well I must get these indoors (TAKES THE POT PLANTS AND LEAVES. JACK COMES AROUND THE CORNER PUSHING A WHEELBARROW)

JACK Hello Mark. How's the fishing then?

MARK Not to bad considering. We're taking Voortrekker round to where she used to be tonight, she's got a leak in the stern gland.

JACK Sure it's not the packing?

MARK No John's checked all that.

JACK Of course, he would have, wouldn't he! ………… So no great excitements then.

MARK No – it's quietened down, thank God. It would have to after last week ………… oh yes – your friend Alf's son was rushed to hospital this morning in an ambulance.

JACK What? (AGHAST)

MARK Alf's son, Fred; He was taken ill on board this morning and they carted him off to hospital.

JACK What happened – do you know? (VERY ANXIOUSLY)

MARK It sounds as though he's got this virus that's going around. It's a pretty nasty thing, from what I can gather. An old lady has died from it already.

JACK Good God! ………. What time are you going down town Mark? (EXCITEDLY).

MARK I'll be leaving in about twenty minutes or so.

JACK Can you give me a lift down please?

MARK Why yes, of course.

JACK Thank you – I'll just go and see your mother and ask her if she minds me going early. (EXITS)

CUT TO MARK'S FACE, A LITTLE PUZZLED BY JACK'S REACTION.

DISSOLVE TO LATER IN THE POLICE STATION.

HELEN IS TALKING TO ROBBIE.

ROBBIE I see Miss ………..?

HELEN White; Helen White.

ROBBIE I see, so you gave him the watch in the afternoon.

HELEN Yes.

ROBBIE And it was in the bedsit when you both left that evening?

HELEN Yes – it was on the shelf above the bed.

ROBBIE I take it that Mr Dugdale and yourself are friends.

HELEN Yes.

ROBBIE Where are you living at present?

HELEN Well, right now I'm staying with Mark's parents – since that dreadful night, that is!

ROBBIE And before that?

HELEN At Mr Dugdale's bedsit.

ROBBIE Ah! I see! (HELEN FLUSHES) Well - in that case there's no more that I have to ask you. Thank you for coming in Miss White (HANDS HER THE WATCH RECEIPT AND THE WATCH). You may as well take these with you.

HELEN (TAKING THEM)   Thank you.

ROBBIE (GETTING UP AND OPENING THE DOOR) Goodbye Miss White.

HELEN Thank you. Goodbye. (EXITS)

DISSOLVE TO EXTERIOR OF HOSPITAL.

JACK GETS OUT OF MARK'S CAR. A STRONG GUST OF WIND CATCHES HIM; HE LOOKS UP AT THE SKY.

JACK She's blowing up Mark – you'd better look smart if you're going round the corner!

MARK I think you're right Jack. I'd better get going.

JACK Right, and thanks for the lift.

MARK Not at all, Jack. Bye.

JACK (WAVING) Bye Mark.

DISSOLVE TO FRED'S BED IN HOSPITAL.

FRED IS HALF SITTING UP WHEN THE NURSE COMES IN WITH JACK.

NURSE I've got a visitor, if you're feeling up to it.

FRED (WITH A WAN SMILE) Yes – I'm alright.

NURSE You're not alright – otherwise you wouldn't be here. It's lucky for you you were brought in in time! (AN ADMONISHING LOOK AT FRED)

JACK Well – I'm sorry to see you here Fred.

FRED You're the first visitor I've had.

JACK I got off early and happened to be down this way………,

FRED Nice of you to come.

JACK Well – I know what it's like your first day in a hospital – oh (DIGS INTO HIS POCKET AND PRODUCES TWO PACKETS OF CIGARETTES) I brought you these.

FRED Thank you Mr Men ……………….

JACK Jack! Call me Jack!

FRED Thanks Jack, but I don't think they'll allow me to smoke. Don't feel like it anyway – my bloody chest feels like it's on fire.

JACK Well – I won't tire you out – the nurse only let me in as a favour anyway.

FRED Alright Jack – thanks for coming and thanks for the cigarettes.

JACK (GETTING UP) That's alright, boy. I'll come again in a few days' time.

FRED OK. Bye then.

JACK God Bless. (TURNS AND LEAVES)

NURSE (COMING BACK AND STRAIGHTENING FRED'S BEDCLOTHS AND SEEING THE CIGARETTES) Oh no, my boy – not for you! (TAKES THE CIGARETTES).

Fred That's alright, nurse, you keep them. I don't want to see another one – ever again!

NURSE Good boy!

FRED If I'm asleep when my mother and father come in will you wake me up please?

NURSE Oh (SMILING) I though that **was** your father! Well, I've never seen two people look more like father and son! (SMILING. LEAVES)

CUT TO CLOSE UP OF FRED'S FACE, HIS BROW FURROWED.

DISSOLVE TO HARMONIES RESTAURANT. IT IS DARK.

ROBBIE, THE DETECTIVE, IS BANGING ON THE DOOR. THE WIND IS WHIPPING ROBBIES' COAT AND HAIR ABOUT. HUGH COMES TO THE DOOR.

HUGH Oh! hello!

ROBBIE I'm sorry to trouble you again Mr Dugdale.

HUGH That's perfectly alright – please come in.

ROBBIE Thank you.

HUGH Have a chair (MOTIONS HIM TOWARDS ONE AT THE FAR END OF THE BAR AND LEADS THE WAY. ROBBIE SITS). Will you join me in a drink? I was just about to have one myself ……………. brandy?

ROBBIE That's very kind of you – thank you.

HUGH GOES AND GETS DRINKS AND RETURNS.

HUGH Here you are (GIVES THE DRINK. RAISES HIS GLASS). God Bless.

ROBBIE Cheers.

HUGH (SITTING DOWN) Now then – what can I do for you?

ROBBIE I just came to return your son's £65. I should have done it this afternoon when Miss White was in the office. (BRINGS OUT THE ROLL OF MONEY AND PUTS IT ON THE TABLE)

HUGH (LOOKING BLANK) I'm sorry I don't understand.

ROBBIE Your son's £65. I should have given it to Miss White.

HUGH I'm sorry to sound obtuse, but I still don't understand ………… What has my son's £65 to do with Miss White?

ROBBIE She's your son's – I mean she gave your son the watch and I should have given this money back to her along with the watch this afternoon!

HUGH Oh you mean Mrs Bishop!

ROBBIE The lady who is staying with you at present! (CONCERNED NOW)

HUGH Yes, Helen Bishop.

ROBBIE Then she's not Miss White?

HUGH Certainly not as far as I know!

ROBBIE You said **Mrs** Bishop!

HUGH Yes that's right!

ROBBIE And is there a **Mr** Bishop?

HUGH Yes there is – a nasty piece of work too – I believe.

ROBBIE He wouldn't happen to be in the area, would he?

HUGH Yes, I believe so. They – or rather he, lives at Creekside ……… she left him about two weeks ago, you know.

ROBBIE No I didn't! (RATHER SHARPLY). Have they lived at Creekside long Mr Dugdale?

HUGH Lord no – a comparatively short time. Such A pity he's such a ………………

ROBBIE (INTERRUPTING) You don't happen to know where they lived before?

HUGH I think my wife told me that Helen Bishop has a family trust in Jersey and that she and her husband lived there …….. (ROBBIE GETS UP)

Robbie Where's your phone?

HUGH (TAKEN ABACK) ……… it's over there in the office.

ROBBIE (HEADING FOR THE OFFICE) Sorry Mr Dugdale, but this is urgent!

DISSOLVE TO ABOARD MALAMUC THE CONVERTED TRAWLER.

TEDDY AND NIGEL ARE IN THE WHEELHOUSE. THE VESSEL IS AT SEA AND HAS BEEN FOR A COUPLE OF HOURS. IT IS PITCH BLACK OUTSIDE AND THE SEA IS ROUGH).

TEDDY We should have waited until this weather had calmed down.

NIGEL We couldn't have! We've got a deadline. They'll only hang on for us for half an hour then they'll go back.

TEDDY Do you think we'll make it on time?

NIGEL Just about. I'll go and have a look at the chart. (GOES AND LOOKS AND SHOUTS AT TEDDY) Yes, we should be able to see their lights in another 15 minutes! But keep her dead on that course, for Christ's sake.

TEDDY I'm doing my best.

DISSOLVE TO POLICE STATION INTERIOR.

HELEN IS SITTING DOWN IN FRONT OF INSPECTOR MACKAY)

MAC And why the devil you didn't volunteer this information before beats me, young lady. I could have you for obstructing the law you know!

HELEN (VERY, VERY SHAKEN) But I had no idea that ………… Oh God! (SHE BURIES HER FACE IN HER HANDS).

SERGEANT DAVE COMES IN WITHOUT KNOCKING.

DAVE They've just radioed in from Creekside. The road was blocked but there was nobody in the house and it doesn't look as if it's been lived in for weeks.

MAC Right – thank you Dave. Well, Miss White, where else could he have gone?

HELEN Well, there's only the boat.

MAC What boat?

HELEN It's one of those fast launches – a big one, blue and white.

DAVE Wait a minute – I remember seeing it tied up where that yacht broker has boats. It **is** the boat that was involved in some trouble near Creekside isn't it Miss White?

HELEN I don't know …………… I …………………

DAVE Your ……………….. Mr Bishop nearly caused a yacht to sink just off there a few weeks ago!

HELEN Yes – I remember now.

MAC Right Dave – get some men to that yacht brokers straight away and if there's no-one there go to his home, or his partner's home, or even his secretary's home – anything as long as they bring back the information on where he is!

DAVE Right (TURNS TO LEAVE).

MAC (CALLING AFTER HIM) And Dave ………….. they don't have to be gentle – there's no time for that!

DAVE EXITS.

MAC Right then (TURNING BACK TO HELEN) Do you have any idea of the whereabouts of Mark Dugdale, Miss White?

HELEN Yes – he's gone with his boat to wherever it is that Mr Dugdale used to keep it.

MAC You realise the implications here, Miss White – do you?

HELEN (LOOKING BEWILDERED) No.

MAC Well – I should have thought it was pretty obvious! (PICKS UP PHONE AND GETS THROUGH TO THE DESK) Dave! Send someone to Harmonies and find out where Mr Dugdale used to keep his boat. His son should be there on it. Then tell them to bring Mark Dugdale back here in protective custody in case this Bishop fellow tries to get him again! (PUTS PHONE DOWN).

HELEN (GASPING IN HORROR) Oh no! He couldn't ……….. O my God! It's all my fault (BEGINS TO SOB TERRIBLY).

CUT TO MAC'S FACE LOOKING AT HER COLDLY.

DISSOLVE TO MALAMUC.

THE STORM IS INCREASING. TEDDY AND NIGEL ARE STILL IN THE WHEELHOUSE.

TEDDY Nigel! (PEERING THROUGH THE GLASS) I think I can see some lights!

NIGEL (COMING FORWARD) Where?

TEDDY Up ahead but slightly off to port – Damn! No – it's gone again now! (BOTH PEERING INTENTLY)

NIGEL There it is!

TEDDY I see it!

NIGEL Whoopee!

TEDDY (GRINNING, THEN HIS FACE BECOMES ANXIOUS) How the Hell can they come aboard in this weather?

NIGEL They won't! They'll sling a rope across and we'll haul it in.

TEDDY Well, let's get on to them shall we? (PUTS HIS HAND UP TO GET THE RADIO INSTRUMENT)

NIGEL (STOPS HIM) No! We always observe radio silence in case anyone's listening in! (GRINS AT TEDDY) Like to suck some eggs?

TEDDY (SMILING) Touche, mon brave! Touche!

NIGEL Cut her down a bit now!

TEDDY (THROTTLING OFF) But damn it Nigel they won't let us have the stuff without the money will they?

NIGEL Depends – sometimes they don't. But one has to be prepared, in case (PATTING HIS JACKET POCKET). In weather like this we normally just take the stuff and I go over to Holland the next day and make the payment.

CUT TO TEDDY'S FACE, AND BACK TO THE GENERAL SCENE.

NIGEL Right! Here we go! You stay at the wheel …………. I'll do the receiving and for Christ's sake try to keep her steady! (OPENS THE WHEELHOUSE DOOR AND STEPS OUT INTO THE STORM).

TEDDY (AFTER NIGEL HAS GONE) Aye, Aye, Sir! (LOOKS DOWN TO HIS RIGHT WHERE THERE IS A BIG PIPE WRENCH AND LOOSENS IT IN ITS HOLSTER).

DISSOLVE TO MINUTES LATER IN THE WHEELHOUSE.

NIGEL OPENS THE DOOR AND STAGGERS IN PUFFING AND LAUGHING.

NIGEL Got it! Got it! (CLAPS TEDDY ON THE BACK). We've got it laddie! Take her away, Skipper! Back to our lovely, leather clad ladies!

TEDDY Where's the stuff?

NIGEL Where I always put it, my dear chap! In the false bottom of the air cylinder! Ha Ha! (LAUGHS HILARIOUSLY). You didn't know that did you! And it's **your** boat! (LAUGHS AGAIN).

THE LIGHTS OF THE OTHER BOAT HAVE DISAPPEARED NOW.

NIGEL Come on then! Get this old tub around and headed for home!

TEDDY I'm waiting for the right wave, for God's sake! (LOOKS PAST NIGEL'S SHOULDER). What bloody lights are those? (NIGEL TURNS AND GOES TO THE GLASS OF THE DOOR AND CUPPING HIS HANDS PEERS INTENTLY. TEDDY WITHDRAWS THE PIPE WRENCH AND SMACKS HIM OVER THE HEAD WITH IT WITH ALL HIS MIGHT. NIGEL FALLS WITH A CRY. TEDDY HITS HIM AGAIN AND AGAIN THEN STRAIGHTENS UP AND ATTACHES A ROPE TO ONE OF THE SPOKES OF THE STEERING WHEEL. HE EMPTIES HIS POCKETS OF ALL IDENTIFYING OBJECTS PLUS HIS WATCH AND SIGNET RING, THEN CHANGES HIS MIND TALKING TO HIMSELF)

TEDDY Silly Billy! What did you want to go and do all that for! Silly boy! (HE PUTS EVERYTHING BACK IN HIS POCKETS, PUTS HIS SIGNET RING ON NIGEL'S FINGER, PUTTING NIGEL'S ON HIS OWN – EXCHANGES WATCHES AND THEN STARTS STRIPPING NIGEL OF HIS CLOTHS.

DISSOLVE TO A FEW MINUTES LATER WHEN TEDDY IS WEARING NIGEL'S CLOTHES. HE IS JUST PUTTING HIS REEFER JACKET ON NIGEL. HE COMPLETES THE TASK AND FINALLY JAMS HIS OWN CAP ON NIGEL'S HEAD. HE OPENS THE DOOR OF THE WHEELHOUSE AND PUSHES NIGEL THROUGH ONTO THE DECK. GETS ON HIS HANDS AND KNEES AND GETS NIGEL HALF OVER THE GUNWALES.

TEDDY Goodbye Teddy Bishop (SHOVES NIGEL'S BODY OVER THE SIDE. GETS BACK INTO THE WHEELHOUSE AND BEHIND THE WHEEL. TAKES OUT NIGEL'S WALLET EXTRACTS A BANK CARD) and Hello Nigel T Armstrong! (LAIUGH LOUD AND LONG. THE NOTE OF THE ENGINE CHANGES AND TEDDY GIVES IS A BIT MORE THROTTLE. THE ENGINE SPLUTTERS, GOES ON FOR A FEW SECONDS AND DIES. TEDDY'S FACE IS SUDDENLY FILLED WITH FEAR. HE OPENS THE HATCH IN THE WHEELHOUSE AND GETS DOWN INTO THE ENGINE ROOM. HE GETS THE ENGINE ROOM TORCH AND LOOKS AROUND, FINDS AN ADJUSTABLE SPANNER, CRACKS THE BLEEDER VALVE ON THE DIESEL PUMP AND NOTHING COMES OUT. GOES TO THE TANK AND KNOCKS IT A FEW TIMES FROM TOP TO BOTTOM. THERE IS PLENTY OF DIESEL. FLASHES HIS TORCH AGAIN AND THE BEAM HITS THE HEADER TANK AND A NOTICE ON IT WHICH SAYS 'HEADER TANK – PUMP FULL EVERY THREE HOURS'. HIS HEAD SAGS, HE GOES DOWN ONTO HIS KNEES). Oh Dear God! Help me! Help me! (HE STARTS TO USE THE SEMI ROTARY PUMP AND WE SEE THE LEVEL INDICATOR RISING. HE GOES AND CHECKS THE BLEEDER. IT IS BLOWING BUBBLES SO HE GOES AND PUMPS AGAIN, HIS FACE IS PANIC STRICKEN. THE FUEL INDICATOR RISES AND RISES. THE BLEEDER VALVE STOPS BUBBLING AND HE GOES AND TIGHTENS IT UP. SAGS BACK ON HIS HAUNCHES – GOES AND OPENS THE AIR BOTTLE, MAKES THE USUAL ADJUSTMENTS TO THE ENGINE AND THROWS OVER THE AIR START LEVER. ALL HE GETS OUT OF IT IS A 'PHFT' – NOTHING HAPPENS. HE TRIES AGAIN – NO NOISE AT ALL! HE SINKS DOWN ON THE FLOOR AND A SOB ESCAPES HIM. HE TRIES AGAIN.

NOTHING! THE AIR BOTTLE IS EMPTY! HE LIFTS OUT THE AIR BOTTLE TO CHECK THAT THE DRUGS ARE THERE. SCOOPS THEM OUT AND STUFFS THEM INTO HIS JACKET ETC. HE LEAVES THE EMPTY AIR BOTTLE WHERE IT IS, PROPPED UP AGAINST THE BULKHEAD. HE DASHES UP THE LADDER, AS HE DOES SO THE AIR BOTTLE FALLS RIGHT ON TO THE SEA COCK. IT'S USELESS. HE COLLAPSES IN A HEAP IN THE WHEELHOUSE, ONE ARM THROUGH THE WHEEL).

CUT TO THE ENGINE ROOM WHERE THE WATER IS POURING IN THROUGH THE BROKEN SEA COCK'S INLET VALVE.

FADE TO END.

PART FIVE, EPISODE ONE

HARMONIES RESTAURANT

INSPECTOR MACKAY IS TALKING TO HUGH AND MARK. THE RESTAURANT IS NOT OPEN BUT PAULINE IS PREPARING TABLES ETC.

MAC No – it was just a hunch we had in fact and a lot of luck. Some sacking had been sucked up into the sea cock and blocked it. I suppose the increased weight of the vessel slowed her down considerably so that by the time the storm subsided she was close inshore. Poole lifeboat took her in and Armstrong, as it was thought he was, was rushed to hospital. The heroin was found in his possession and when his secretary was taken down there to identify him it all turned out that Armstrong was Bishop. He's going away for a very long holiday – in fact chances are that he'll end up in Broadmoor (TAPPING HIS HEAD) and he'll never see the light of day again! (LIGHTS HIS CIGARETTE AND THROWS MATCHES ON THE TABLE AND LEANS BACK IN HIS CHAIR). You were extremely lucky young man – extremely lucky! (PAUSE) . What's happened to Miss White.

MARK (SLOWLY) I'm afraid she's not coming back. As you know she had to go and corroborate the secretary's identification and ………….. well – she rang and said she wouldn't be coming back as this part of the country had too many bad associations.

MAC Well – I suppose it's a lot for a young lady to take.

MARK It's quite a bit for anyone to bear! God – how could she have been fooled by a man like that!

MAC They're very clever these paranoid types – you'd be surprised the number who have latched themselves on to rich women. Maybe it's that little bit of craziness glimpsed sometimes which makes them attractive to that kind of woman.

HUGH Poor girl! Tragic!

MAC Well – I thought I'd come and have this final little chat to clear up any misunderstandings you might have had.

HUGH Thank you very much, Inspector. We much appreciate it, believe me!

MAC Right! Well (GETTING UP) I've got to go and see a man about a dog now.

HUGH (LAUGHING) Really?

MAC Yes. The man's dog has been stealing his neighbour's underwear off the line and the neighbour is convinced it's the man himself who's doing it. And that he has sinister intentions of a sexual nature upon her body. Poor chap – all he's done is train this scruffy mongrel to jump up and take things from his hand! (LAUGHS) Thank God there's a funny side to some of our work! We'd **all** be in Broadmoor otherwise!

HUGH (LAUGHS) Well thank you again Inspector (SHAKES HIS HEAD). Please call again, any time, we shall be glad to see you!

MAC Thank you. Goodbye young man. Try not to take it too hard!

MARK (GETTING UP). Thank you, Inspector.

HUGH (TAKING MAC TO THE DOOR AND LETTING HIM OUT) Goodbye Inspector! (CLOSES DOOR AND RETURNS). Well – that's over and done with! How do you feel about it all now, Mark?

MARK Not too good (SOFTLY).

HUGH Mark …………… I don't want to pry but ……….. did Helen mean anything to you?

MARK (AFTER SOME THOUGHT) In a way ………… yes. I was very fond of her.

HUGH Well, my boy ……….. it's one of the sad things in life. People aren't always what they seem to be!

MARK (LOOKING RATHER SAD) Dad ………… I ………… I think I'll go away for a while.

HUGH (CONCERNED) Well …….. if you feel you have to, my boy …………… I suppose you must ……………… Where did you think of going?

MARK I don't know ………… I might even go back deep-sea.

HUGH Well ………. Whatever you think would suit you best.

MARK I'd better go and have a chat with Martin and John.

HUGH Yes ………. I should let them know fairly soon if I were you – in all fairness to them.

MARK Is there anything that I can do here for you?

HUGH No thank you, my boy …………. You go on and get your own business sorted out.

MARK Right! Well – I'll get going then.

HUGH Shall we see you later?

MARK Sometime – yes (STILL "PIANO" AND GETTING UP GOES TO THE DOOR) Cheerio, Dad. (RAISES HIS VOICE) Cheerio Pauline!

PAULINE Cheers Mark! (PAULINE COMES TO STAND BY HUGH'S CHAIR).

HUGH Well, Pauline ………….. I think we've got a very sad boy there.

PAULINE Yes …………. Hit him hard, alright! ……………. he'll get over it …………… given time!

DISSOLVE TO THE JENKINS FARMHOUSE INTERIOR.

ELIZABETH IS TALKING TO MR JENKINS.

ELIZABETH I hope it's not too much of a rush; we could always make it next time if you wish!

JENKINS No, no! Tomorrow will be just champion, I'll go and leave a message for Michael and Margaret with Mrs Tripp.

ELIZABETH Oh dear – I'm sorry! I'd forgotten they are due back tomorrow aren't they?

JENKINS That's right ………… It doesn't matter, my dear. I shall see Margaret when we come back. In any case I'm sure they'd like to settle in by themselves without the fuss of moving me up there and all that.

ELIZABETH (GETTING UP) Well – if you're sure ....

JENKINS Yes – yes, absolutely!

ELIZABETH Well – I'll pick you up at half past nine then – will that be alright?

JENKINS Fine! (TRYING TO GET UP).

ELIZABETH No, please, don't get up! Oh – I've got the paper if you'd like it! (PUTS NEWSPAPER ON THE TABLE).

JENKINS If you've finished with it ....

ELIZABETH Yes – there's never much in it anyway (TURNS AND GOES TO DOOR) – half past nine then!

JENKINS I'll look forward to it!

ELIZABETH Bye (EXITS).

JENKINS Bye, bye! (SMILES, THINKS FOR A MOMENT, PICKS UP THE PAPER AND UNFOLDS IT. WE SEE THE HEADLINES "PLANS FOR RE-OPENING THE WHEAL CLIFFORD TIN MINE" ETC).

DISSOLVE TO HOSPITAL.

FRED IS MUCH BETTER AND SITTING UP IN BED. HIS FATHER (ALF) AND DANNY ARE AT HIS BEDSIDE. THEY ARE ALL IN A GOOD MOOD.

FRED It's not so bad when you get into the swing of it Danny! (SMILING) Go on! You're like an old woman!

DANNY Those bloody hooks scare the daylight out of me, Fred!

FRED (LAUGHING) Some bloody fisherman you turned out to be! You'd be better off with a pick and shovel down the mines! (LAUGHS)

ALF Damn! I forgot to show you, Fred! (BRINGS A COPY OF THE PAPER FROM HIS POCKET, UNFOLDS IT AND LAYS IT ON FRED'S LAP).

FRED (SEEING THE HEADLINES) Bloody Hell! I **thought** something had bucked you up a bit today! .... Does that mean your shares will be worth something now?

ALF We shall have to wait and see. I'll go and have a chat with Jack – see what he says!

FRED You know he's been in to see me a couple of times, Father?

ALF (NODDING) Yes.

FRED (AFTER A PAUSE) I know who he is now!

ALF Oh! .... I see!

FRED (SMILING GENTLY NOW) and I've had a lot of time to think, ... lying in this bed. It's alright Father – I don't feel the same any more (TAKING ALF'S HAND). We've only got one life to live and we should live it without regrets or bad feelings.

ALF I'm so glad to hear you say that Fred!

FRED (TO DANNY) Danny – I hope your father is as good a father to you as this one is to me.

DANNY Dunno ……….. never thought about it much …………… Yes – reckon he's alright, my old man. Aye – he's alright!

FRED AND ALF BURST OUT LAUGHING AT DANNY'S NEWFOUND REALISATION THAT HIS FATHER'S "ALRIGHT".

DISSOLVE TO ALAN AND STUART ON A QUAY SORTING OUT SAILS.

ALAN Just as well we had a look at these. I didn't know about that tear (NODDING).

STUART Yeah – wouldn't like to put that up in a gale of wind.

ALAN Well! Spare sails or not they're not worth carrying if they're like this – I'd rather run with bare poles!

STUART Well – thank God we didn't set out when that storm was here!

ALAN Just goes to show you mate! One minute it's lovely and an hour later you're in a bloody hurricane. …………… Sophie alright now?

STUART Just about …………. We're going to get married when I come back from France.

ALAN Well …………. proper thing to do isn't it, mate? Can't go around leaving bastards all over the place ………… Mind you – you'll have to watch your step in France! (LAUGHING)

DISSOLVE TO A FEW DAYS LATER AT THE DUGDALE RESIDENCE.

RACHEL What about your car, Mark?

MARK Oh – I'm lending it to John – he'll take good care of it and do anything that's needed …………. Well – goodbye Grandpa! (THEY BOTH SHAKE HANDS).

GRANDPA God Bless you, my boy! Send me a naughty postcard!

MARK (LAUGHING) I shall, I promise! (EMMA, RACHEL, MARK AND HUGH LEAVE THE ROOM. GRANDPA SITS DOWN AGAIN IN FRONT OF THE TELEVISION SET AND LOOKING AT THE PAPER. THE TV IS ON AND WE SUDDENLY HEAR THE ANNOUNCEMENT THAT THE ARGENTINIANS HAVE TAKEN SOUTH GEORGIA. GRANDPA'S EYES GO WIDE OPEN AND HIS JAW DROPS. HE GETS UP, LEAVES THE ROOM AS FAST AS HE CAN AS WE HEAR CRIES OF "GOODBYE" FROM RACHEL AND EMMA AND THE SOUND OF HUGH'S CAR DRIVING AWAY.

GRANDPA Stop! – Stop them! (BUT IT IS TOO LATE).

RACHEL (COMING INTO THE KITCHEN; - IT'S AS FAR AS GRANDPA HAS GOT) Whatever is the matter? Are you alright?

GRANDPA It's those damned Argies – Hijos de putas! (HE SHOUTS) They've taken South Georgia!

DISSOLVE TO TOM (DANNY'S BROTHER) SETTING OFF IN HIS INFLATABLE FROM THE QUAY OUTSIDE THE CHAIN LOCKER. WE SEE HIM THROUGH THE PUB WINDOW. AS HE GOES ROUND THE CORNER WE PULL BACK AND PAN TO WHERE ALAN, BERT AND THE REST ARE HAVING A DRINK.

ALAN Well – couldn't leave without a last pint could we?

RON Aren't your ladies coming to see you off?

ALAN They already have when we pushed off from the quay up river. They think we're well out to sea by now – (ALL LAUGH). Well – got to get your priorities right, haven't you! (MORE LAUGHTER. ALAN FINISHES HIS DRINK AND LOOKS AT STUART).

ALAN Well – come on then mate! Let's do it!

BERT We'll come and cast you off! (CHORUS OF "YES").

ALAN All right then – come on!

THEY ALL TROOP OUT – HALF DOZEN OR MORE, ALL (EXCEPT ALAN AND STUART) WITH GLASSES IN THEIR HANDS. THEY TROOP OUT OF THE DOOR SINGING AND DANCING BEHIND ALAN AND STUART. WE FOLLOW THEM THE FEW YARDS TO THE QUAY. ALAN AND STUART SCRAMBLE DOWN THE LADDER. ALAN IMMEIDATELY STARTS THE ENGINE – LOOKS UP AT THE MEN ON THE QUAY.

ALAN Alright boys – cast her off!

BERT (LOOKING AT THE OTHERS WITH HIM) The Benediction lads?

ALAN On no! Quick Stuart.

THE LOT ON THE QUAY POUR THEIR BEER ALL OVER THE BOAT AND THE TWO LADS UNZIP THEIR TROUSERS AND START TO PIDDLE OVER THEM AS WELL; THE BOAT IS CAST OFF, PIDDLING STILL CONTINUING AND BERT RAISES HIS ARM AND CONDUCTS HIS COLLEAGUES IN A CHORUS

ALL Piss off .... Amen (LIKE A RESPONSE IN CHURCH, THEN THEY ALL FALL ABOUT WITH LAUGHTER.

ALAN AND STUART SHAKE THEIR FISTS AND SHOUT.

BERT (SHOUTING BACK) Egg-zackly! (IN REFERENCE TO THE EGG ESCAPADE AND STICKS TWO FINGERS IN THE AIR LAUGHING ALL THE TIME).

THE YACHT PULLS AROUND THE CORNER OUT OF SIGHT, THE TWO LADS STILL SHOUTING AND GESTICULATING.

DISSOLVE TO ROSEBRAWSE.

ELIZABETH IS SITTING DOWN WITH MICHAEL AND MARGARET. M & M LOOK VERY HEALTHY AND HAPPY.

ELIZABETH Well – there's no need to worry, I promise you!

MARGARET I know but some people get rather withdrawn when asked to live with their newly married offspring.

ELIZABETH Not **your** father (HOOT OF LAUGHTER). All I've heard is how Michael plans to do this and that and how **he** is going to help him! Goodness no! …………and I'm sorry I can't tell you what he's up to – it's a dark and terrible secret (SMILES). He had hoped to come back with me the next day but the – oops – nearly gave it away (LAUGHS), but he's had to stay rather longer and he'll come down with Simon tomorrow or the day after.

MICHAEL Ah hah!

MARGARET Now Michael! These men don't understand; please excuse my husband, my dear! (SMILING HUMOUROUSLY)

ELIZABETH And how is your guest settling in?

MICHAEL Hard to say yet – he only arrived this morning.

ELIZABETH Well – the pictures are certainly worth keeping. What you have there you know, Michael, is a complete architectural history of Cornwall in the 1800s. Lots of those houses in the paintings have changed enormously and, sadly, most of them no longer exist.

WE HEAR A VOICE FROM OUTSIDE THE ROOM, AND SOME COUGHING.

JOHN WILLIAMS Oh – I don't know – all these stairs (TALKING TO HIMSELF) (COUGH! COUGH!) Hello! Where is everybody?

MICHAEL In here! (GOES AND OPENS DOOR). Come in John! (ENTER JOHN WILLIAMS, A MAN IN HIS SIXTIES, VERY SPRIGHTLY AND RUDDY FACED; HE IS OF MEDIUM HEIGHT. THE ONLY RESEMBLANCE HE HAS TO MICHAEL IS IN THE SET OF HIS EYES AND SHAPE OF THE EYEBROW). Elizabeth, may I introduce my long lost cousin John Williams. John – Elizabeth Labron.

JOHN W How do you do! (HE HAS A CULTURED VOICE WITH A SLIGHT WELSH INTONATION WHICH COMES OUT SOMETIMES WHEN EXCITED).

ELIZABETH How do you do! I've been looking at some of the paintings you brought down with you.

JOHN W He – what? Oh – yes! Don't know much about paintings! Like a good landscape though! Plenty of hills and rivers and that kind of thing! (MARGARET AND MICHAEL SMILE AT EACH OTHER). Words! That's what I like! A good book, well written with a bit of mystery – you know! Well! Is the Sun over the yard arm yet?

MICHAEL It certainly is! Ladies! What will you have?

ELIZABETH Gin and tonic, please.

MARGARET The same for me, please.

MICHAEL John! What will you have?

JOHN Scotch please, with water – fifty fifty!

MICHAEL GOES TO GET DRINKS.

MARGARET Is your room alright John?

160

JOHN Splendid, absolutely splendid!

MARGARET I apologies for any mess but we haven't been back long from the Scillies.

JOHN Ah that's somewhere I want to go next week!

MARGARET You'll love it – it's quite Heaven!

JOHN Is it possible to hire a boat to go across?

ELIZABETH Yes, but the weather is a bit unpredictable here at this time of year. You'd be better going on the Scillonian or even by helicopter.

JOHN No, no. Not flying – if God had meant us to fly he'd have given us wings. As it is I find swimming exhausting enough! (THEY ALL LAUGH). No – I love the sea anyway ……… You know …………… at home I get what I call sea hunger and I just **have** to go out in a boat. Even if I only walk the shore it makes me feel renewed.

MICHAEL (COMING BACK WITH THE DRINKS). Funny you should say that – I feel exactly the same.

JOHN No – it's not really funny Michael. You see you and I come from a long line of seafaring people.

MICHAEL Good Lord! That's the first I've heard of it!

JOHN Oh yes! And some of them were a bit naughty, you know! In fact, on one side of the family – I'm going back two hundred years now – one of our common ancestors had a gang called "the silver hatchet gang" and used to lure ships on to the rocks with false beacons!

MICHAEL Good Heavens!

ELIZABETH Wreckers! (LAUGHS). Margaret! You've married a wrecker! (THEY ALL LAUGH EXCEPT JOHN).

JOHN I know what used to happen you know ……… it was terrible. Terrible!

MARGARET But that was ages ago John!

JOHN It's the same blood as runs in these veins today, my dear! Terrible ………… Yes, as I was saying – after the ship was wrecked the men would go around the rocks butchering all who had survived and then they cut off their fingers or even hands – to get at rings and bracelets.

MARGARET Ghastly!

JOHN Yes! And their activities weren't only confined to Wales you know – oh no they came across to Cornwall as well……………

ELIZABETH Of course! The Celtic cousins!

JOHN No, no, my dear; more than cousins! Brothers! Did you know that in the ninth century Cornwall was known as West Wales and one hundred years **before** that Cornwall **and** Devon was West Wales! And the language they call Cornish, if they were to speak it properly, is really only a dialect of Welsh. You can still hear the same basic dialect today in the Aberdare region of Wales. And, incidentally, if this Cornish Nationalist party were only to admit to that fact – do you know what it would mean? Well – think of it – if Cornish is a dialect of Welsh then, by law it would have the same official **standing** as Welsh – yes – it would be an official language here, equal with English!

MARGARET Goodness – don't tell them that or we'll have even more Mebyon Kernow candidates pounding on our door.

JOHN Well – it stands to reason doesn't it! I mean the Yorkshire or any other dialect isn't arbitrated against for being what it is! So why shouldn't Cornish have an equal right. It's time the Board of Racial Equality started turning its eyes on our **native** inequalities apart from those of any immigrants. And what about all these politicians who go on about England this and England that. Don't they know that this is the **United** Kingdom now? I know quite a few Welshmen who get rather hot under the collar when they hear that kind of thing as I do myself. Good God! I didn't fight the Germans for **England**! I fought them for Britain and the **British** people, not just the English, or Welsh, or Irish or Scots!

MICHAEL Bravo! Bravo, John! I've never heard it stated before but, by God, you're right.

JOHN Well – there you are! Britain, or as it's correctly called **Prydain**, has existed in our Celtic culture for possibly as long as eight thousand years. Why should people who have only been here for five minutes try to change it! Hah! ……………… God Bless! Everyone! (THE GIRLS ARE QUITE TAKEN ABACK BY ALL THE RHETORIC AND ARE STILL THINKING ABOUT A LOT OF WHAT HE SAID)

ELIZABETH Er – yes – cheerio.

MARGARET God Bless.

MICHAEL (WANTING TO GET JOHN OFF HIS SUBJECT) John – why don't you come and look at these paintings that Elizabeth has restored!

JOHN (LOOKING AROUND) Oh yes – I'd like to have a look!

THE GIRLS ARE NOW GIVING EACH OTHER GLANCES IN REFERENCE TO JOHN'S OUTBURST. WHILE MICHAEL TAKES JOHN AROUND THE ROOM).

MICHAEL ………………and it seems, according to Elizabeth that these two paintings are of the same house – you see? (JOHN LOOKS AT THEM)

JOHN Hm (NOT TERRIBLY INTERESTED).

MICHAEL And this one (POINTING) was done by our common ancestor, John E Williams.

JOHN (LOOKING MORE CLOSELY) Oh – it's very good isn't it!

MICHAEL ……………and even more interesting is the fact that on the back is what we think is the name of the house (TAKES THE PAINTING OFF THE WALL AND TURNS IT OVER).

JOHN (LOOKING AT THE NAME) Ah – Crugsaeth (PRONOUNCES IT PROPERLY "CREEG-SAHEETH")

MICHAEL Surely it's Crugseeth!

JOHN (LAUGHS) Since when did you speak Welsh! - ?

MICHAEL Welsh? But we thought this was in Brittany!

ELIZABETH NOW GETS UP AND JOINS THEM.

JOHN Oh it could be but old John M wrote everything in welsh in his diaries, all through his long search for his father – everything is Welsh! (LOOKING BACK AT THE PAINTING RIGHT SIDE UP AND GIVING IT BACK TO MICHAEL). Yes – it's obvious it's the same house (POINTS TO THE DE TRAPENARD) - there's the arrow!

ELIZABETH What do you mean?

JOHN The arrow! Crugsaeth translated into English means "the ridge of the arrow" (POINTS). There's the arrow in the rock formation and it's the beginning of the ridge that goes back up there in the painting!

ELIZABETH (CLAPPING HER HANDS TOGETHER) What a marvellous piece of detective work!

JOHN Nonsense! Pure translation. All Celtic place names are descriptive of where they are or what they are – as is this – Arrowridge!

MARGARET How beautiful!

JOHN Not at all! This place of yours for instance means "big or large moor"!

MARGARET Oh how lovely! I can see we're going to have a lot of useful information out of you.

MICHAEL Would place names have had anything to do with farming?

JOHN Of course, the names tell you what was grown here in the past when the land was homesteaded. There are lots of instances where the kind of tree or animal prevalent is inherent in the name! Sometimes these names go back thousands of years! ………. Incidentally Michael, I've got the translation of John M's diaries at home – I did the translation when I was about 17 and haven't even looked at it since.

MICHAEL Why on earth not?

JOHN (HOLDING UP HIS GLASS) Too many other distractions (LAUGHS).

MICHAEL Would it be possible to have a look at them sometime?

JOHN But, of course! I'll send them on to you when I get back.

MICHAEL Gosh – I'm terribly sorry – I've been neglecting everyone's drinks! (LOOKS OUT OF THE WINDOW). I say that wind's picked up! I hope we're not going to have another storm like last week's! (IT IS GETTING DARK)

DISSOLVE TO STRONG WIND AND ROUGH SEA.

TOM IS IN HIS INFLATABLE TROLLING FOR BASS; THERE ARE HALF A DOZEN IN THE BOAT. HE IS INTENT ON THE FISHING AND DOESN'T TAKE IN HIS SURROUNDINGS OR THE CONDITIONS. THE ENGINE STOPS.

TOM Damn! (HE THEN LOOKS AROUND AND SEES THE STATE OF THE SEA). Bloody Hell! (HE PULLS IN HIS LINES AND STOWS THEM IN A BOX. HE PULLS THE STARTING ROPE – THE ENGINE DOESN'T START. HE TRIES AGAIN AND AGAIN. THE WIND IS BLOWING HIM OUT TO SEA AND IT IS GETTING DARK. HE KEEPS ON TRYING TO START THE ENGINE).

DISSOLVE TO MARTIN POLGLAZE'S HOUSE.

MARTIN Yeah – I can quite see your point, old mate, but we'll have to get the final word from the Boss! (TO JOHN)

SUE (COMING IN, TAKES IN THE END PIECE OF THE CONVERSATION) Oh yes – **now** what do you want me to take the blame for?

MARTIN John here is worried about Pauline staying at the flat. She's been a bit nervy ever since that murder.

SUE I should jolly well think so too. All you men are so damn selfish! All right for **you** when you're at sea, but what about us women stuck here by ourselves!

MARTIN (SMILING AND OPENING HIS ARMS IN MOCK SURRENDER). And now I suppose you're going to say that Pauline should come and live with us in the new house! - ?

SUE Yes! (ANGRILY)

MARTIN And that she can have two rooms and John can do the work needed to convert it and only charge him £10 while the place is still being converted!

SUE Yes, of course! (PUFFING UP LIKE A BANTAM HEN) and when he's finished the converting ………… (SHE TAILS OFF AS SHE REALISES THAT MARTIN HAS GOT ONE OVER ON HER; GETS VERY RED, GOES OVER TO MARTIN AND STARTS TO SLAP HIM, HALF IN ANGER, HALF LAUGHING AND FINALLY THEY BOTH LAUGH HILARIOUSLY AND SHE FALLS INTO MARTIN'S LAP AS MARTIN IS TRYING TO FEND HER OFF).

MARTIN Mental Judo that was mate! (GIGGLING)

JOHN (ALSO LAUGHING) How's that!

MARTIN Using your opponent's strength to beat him! (THUMP ANOTHER DIG IN THE RIBS FROM SUE). Alright then! – seriously now Sue! – Hey! Stop it!

SUE Hey yourself! (GETS UP AND STANDS IN FRONT OF THEM). When are you lot going off again?

MARTIN Three or four days time, I suppose, as long as we can get a decent replacement for Mark by then.

SUE Well – in that case – John! You bring Pauline's things over here the day you're due to leave. I'm not having that girl sleep in that flat all alone any more. She can stay here for the week and help me pack and move on the next weekend. And I'm not hearing any more about it so there! Now, get out the two of you. This is house cleaning night! (THE TWO MEN FLY OUT OF THE DOOR AND THEY HEAR SUE SHOUT AFTER THEM) - and don't you come back here pissed or I'll cut off your rations! (MARTIN AND JOHN HALF DOUBLE OVER, GIGGLING AND EXIT QUICKLY)

DISSOLVE TO SHOT OF THEM GETTING INTO THE CAR – THE WIND IS VERY VERY STRONG.

DISSOLVE TO CHAIN LOCKER. MOST OF THE LADS ARE THERE. ENTER MARTIN AND JOHN.

BERT Hello lads – what are you having?

MARTIN) Pint please!
JOHN   ) Thanks Bert – pint!

BRIAN You missed the send off today! (PULLING PINTS)

JOHN What was that?

BRIAN Alan and Stuart went off to France in their ferro boat!

MARTIN In this weather? (INCREDULOUSLY)

BERT No – it was lovely this afternoon!

BRIAN We gave them the Supreme Benediction.

MARTIN You didn't!

BERT We did! (MARTIN AND JOHN LAUGH)

MARTIN Oh I'd like to have seen that! ………… What about this weather though – it's nearly as bad as that last storm we had!

JOHN Is the boat up to the mark?

BERT Oh it's a lovely boat!

RON Yes – strong too.

MARTIN What kind of radio has he got?

BERT Radio? What? ……………

BERT AND RON EXCHANGE GLANCES.

RON Oh no! Don't tell me he didn't put the radio in!

BERT I don't know Ron.

RON Oh I **am** a bloody fool!

JOHN He might have one of those new ones with a small aerial!

RON Let's hope and pray you're right.

BERT Amen to that! No – Alan wouldn't be so stupid. Got his head screwed on he has!

BRIAN Yes, of course he has!

JOHN (QUIETLY TO MARTIN) I've just thought of something.

MARTIN What?

JOHN Well, Fred will be out of hospital soon, and that means Janner will be out of a job!

MARTIN Yes (LOOKS AT JOHN) .... Oh! I see! Yes – boy! Yes – Janner's our man! Well done John! (GRINS AND SHAKES HIS HEAD).

JOHN Any word from Michael?

MARTIN Oh yes – I forgot. He rang up and thanked us for fixing him up with Janner and he's going to take us out for a drink this weekend. He said Danny was playing up a bit about long lining and that if Fred wasn't out of hospital soon he'd be there himself! (GRINS)

JOHN Who? .... Michael?

MARTIN No! .... Danny! What's the matter with you? Out of practice with the beer or what?

JOHN No – I was thinking it was such a shame that Mark had to go.

MARTIN Yes. I don't blame him though; - do you?

JOHN Not a bit of it.

BRIAN Martin!

MARTIN Yes Brian.

BRIAN What's the name of the ship your mate Mark has joined?

MARTIN Atlantic Conveyor.

BRIAN There we are Bert – I told you it was! (RON IS TALKING TO SOMEONE ELSE AND TURNS AROUND – HE TOO IS PART OF THE DISCUSSION ABOUT MARK).

RON What is it Brian?

BRIAN The Atlantic Conveyor.

DISSOLVE TO ROSEBRAWSE.

DINNER HAS JUST FINISHED AND MARGARET, MICHAEL AND JOHN ARE HAVING COFFEE IN THE SITTING ROOM.

JOHN That was a most delicious meal, Margaret, thank you very much.

MARGARET Not at all, I'm glad you like it.

MICHAEL John! What's for you? Brandy? Whiskey?

JOHN You wouldn't happen to have any Spanish brandy?

MICHAEL Afraid not!

JOHN Calvados?

MICHAEL Yes, indeed we have! Hang on a minute! (GOES TO NEXT ROOM AND RETURNS WITH A FULL BOTTLE). Voila! This was a wedding present from my best man, along with a host of other things and another eleven bottles of the same!

JOHN Well – that's what I call a wedding present!

MICHAEL It is rather – isn't it!

MARGARET I didn't know Simon had given us all that!

MICHAEL My dear – I don't think you've seen **half** the presents! (THE TELEPHONE RINGS). Who the devil can that be! It's half past nine – you'd think people would know = wouldn't you! Excuse me. (MICHAEL LEAVES AND GOES TO THE PHONE AND COMES BACK IN A FEW SECONDS). It's for you John – a lady.

JOHN (STARTLED, GETS UP) Oh! Right! …………..

MICHAEL I hope there's nothing wrong. She sounded a little shaky.

MARGARET Who was it?

MICHAEL I don't know – just a lady.

MARGARET Wife – do you think?

MICHAEL Could well be. Certainly didn't waste any time on formalities! (JOHN COMES BACK INTO THE ROOM LOOKING SHAKEN).

JOHN I'm very sorry but there's been an accident at home ………. My second son (PUTS A HAND TO HIS FOREHEAD) – there's a terrible storm and one of the old elms fell across the road and his car smashed into it. He's badly hurt ……………. I must go.

MICHAEL AND MARGARET SPRING UP.

MARGARET Oh dear, I'm so terribly sorry!

MICHAEL I'll phone to see if there's an early train! (EXITS)

JOHN Isn't there a train tonight?

MARGARET No – the first practical one from here is about 2.00 am. The ones that run at this time of night will get you there about the same time.

JOHN Oh Damn!

MARGARET Do you now know more than that there's been an accident?

JOHN No – the police phoned my wife immediately and they told her very little.

MICHAEL (RETURNING) 3.40 – that's the best one John. I'll drive you to the station, of course ……………. I'm sorry but Cornwall is stuck out on a limb as far as trains and things go. (THERE'S QUITE A CRASH FROM OUTSIDE SOMEWHERE AWAY FROM THE HOUSE). What was that? - !

MARGARET Well – it's not the time to go looking right now, Michael. I think we'd all better get to bed if we're to be up at 2.30!

MICHAEL Good idea! Oh – before I forget! (EXITS AND COMES BACK CARRYING A BOTTLE OF CALVADOS). There we are John – that'll keep you going on the train until you get home!

JOHN Oh dear! Thank you so much. I had so much looked forward to staying the week here!

MARGARET I'm sorry too. I hope you'll come again and soon.

MICHAEL Yes, indeed!

JOHN Thank you so much.

DISSOLVE TO RON, COXSWAIN'S BEDROOM. MEDIUM CLOSE UP ON HIM. IT IS JUST BEFORE DAWN. HE SUDDENLY OPENS HIS EYES AS IF SEEING DANGER; SITS UP IN BED AND LISTENS FOR A MOMENT, THEN GETS UP AND DRESSES. THE WIND IS STRONG.

DISSOLVE TO SOPHIE AND A GIRL FRIEND IN A FLAT. SOPHIE IS BEING SICK IN THE BATHROOM, HER GIRL FRIEND IS OUTSIDE THE DOOR. IT IS DAWN.

JUDY(KNOCKING THE DOOR) Sophie! ………. Are you alright? ………… Sophie! ……….. (THE DOOR OPENS, SOPHIE SLUMPS AGAINST THE DOOR, CRYING).

JUDYWhat's the matter Sophie? Are you alright? (TAKES HER IN HER ARMS).

SOPHIE Alright? (HYSTERICALLY) No! I'm not …………I'm having his baby! ………….. (THEN SHRIEKS). Oh Stuart!

DISSOLVE TO FERRONUFF AT SEA IN A STORM.

ALAN IS IN THE COCKPIT ALONE. STUART IS DOWN BELOW MAKING SURE THE ENGINE IS OK.

ALANStuart! …………. Stuart! …………. Stuart! ……………..(STUART'S HEAD APPEARS AS HE SLIDES BACK THE HATCH COVER).

STUART (SHOUTING) What? ……………. ?

ALAN(POINTING) Up ahead …………… a dinghy ……………. someone in it! (STUART SCRAMBLES THROUGH THE HATCH, QUICKLY CLOSING IT AFTER HIM. TIES HIMSELF ONTO A CLEAT, AS HAS ALAN, AND HALF STANDING LOOKS ATEAD).

STUART Yes ……………. you're right!

ALANGo forward and take a rope! ………… If you miss him there's a chance I'll get him! (STUART NODS AND VERY **VERY** CAREFULLY GOES FORARD).

CUT TO INFLATABLE DINGHY. OCCASIONALLY AN ARM COMES OVER THE SIDE AND EMPTIES A TIN OF WATER. STUART COILS HIS ROPE. AS THE YACHT COMES UP TO THE DINGHY STUART THROWS THE ROPE – HARD. THE ROPE **SMACKS** INTO THE INSIDE OF THE DINGHY, FRIGHTENING THE OCCUPANT WHO LOOKS UP IN FEAR – IT IS TOM -)

STUART The rope! - Take it!

TOM GRABS THE ROPE AND MAKES IT FAST TO HIS PAINTER. STUART PULLS IN THE SLACK
UNTIL THE DINGHY IS PARALLEL WITH THE AFTER END OF THE YACHT. ALAN STICKS HIS ARM
OVER AND GRABS TOM'S ARM AND PULLS HIM INTO THE COCKPIT. STUART SCRAMBLES
BACK TO THE COCKPIT, OPENS THE HATCH AND BUNDLES TOM INTO THE ACCOMMODATION,
LOOKS AT ALAN, GIVES THE "THUMBS UP" SIGN AND GRINS. ALAN RETURNS IT. STUART
SHOUTS, POINTING AT THE DINGHY.

STUART Shall I cut it loose?

ALAN No! ………. It'll do as a sea anchor perhaps!

STUART Where do you think we are? ………?!

ALAN I think we must have been driven back to Lyme Bay by now!

STUART GIVES THE "THUMBS UP" AND MAKES FOR THE HATCH.

STUART I'll see if I can hold the kettle still enough to make a cup of coffee!

ALAN What ……….?

STUART MAKES DRINKING FROM A VESSEL MOTIONS WITH HIS HAND. ALAN SMILES AND
GIVES THE THUMBS UP.

DISSOLVE TO RON ON THE POINT OF A HEADLAND, LOOKING OUT TO SEA WITH HIS
BINOCULARS. HIS CAR IS PARKED BEHIND HIM. PUTS BINOCULARS DOWN. HIS EYES ARE
TROUBLED. PULL BACK.

FADE TO END.

PART FIVE, EPISODE TWO

CONTINUING THE SHOT OF <u>RON</u> LOOKING OUT TO SEA FROM PART ONE.

<u>RON</u> GETS BACK INTO HIS CAR AND DRIVES OFF.

DISSOLVE TO COASTGUARD STATION.

<u>RON</u> WALKS INTO THE "OPERATIONS ROOM")

<u>RON</u> Morning Gerald!

<u>GERALD</u> (TURNING ROUND) Hello Ron, boy, what are you doing here?

<u>RON</u> Couple of mates went off to France yesterday – yacht called Ferronuff. Wondered if you'd had any report on her.

<u>GERALD</u> Not as far as I know, Ron; I'll have a look at the book – one of the others might have reported something. (PICKS UP A LOG BOOK AND TURNS THE PAGE) .... No! .... nothing here. No sightings, no reports .... nothing!

<u>RON</u> Well – I just hope and pray that everything's alright. .... No radio messages? You're sure?

<u>GERALD</u> No – you know **that**, Ron; it would be down here otherwise! (TAPS THE BOOK WITH HIS FINGER). Listen! (HOLDING OUT HIS HAND FOR SILENCE). The wind's dropped! Let's have a look at the anemometer! (GOES OVER AND LOOKS; NODS). Yes, dropped right down. (LOOKS AT HIS WATCH). That's about right – this is what we expected. Give it another half an hour or so and it'll clear up altogether.

<u>RON</u> Well, that's something then! (THERE'S A KNOCK AT THE DOOR AND A BOBBLE-HATTED HEAD STICKS THROUGH; IT IS DANNY).

<u>DANNY</u> Is it alright to come in here?

<u>GERALD</u> Depends what you want!

<u>RON</u> Hello Danny. Yes – come on. Gerald here's not going to eat you!

<u>DANNY</u> (COMING IN) My brother didn't sleep in his bed last night!

<u>GERALD</u> Well .....? ......! Does that mean you suspect him of fornicating or what? ...?

<u>RON</u> Hold hard, Gerald! .... Is his dinghy where he normally keeps it?

<u>DANNY</u> No!

<u>RON</u> Oh bloody Hell! .... Where does he go when he takes the dinghy out?

<u>DANNY</u> Dunno! He won't tell anyone! Gets nasty when you ask him!

<u>RON</u> Well .... where the Hell do you start looking? Kids, Gerald! Kids in dinghies!

GERALD How old is this brother of yours then?

DANNY Sixteen.

GERALD Is he a young sixteen or an old one?

RON He can handle a boat – I can tell you that! Trouble is he's got no respect for the sea; just hope the sea hasn't kicked him too hard in the arse this time. (CLAPS DANNY ON THE SHOULDER)..Hope Danny! Hope and pray! Don't let any other thoughts enter your head! ……… Did you walk up here?

DANNY Yes.

RON Well, come on, I'll give you a lift back. Gerald will give me a ring as soon as he hears anything. Won't you Gerald? - !

GERALD I certainly will.

RON There you are! ………… As soon as I get news I'll drive up to your place and let you know! Alright?

DANNY Thanks Ron (LOOKS AT GERALD). Thanks!

GERALD That's alright boy – that's what we're here for.

RON (PUTTING HIS ARM AROUND DANNY'S SHOULDERS) Come on my boy; you come on back to town with me! Might even get the missus to fix us both some breakfast …………… Bye Gerald …………… And thanks!

GERALD Bye Ron, bye sonny. (THEY TURN AND EXIT)

DISSOLVE TO A FEW HOURS LATER AT ROSEBRAWSE.

MICHAEL HAS JUST COME IN TO THE KITCHEN IN A HURRY.

MARGARET Hello dear – cup of coffee?

MICHAEL Love one please…………. Well – fairly obvious what that noise was last night!

MARGARET What was it?

MICHAEL All the galvanised roofing on your sheds has been blown off!

MARGARET Oh no!

MICHAEL That's not all, there are a lot of tiles missing on the house and one of the chimneys has broken off and fallen straight through the roof, smashing your father's bed!

MARGARET (HANDS TO THROAT). Oh my God!

MICHAEL I think you'd better come and have a look at it, but have a coffee first with me; I want to put a few suggestions to you about the repair of your place ……….. you mentioned coffee!

MARGARET Oh yes – sorry! (STARTS MAKING COFFEE).

MICHAEL Well (SITTING DOWN) you'll see what I'm talking about when we get down there, but I think it's well worth considering turning your place into a holiday home – or should I say, a **fantastic** holiday home …………   You know how all your buildings and house are all joined together in the shape of a half square?

MARGARET Yes (DOUBTFULLY).

MICHAEL Well, the whole thing faces South, and it occurred to me while I was down there just now that if you brought the height of the house down to the level of the buildings, and roof it with one long continuous roof – solar panels and that sort of thing with a swimming pool in the middle of the square – well – what do you think!

MARGARET Oh Michael! – it's very difficult for me to comment – it's been my home for so long! ………   I do see what you mean though, but it also seems to be an awful lot of work.

MICHAEL It's half done already! Wait till you see what the storm did! You may have quite a shock! ……….   Has the post arrived, by the way?

MARGARET Sorry – yes – it's still in the hall (MICHAEL GETS UP AND GOES TO GET THE POST).

DISSOLVE TO MICHAEL COMING BACK WITH LETTERS IN HIS HAND, SELECTS A LARGE WHITE ENVELOPE.

MICHAEL If this is what I **think** it is (SLITTING ENVELOPE AND TAKING OUT DOCUMENT/DEEDS TYPE SHEAF OF PAPERS – TAKES A SINGLE SHEET OF PAPER FROM THEM – IT IS A LETTER) Ah haha! ……….. Mmmm! (GATHERS UP ALL THE PAPERS, DUMPS THEM ON THE TABLE IN FRONT OF MARGARET)   Creekside!

MARGARET Oh! Is it something about that poor girl? Oh! That dreadful man! I can't help thinking how lucky I am! (STARTS TO PICK UP THE PAPERS).

MICHAEL I've bought it for you! It's my wedding gift to you and our children. It can never ever be sold. It's been arranged that way – whatever happens!

MARGARET Michael! ………   I …….. I ………... Oh! **Thank** you! ……..(GETS UP AND KISSES HIM) ….. But how did …….. ?

MICHAEL (INTERRUPTING) The day before the wedding I think it was – yes, Simon was here; that poor girl came and poured out her heart to me and offering Creekside at the same price as she paid for it, and well, there you are! Fait accompli!

MARGARET (CLASPING HER HANDS TOGETHER) Oh Michael; Thank you so much! Oh! (EXCITEDLY) Let's go down there and look at it!

MICHAEL Yes, of course, dear; but let's look at your father's place first. ………   Oh yes ……… if you like I'll get Ben on the tractor this morning and open up the roadway to Creekside.

MARGARET That would be marvellous! (GOES TO HIM AND EMBRACES HIM AGAIN). Thank you darling ……..   for everything! (THEY KISS. THE PHONE RINGS).

MICHAEL Damn! I used to think phones ringing at this kind of time only happened on the movies! (LAUGHS). I'll get it. (EXITS WHILE MARGARET OPENS THE DOCUMENTS)

DISSOLVE TO MICHAEL RE-ENTERING.

MICHAEL That was cousin John. He's arrived home and things are not so bad as expected. However, his boy has multiple factures to one leg, broken ribs and wrist and fractured nose and cheekbone.

MARGARET Oh! How terrible.

MICHAEL Yes – it's the same storm that hit us here, of course. There must be chaos all over the West of Britain............... Oh yes! He saved the Calvados for drinking at home and he's already expressed to me the translation of the John M Williams diary he did when he was 17 – it should get here tomorrow morning – with a bit of luck.

MARGARET How kind! He **was** nice – I liked him enormously!

MICHAEL Wasn't he! .... A breath of fresh air! Poor chap! .... I hope the boy's injuries heal well anyway! (PAUSE) .... Right! Shall we get going?

MARGARET (GETTING UP) Yes of course, I just need to put a cardigan on. Oh Michael!

MICHAEL Yes?

MARGARET This isn't an April Fool Day's joke, is it?

DISSOLVE TO LATER IN THE DAY AT ROSEBRAWSE. TEATIME. MICHAEL AND MARGARET ARE HAVING TEA.

MICHAEL Yes, well, quite honestly I think it should have been quite obvious to everybody; the world price of scrap has dropped most dramatically this year, and there's this chap David off going to south Georgia to take away all that's left of the whaling station. It doesn't add up! .... So now they're on the island and have run up the Argentine flag – what impertinence! But there – if we hadn't announced that we were going to take the Endurance away, perhaps they wouldn't have become so cheeky. All I hope is that it doesn't escalate into .... (HE IS INTERRUPTED BY THE NOISE OF A CAR DRAWING UP ON THE GRAVEL). Hello – we have visitors! (STARTS TO GO OVER TO THE WINDOW WHEN THERE'S THE SOUND OF THE FRONT DOOR OPENING).

JENKINS Hello – hello!

MARGARET (JUMPING UP) It's Daddy! (TURNS TO GO TO THE SITTING ROOM DOOR WHEN MR JENKINS OPENS IT AND COMES IN, WALKING OVER TO MARGARET).

JENKINS April Fool! (MARGARET GOING TO HIM)

MARGARET Daddy! How lovely to see you!

JENKINS My girl! I did miss you! (THEY KISS AND EMBRACE). Michael! (OFFERING AND TAKING HIS HAND). It's good to see you my boy! .... Well, you both look very well indeed!

MICHAEL So do you! – I'm sure you seemed to be moving much more easily when you came in!

JENKINS Ah .... probably the release of tension after the car journey.

MARGARET Oh yes – Simon! Where is he?

JENKINS He's just checking the oil; he said the engine was overheating .... Ah! Here he is!

SIMON (ENTERING) Hello chaps! (GOES AND KISSES MARGARET, SHAKES HANDS WITH MICHAEL). Well – how was the honeymoon?

MARGARET Perfect! I think we'll go to the Scillies again.

MICHAEL Rather! ………… Well – sit down and have some tea – or would you prefer something stronger? (CHORUS OF NO'S; MARGARET GOES TO GET MORE CUPS). Well – how did you enjoy London?

JENKINS I met some very nice and decent people and enjoyed myself the whole time in their company but, as for London itself, I can think of no place closer to Hell!

SIMON (LAUGHING) I think I must agree with you Mr Jenkins, but the change from weekdays to weekends is quite dramatic…………it's only the traffic that makes it Hell.

JENKINS Well – traffic or not, I don't care if I never go there again.

MARGARET (COMING IN) Where's that dear?

JENKINS London.

MARGARET Gosh no – I don't know how you stood up to it, Daddy! What on earth did you go there for anyway?

JENKINS Ah! (WAGGING HIS FINGER). That is a secret between myself and Elizabeth.

SIMON Oh – may I use your phone, please?

MICHAEL Of course. (SIMON LEAVES).

MARGARET Oh Daddy! We haven't told you about Creekside!

DISSOLVE TO LATER THAT EVENING IN HARMONIES.

SIMON AND MICHAEL HAVE COME OUT FOR A DRINK AND TO SEE HOW SEA CELT IS GETTING ON.

HUGH We haven't heard from him yet …………….. I thought he might have gone chasing off after that poor girl from Creekside, but he went back to the Merchant Navy instead.

MICHAEL Oh yes – I knew I had something to tell you – I've bought Creekside.

HUGH Congratulations. My word you were quick off the mark!

MICHAEL Actually the lady you just mentioned came to me and asked me to buy it!

HUGH Well – good luck to you anyway.

MICHAEL (LOOKING AT HIS WATCH) Time we went to look for my skipper I think. Ready Simon?

SIMON Yes; I promised I'd look in on Elizabeth tonight – she's going to take me sailing tomorrow – so I don't want to be too late.

MICHAEL Come on then……………. Well cheerio Hugh.

HUGH Bye bye now.

MICHAEL See you next week probably (THEY TURN AND LEAVE).

DISSOLVE TO OUTSIDE THE CHAIN LOCKER PUB.

A LARGE GROWD IS ON THE QUAY, ALL THE REGULARS ARE THERE AND THEY ARE
WATCHING AND WAITING FOR A BOAT TO COME INTO VIEW. SIMON AND MICHAEL JOIN THE
THRONG – GO OVER AND STAND NEXT TO RON THE COXSWAIN.

MICHAEL Hello – what's up?

RON Oh hello! I didn't recognise you there ………….. The coastguard has just let us know that a boat
we thought had been lost is coming in. We're all here hoping it's the right one (RETURNS HIS GAZE TO
THE POINT. A BOAT COMES INTO VIEW. RON PUTS HIS GLASSES UP. AFTER A MOMENT OR
TWO SHOUTS). Yes! Yes it is – I can see Alan and there's Stuart! (LETS HIS GLASSES HANG
AROUND HIS NECK AS EVERYBODY GIVES A CHEER, HE JOINS IN. PUTS THE GLASSES UP
AGAIN). What the ……………! (TURNS AND LOOKS FOR DANNY) Danny! (SEES HIM AND WAVES
HIM FORWARD).

RON Come here! Quick! Come on! (DANNY COMES ON, NOT LOOKING VERY HAPPY AS HIS
BROTHER TOM IS STILL MISSING. HE COMES UP TO RON. RON PUTS HIS GLASSES AROUND
DANNY'S NECK, GOES BEHIND HIM AND SETS HIM LOOKING STRAIGHT AT THE YACHT BY
HOLDING HIS SHOULDERS). Put the glasses up Danny! (HE WHISPERS IN HIS EAR. DANNY PUTS
UP THE GLASSES. WE SEE HIS FACE START TO BREAK AND TEARS TRICKLE DOWN HIS
CHEEKS AS HE BRINGS THE GLASSES DOWN AGAIN. HE HEAD SAGS FORWARD, HE TAKES A
DEEP BREATH, LIFTS HIS HEAD TO THE SKY AND HALF LAUGHS, HALF SHOUTS IN JOY. ALL
THE OTHERS JOIN HIM AND START CLAPPING AS THE LITTLE BOAT DRAWS NEARER. SIMON
AND MICHAEL LOOK AT EACH OTHER AND SMILE).

DISSOLVE TO LATER, INTERIOR OF CHAIN LOCKER.

THE SURVIVORS ARE DRINKING THEIR FULL. THERE'S ALMOST A CARNIVAL ATMOSPHERE IN
THE PLACE. SIMON AND MICHAEL ARE TALKING TO JANNER).

MICHAEL (TALKING TO JANNER) There's no need to apologise Janner; the boat's paying her way and
giving you both a living wage. I know Danny's not too keen on long-lining but he'll get used to it one
day…………… Anyway when Fred gets back he'll go over to bottom trawling again, I suppose
…………… What about you Janner? Have you got anything fixed up after this?

JANNER Yes – bit of luck there! Martin and John asked me to work on Voortrekker.

MICHAEL Well – that **was** a bit of luck …………… Any news of Fred? I haven't been able to get to see
him yet.

JANNER There's Alf – now come in – he'll know. (MICHAEL TURNS TO SEE ALF COMING
TOWARDS THE BAR AND SMILES AT HIM. ALF COMES OVER).

MICHAEL Hello Alf – will you have a drink?

ALF Oh – thank you. Pint please.

MICHAEL Brian! – another round here please (TURNS TO ALF). How's Fred?

ALF Coming along fine, thanks.

MICHAEL Well, that's good news! When will he be coming out?

ALF Next week, they say! (<u>DANNY</u> COMES OVER).

MICHAEL Hello Danny! How are things?

DANNY (PISSED) First bloody class

MICHAEL Janner was telling me your brother had a lucky escape.

DANNY Yep! ………. S'right! ……… So we celebrating and I want to ask Alf for a job in his mine cos I can't stand they bloody hooks, I can't. honest Janner, I bloody hate them.

JANNER Never mind, Dan – Fred'll be back in a couple of weeks and you'll be pulling up the trawl again.

DANNY Thank God for that! (TURNS AND LURCHES BACK TO <u>TOM</u>).

JANNER What was he talking about a mine for Alf? Excitement has gone to his head I'd say.

THE DRINKS FINALLY ARRIVE AND <u>MICHAEL</u> PAYS AND DISTRIBUTES THEM.

MICHAEL Cheers.

CHROUS OF CHEERS.

ALF (TAKING A SIP) No – he was on about Wheal Clifford mine opening up again that's all.

SIMON Oh yes – I heard about that. Quite a bit of speculation on it.

MICHAEL Really?

SIMON Rather. The newest thing to be in on as far as I can make out.

MICHAEL (TO <u>ALF</u>) Simon's father is in the City!

ALF What – Truro?

MICHAEL (SMILING) No Alf – it means that he's involved in banking, Lloyd's and that kind of thing.

ALF Oh! So he'd know a bit about shares and that!

MICHAEL Of course.

ALF Well – what about shares in Wheal Cliffod then – would they be worth anything?

SIMON (LAUGHING) Worth anything! ……….. Why it's one of the hottest things this month!

ALF If you had some, would you sell them or hang on to them?

SIMON I should hang on to them for the time being and see how the market lies the middle of next week ………… Why? ………….. You don't have any – do you?

ALF (SMILING PROUDLY) Reckon I do!

SIMON Good God! And there's father who's been in the City for years – he'd give his back teeth for a few hundred.

ALF (LAUGHS) Oh! Reckon I got a damned sight more than a few hundred!

SIMON Do you know how to go about getting rid of them at the right time?

ALF Well ,,,,,,,,,,,,,,,, er – no – I suppose.

SIMON You're obviously a friend of Michael's here so I'll let you know what to do and when to do it – **but** (HOLDING UP A FINGER) you will have to do it at exactly the time I say! .... To within a couple of hours – that is!

ALF Well .... I ....

SIMON But **whatever** you do – do **not** get rid of them until you hear from me. You've got quite a few thousands of pounds coming to you if you've got as many shares as it seems you have!

CLOSE UP ON ALF'S FACE AND

DISSOLVE TO ROSEBRAWSE NEXT MORNING. IT IS BREAKFAST TIME.

JENKINS (LOOKING UNHAPPY) I never thought there could have been so much damage. I was sure that those slates were well fixed; and when I think of what the chimney did! .... It's a good thing I was in London! I have Elizabeth to thank for that.

MARGARET (SHUDDERING) Let's not talk of it, Daddy. It's too horrible to think about! .... Simon's late coming down, Michael!

MICHAEL (HE IS READING THE POST – THE DIARIES OF JOHN M WILLIAMS IN PARTICULAR) Mm? ...... What? Sorry darling!

MARGARET I said Simon's late.

MICHAEL Oh yes! .... I think he may have left already. He said Elizabeth was taking him sailing this morning. They're going to pop into your creek and come up for lunch.

MARGARET Oh that will be nice! I think we'll have fish pie as it's Friday.

JENKINS Lovely – I haven't had fish for a week!

MARGARET Well, that settles it then – fish pie it is. What vegetables would you like with it?

JENKINS Oh, your usual thing, my dear.   That will be lovely!

MARGARET Michael?

MICHAEL (IN THE DIARY AGAIN) Mm .... yes (VAGUELY)

MARGARET With mangolds, some kale and a handful of molassine meal – how's that?

MICHAEL (NOT LISTENING, OBVIOUSLY) Mm – yes – wonderful. (MARGARET AND JEMKINS LAUGH). .... Mmm – what – what's going on? (TAKING NOTICE AT LAST).

MARGARET It's alright my dear – you carry on .... What's so interesting anyway?

MICHAEL Well – it seems from this translation, that John M Williams had followed his father's footsteps all over Wales. I'm just getting to where he is preparing to get a crew together to fight the French – John M states here that the local people had no love for him and thought he was a monster. It seems he had flogged a young man to death for disobeying his orders. There's also the occasional reference to how he treated his mother. Incidentally he refers to his father as the Captain. …………….. Writes very well – can't be sure, I suppose, as it's in translation, but it's quite beautifully laid out in parts – oh yes – something quite interesting here (FOLLOWS THE SCRIPT WITH HIS FINGER) listen……… " the old lady told me that she remembered the Cadpen Gwilym because he had tried to steal her sister when she was in her youth", So – he was obviously a womaniser or worse and it's this Cadpen Gwylim which intrigues me – perhaps it's the origin of Williams ………… I must write and ask John about that.

MARGARET That's certainly very interesting but he doesn't sound like a very savoury character, Michael.

MICHAEL Afraid not ………… Do you know – I think I might get all this photocopied. Perhaps John would lend me the original – I could have it and the translation printed and made into a book………. Oh dear! I wish I could spend the morning reading it – it's fascinating!

JENKINS If it's Ben clearing the Creekside gateway you're worrying about, I can go and get him started.

MICHAEL No – I couldn't expect you to go all the way ………….

JENKINS Not a bit of it! I would like to see to that for you.

MICHAEL Would you really? I say – that would be a kindness if you would ……….. I'm not a bookworm by any means, as you know, but I just can't put this down.

MARGARET Well dear, why don't you take it into your study and read it there while I clear away the breakfast things? …… I'll bring you a cup of coffee in a while.

MICHAEL Right (GETS UP AND GOES OUT OF DOOR, PEEPS BACK IN, LOOKING AT JENKINS) and thanks again!

JENKINS Not at all, my boy (RAISING HIS HAND. MICHAEL EXITS. JENKINS GETS UP) Well, my dear, I'll get on down to see Ben – he's probably picking up the slates already.

MARGARET Daddy!

JENKINS Yes.

MARGARET Michael has some suggestions about the house and buildings.

JENKINS Good!

MARGARET Well – I don't know if you'll think they're good when I tell you that he has suggested bringing the house down to the level of the buildings with one roof covering the lot and a swimming pool in what he calls the courtyard.

JENKINS What? ……… Brilliant! What a brilliant idea!

MARGARET (ALMOST SPEECHLESS) But Daddy! …….. I thought you'd be horrified by the idea! You've always been so traditional in all things!

JENKINS Yes, my love, I know; and it's probably cost me a lot too………… This last week I've learned that what things seem to be isn't always true ………… oh yes – I've always known that; but I've always rejected new ideas and practices out of hand. But not any more! No – by damn! (THUMPING THE AIR) Not any more! No! Let Michael do what he likes with the place! Whatever he does will be a change for the better. …………… You just wait six months, my dear! That old house ………… **and** me! You won't recognise us! (WALKS OUT OF THE ROOM. MARGARET IS LEFT SITTING THERE, WONDERING WHAT THE HELL HAS HIT HER!)

DISSOLVE TO ELIZABETH'S 20FT YACHT – A NICE LITTLE TRAILER SAILER.

SHE AND SIMON ARE HAVING A HAPPY TIME. SIMON IS TRYING TO HELP BUT DOESN'T KNOW MUCH ABOUT THINGS. IT IS LOW WATER SO THERE'S NOT A LOT OF ROOM TO MANOEUVRE WHEN GOING UP THE RIVER).

SIMON Well – as you can see there's not much seafaring blood in my veins!

ELIZABETH Nonsense! We're an island race! All you need is practice.

SIMON I think I'd be better employed taking Polaroid pictures of you and the rest of the beautiful scenery!

ELIZABETH Well – what can a lady say to such a compliment! (LAUGHS)

SIMON (GROPING IN HIS BAG) Right – here we are – instant masterpieces! (HE STARTS TAKING PHOTOS, HOLDING THEM UP TO ELIZABETH).

ELIZABETH No – it's no good – I can't look at them now. I'll wait till lunchtime!

SIMON All right (CONTINUES SNAPPING AWAY. HE TAKES A FEW WHILE THE BOAT IS ON THE OTHER TACK WITH CREEKSIDE IN THE BACKGROUND).

ELIZABETH How about going down as far as the Harbour? We can come back up with the incoming tide which will give us enough water to go into Margaret's creek! …….?

SIMON Lovely! I've got more film here!

ELIZABETH Well – just don't ask me to restore them for you! (THEY BOTH LAUGH).

DISSOLVE TO THE FISH QUAY SAME TIME AND DAY.

VOORTREKKER IS ALONGSIDE, TIED AHEAD OF SEA CELT; MARTIN AND JOHN ARE FINISHING SOME WORK ON DECK.

MARTIN Here comes young Tom. (TOM APPROACHES WITH DANNY). Welcome home, young man!

TOM (SHEEPISH GRIN) Thank you! ……… and thank you for selling me the inflatable. If I'd been in my old one I wouldn't be here now!

JOHN That's alright boy ……….. but, in fact, if you hadn't had the inflatable you wouldn't have been there then anyway!

TOM Well ………… suppose so but it was that bloody engine that did it anyway!

JOHN Have it long?

TOM No – only a couple of days.

MARTIN Well – next time you'll know! Won't you!

TOM Won't be a next time!

MARTIN I'm glad to hear it! Where did you get the engine from anyway?

TOM Well – it doesn't matter any more, so I can tell you. I bought it from Harry; down at the fish quay.

MARTIN Harry? ……….. Didn't know he had an engine for sale!

TOM No – it was his brother's or something ……….. Anyway I used to sell him fish and he said it was time I got a bigger and more reliable boat and engine.

MARTIN Oh! I see! What fish did you sell him, Tom?

TOM Bass.

MARTIN Bass! By God, Tom – if you can catch Bass you're a good fisherman! Did you catch many?

TOM Oh yes! Never less than 35 to 40!

DANNY I **thought** you had a lot of money! Bass! – you must be a bloody millionaire by now!

MARTIN Yeah! (LAUGHS) At £1 a pound you should really be in the chips!

TOM £1 a pound! He was only giving me 50p!

MARTIN No – that's impossible Tom! It's never been less than £1 a pound; the price is regulated by the market.

TOM No! I tell you – he only gave me 50p a pound.

MARTIN Did he give you receipts?

TOM Receipts? - No! – why?

JOHN Hello, hello! ………. We've seen this before – haven't we Martin?

MARTIN Too bloody true we have!

TOM Why? How come?

JOHN Well – someone who sells fish on a quay is in the best position to sell his own fish – isn't he?

TOM Yes.

JOHN Well – that's probably what Harry's been doing – buying your fish and selling it to the customers instead of the fish from boats like us. That way he's not only getting his salary from the co-operative, but he's selling his own fish at 100% profit. How much fish did you sell him on average?

TOM Oh, between £85's worth and £160's worth a week.

JOHN Well, that's how much extra he's been making on top of his salary then! .... I don't mind that so much, but I do mind that you didn't get the right money! (THROWS DOWN THE RAG HE WAS USING TO WIPE HIS HANDS). I don't know about you Martin, but I'm going down there right now. Soon sort this Harry out!

TOM Hey! I don't want to make a fuss!

JOHN No fuss, lad – but we'll see to it that you get your money **and** a decent engine instead of the one he sold you! Come on Martin; let's go and get this fisherman his dues! (CLIMBS UP THE LADDER FOLLOWED BY MARTIN).

DISSOLVE TO ROSEBRAWSE.

IT IS LUNCHTIME. ALL ARE SEATED AND EATING THEIR PUDDING.

MARGARET I wondered why Simon was so keen to come down here, now I know – it's the sailing!

ELIZABETH LAUGHING Yes – I'm sure it must be!

SIMON Didn't you know? (LAUGHS). I'm the expert on it. Oh yes – travel all over the country lecturing to people on how to go up a 2ft deep channel in a 3ft deep boat! Very clever that! (THEY ALL LAUGH) All illustrated with slides too! Good Lord – I'd forgotten about the Polaroids! Excuse me please! I'll go and get them! (LEAVES TABLE).

MICHAEL Is he still crazy with the camera?

ELIZABETH I think he must be.

MICHAEL (LAUGHING) I took him out deer stalking once and he came back with about 50 pictures of a mountain (THEY ALL CHUCKLE AS SIMON RETURNS).

SIMON Here we are everybody! I'll pass them round and you can swap them over. (DISTRIBUTES PICTURES).

MARGARET Oh dear! Elizabeth! They haven't done you justice! Oh – I don't know .... this one's quite nice – yes – mm! A nice one of Creekside with you at one side and **another** of Creekside; now here's a nice one ....

MICHAEL Pass them on dear (MARGARET PASSES THEM ON). Oh yes – good – mm that's nice.

ELIZABETH May I see some? I haven't seen them yet.

MICHAEL (PASSING THEM ON IMMEIDATELY) I'm so sorry!

ELIZABETH Thank you .... (LOOKS AT THEM ONE BY ONE). Oh yes I see! (LAUGHS) mm yes that's my father's nose alright! Dear! Look at this one (HOOTS). Hm – yes .... Wait a! (SUDDENLY SERIOUS) .... Yes – my God (GETS UP WITH THE PHOTOGRAPH AND GOES TO THE TWO PAINTINGS ON THE WALL AND LOOKS FROM THE PHOTO TO PAINTING AND BACK AGAIN). Michael! Yes – of course! I knew it struck a cord when John said it in Welsh – Crugsaeth – Creekside! Don't you see? (ALL GET UP, MICHAEL RUSHES TO HER).

MICHAEL What are you saying?

ELIZABETH Look! (POINTING TO THE **VERY SAME** ROCK IN THE PAINTINGS AND THE PHOTO). It's Creekside! The house was Creekside all the time! (SHOUTING EXCITEDLY NOW).

MICHAEL Good God Almighty! You're right – you're absolutely ……… hang on!

MICHAEL I've just come to a place in the diary! (SHOOTS OUT OF THE ROOM WHILE THE OTHERS COME AND LOOK AND TALK EXCITEDLY. MICHAEL RUSHES BACK IN). Listen everybody – listen! (reads from the diary) ………… " and I knew that I had finally found the captain's final dastardly deed. Oh that a son should have to bear this after a lifetime's search. I have turned over one stone too many and the viper has struck. I shall, I think, never recover from this, my father's last shameful act. My last memory of the accursed Crugsaeth is that of the South gable crumbling as I put away from shore. May the flame that I kindled and the destruction thereby be a memorial to those who suffered so terribly at his hands. This is the final entry that I make; I think I shall not recover from my shame – ever!" (SILENCE FOLLOWED THE READING. THEY ALL LOOK AT MICHAEL WHO IS IN DEEP THOUGHT AS THE REALISATION HITS HIM. FINALLY -)

MICHAEL Margaret – do you know what this means?

MARGARET Yes, my dear (HOLDING HIS ARM).

Michael (PUTS HAND TO FOREHEAD) It's unreal – it's almost ………….. supernatural! I've just bought the house that my ancestor built and where French prisoners were murdered – **He** murdered them! My God! (GOES AND SITS AT THE TABLE, HEAD IN HANDS, THE OTHERS LOOK AT HIM – HE SUDDENLY SITS UP). There's only one way to make certain! (LOOKS AT JENKINS). Is the tractor and fore-end loader still down at Creekside?

JENKINS Yes – it is!

MICHAEL Is the gateway clear?

JENKINS Yes.

MICHAEL Come on them – all of you let's drive down there – I may need your help (GETS UP AND LEAVES. ALL THE OTHERS EXCHANGE GLANCES AND THEN FOLLOW HIM OUT).

DISSOLVE TO CREEKSIDE.

MICHAEL IS ON THE TRACTOR DRIVING IT TO ITS LIMIT. HE HAS A VERY DETERMINED LOOK ON HIS FACE. HE SUDDENLY STOPS).

MICHAEL Margaret! Go to the house please and get the big torch and the gas lantern! We may need them! (HE GOES BACK TO HIS TASK, PUSHING IN THE FORE-END LOADER TO WHERE THE ROCK GARDEN IS. IT IS WHAT'S LEFT OF THE SOUTH HALF OF THE HOUSE. HE DIGS FRENZIEDLY – NOT SPARING THE MACHINE. HE SHOUTS OVER HIS SHOULDER)……….. and bring some shovels!

DISSOLVE TO AN HOUR LATER.

MICHAEL HAS CLEARED AN APPRECIABLE SPACE; HE HAS JUST PULLED BACK IN ORDER TO DRIVE FORWARD AGAIN WHEN SIMON CRIES OUT).

SIMON Stop! Stop Michael! (POINTS) Look! (WE SEE A LARGE FLAG STONE WITH RING IN IT AT THE SIDE FURTHEST AWAY FROM THE TRACTOR, MICHAEL JUMPS OFF THE TRACTOR AND STRIDES TO IT. HE TRIES TO LIFT IT BUT FAILS).

MICHAEL Damn! Give me a hand here Simon! (THEY BOTH TRY BUT TO NO AVAIL. THEY STAND UP – PUFFED).

SIMON   The tractor, Michael!

MICHAEL Of course! (GOES TO THE REAR OF THE TRACTOR, GETS A CHAIN OUT OF THE BOX,
DRAGS IT TO THE RING AND PUTS THE CHAIN THROUGH. GOES BACK TO THE TRACTOR AND
GETTING ON, DRIVES IT SO THAT THE FORE-END LOADER IS ABOVE THE RING. HE DROPS
THE FORE-END A FEW FEET, PUTS THE BRAKE ON, GOES ROUND TO THE FRONT, PUTS THE
RING OF THE CHAIN OVER A PROJECTION ON THE FORE-END LOADER AND THE HOOK OVER
ANOTHER, JUMPS BACK ON THE TRACTOR. ALL THE OTHERS NOW COME CLOSE TO SEE THE
STONE BEING LIFTED. HE ENGAGES THE FORE-END LOADER AGAIN AND STARTS TO RAISE IT.
THE FRONT OF THE TRACTOR BEGINS TO GO DOWN. MICHAEL STARTS LIFTING THE LOADER
IN JERKS).

SIMON   (LIFTING HIS HAND) Hang on Michael! (SIMON GOES FORWARD WITH A SHOVEL AND
STARTS TO SCRAPE THE CRACK AROUND THE FLAGSTONE WITH THE EDGE OF THE SHOVEL.
STEPS BACK AND SIGNALS TO MICHAEL). Ok, try it again! (MICHAEL STARTS LIFTING IN JERKS
AGAIN AND SUDDENLY THE STONE LIFTS CLEAR AND DROPS BACK IN PLACE AGAIN. CHEERS
FROM EVERYONE, MICHAEL'S FACE RELAXES AT LAST AND HE WIPES HIS FOREHEAD WITH
HIS SLEEVE AND THEN CONCENTRATES AGAIN. THE LOADER RISES AGAIN AND THE STONE
LIFTS SLOWLY UNTIL IT IS HANGING FROM THE FORE-END AND SWINGING GENTLY. HE
REVERSES THE TRACTOR A FEW FEET AND SWITCHES OFF, LOWERING THE STONE TO THE
GROUND. SIMON STARTS TO GO TOWARDS THE HOLE).

MICHAEL No Simon. It has to be me! ……… Margaret! The torch and the lamp (HOLDS HIS HAND
OUT AND IS GIVEN THEM ALMOST IMMEDIATELY. SWITCHES THE TORCH ON AND GOES
FORWARD. WE SEE STONE STEPS LEADING DOWN. MICHAEL STEPS SLOWLY DOWN, HIS
TORCH LIGHTING THE DARKNESS. STOPS WHEN HE IS AT THE BOTTOM, TURNS, LOOKS UP).
Pa Jenkins! (JENKINS COMES TO THE EDGE OF THE HOLE).   Come on – this is the dungeon you
never found when you were a child. You come down next! And you Simon! (THE TWO MEN COME
DOWN). Margaret! ……… you and Elizabeth stay there for a while please! (RESPONSE. MICHAEL
SHINES HIS TORCH AND WE SEE BARE COBWEBBED WALLS – A STONE BENCH WITH A BOX
ON IT; MANY EMPTY BOTTLES SCATTERED ALL OVER THE PLACE AND A STACK OF FULL
BOTTLES OF WINE IN THE CORNER. LIGHTS THE LAMP. IN THE OPPOSITE CORNER IS A
DOORWAY AND A HEAVILY BARRED DOOR WITH A GRILL IN IT. AT THE SIDE OF THE
DOORWAY IS A PAINTING. IT IS COATED IN COBWEBS AND DUST. THERE IS NO FRAME
ABOUT IT – JUST THE CANVAS ON ITS STRETCHERS. THE THREE MEN GO FORWARD VERY
CAREFULLY – THE AIR IS COLD BUT NOT DAMP).

MICHAEL What on earth - !! (GOES TO TOUCH THE PAINTING AND STOPS HIMSELF).. Simon get
the girls! I want Elizabeth to look at this! (SIMON GOES OFF, MICHAEL AND JENKINS LOOK
AROUND AT THE EMPTY WINE BOTTLES, NOT DISTURBING THEM. MICHAEL GOES TO THE
BOX. THE LEATHER HINGES AND FASTENINGS CRACK AS HE TOUCHES THEM AND THE LID
LIFTS UP. HE SHINES THE TORCH INSIDE AND GASPS). Look! Look here! (JENKINS COMES
OVER AND WE SEE A HAT OF NAPOLEONIC TIMES, A PISTOL AND SASH, A BOOK, A SMALL BOX
AND A LARGER BOX. MARGARET AND ELIZABETH COME DOWN. MICHAEL SHINES THE TORCH
FOR THEM.

ELIZABETH (SHIELDING HER EYES FROM THE GLARE OF THE LAMP). Simon said there was a –
oh – there! (COMES OVER TO IT). Good God – what is it?

MICHAEL That's what I want you to tell me!

ELIZABETH Simon – see if you can find me something like a feather outside! (SIMON GOES BACK UP
THE STEPS. ELIZABETH LOOKS AROUND). Margaret was telling me the legend – but I can't see any
skeletons!

MICHAEL There's still that doorway there to go through!

ELIZABETH Oh my God! The very thought! (SIMON RUNS BACK DOWN WITH A FEATHER AND HANDS IT TO ELIZABETH WHO TURNS TO THE PAINTING). Bring the light closer – stop! Not too close! (SHE STARTS TO LIFT UP THE COBWEBS WITH THE FEATHER IN ONE CORNER). This is in perfect condition, Michael! No cracks! (GOES ON PEELING OFF THE COBWEBS UNTIL SHE'S GOT A COUPLE OF SQUARE FEET AND SUDDENLY A FACE APPEARS). Handkerchief please! (SIMON HANDS HER ONE. SHE BLOWS ON THE FACE AND HITS IT VERY GENTLY WITH THE ENDS OF THE HANDKERCHIEF AND SUDDENLY CRIES OUT. Oh Michael! It's your face!

MICHAEL What? (PEERS). My God! How ……….. what on earth!

MARGARET Oh how horrible! (SIMON RELIEVES THE TENSION BY SAYING).

SIMON (LAUGHING) I thought you said he was the handsomest man you'd every seen! (THEY ALL HAVE A LITTLE LAUGH AND TAKE DEEP BREATHS).

MARGARET Isn't the air good in here!

ELIZABETH Amazingly good! Accounts for the perfect condition of the painting, of course! (BY NOW SHE HAS UNCOVERED MOST OF THE FIGURE AND STARTS BLOWING AND SMACKING WITH THE HANDKERCHIEF AGAIN, AND WE SEE THAT THE FIGURE IS IN CHAINS AGAINST A WALL, AND THAT SCORCHED ONTO A BOARD AND HUNG IN CHAINS AROUND HIS NECK IS A PIECE OF WOOD WITH THE WORDS "C'EST PAYEE). I know this brush work, Michael. You have it hanging on your sittingroom wall!

MICHAEL (ASTONISHED) My great great ? ……………

ELIZABETH No! It's de Trapenard! We'll soon find out! (GOES TO THE BOTTOM OF THE PAINTING AND STARTS LIFTING THE COBWEBS AND THEN BLOWS AND FLICKS).

ELIZABETH Voila! What did I tell you! (WE SEE E DE T IN THE CORNER).

MICHAEL But how on earth! I don't understand!

ELIZABETH I think I'm beginning to! ……….. Michael – just open that door and see what's inside.

MICHAEL No need to – there's a grill I can shine (SHINES HIS TORCH THROUGH). Good God Almighty!

MARGARET Oh Michael! What is it? (TERRIFIED).

MICHAEL It's a skeleton hanging in chains! Just like the painting!

ELIZABETH I thought it might be …………… Before we go any further I think we should get your cousin John down here with any more diaries written by John E Williams.

MICHAEL But why? He's only just gone back!

ELIZABETH Well – we'll need written evidence to back it up, but I have a very strong feeling about this!

MICHAEL But what?

ELIZABETH I think that when you look at that skeleton in chains, Michael, you're looking at your ancestor – The Captain! …………… Look at the painting – the face – the insignia, and have a look at the wall in the dungeon and the painting.

MICHAEL My God – you're right!

ELIZABETH Right now then – Michael! I want you and Simon to lift the painting off the iron pegs and put it in the back of my estate car. Then I'll take it back to my studio this evening. Is there anything else here?

MICHAEL Yes, that box has things in it!

ELIZABETH Very well, bring it along. Then I advise you to seal the place up again until John Williams gets here. For God's sake do what I say Michael. You may be on the brink of something very very important! – to yourself and to history.

ZOOM IN ON PAINTING'S FACE.

DISSOLVE TO ROSEBRAWSE. CLOSE UP OF MICHAEL WILLIAMS' FACE, PULL BACK AND WE SEE THEY'RE ALL SITTING DOWN HAVING STRONG DRINKS.

MICHAEL I don't think I've ever had such a traumatic day. (SAGS IN HIS CHAIR – WHACKED). Switch on the radio dear – let's see what we've been missing!

ZOOM IN ON RADIO AS IT'S SWITCHED ON GIVING FALKLANDS NEWS.

DISSOLVE TO TV SET IN DUGDALE RESIDENCE. THE ANNOUNCER IS JUST GIVING DETAILS OF THE INVASION.

CUT TO FACES OF GRANDPA AND RACHEL. GRANDPA IS ABSOLUTELY LIVID, TIGHT-JAWED, STARING EYES).

RACHEL Oh! Thank God my dear boy is not in the Royal Navy! (LOOKS OVER AT PHOTO OF MARK).

CUT TO PHOTO OF MARK ON A DRESSER WITH A POSTCARD OF A SHIP PROPPED UP AGAINST IT. THE SHIP IS THE ATLANTIC CONVEYOR, THE SHIP IN WHICH MARK IS A DECK OFFICER.

ZOOM IN ON BOTH AND FADE TO END.

ABOUT THE AUTHOR

John Dillon was born in Wales in 1933 and was educated at Christ College, Brecon, a Public School founded in 1541 by Henry VIII. A movie actor, John had the lead in *Mind on the Run* and BBC TV *Sadwrn* in 1965, and had bit parts in *Solomon and Sheba, King of Kings, El Cid,* and *Custer of the West.* He also had roles in many TV and radio plays. John ended his film career as Assistant Director for Lieder Films in 1968 and retired to Ireland. Horse-breeder, share fisherman, refugee aid worker, he also worked alongside his wife for 30 years as her assistant in Paintings Conservation. The work was varied and included oil paintings and polychromed wood surfaces in the West of England, including many churches in the South West. The last eleven happy years were spent in rural France within sight of Mont Saint Michel. They have one grown-up daughter now engaged in worthwhile work helping young couples, and others, to get started on the ladder of owning their own homes.

John says, "I finished all my film work in 1968 but a mysterious "other" John Dillon appeared in 1984! This person has nothing to do with me and, when I complained to British Actors Equity about it they said it was beyond their jurisdiction!! I wonder why on earth I paid them all those Equity dues then – what possible good have they ever done me? Even as far back as 1965 when the Beeb was looking for a person to front a Welsh language programme for education and the job was given to someone other than an actor, the Equity representative refused to do anything because he said the BBC would never again give him a job. He was an actor. Disgusting stuff eh?!! – "

John's second book, *Tales of Scilly, Podgy and The Delightful Company,* was recently published. For children, the book provides beautiful illustrations, great suspense, and unforgettable life lessons. For adults, it contains an imaginative, thoughtful, and humorous perspective of life beneath the sea, and teaches compassion and freedom for its creatures.

Printed in Poland
by Amazon Fulfillment
Poland Sp. z o.o., Wrocław